D1103713

Fire and Rain

H. A. Covington

Writers Club Press
San Jose New York Lincoln Shanghai

Fire and Rain

Writers Club Press
an imprint of iUniverse.com, Inc.

For information address:
iUniverse.com, Inc.
5220 S 16th, Ste. 200
Lincoln, NE 68512
www.iuniverse.com

ISBN: 0-595-14220-6

Printed in the United States of America

This is for the real Mary Jane. Rest in peace, angel.

Author's Note

Some of the persons and events in this book are based on real people and real incidents that took place a generation ago in Chapel Hill. Some are not. Which are which, and precisely who is referred to, is for the author to know and you, the reader, to speculate upon. This book is "...a play to catch the conscience of the king." Enjoy!

Introduction

Saturday Morning
October 24th, 1970
Chapel Hill, North Carolina

The murderers stepped into the cold autumn darkness, leaving the house of the dead behind them. One of them quietly closed the door to the tomb, his gloved hands leaving no fingerprints. He glanced at his watch; it was not quite one thirty in the morning. He turned and stepped off the back porch, carefully scuffing his shoes in the wet grass to remove the blood they had all been walking in down in the basement.

He had killed one of the girls himself. She'd been brave at the last, he granted her that. No screaming or begging for mercy like the other one. Just silent tears sliding down her cheeks. "Won't you even tell me why?" she had begged him in a soft, strained voice as he slipped the noose around her neck. "Please, tell me! If

I know why maybe it won't be so bad. Please don't make me die not knowing why, with anger and fear and hate for you in my heart. Please, tell me why!"

"Because it has to be this way," he told her. "I'm sorry. Sometimes there is no better reason than that." Then he had jerked the cord tight and held it firmly closed until she was dead.

The second murderer looked at the third. "This was a mistake," he said. "This should never have happened. You are responsible."

"I know," said the third killer.

"We must discuss this, quite seriously," said the second man.

"Yes, I know. But let's get out of here first," The killers moved around the house, and checked the silent empty street beneath the pale electric lights. No one was about. They headed for their car. The second man looked back at the house and spoke to the first. "I thought you turned off all the lights?" he demanded.

"I did," said the man who had strangled the girl.

"I thought I saw a light in the upstairs window. No, no, it was nothing," he said, looking again. The first man turned and looked up at the window. The dead girl's room, the one he had killed. For a moment he thought he saw a light too, a face framed in the window. But that was impossible. He had made sure she was quite dead, and now there was nothing in the window but blackness. They all turned and walked away.

Fire and Rain

"...I've seen fire, and I've seen rain.
I've seen sunny days that I thought would never end.
I've seen lonely times when I could not find a friend,
But I always thought that I'd see you again..."

—James Taylor*

July, 1996

I

"Before we proceed, I have to discuss something with you," began the real estate broker tentatively. "The house you want to buy has a history. A rather unpleasant history that you might not be comfortable with."

"Oh, Lord!" responded Heather Lindstrom in alarm. "I get the feeling I'm about to learn why a five-bedroom house in downtown Chapel Hill is going for less than a hundred thousand dollars. Don't tell me, it's built on an old Indian burial ground and it's haunted by ectoplasmic Stephen King type thingies?"

"No, no, nothing so melodramatic," laughed Mike Mangella. They were sitting in his carpeted office on Rosemary Street. Outside the pavement shimmered in the crushing muggy heat of a Carolina July. "I've given this little presentation a number of times, and I must confess I've never quite gotten the hang of it. The fact is that many years ago, there was a double murder committed in the house. Two teenaged girls were killed and the slayer was never identified or arrested. In answer to your question, no, there have been no complaints of pale sheeted figures or rattling chains or shrieks in the night. But I'll be honest with you, several past residents have sold because even after living in the house for a while, they simply didn't feel comfortable there. It is my understanding this is the case with Linda Boothroyd, the present owner. You have a teenaged daughter yourself, Heather, and I can see where you might have a problem with the knowledge that two girls near Tori's age died violently in the house."

"That's not melodramatic?" whistled Heather, pursing her lips. "It's a bit of a shock, I admit. Never caught the guy, you say?"

"No. At one stage it was thought the murders might have some connection with the Jeffrey McDonald case down at Fort Bragg, which took place that same year, 1970, but the authorities eventually ruled that out. Heather, I know I don't have to point out that you would be lucky to get a decent condo anywhere in Orange County for this price. If you decide you can live with this situation you'll be getting a fine piece of property at a real steal. Not only is there the exceptionally attractive price of the house itself, but the walking distance to the University will save you a small fortune in commuting costs."

"I'm acutely aware of that," said Heather. "Tell me more about these murders in 1970, and what's happened with the house since then."

"The girls were students at Chapel Hill High School, and their parents were UNC people," said Mangella. "One of the victims was the daughter of Margaret Mears."

"*The* Margaret Mears, as in prominent progressive Congressperson from New York?" asked Heather, astonished.

"That's her," said Suzanne Lentoff, the Barbie doll real estate agent who was handling the listing. "The elegant lady we see every night on the six o'clock news campaigning for the Clintons' re-election. In 1970 Dr. Mears and her husband were both professors here. They left town after their daughter's death and they divorced soon afterwards. I think he went over to N. C. State in Raleigh and he still teaches archaeology or something there, but Dr. Margaret Mears moved to New York City and began her political career. Actually, she was already very well known politically. She first gained national prominence as a very active member of anti-Vietnam war protest movement here in Chapel Hill."

"Yes, I've heard of her," agreed Heather. "And you know, I think I recall hearing that she'd lost a daughter in some kind of bad circumstances."

"It was pretty bad," admitted Mangella. "The house that you're hopefully going to buy belonged to the Mears family in 1970. In October of that year the parents were away at an anti-war symposium Washington, D.C. The girls...I'm sorry, I never can recall their names, which I know is callous of me, but after all, it was a quarter century ago...Dr. Mears' daughter had a friend sleeping over with her. Somebody broke in, sexually assaulted them, and murdered them. I don't know many of the details, but I understand it was a horrific crime."

"And the cops never had any clue at all who did it?" asked Heather with a frown. "That's pretty chilling."

"Well, they never actually charged anybody," Mangella said. "There were all kinds of rumors, needless to say, and please bear in mind this is just what I've heard bandied about during the ten years I've lived in Chapel Hill myself. But I'm told the police picked up some trailer trash kid from over in Durham who'd been an on-again, off-again boyfriend of one of the girls, and they really put him through the wringer. They just couldn't find any proof to make it stick."

"I heard it was bikers," put in Suzanne. "A motorcycle gang thing. One of the girls was supposed to have been partying with the Hell's Angels and it got out of hand."

"That's another possibility," agreed Mangella. "There have also been persistent stories about drugs and devil worship, but you need to understand, Heather, that would be pretty much standard in any case where a couple of teenagers are murdered with no arrest or conviction. I've never seen or heard any proof that it was anything other than a straightforward brutal rape and murder, but that's certainly bad enough, and as I said, a lot of people move in only to find they can't really get comfortable there."

"So the house comes on the market fairly often?" remarked Heather suspiciously. "Sure there's no specters? No ghostly girls in bloody nightdresses? Pardon me, I don't mean to sound facetious, I know it was an awful thing."

"No, nothing like that," Mangella assured her with a warm smile. "I think quite honestly it's mostly due to the peripatetic nature of the academic world. University towns are almost as bad as army towns for a nomadic population. The people who have owned the house since 1970 have almost all been connected with the University, like you, except there was one couple who worked in the Research Triangle Park for a major pharmaceutical research firm. They got transferred to California."

"I'll level with you, Mike," said Heather with a sigh. "Yes, it bothers me. It bothers me a lot, and if I had known this before I looked at the house I probably would have had second thoughts. But it's a great deal and you're right, it could be a lovely home for me and for my kids. We've agreed that my son Greg and his wife will be moving in when they get married, and with a mortgage this low, and them paying half the bills and upkeep, this is a chance for me to recoup financially I can't pass up. Let's get the ball rolling. How soon can we close?"

"I don't see any problem in getting you in by Labor Day," said Mangella, beaming. "I got a call this morning from your bank, and the financing package is acceptable to them. We'll go ahead and get started. There's literally several pounds of paperwork we have to go through. I hope your signing fingers are nice and limber. Would you like coffee or a soda?"

"A Diet Coke if you've got one."

"You know, Heather, I still have difficulty believing that you have a son old enough to get married," gushed Suzanne, flashing her a brilliant smile of perfectly capped teeth. "You look like you're barely thirty!"

"Thanks, but I've got forty-two big ones racked up," Heather replied. "Married young, too young as it turned out. I was only eighteen when Greg was born. Speaking of kids, Tori's kicking her heels in your vestibule. I'm sure we're going to be in here for a while. Let me cut her loose." Heather stepped out of the manager's office. Her teenage daughter Tori was sitting, or rather slouching on a sofa, idly thumbing through a magazine. She resembled her mother at sixteen, tall and slender with just enough rounded curve below the waist and below the shoulders to catch the notice of boys. The major difference was that Tori's shoulder-length hair was a warm amber, more than brown but not quite red. Her mother's hair was long, silky ash blond, the growing number of silver hairs creating an overall platinum effect rather than gray. It cascaded down her back to her waist. Heather had worn it like that since she was Tori's age. She had always refused to cut it, because she was convinced, with some justification, that if she did she'd look like a blond Olive Oyle. "Sit up!" Heather commanded absently, out of force of habit. Tori's body inclined to an angle just barely compatible with the broadest possible definition of sitting up. Heather fished around in her purse. "I'm going to be in there with Mr. Mangella and Ms. Lentoff for a couple of hours. Here's twenty dollars. You can go look around in the stores up on Franklin Street. Be back here by one o'clock and then we can go someplace for lunch."

"Can I take the car?" asked Tori, spitting out her gum and sticking it under the table.

"Don't do that," said Heather with a scowl. "Put it in the trash can. You don't need the car to go to Franklin Street. It's just one block up."

"I could go to University Mall. Where's the trash can? They don't have one."

"Well, find one! Don't put chewed gum under furniture. It's dirty and vulgar and you know better than that."

"They should have ash trays."

"No they shouldn't, and if I catch you smoking you might as well give that new license of yours back to the state of North Carolina, because you're not getting behind the wheel of that car for a good long time. What do you want at the mall? Never mind. We'll go there for lunch if you like. There's plenty of interesting things on Franklin Street."

"It's not as good as Seattle. This is a hick town," said Tori with a pout.

"No, dear, this is a *small* town. It's one of the most cosmopolitan places in the country and you'll find everything here you could ever want or find in Seattle, you'll just find it in a smaller package."

"We gonna buy that house on Boundary Street?" asked Tori.

"We sure are," said her mother. "You like it?"

"Ah, it'll be OK I guess," said Tori uncomfortably. "Thanks for the shekels, Mom. I'll go to Goodvibes."

"Oh, God, more grunge rock or whatever it is nowadays? You young whippersnappers don't know what rock and roll is! When we get all our stuff out of storage I think I may unlimber the old eight-track. Grand Funk, Led Zepp, Three Dog Night, Jefferson Airplane..."

"Oh, yeah?" laughed Tori, standing up. "Let's match your eight-tracks against my CDs when we get everything out of storage. I'll bet I've got more stuff from the Seventies than you do. I bet I can even sing it better than you can, at least a lot better than you were doing the other day when we were at the house."

"Pardon me?"

"Sing better than you. Remember when we were looking over the house and you were upstairs and you started singing that old Three Dog Night number? You know, 'Celebrate, celebrate, dance to the music'? You were too soft and too slow. See you at one o'clock." She almost skipped out the door. In some ways Heather thought her daughter was very young for her age, in others Heather thanked her stars Tori had hit sixteen and still stayed as relatively innocent as she was. As she turned to go back in to the waiting realtors, Heather's brow suddenly furrowed.

Odd. She was sure that when they had spent those several hours last week going over the empty house she was about to buy, she had not at any time begun to sing, Three Dog Night or anything else.

*   *   *

On the same day in Raleigh, Agent Matt Redmond of the North Carolina State Bureau of Investigation tapped on the door of the director's office. Under his arm he carried a large sheaf of manila file folders, bulging with documents and photographs. "Come on in, Matt," said Director Hightower, a rotund man in a pin-striped shirt, red suspenders, and a string tie. Redmond came in, closed the door without asking, and sat down. "Real nice job on that business down in Duplin County. I just got a call from Haskins, the D.A. down there. Antonio Johnson's lawyer called him, wants to cut a deal."

"What, plead him down to second degree or manslaughter?" demanded Redmond. "That's outrageous bullshit, Phil!"

"Yeah, I know. That's what Haskins told the shyster. He said the best deal his client's going to get is guilty to murder one with no death penalty, and he testifies against Kenny Atwater. Johnson will do a good twenty at least, and Atwater gets the needle. D.A. thinks they'll go for it, and the way things are going right now with the legislature and the Supreme Court trimming back all these goddam appeals we might actually see Kenny get the juice in five or six years instead of the usual ten or fifteen. If you hadn't found Valerie Seawell and turned her we'd have been lucky to get them at all. Congratulations again on a job well done, Matt."

"What's Miss Valerie's future looking like?" asked Redmond.

"Oh, she cut a deal for five years in Bragg Street and she thinks after that she's going to go into the Witness Protection Program and spend a few years munching nachos and watching color TV," chuckled the director. "But since you pointed out that outstanding warrant in Georgia, I think the folks down there can protect her a lot better in one of their women's prisons than our overburdened Federal judicial system can. Valerie don't know that, of course, and we're going to make damned sure she don't find out until after she testifies."

"She'll only get another five or ten years in Georgia," commented Redmond, his lean face scowling. "Dammit! All three of them ought to be wheeled into that little green room down there in Central Prison and get three needles stuck in their arms, hooked up to one family-sized jug of cyanide! Kay Wicker was a trashed-out whore and a junkie, but the baby was only eighteen months old, for Christ's sake!"

"She probably would have ended up like her momma," commented the director. "Or like our Miss Valerie."

"We don't know that for sure," said Redmond morosely. "Now we'll never know."

"Look, Matt, we got the bad guys! One of them's headed for the green room eventually, and the other two will be off the street for a good long while. With the system today, that's as good as it gets. If it weren't for you they'd still be out there selling poison to kids and killing more people. Another case closed for the Southern Sherlock Holmes!"

Redmond groaned in disgust. "You'd think you'd have better things to do with your time than watch tabloid TV," he said.

"Better than Two Gun Matt," laughed the director. "You ask for it, you know, wearing that fedora hat all the time and going around looking like you're Indiana Jones. Look, you said you wanted to see me. What's up?"

Redmond fished a sheet of paper out of his pocket. "Vacation request form. Starting October 1st. Three weeks accumulated vacation, all my sick leave, and all my comp time for the past two years off every case I ran for days without a break, time I never took. Total six weeks. I checked with Human Resources and this is all legit, I'm entitled to it. I want it all. If I can't work this out vacation-wise then I'll take an unpaid leave of absence, but I want the time off."

"Jeez, Matt, I don't know, six weeks..." said the surprised director doubtfully.

"Don't worry, I haven't forgotten I've got court in the Ming Ho murder and the Armaco fraud case coming up during that time frame," Redmond assured him. "I'm not going to the North Pole or anything. I'll still be in the area. I'll make all my court dates and testify with bells on. I want to take this time for a personal project."

"What project?"

Redmond pulled one of his Dominican cigars out of his pocket. "You mind?"

"Only if you don't give me one." Redmond handed him a cigar. "Hang on a minute," the director said, his mouth watering. He got up and went to the door, which he locked. Then he went to the window air conditioner rumbling in the far wall. "Too damned hot outside to open a window," he said, turning the unit on high and also turning on an electric fan which sat on his desk. Papers started ruffling around the room and lifting off the desk; the director slammed assorted objects down as paperweights to keep them from taking flight. They both lit up and leaned back in their chairs, luxuriating in the fragrant smoke. "The smell of these will be all over the building in ten minutes," chuckled the director gleefully. "Then that politically correct bitch Betty Springer will spend the next twenty running up and down the halls in a self-righteous frenzy trying to catch the unreconstructed reactionary male lawmen who are violating the state's sacred no-smoking policy."

"Phil, do you realize that if anyone besides me overheard you make those remarks you could lose your job?" said Redmond seriously. "Plus Assistant Director Springer could file a lawsuit claiming that you were creating a hostile sexist atmosphere in the workplace that might cost you your life savings, your home, and everything you own? You'd be better off getting caught with your hand in the till. If you were just stealing money the attorney general and the governor might could cover your ass. Get hit with any kind of PC violation and they'll run for cover like spooked rabbits."

"I am well aware of it," replied Hightower bleakly. "Bucking for my job, Matt? Why don't you report me?"

"I'm going to forget I heard that," said Redmond.

"Sorry," sighed Hightower. "What's sickening is that there's some in the bureau who would go running to Betty Springer about my smoking a cigar or rat me out to the news media if I told a nigger joke. My God, sometimes it's like living under Stalin! I expect to come in some morning and see posters on the wall telling me Big Brother is watching!"

"Big Sister," chuckled Redmond.

"Anyway, getting back to you, this personal project that's going to take six weeks we can ill afford to give you is...?"

"You remember once or twice over the past three years you've asked me why I left Justice and joined the SBI?" asked Redmond.

"I do indeed," said the director, puffing away. "I never really bought the Waco story. I've always wondered why you really resigned from a job with a six-figure salary and enough perks and bennies effectively to double your pay, and an incredible retirement package. You tossed all that aside, and what did you do then? Did you join one of the two dozen law enforcement agencies in this country or in Europe who would have gone down on bended knee for your experience and expertise? Nope. Instead you came back to tobacco country to sign on with a pissant little state investigative agency with no real power, authority, or resources. This job pays less than a good secretary in the Research Triangle Park earns, we just barely have powers of arrest, and we're so politicized that someone with the right connections in the Democratic party can publicly buttfuck animals in the Asheboro zoo and still escape prosecution."

"How's Wiley's therapy coming?" asked Redmond.

"Hell, I don't know, ask the judge. Ask his damned shrink."

"Well, now, you got to remember Wiley didn't get off scot free," reminded Redmond. "The llama bit him in the ass." The director snorted. "Look, you asked and I'll tell you the whole story now. Waco was true enough as far as it went. I wouldn't have stayed Federal after that no matter what, but as to why I joined your little band of merry men specifically, the SBI has something I want."

"And what might that be?" asked the director curiously.

"Jurisdiction."

"Huh? I don't follow," said Hightower, puzzled.

Redmond slid the file folders across the desk to him. "The SBI has jurisdiction over this," he said quietly. "I want this case, Phil. I've been here three years and not taken a single day off specifically so I can accumulate enough vacation to work this case on my own time, concentrate on it without worrying about twenty others on my board. I'm asking for this leave starting October 1st. That gives you over two months' notice. That gives me two months to clear everything off my desk. I'll leave you with a clean slate, every i dotted, every t crossed. In return I want all six weeks I'm asking for. This investigation was never closed. I want you to assign it to me officially, so I have proper authority and so I can use the archives, use the lab if I need it, get assistance from the local cops in Chapel Hill and the Orange County Sheriff, so forth and so on, whatever I may require. I don't want you calling me in for anything or trying to cut me short. I don't give a damn if Peaches the transvestite whore bites off Billyboy's dick during a blow job under the statue of the Confederate soldier down on the Capitol grounds. If that happens you call the Secret Service, not me. *I am going to find the bastards who did this!*"

The director looked at the files. There was a faded rubber stamp in large lettering, *"Investigation #89945-70. Opened: October 24, 1970. Closed: _____."* The closure date was blank. "Orange County. Offense: Multiple Homicide" he read aloud from the jacket. He opened the first file. "Mary Jane Mears, female Caucasian, aged 16. Allison Jean Arnold, female Caucasian, aged 17." He looked up. "You know, Matt, it's odd. Ever since you came here, I've always had it in the back of my mind to ask you to take a look at this one, what with you being Sherlock Holmes and all, and I don't mean that in a facetious or disrespectful way. Tabloid bullshit aside, I got to say you're the best I've ever seen at looking at a crime scene and figuring out just what the hell happened, and then going out and bringing in the right people. Hell, yes, you can have your six weeks and you can have this case! But why? What got you interested..oh, sure, that's right, you're from Chapel Hill, aren't you?"

"Carrboro, actually, but it's the same thing. I grew up out of Carrboro along Highway 54, just a few miles from where I live now, and I went to Chapel Hill High School. I'd just turned 17 when it happened. I knew both the victims. Some time ago, I couldn't even exactly tell you how or when, I made up my mind that this is something I'm going to do for Mary Jane and Jeannie."

"What if you can't turn up anything new in six weeks?" asked the director. "This was twenty-five, almost twenty-six years ago. Trail's mighty cold and a lot of your witnesses are going to be long gone, dead or scattered to the four winds."

"Then I'll work another three years with no vacation and take another six weeks off," replied Matt. "I'm going to get these guys."

"What if you can't get them?" asked the director. "What if you just can't find any new leads after all this time? The agents who legged this in 1970 weren't fools, Matt, and two teenaged girls raped and murdered wouldn't have been a politically protected case. The SBI wouldn't have gone that far for anybody, not a double sex murder."

"I know that, Phil."

"Worse yet, suppose you come up with a theory and the men turn out to be dead? Or worst of all, you become sure you know and you just can't prove a damned thing? That kind of situation drives any lawman crazy. I know. I've had my share."

"I'll take my chances on that. If that's the way it plays out, at least I'll know, and I'll make damned sure they know I know it," said Matt grimly.

"You keep saying they, plural. Why is that? As I recall, our guys never even got a glimmer on this one. You got an idea already?" asked the director.

"I'm sure it was at least two killers, maybe three but no more," said Matt. "I've just about memorized those files over the past three years. There was no sign of forced entry and the investigators never figured out for sure how the killer or killers got in. The obvious deduction is that one of the girls knew them and let them in, but there's no proof one way or the other. The family dog was found in a hallway, its neck broken by a powerful twist."

The dog was a little mutt named Grouch, Matt recalled. *Mary Jane loved animals and would have turned the whole house into a menagerie if her mother had let her, but she doted on Grouch. Did the monster kill her dog in front of her eyes?* "Granted, one man could have committed these crimes if he were armed with a gun or a knife and could intimidate the girls into submitting," Matt went on, "But the MOs in each killing were different. To me that says two killers. Both victims were discovered nude and both had been raped, but there the patterns diverge, at least enough to suggest that the actors paired off, each with a victim. Mary Jane Mears was found in her bedroom upstairs, bound or strapped into a chair with swathes of heavy masking tape, tightly and efficiently wound. A belt belonging to her father was strapped around her waist, pinning her midsection to the chair. Beyond the sexual assault she was not tortured or manhandled. She was strangled swiftly and efficiently with a ligature believed by the medical examiner to be an Italian-style garotte, basing this conjecture on a bruise at the left side of her neck where the knot had been twisted tight, which indicates the killer was most likely left handed. Imprints in the flesh indicated the ligature was made of rope and was removed by the killer when he left. The scene in the photos is reminiscent of a judicial execution in the electric chair or the gas chamber. There is a distinct air of ritual display about it, at least to my perception, which as you know is a common element with many serial killers."

She knew she was going to die, thought Redmond to himself. For long minutes, she knew that it was all over for her at sixteen, that morning would never come again. She knew that she was going to be hurled against her will out into the cold empty darkness while the rest of us were to be allowed to stay behind here in the light and the warmth and the being. She must have cried out in her soul at the unfairness of it. I know I did. I still do. My love, my dearest in life, God forgive me this selfish thought which has always obsessed me, but in your last moments, did you think of me?

"So the difference in the two MOs was...?" prompted the director.

"Jeannie Arnold was found in the basement, also nude, also raped. Her wrists and ankles had been restrained by handcuffs or manacles, not masking tape. These were also removed from the scene by the killer when he left. Maybe he thought we could trace them. Jeannie's body was not bound in place like Mary Jane's, simply left lying on the laundry room floor, almost like she had been thrown away once the killer had no more use for her. Her body showed trauma caused by extensive torture. She had apparently been suspended by her wrists from an overhead water pipe and brutally flogged with a homemade whip or scourge which left indentations in the flesh identifiable by the pathologist as electrical cord. She received over fifty identifiable lashes. That's an extremely heavy beating even for a sexual homicide. She was also burned with cigarettes or a lighter on her breasts, genitals, and other places. The skin had been flayed from the soles of her feet with a knife or razor blade. Pins or needles were inserted into her flesh in 36 places, all her toenails and fingernails were ripped off, and a light bulb had been forcibly inserted into her anus and shattered. She was killed by a thrust from a long, thin-bladed weapon through her left eye into her brain, probably meaning that unlike suspect number one, Jeannie's killer was right-handed. The weapon wasn't found on the scene, like the other items taken away by the perpetrators, who mopped the floor after them in order to obliterate any bloody footprints."

She lay on the floor like a broken doll, Matt thought. *She had danced before us all earlier that night, her golden body a living flame. I loved Mary Jane, but I admired Jeannie openly. Mary Jane wasn't jealous, for everyone admired Jeannie, longed for her. A few hours later the fire maiden I remember was lying on a cellar floor broken and dead, after an ordeal of agony which must have driven her mad. By the time the end came she probably welcomed death, greeted it with joy and relief. Yet to me she's just another crime victim like the hundreds I've seen, more pathetic than most. Why can't I feel for Jeannie like I feel for Mary Jane? She was just as warm and alive, the crime against her just as evil. Why should I always think of this case as Mary Jane and sometimes almost forget poor Jeannie? That's not right, and I have to do this right. It's what I promised them.*

"Whew, my God, what a damned sadist!" growled the director, looking at the crime scene photos from a quarter century before. "How can some of these creeps get this sick?"

"I don't think Jeannie was tortured for sexual pleasure," said Redmond quietly. "I think she was tortured for information."

"Huh?" said the director. "What do you mean?"

"An interrupted burglary has never made much sense here," explained Redmond. "Nothing was stolen from a house full of valuable small appliances and knick-knacks. Dr. Margaret Mears' jewelry box was in plain sight, Dr. Andrew Mears' several expensive cameras were left alone. These guys stayed in the house for a minimum of three hours, yet they didn't take a dime or a spool of thread, not even so much as a beer from the fridge. They came to kill both those girls, and they came to interrogate Jeannie Arnold about something they believed she knew or something she had done. The killers brought with them the necessary tools to restrain their victims and the instruments of torture to use on Jeannie Arnold. Mary Jane Mears was killed execution style by someone who used masking tape and a pre-prepared ligature as an instrument of death, and I have come to believe that her death was almost incidental, or at least secondary to the main target, Jeannie Arnold. Jeannie was fiendishly tortured by someone who used handcuffs, not masking tape, and she was then killed with a bladed weapon, not strangled. If there was only one perp why didn't he kill Jeannie with the same ligature he used on Mary Jane? Why use two weapons? If we have a sadist here who tortures women for kicks, then he's alone in a house with two beautiful, naked young girls whom he has completely in his power. We assume he knows the parents are out of town and he won't be interrupted. That's sade heaven. Why not make a meal out of Mary Jane the same way he did Jeannie?"

"But they were both raped," pointed out the director.

"Were they?" asked Redmond. "Check the lab report. No semen was found in either body. The rape diagnosis was based on the pathologist's discovery of trauma, bruising and tearing in the vaginal and cervical walls of both victims. This has always been written off to the idea that our man or men can't ejaculate, a common phenomenon with sex offenders. I don't believe sexual gratification was the purpose. I think the rapes were committed with a broom handle or a dildo or something to make it look like a sex crime."

"While the victims were alive," breathed Hightower.

"While the victims were alive, aware of what was happening and possessed full capacity for suffering and humiliation, yes."

"If your foreign object rape theory is correct, then you realize you could also be looking for a woman?" pointed out the director. "Unlikely, but possible."

"I agree," said Redmond. "Unlikely but possible. I believe that Jeannie Arnold was tortured to make her reveal some information which the actors thought so vital that they were willing to commit a time-consuming, elaborate double murder in the middle of a populous town in order to obtain it."

"What kind of information could a 17-year-old high school girl have that would justify an act like...like this?" demanded the director, gesturing at the files.

"I have no idea on earth," said Matt. "That's what I'm going to take six weeks off to try and find out."

"That is a wild theory, Matt," said the director, shaking his head. "Have you got anything other than supposition to back it up?"

"The timetable of the crime fits my theory," said Matt. "The medical examiner on the scene gave the opinion that Mary Jane Mears died at approximately eleven o'clock, give or take half an hour. Jeannie Arnold's time of death is given as approximately one A.M., almost two hours later. Both girls were at the Harvest Ball dance at Chapel Hill High School that Friday night, October 23rd. The dance ended at ten o'clock. Mary Jane stayed on in the parking lot until about twenty past, when both girls drove home to the Mears house in Jeannie Arnold's car, a 1968 Plymouth Fury..."

"How do you know all that?" asked the director.

"Because I was with her." Matt hefted the files. "My first contact with law enforcement was being interviewed by the Chapel Hill Police and the SBI about this case at age 17. Fortunately, I went straight home after the dance, came in just as the eleven o'clock news was coming on and my father was starting in on his second case of National Bohemian beer. He went into one of his roaring tirades which woke up my mother, so both of them could vouch for my whereabouts at the crucial time. As the boy friend of one of the girls I would have been a prime suspect otherwise. As it is, I'm sure Daddy has always regretted not finding some way to frame me for the killings."

"I gather he's not beyond it. No offense, Matt."

"None taken. My father is the only man outside the narcotics business I have ever known whom I consider to be genuinely devoid of a single scruple, yes. Anyway, getting back to my point, if Mary Jane was killed about the time I was listening to that sodden bully bellow at me, allowing ten to fifteen minutes for her and Jeannie to drive home, then the killers must have been waiting for them. They killed Mary Jane almost immediately. Why? A person or person breaks into the house. They steal nothing. Instead they wait for the two girls to come home, then overpower them and bind them. Jeannie Arnold, the most important, is bound in handcuffs to make damned sure she can't get away, and she is taken to the basement where her screams will not be heard while she is tortured. Mary Jane Mears is taken upstairs to her room, forced to strip and submit to the violation of her body, either sexually or with a foreign object. Then she is bound into the chair, quickly and efficiently put to death, the killer puts his garotte in his pocket and goes elsewhere. Meanwhile downstairs Jeannie Arnold is being methodically beaten and tortured with instruments brought to the scene for that purpose. This goes on for a good two hours, during which the killers already have one dead body in the house and no guarantee that some alert neighbor hasn't heard or seen something which awakens suspicion and called the cops.

"Now, Phil, this is what we *know* happened due to the evidence found on the scene and the medical examiners' report. Does this sound like a burglary gone bad to you? After two hours I think the killers either got what they wanted from Jeannie or decided they would never get it, and they put Jeannie to death with a blade. Another thing which makes me feel there were two of them, by the by, is the fact that there is a recognized psychological difference in stranglers and blade killers. It's certainly not out of the question for a murderer to use different weapons, but it's sufficiently uncharacteristic to raise questions. The actors departed and not one trace of them has been found from that day to this. How many common or garden-variety criminal low-lifes have you known who could keep a secret like that for twenty-six years, Phil? If it was run-of-the-mill scumbags, black or white, somebody would have been running their mouth about it. So far as I can tell, the SBI investigation was handled completely professionally and on a high priority basis. They simply could not find a single solitary clue. That's because they were thinking in terms of ordinary criminals or sex offenders. Whoever these guys were, the one thing they weren't is ordinary."

"I don't know. It's got more holes than a Swiss cheese, Matt," said the director, shaking his head dubiously.

"Well, I think I can turn it into a nice solid cheddar."

"If that's true and these killers are somebody special, and if they're still around, they might not like you poking a stick at this after all these years," warned the director. "They might try to get you before you get them."

"I hope so, Phil," said Redmond softly, a thin smile playing around his lips which made the director shudder inwardly. "I certainly hope so."

II

It was almost five o'clock on the afternoon of Friday, August 30th, when the moving van left, a gigantic behemoth easing gently out of the driveway of the house on Boundary Street and down the narrow street. Heather was thankful her biweekly paycheck had direct-deposited the night before, otherwise she could not have given the moving men the $50 tips each that she had to admit they richly deserved for their help. As it was, she and Tori would be eating out of cans for the next two weeks. Every item of furniture they had brought from Seattle and seventy-odd cardboard cartons of various sizes, which had been sitting in storage in a Raleigh warehouse, were now piled up in various rooms of the house in no particular order. "One last culinary splurge and then it's Chef Boyardee time," Heather warned as she gave Tori ten dollars and some loose change and allowed her to take the car on an expedition to McDonald's. "And make sure you get it back here before the food is cold!" she commanded. "We haven't got the microwave unpacked yet, and there's nothing more gross and disgusting than cold fries and a gooey cold Big Mac." The thought of ordering in a pizza had occurred to her, but Heather decided she wanted a little time alone in the house, to feel it out.

When she heard the car pull out of the driveway Heather collapsed onto the newly-unloaded sofa in the big living room and pulled off the bandana from her hair. Her jeans and blouse were damp and sweaty from helping the movers heft and tote. *Definitely early to bed tonight,* she thought. *We've got the whole Labor Day weekend to unpack. God, it's hot in the South! Isn't that air conditioning working at all?* She knew it was; she could hear the rumble and feel the cool air from the vents on her face. There was no question that other than the one macabre aspect of her new home's history, this house was an unbelievable bargain which someone on her salary had no right on earth to expect. Two stories of gleaming whitewashed brick with bright green shutter and trim, a newly refinished roof, a fully fitted kitchen with an electric range (Heather had always been paranoid about natural gas), a beautiful back garden and a stately oak on the front lawn were more than she'd dreamed possible. There were sixteen spacious rooms and four bathrooms, four bedrooms (one with a balcony) and a sewing or recreation room with skylights on the upper floor, another bedroom, a den and a library with fitted shelves downstairs, a large glassed-in conservatory, an oak-paneled formal dining room and breakfast nook. Heather simply could not believe her good fortune. The neighborhood was quiet and leafy, with wide sidewalks and picturesque small ravines cutting through it.

In Seattle it had taken her an exhausting and nightmarish hour-long commute under even the best of rush-hour traffic conditions to get from her home in Ballard to Microsoft on the East Side. It was onto Interstate 5 South at 85th Street, then a lengthy battle to get into the far left lane, then onto the 520 and over the long Rosellini bridge across Lake Washington, then onto the 405 until she could exit, then a crawl through street traffic, only to do the same in reverse at five o'clock. And God help her if she couldn't make it into that far left lane on I-5 in the mornings; if she missed the 520 she could only go with the traffic flow through downtown Seattle, take I-90 East across the lake and get off in Bellevue, a good extra hour. Or God help her if there was an accident or tie-up on any of the freeways; there were times when she had not arrived home until eight o'clock at night, and had spent her time sitting in traffic desperately trying to keep track of Tori by cellular phone. Now Heather was within ten minutes' brisk walk of her job, no more than five if she caught the downtown shuttle bus at the corner of Franklin Street and Boundary. She could come home for lunch. The very idea overwhelmed her. The house was an incredible stroke of luck at a time in Heather's life when she most needed it. Surely a minor matter of past unspeakable horror could be lived with? Beyond the sound of the air conditioning there was silence throughout the house now. "Should I plug in the radio and get some electronic noise in here?" Heather asked herself aloud. Instead she decided to take a quiet personal inspection tour of her new abode, based now on her recently acquired knowledge of the events of 1970.

What she had learned about the house came from old back issues of the brilliantly named Chapel Hill *Newspaper,* which in those days had been called the Chapel Hill *Weekly.* Heather recalled her shock as she suddenly saw her house looming on the front page in the microfilm reader screen. It was quite recogniza-ble, the same two-story white brick structure, the same dark green shutters, although there was a slightly different portico. Sometime in the intervening years someone had replaced the wrought-iron trellis work of those days with the Doric columns of today. The big oak at the corner of the lot was still here, but there had been a few more trees in the yard twenty-five years ago, a couple of maples and what looked like a chinaberry tree. Crime scene tape was strung in front of the door and a young black police officer standing guard managed to look as pale as a black man could look as he stared into the photographer's lens. A 1968 Plymouth Fury was parked in the driveway in front of the garage.

Heather got up from the sofa and climbed the broad carpeted front stairs to the second floor. She could find out little detail from the newspaper stories except that the killings had been brutal. The Mears girl had been found upstairs in one of the bedrooms while the other victim, Allison Jean Arnold, had been discovered in the basement. Heather stepped slowly through all the upstairs rooms. There was no way she could tell in which bedroom the murder had taken place. She even looked closely at the parquet floors for bloodstains, but she could see nothing. She went back downstairs and into the basement through the door in the kitchen. She had been down there when she toured the house before and seen the washer and dryer hookups, but she had not known then that it had been the scene of a murder. She snapped on the light at the head of the wooden stairs, then slowly descended, one step and a time, looking around her. It didn't look like a murder scene, but then what did a 25-year-old murder scene look like? The basement was warm and musty, but that was all. But what would Tori experience here?

Heather had always tried to avoid thinking about certain incidents in Tori's past. Life had been confused and complicated enough without trying to deal with the fact that her daughter appeared to be psychic or sensitive to some kind of supernatural world. There were occasions from the girl's earliest childhood where she had claimed to see things no one else could see, so insistently and graphically that it was hard to accept them as pretend. There had been times when Heather would pause outside the toddler's bedroom late at night and hear her talking baby-talk in a normal tone of voice as if she was carrying on a conversation, and sometimes giggle in a certain way she only laughed if she were being tickled. When Heather would snap on the light and ask who little Vicky, as she was known then, was talking to, it was never to stuffed toys or imaginary animals with fantasy names, but children with real names like Donald and Karen and Steven and Nita. When she was five there had been the invisible "granny" no one else could see. At her first school there had been the unpleasant old man on the playground who frightened her, but whom none of the teachers could see every time the child ran crying to them. After a parent-teacher conference over these sightings it seemed to Heather that Tori had finally come to understand that some things were real and some weren't, that real meant what others could see, and that if she saw or heard anything else it was a very good idea to keep quiet about it.

There had been a few strange occurrences since then, notably the night when ten-year-old Tori had awakened screaming and sobbing the house down, wailing over and over that her Daddy was hurt and bleeding. It wasn't until noon the next day that Heather got a call from the police in Florida telling her that her ex-husband had checked into a rundown Orlando motel, consumed a 3-liter glass jug of Gallo Rosé fortified with a pint of vodka, and about three o'clock in the morning had laid down on the bed and cut his own throat with a newly purchased K-Mart carving knife. Allowing for the time difference between Orlando and Seattle, Bill had died at the same time Tori had her seizure.

Greg had been a senior in high school when it happened, always passionately protective of his mother and angrily hostile to his father, and he made no secret of his lack of any grief. "The guy was a louse, Mom," was his view. "He was a drunk and he hit you." Tori was almost catatonic for two days and Heather was about to have her admitted to the hospital when the girl suddenly snapped out of it. "I want to go to Daddy's funeral," she had said. So she had gone with Heather and Greg down to California, her first time on an airplane, looking out the window onto the tops of the clouds and saying nothing. She had been silent throughout the funeral, silent as the coffin was lowered into the ground, and from that day on had never mentioned her father again. To all appearances she was now what passed for a normal and well-adjusted teenager, admittedly a hard thing to quantify in 1996 when some sixteen-year-olds carried submachine guns and others couldn't read on a nine-year old level. For reasons she could not fully explain, Heather was perpetually worried sick about her, terrified for her future. She had an idea that she was afraid Tori's life would end up being as full of pain and hardship and disappointment as hers had been.

But she could not get out of her mind Tori's casual comment about hearing singing in the empty rooms of this house. It bothered her. A song Heather remembered from her own youth. A song from 1970.

She was digging around in a cardboard box for plates and utensils when Tori pulled back into the driveway and came bouncing in with a big white Mickey-D's bag which filled the breakfast nook with the glorious aroma of grease and cholesterol. Big Macs, McNuggets, McChickens and fries appeared from the bag. "I bought you an extra McChicken with my own money," said Tori, blithely ignoring the fact that Heather gave her the allowance to begin with. "You're too skinny. You need some meat on your bones if you're going to get a boyfriend at your age. Your Coke may be a bit watery from all the ice. I got a milk shake. Who's here?"

"Beg pardon?" asked Heather, her mouth full of Big Mac.

"Who's that girl upstairs?" asked Tori. "I saw her looking down at me through the window as I was coming in. Does she want some fries?"

Heather's heart began to pound. She calmly put down her burger. "There's no one here, Tori," she said.

Tori looked up quickly, then shrugged. "Oh, okay. I guess I must have mistook her for something else."

"Mistaken something else for her," corrected Heather. "Tori, what did this girl you saw in the window look like?"

"I told you, I must have made a mistake. I didn't see anybody," said Tori.

"Does it happen often, honey?" asked Heather carefully. "You can talk to me about it, you know. I promise I won't ridicule you or disbelieve you. Do you want to talk about it?"

Tori looked down at her plate. "Uh, I don't think so. Can I pass on that one, Mom?"

"All right, if that's what you want," said Heather. *God, how do you deal with a subject like this?* she thought despairingly. *Now dear, be a good girl and tell Mommy about all the dead people you see?*

They ate for a while in silence. Tori finished and stood up. "Daddy still loves you," she said simply. Heather looked up, shocked, realizing that her daughter was entirely serious and was perfectly certain, whatever the source of that certainty might be, that she was stating a fact.

"I'm glad," whispered Heather, her eyes filling with tears. "Thank you for telling me that, honey. You know I still love him too, in spite of everything, don't you?"

"I know," Tori replied. She leaned over and kissed her gently, then left the room.

For the rest of the evening they unpacked and sorted, with the boom box in the kitchen turned up loud enough to be heard all over the house. There was a brief war over the station. Tori wanted rock and Heather wanted National Public Radio. Spinning the dial up and down, there seemed to be an inordinate number of country stations. "Why not listen to some of that for a while?" suggested Heather. "We're in the South now, we need to start becoming accustomed to the native culture."

"Chapel Hill isn't the South, it's more like New England, everybody here says. They don't want to be part of the South here and if that's their music I don't blame them," said Tori in a huff. "All it is, is some guy howling about how his woman done left him, his mama's in prison, he lost his job, his dog died, his pickup truck's been repossessed and he's out of beer. Let me play my Cheryl Crow CD."

"If I can play my Nancy Griffith afterwards," said Heather.

"Totally mush!" complained Tori. They finally compromised on an oldies station. Heather was in the middle of a box of sheets and pillowcases when she heard Three Dog Night with a sudden shiver: "*Celebrate, celebrate, dance to the music...*" But it was the radio.

About ten o'clock, they went upstairs where the beds were disassembled, mattresses and frames leaning against the walls in the hall. "Okay, decision time," said Heather. "Which room do you want? You and me will be up here. I'm pretty sure Greg and Sheri will want to occupy the downstairs bedroom when they move in. More privacy and further away from the battle-ax mother-in-law."

"They'll want to be down there where we can't hear the mattress shake," sniggered Tori.

"Don't knock it, kiddo, you'll be making the mattress shake in a few years yourself," said Heather with resignation.

"What makes you think I'm not already?" asked Tori mischievously.

"You're not, are you?" asked Heather sharply. "I mean, when would you get the time?" she continued, trying to lighten her tone. "I watch you like a hawk."

"You sure do," giggled Tori. "Sorry, Mom, didn't mean to give you any more gray hairs. Nope, no mattress-shaking in my life as yet, although if I'd gotten my license in Seattle and Tim Brewman wised up and dumped that skag Connie Michaels this year, you might have had something to worry about."

"Mmmm, let's see, Tim was the football player?" asked Heather, smiling, secretly relieved.

"You got him. A hundred and eighty pounds of prime USDA inspected beef."

"And the official line is only men can be sexist!" said Heather in exasperation. "I don't suppose it's possible that this boy might have a mind as well?"

"I dunno," said Tori with a shrug. "Anything's possible, I guess."

"I *hope* that's the beginning of what will blossom into a very dry, witty sense of humor," returned Heather. "Now, which bedroom do you want?" Tori walked without hesitation into the first room on the left.

"This one," she said.

"Is this the window where you saw the girl's face?" asked Heather. Tori stopped and stood silently. "Honey, I'll say my piece and then I promise I'll shut up about it until such time, if ever, that you want to talk to me about this part of your life. Just before I bought this house, the real estate people had a talk with me about something pretty unpleasant that happened here a long time ago."

"The two girls who were murdered," said Tori. "I know, Mom. They're still here."

"Oh, God," breathed Heather, feeling faint. "That's right. Two girls about your age were killed in this house. I went ahead and I bought the place because frankly there is no way in hell we would ever get a deal like this for the money I make, no place where we could all live together, which is what we're going to have to do if Greg and I are going to make ends meet and get you through college. I don't believe in ghosts or curses, but I think you have a different perspective than I do, and I respect and acknowledge that fact. If at any time you feel that there is something, well, *wrong* here, I want you to come to me and tell me. You won't be laughed at or disbelieved, I promise. I don't know what we can do about it, but we'll cross that bridge when we come to it. OK?"

Tori turned to her. "You mean is there something eeeee-viillll in this howssse, ya ha ha, no. I don't think we'll see any blood dripping out of the faucets and I won't be turning my head around and around and spewing green glowing puke all over you any time soon."

"Well, that's a relief," admitted Heather. "You haven't done that since you were two."

"I'll tell you what there is, though. There's a lot of terrible grief and unhappiness, most of it up here, in this room. I want this room because she's very lonely and sad and I think she wants me here. Downstairs in the laundry room there's something really bad, fear, panic crazy and sick-making. The girl who died down there died real bad, Mom, real hard. I'd rather not go down there if that's all right with you."

"That's fine, honey," said Heather with a nod. *Great,* she thought, *Now I have to go down there by myself.* "Do you think we're going to have any, er, problems with our, ah, previous tenants? Are they going to, oh, object to our presence?"

"Mom, I don't know how to explain this," said Tori slowly, "But I'm not sure either of them know where they are, how much time has gone by, or who we are. They're kind of stuck here. The one up here can communicate, I think, a little bit. The one downstairs is out of her mind with pain and terror. She's been dying down there for all these years."

"Oh, God," breathed Heather again, stunned. "Is there anything we can do, honey?"

"Catch the bastards who did it to them," said Tori without hesitation. "They can't leave here because it's not over for them. It can't be over until everyone knows who did it to them."

"Hoo boy," groaned Heather. "Look, are you going to be able to sleep in here tonight?"

"Are you?" asked Tori.

"We'll see. Okay, let's get your bed in here."

Later that night Heather lay in the darkness in the king-sized bed she had shipped from Seattle. "Mighty big bed for a single mother," Tori had quipped slyly.

"Hope springs eternal," Heather had returned with a wry smile. She'd long since given up in her own mind any hope that she would ever get married again, but at the same time she was emotionally starved, bitterly depressed, and she desperately missed sex. True, she was a young-looking 42, but she was also tall and still a bit gawky as she had been when she was an adolescent. She was in the genteel poverty tax bracket, and she came with a nubile teenager attached whom Heather was honest enough to admit to herself she feared as a temptation to any man in her life. *But damn, it's been a long time since I got laid!* she thought as she stretched her legs under the sheets over the expansive mattress. *I need to remedy that while I can still attract some decent one-night stands. I need something more to remember when I'm old and sitting by the fire with my knitting and my cat, a time of life which is getting closer by the day. Better let the guys at work alone, and no married men, but surely I can latch on to some horny professors? Maybe a grad student or two? What about other women? That's a possibility too, just so long as they look like women. No bull dykes or butches. A woman isn't as good as a man, but she's better than jacking off.* In the ten years since she had divorced Bill, there had been eight sexual liaisons, three of them lesbian, all of them brief and not overly satisfactory. *Hmm*, thought Heather, finally drifting off to sleep, *Better be careful if I do end up with a female lover. Always her place or the No-Tell Motel. Greg would just plain freak and Tori—-well, just because I do it doesn't mean I want her doing it.* She reflected on how hypocritical she would have found such an attitude when she was young, before she had children of her own. *Do as I say, not as I do, right, Mom? Damn, I hope Tori's never so desperate for a little comfort she has to take another woman to bed!*

✶   ✶   ✶

Some time later Heather awoke. The house was quiet; the air conditioning had stopped. The very first twinges of light in the east showed outside through the curtainless windows. She got up and shuffled into the bathroom, urinated, came out and was about to crawl back into bed when she heard something outside her door. She reached for the bedside lamp and then remembered it was on the floor; they hadn't brought up the nightstands yet. She reached down and turned on the light, then pulled her robe off a cardboard box and put it on. She opened the door. Then the sound came again. Someone was crying, a woman or a girl, weeping softly, desolately.

Trembling, Heather turned on the hall light. The sound stopped. She tiptoed to Tori's bedroom door and quietly opened it. The light shone in on her daughter, lying on her back, her head to one side, breathing deeply, sound asleep. It had not been Tori who wept. Heather closed the door and turned out the hall light, then turned on the overhead light in her bedroom and sat on the bed. After a while she muttered to herself, "Bullshit! This is an emergency!" From her purse she fished out an unopened pack of cigarettes and a Cricket lighter. She tore open the pack, mangling it so badly that it broke open and the cigarettes spilled all over the floor. She picked one up and lit it, her hand shaking as if she had the ague, inhaling it in three long drags. She went into the bathroom, threw the butt into the toilet and lit another cigarette. Just as she finished it the sound of a girl's weeping came again from down the hall, soft and unmistakable.

Heather buried her face in her hands. "Dear God," she whispered. "Have mercy. Tori needs me. Don't let me go insane in this place."

III

On the first day of October the summer heat finally broke for a bit, and autumn arrived. The leaves along Franklin Street were perceptibly turning color now. Matt was wearing a light windbreaker as he crossed the parking lot at University Mall to the Kerr Drugs.

It was his first day off on his long leave. He had spent the day in his Carrboro apartment going over the entire SBI case file yet again, from beginning to end. He cleared off the one full-sized table he owned, broke the files down and laid them out in separate stacks: medical reports, witness interviews, agent reports, crime scene photos and inventories, newspaper clippings, and a large stack he designated "the MacDonald mess", documents dealing with SBI attempts to determine what linkage if any there was with the Jeffrey MacDonald murders in Fort Bragg on February 16th, 1970. Matt was completely convinced that the whole MacDonald thing was a dead end, and he was eager to leap right in to doing legwork, but he knew that his first task, however reluctantly, was to go over the MacDonald stack and make 100% sure it was a dead end. Something might leap out at him that would knock his theories into a cocked hat. It wouldn't take him long. He already knew the whole huge file by heart.

By six o'clock the rush hour had died down and Matt decided to run down to the mall and get a few things, as well as stop by his tobacconist and stock up on cigars and pipe tobacco. The guys at the bureau had taken up a collection on his first birthday with the SBI and had bought him a sardonic but pleasant gift: a big Sherlock Holmes-style clay meerschaum pipe. Matt made sure he never lit it up in the bureau's designated smoking area, i.e. the public sidewalk, but he found that smoking the monster at home genuinely did relax his body and concentrate his mind. This was definitely going to be a three-pipe problem. Daylight savings time was still in effect, so it was light outside. The air was crisp and bracing in the parking lot and downright chilly inside, because the mall air conditioning was still on. Matt spent about twenty minutes buying and batting the breeze with Derek Bentley, the seedy little Englishman who owned the Up In Smoke Shop, while Bentley mixed up a pound of Matt's personal blend. Matt needed a few toiletry items as well, and he stepped into Kerr Drugs and picked up a basket. "Hey, Maggie," he said with a cheerful nod to the full-figured black woman who managed the store, a casual acquaintance.

She beckoned him over and whispered to him, "Mr. Redmond, could you stick around for a a bit? There's a gentlemen down on aisle five who's putting merchandise in his pockets. I can't say or do anything until he actually leaves the premises without paying, that's our procedure, but to tell you the truth I'm a bit scared to approach him. I know you're SBI and not a Chapel Hill cop, but…"

"I can apprehend someone committing a crime if I see him doing it, anywhere in the state of North Carolina. Do you think he may be armed?" asked Matt, quietly turning his head to try and catch a glimpse of the shoplifter. All he could see was the tangled, uncombed back of the man's head.

"No, I don't think so, but I know he's crazy," said the woman worriedly. "I seen him around the mall a lot. He's always talking to himself, and he looks really spacey. I think he may be on drugs. He's not a homeless person or a trashy type, he's always well dressed, but he don't bathe regular and sometimes it's pretty intense getting downwind of him. He obviously ain't right in the head. I don't know why security don't ban him from the mall. He scares people."

"Wait here, and stick this behind the counter for me," said Matt, handing him his bag from Up In Smoke. Matt eased down the aisles and peeped around the corner. The man was over six feet tall and looked late thirtyish, with a pasty pale complexion and unkempt brown hair that fell down over his collar. He was studying the paperback book rack, mumbling to himself, oblivious to everyone and everything else. Abruptly he reached out, took a book, and stuck it into the pocket of his expensive sport coat. Both pockets swung and bulged from whatever he had stuffed into them. Matt grinned and withdrew.

Back at the counter he said, "Yes, you're right. He's crazy as a loon and he's probably on drugs, prescription medication to keep him from collapsing into a dangerously violent schizophrenic state and going berserk with a chain saw or something equally spectacular. You were smart not to approach him on your own. He hasn't done anything really bad since he was young, at least not that I know of, but there have been a whole series of assaults, petty thefts and destruction and a couple of unexplained small fires. The potential is always there for him to lose control. He shouldn't be at large in society, he should be in an institution, but his father is one of the wealthiest men in the South and unless this fine young cannibal freaks out someday and just plain kills somebody, he'll never see the inside of Dorothea Dix. I might add that he is also the darling of the Chapel Hill artsy-craftsy touchy-feely New Age set, a brilliant pianist who gives regular recitals around the country, and a composer of no little talent who had his first symphony performed at the age of 15. I've often wondered how that high-toned crowd he hangs with deal with his occasional outbursts of hysteria and random violence."

"You know him?" asked Maggie in surprise.

"Oh, yes, I know him. He knows me, too, and if we're going to catch him out he mustn't see me. I'm going to stand over here by the paper racks with a newspaper in front of my face like I'm reading it. I can watch him in the overhead mirrors. If he leaves without paying for all that stuff in his pockets, I'll follow him out and bust his stinky ass while you call 911." The subterfuge with the newspaper wasn't even necessary. The man didn't go through the checkout line at all, he simply shuffled out the far door into the parking lot. "That's it," called Matt as he headed out the door. "Make that call, Maggie."

Matt caught up with the tall, shambling figure at the first row of cars. He gripped the suspect's arm like a steel vise, and the man's face went slack with astonishment. *"You!""*gasped the thief.

"Excuse me, sir, I am an SBI agent and I have reason to believe that you have removed merchandise from the drug store without paying for it," said Matt formally. "Accordingly I am going to search you. Put your hands on the trunk of this car, feet back and spread them..."

"Motherfucker! Swine! Son of a bitch!" screamed the man, eyes rolling, spittle flying from his mouth, his face twisting in sudden lunatic rage. *"Bastard! I'll kill you!"* Matt expected a wild punch and braced to block it and retaliate with a knockout blow, but instead the suspect snarled like a beast and literally went for his throat, grabbing the back of Matt's head and pulling his face forward, his jaws open to bite and tear at Matt's jugular vein with his teeth.

"Jesus shit!" cursed Matt, shooting out one hand to push the madman away and giving him a sharp knee intended for the groin, but his opponent had twisted around so the knee only caught the meaty part of his thigh. The shoplifter staggered back and flailed his fist in an enraged punch which Matt blocked easily, sinking his own fist into the man's belly once, then twice, then a right to the mouth which sent him to his knees, then another right, then another, as Matt completely lost his temper and hammered the swaying thief's face. He collapsed on to sidewalk and Matt kicked him in the ribs. "You goddamned fruitcake!" he breathed. "Not so easy picking on a full grown man as it is to torture cats and guinea pigs to death, is it? Not so easy as beating up a twelve year old girl and buttfucking her, is it?"

"You're the crazy one," said the broken thief on the ground. "You tell lies. You tell lies about Mama and Daddy. You're hateful and evil. You try to get money from Daddy by extortion and threats. You deserted your wife and your children and left them starving with no money at all." He tried to get up, his face dripping blood in gobbets. Matt launched another kick.

"Stay down!" he yelled. "You say one more word and by God I'll kick every tooth in your head out! You yellow, contemptible piece of trash!" He reached down into the man's pockets and pulled out the paperback book, a Barbara Cartland romance of all things, along with several women's cosmetic items, a plastic bottle

of STP gas treatment, a small china figurine of some generic European peasant girl, four Zodiac key rings, a pack of four AA batteries, a child's school pencil sharpener, a packet of peanuts, and a UNC Tar Heels swizzle stick. "What is this shit, Sid?" demanded Matt angrily. "This is trash! Why are you stealing trash?" He pulled out Sid's wallet from his pocket and opened it, finding six $100 bills and a thick wad of tens and twenties. "You're walking around here with more than I clear in a single paycheck, and you're stealing stupid little crappy things like this? Sid, do you understand that this is crazy? Do you understand that *you* are crazy? Do you understand that you are deeply sick in your mind and you need real help in a real mental institution, not those asshole tame shrinks over at Duke that Daddy pays two hundred bucks an hour just to keep you doped up and ambulatory? When in God's name will you understand that Daddy *is not your friend?* That he *does not want to help you?* That he wants you to be like this forever?"

"You're a liar and a murderer. You murdered those men in Mexico even though you knew they were innocent. You murdered a Mexican woman, too."

"*Shit!*" howled Matt in rage and frustration, in his fury kicking Sid in the side yet again. Sid fell to the pavement and began to weep like a child. A small crowd had gathered, but no one intervened, all of them awestruck at Matt's fearsome rage. "Far out, man!" came a voice from among the spectators.

"*That's enough!*" came a sharp voice of command. Matt looked up and saw a tall, muscular young black man in uniform getting out of a Chapel Hill police cruiser that had pulled up behind him. "What's going on here? Oh, hi, Matt. This our shoplifter? Man, you really worked him over, didn't you?"

"Hi, Jamal," said Matt wearily. He pointed to the incongruous collection of bric-a-brac on the ground. "That's what crybaby here was stealing. Crap. He's not a thief, really, he's a klepto, among other things. He won't get help, real help from somebody who wants to straighten him out." The Chapel Hill cop drew Matt over to the police cruiser.

"Uh, Matt, I saw that last kick as I was pulling up, and no way was it called for," he said in a worried tone. "We may lose this one on excessive force. That's not like you, man. What's the situation here? You know this guy? What's his name?"

"Sid Redmond," said Matt with a sigh. "He's my brother. We both inherited the same asshole gene from our father, but he can't seem to keep his under control like I can. Usually I can, anyway. I'm sorry if this gets tossed on excessive, but believe me, that kick was called for. He's had it coming for a long, long time."

*   *   *

It was the next nightfall. Matt had spent the day going over the MacDonald mess and reassuring himself that there was no conceivable link between the Chapel Hill murders and the Jeffrey MacDonald massacre; the stack of pertinent documents had been returned to the file. He sat in his armchair under a single pool of light from a standing lamp, nursing a National Bohemian beer and debating idly whether he had enough energy to pick up the remote and turn on CNN. He looked at the beer. *National Bo. Daddy drank National Bo. Probably still does if he can get it down in Charleston. Why do I drink it? It's horse piss. Even with the crappy salary the bureau pays me I could afford to buy the odd six-pack of some good microbrew. Something deeply psychological here. Am I interested? Naaah.* The phone rang; Matt listened to his answering machine run through the greeting and waited to see who it was. A male voice spoke hesitantly. "Uh, hi, ah, look, Mr. Redmond, I mean Agent Redmond, I'm, ah, kind of a friend of the family out there on Mile End Road, and I was wondering if maybe there wasn't some way we could handle the incident last night regarding Sidney Redmond on an out-of-court basis..."

Matt laughed out loud and picked up the phone. "Steve, I know it's been a while, but those times I called you did say enough before you realized it was me and hung up so that I can recognize your voice. How's it been going?"

"Ahh, oh, it's going OK," said Steve, flustered.

"You should have stayed on that Dew Drop Inn murder case over there in Smithfield," Matt admonished. "You would have gotten to cross examine me."

"Uh, that was why I recused myself and withdrew from the case," said Steve. "It would have been conflict of interest."

"Bullshit. You withdrew because you would have had to sit in the same courtroom with me, pay attention to my testimony, and cross-examine me, all of which involve acknowledging the fact that I exist. You withdrew because Daddy has your balls in a vise through the trust fund. Jesus, Steve, it's not as if lawyers don't make any money in this country! You're not like Sid, you can make your own living. You're not dependent on Daddy."

"Oh, so now you're an expert on legal ethics?" snapped Steve. "Gee, it must be great to be an all-knowing infallible oracle on every topic under the sun. Daddy's right, you aren't anywhere near as smart as you think you are. You're ten per cent brains and ninety per cent ego."

"You've had your law degree how long now?" asked Matt. "Five years? Six? I've been in and out of military and civilian courtrooms for the past twenty-odd years and I have seen lawyers pull tricks your professors down on Duke campus don't even dream exist. Yes, Steve, in some respects I do know more than you do about the law, albeit from a cop's perspective. I know enough to be aware that what you are now trying to do regarding Sid's sticky fingers is unethical and possibly illegal, depending on how far you and Daddy are willing to go to pull Sid's chestnuts out of the fire. Don't worry, I won't turn you in. I'm not recording this but I don't mind if you do."

"I'm not recording this conversation!" protested Steve.

"I have to get my bugsmasher fixed, then," said Matt flatly. "The little flashing red light tells me there's a recording device on the line. That's illegal, by the way. FCC regulations state that you're supposed to have a beep at fifteen second intervals, otherwise it's a Federal offense. I won't bust you on that either, though. Go ahead and make your pitch. I'm curious."

There was a moment of silence, then the small red light stopped flashing, indicating that the recorder on the other end had been turned off. Matt made no comment. "Look, Matt, I'm going to level with you. This is a bad situation. It could develop into a dangerous situation. I spent most of today out at the Plantation trying to calm Sid down. He claims you beat him up while some Chapel Hill cop, a black guy, an Officer Jamal Watkins, held him down. We're filing a civil action against Officer Watkins and the police department alleging excessive force, but Sid keeps saying he's going to start carrying a gun and he'll kill you if you ever lay a hand on him again. Me and Michelle between us pretty much had him settled down, then Daddy calls from Charleston and Sid tells him the whole tale and by the end of it they're both roaring. I could hear Daddy as well as if he was on the speaker phone, which he wasn't. I've never heard him bellow like that since we were kids, honest, Matt. I didn't think he still had it in him."

"Still gets to you, doesn't it, Cheetah?" asked Matt softly. In his memory he could hear it still. There had been some beating in those days, of course, just enough to give bite to Daddy's bark, but always there had been the constant roaring, the bellowing, the abuse, the insults, all delivered at the drop of a hat in a stentorian voice that shook the very walls of the house. Matt thought of his childhood largely in terms of hills and valleys in the decibel level; the rare intervals of silence always stuck out. "Don't worry, Cheetah. It would get to me if I heard it again."

"Don't call me that, Matt. We're not kids any more." Matt had been Tarzan, while Steve, seven years younger, had been Cheetah. "Matt, I think we can get Sid off this gun thing," continued Steve in a worried voice. "Needless to say, Michelle and I have always made sure there's never any guns in the house. Actually, a while back she threatened to leave him if he ever got one and Daddy backed her up."

"I imagine even Daddy has sense enough to be scared of the idea of Sid with a piece," remarked Matt drily.

"Well, that's none of your business. I'm not going to discuss Daddy with you."

"That's a large part of the problem. You never do," said Matt. "I wish you would. We both might learn some things."

"Dammit, Matt, will you listen? Anyway, Mickey will keep a weather eye out for any weapons he might get hold of, and if it comes to that, I'll tell the Orange County Sheriff's people about Sid's mental history and they won't issue him a permit. But Daddy is another matter. Sid is damaged and weak. Daddy is..."

"Daddy is cold sane and as dangerous as a cobra. Yes, Steve, I know. I haven't forgotten the stripped lug nuts on my Buick. I haven't forgotten that .30-06 bullet that eased on through my window last summer."

"That was those damned dopers you chase around for a living!" exclaimed Steve. "You know, Matt, you're not a well person. Your paranoia about our father really sickens me, especially the way you blame Daddy for things like that which you bring on yourself through your own behavior!"

"Steve, I'm a cop. For a long time I was a DEA cop. We make it a point to know at any given time just who's gunning for us, so if somebody takes a pot shot or tampers with our car we know where to look. We have to know these things. It's a matter of survival. Both of the incidents I mentioned were the work of petty criminals with no involvement in any case I ever handled, punks who were suddenly flashing a lot of money before the attacks, who within hours of their arrest mysteriously acquired the best criminal defense attorneys in the state of North Carolina, who did minimum time, and who are now driving late-model Cadillacs. Don't piss down my back and tell me it's raining, Steve. And I damned sure haven't forgotten Jack Conley either."

There was a short silence. "Daddy denies that."

"He would."

"Matt, things are bad in this family and they're not going to get any better," sighed Steve. "That situation's going to be pretty much permanent until Daddy dies. After he's gone I can't think of any way he can enforce The Rule, so at least maybe you and me could have lunch together every now and then, but let's face it, we don't really have much in common, do we? After all that's happened it would always be strained. But this thing last night crossed the line, went way out of bounds, Matt, even for you. For the first time, it's escalated into violence. I don't want it to grow into murder one day. Mama wouldn't want that, Matt. Surely you know that."

"Amazing," chuckled Matt. "Fucking amazing! For the first time it's gotten violent, huh? Daddy tries to kill me twice, not to mention all the stuff Sid did when he was young, and needless to say the fact that Sid was breaking the law and stealing last night has already vanished completely from the picture. But the minute that I lay a hand on Sid, who is in the process of resisting lawful arrest, all of a sudden wicked horrible *violence* has reared its ugly head! Sorry, I forgot Subparagraph A of The Rule. Above and beyond the fact that I don't exist, everything is always my fault. Look, we've gotten off the track. I believe you were trying to corrupt a law enforcement officer? Daddy's wrath is presumably the stick, as if I weren't used to it after a lifetime of living with it. What's the carrot?"

Steve drew a breath. "Sid and I are willing to come to an arrangement with you. Not just about this incident at the mall, although your dropping that is a priority, of course. In return we'll drop our suit against Officer Watkins and the Chapel Hill police department…"

"Why am I not being sued, by the way?" asked Matt. "I'm the arresting officer and I'm the one who administered the aforementioned most righteous ass-whupping upon Sid's odoriferous carcass. I seem to be significant by my absence in your legal complaint. That's going to look funny in court."

"Well, you're a state employee and there's jurisdictional considerations…"

"Oh, *bullshit*, Steve! That's utterly lame and you know it!"

There was another silence. "You know The Rule," said Steve finally.

"I do indeed. A vermilion decree handed down from the Imperial Throne itself. Not one hint, not one whisper, not one act of commission or omission, which would acknowledge the fact that I exist, or ever existed."

"That's pretty much it, yes," admitted Steve.

"I'm curious, Steve. What about all those photos and color slides we took on vacations and camping trips, birthdays and Christmases?" asked Matt. "There must have been hundreds of those things, especially the slides. Am I cut out of the picture? Is somebody else's face pasted over my body? Am I airbrushed out of the photo like they used to do under Stalin when some bigwig Bolshevik got purged?"

"Sid and I have been given selected copies of our old family slides and pictures," said Steve carefully. "Just the ones showing me and Sid and Mama and Daddy and Papa Bowman, our cousins, so forth and so on. No pictures with you in them anywhere, although I think there's some you may have taken showing the other four of us. Daddy and Pauline have all the originals and the negatives down in Charleston, stored away somewhere. I don't know where all the ones with you are, and I can't ask. That would break The Rule."

"The Rule you live by," said Matt wearily. "How much does living by The Rule get you, Steve? How much does blowing your brother and a good hunk of your childhood down the memory hole net you in cold cash?"

"A lot," conceded Steve. "The trust funds are over five million each now, plus Daddy is very generous. He sends Kevin and Annabelle Christmas cards with four-figure checks."

"To a four year-old and a two year-old?" asked Matt incredulously.

"For their college fund, of course," said Steve.

"How much does he send Evie and my children?" asked Matt. "Last I heard it was five hundred a month for all five of them. Oh, I know that's a lot of money in Mexico. I shouldn't complain, I suppose. I suppose he has to pay them something, else Evie might contact me. We might talk. We might remember we loved each other once. We might compare notes about the behavior of a certain Mr. Jack Conley. My wife might all of a sudden realize that she was seduced in more than one sense of the word, totally lied to by a gigolo in the pay of my father."

"Look, we're getting off the subject," said Steve desperately. "I'm trying to tell you that Sid and I are willing to do the right thing in order to end all this and make sure there are no repetitions of the incident which occurred yesterday evening. We will pay you five thousand dollars a month, each of us, from our trust fund income. That's ten thousand dollars a month, Matt. We'll send it to you in the form of money orders or cash by courier if you like. You being a good cop and all, we'll rely on your honesty and respect for our country's laws to report this income to the I.R.S. on your tax return."

"I see. And in order to earn this largesse?" asked Matt.

"Leave the state. The farther away the better, but it has to be west of the Mississippi for sure. Idaho, Washington, British Columbia, California, Colorado, beautiful places, Matt! With a hundred and twenty grand a year you'd never have to work again in your life. If you like being a cop you could become Andy of Mayberry, Idaho. Or you could go to work for some major law enforcement agency like the LAPD or the Seattle police department and make a sizable second income, put you over two hundred grand a year eventually. You're 42 now, right?"

"Just turned 43," said Matt.

"Work for your living expenses and bank what Sid and I give you and you can retire at 50 as a millionaire! Christ Matt, who in their right mind would turn down a deal like that?"

"I'm not in my right mind, Steve. Thanks for the offer, but I'd rather have the kind of fun I had last night. Besides, it's just as illegal for me to accept a bribe as it is for you to offer one."

"My God, you really are crazy!" breathed Steve.

"No, Steve. Just determined to do what I can to balance the scales. That's more important to me than money. I'll take revenge if it's all I can get. I'd prefer justice, but that's no longer possible. Justice has to come from Daddy, not you and Sid, and you don't need to tell me you're making this offer without his knowledge. You're basically OK, Cheetah. I won't even call you spineless, because children and a wife you love can change a man's perspective. I know. I used to have them. Money's all that's left to hold onto in the world of today. Money's the only way you can buy your way out of the madness and the crap and still have a little stability and tranquility for your family. Hard work won't do it, talent won't do it, loyalty and dedication and honesty are not only meaningless, today they're countersurvival."

"You're really cynical," replied Steve.

"No, I am *skeptical.* The people who run this society are cynical, among other things. Anyway, I'm turning you down. Tell Sid if I catch him breaking the law again, or if he so much as looks at me cross-eyed on Franklin Street I'm going to give him another thumping."

"Why do you hate Sid so much?" demanded Steve. "I know you didn't really get along when we were kids, but I never recall it being this bad."

"You simply don't believe it," replied Matt. "Or rather you refuse to believe it, which I think is contemptible, but it's understandable."

"Shut up," said Steve.

"Money does things to men's minds, Steve, and I'm sorry it's blinded you to the truth. But Sid's different. He's not blind. Sid knows. He knows, Steve! He was there when it happened. I think he may have helped, or at least helped Daddy cover it up."

"Jesus, not that shit again!" shouted Steve angrily. "I will not listen to this!"

"He killed her, Steve," said Matt flatly. "Our father murdered our mother." There was a click as Steve hung up.

*   *   *

After his brother hung up, Matt yielded to temptation and watched half an hour of CNN news. Then he spun the dial for a while and was halfway through a Discovery Channel archaeology program on excavating Roman Britain when his doorbell rang. Matt snapped off the television, slipped his .357 Magnum into his belt, and turned on the outside light. He looked through the peephole, saw who the visitor was, and opened the door. "Hi, Michelle."

"Hi, Matt," said his sister-in-law, stepping inside without being asked. She was a short, voluptuous woman of about 30, with a foaming mass of very dark brown hair. She wore a tweed skirt with a woolly Aran sweater tonight against the autumn chill outside. Suddenly a furry orange ball oozed between her legs and stalked into the apartment. "Hello, Trumpeldor, kitty kitty!" cooed Michelle, bending down to stroke the cat. Trumpeldor rolled over on his back, batted at Michelle's hand, and then perfunctorily chewed on her finger for a bit before consenting to stretch out and have his belly rubbed.

"Take the armchair," said Matt, gesturing. "The one at my work table squeaks." Michelle picked up the cat and sat down, playing with him on her lap. He lolled over the edge of the chair and purred. "Do you want a beer or some coffee? I've also got some orange juice and Diet Coke."

"A Diet Coke would be nice," she said. As soon as the refrigerator door opened, Trumpeldor was off Michelle's lap like a shot and trying to batter past Matt's legs to get into the fridge. "Piss off, beast!" ordered Matt, shoving him back. "That chicken is mine, dammit!" He got Michelle her soda as well as another beer for himself, and sat down at the table.

She looked over curiously at the stacks of documents spread out on the table. "What's all that?" she asked.

"Nothing. Just paperwork on an old case I'm going over," he said. "Where are you supposed to be tonight?"

"New Age yoga class and stress relief through meditation," she said. "I can definitely use the stress relief, especially after your over the top performance last night. Did you have to beat him up that badly, Matt?"

"Your husband tried to rip my throat out like a goddamned werewolf, Mickey, but yeah, I did get a bit carried away. He had it coming but I'm sorry about the trouble it's caused you. Sid never check up on you?" asked Matt.

"No, why should he?" replied Michelle. "He trusts me."

"If anybody in the family ever found out that we get together every now and then, it would mean a divorce," said Matt. "Violating The Rule. Daddy would make Sid divorce you. If your loving husband holds you in particular affection, he might even hold out for a whole five minutes before he crumples and gives you the heave."

"Yes, I know that." Trumpeldor came stalking into the living room, walked up and bit Matt mildly on the ankle, then jumped back up on Michelle's lap. "She's not going to give you that chicken either," said Matt to the cat. "Let me guess. You want me to drop the shoplifting charge against Sid?" speculated Matt.

"Mmmm hmm," said Michelle.

"Steve already called me. Offered me ten thousand a month from the two trust funds to do the old Horace Greeley trick and go west, young man."

"Did you accept?" asked Michelle, slurping slightly on her Diet Coke.

"No."

"I didn't think you would. Are you going to push this thing with Sid? Please don't, Matt. Things have been on a pretty even keel out there for a while. I really don't need something like this keeping Sid stirred up. He won't be able to compose or play he'll be so upset all the time, raving about all the horrible things he thinks he's going to do to get even with you, working himself up into an impossible state."

"Why does he steal?" asked Matt. "Or let me rephrase that, why does he steal pocketfuls of strange little thingummies like what I caught him taking last night? He was always into sneaky petty violence and destruction. The stealing is a new one on me."

"Those things were presents for me. He does that every now and then. He goes out and buys twenty or thirty little odds and ends and then puts them on my pillow or heaps them up on the piano with a little sign sticking out with my name on it. It's kind of cute, the heterogeneous selection of knickknacks he comes up with. Usually he pays for them."

"Jeez," sighed Matt. "I mean, okay, I suppose it's romantic in a *non compos* kind of way, but my God, all that money…you'd think a man that rich could find something better to do with his life than wander through it in a medicated daze."

"His music is his life. He's a true artist when he plays, and his CDs will immortalize his gift. He's not a great composer, but he gets within shouting distance of greatness sometimes, and his work is performed. He will leave behind a body of creative accomplishment. You will only leave dead bodies. Who will come out on top a century from now?"

"*Touché,*" admitted Matt.

"I hope you're not offended," she said.

"The truth can often be uncomfortable, annoying, sometimes purest agony," replied Matt. "It can never be offensive. Truth simply is. A wise man is no more offended by the truth that he is offended by the ocean. It is something that exists and there's an end to it."

"Will you drop the charges if I asked you to do so? For me?" pleaded Michelle.

"I don't think it will come to that, Mickey," said Matt with a wry smile. "Steve's got a point. I got a bit carried away yesterday. Gave Sid a bit of the boot any judge is going to rule out of order.

Ironically that black cop, the one Sid and Steve are sueing, witnessed my use of excessive force. Diplomatically suggest to Steve that he have a word with Lieutenant Frank Perry at the Chapel Hill police station. He's court liaison. He should be able to work a trade-off, dismissal of the shoplifting charges in exchange for dropping the lawsuit. Kerr Drugs doesn't come into it because I filed the complaint as arresting officer based on my eyewitness of the act of theft, not the store manager. Steve's probably already thought of it, but your bringing up the idea will enhance your reputation for serene earth-motherly wisdom."

"Thank you," said Michelle. She toyed with her soda for a while and then spoke again. "There's another reason I came, Matt. You know what I want. You've been kind enough to give it to me before. I'd like to do it tonight."

"Are you sure?" asked Matt. "Remember what I told you before, Mickey. I haven't been able to kick Sid physically until last night and I won't be able to make a habit of it. I go along with these little sessions of ours purely as way of kicking Sid metaphorically, kicking that whole scene out there on Mile End Road, kicking Daddy by messing with his world. I've never concealed that from you. I'll never tell Sid or anyone else, because it amuses the hell out of me that this happens every now and then, and besides I don't want them on your case as well as mine. I want it to keep happening, but only every now and then. No affair as such. Total up-front honesty, nothing promised, nothing's going to come of it."

"I know," said Michelle. "If I thought you were falling in love with me or that there was any risk you'd betray me I wouldn't do it." She put Trumpeldor on the floor. "Let me use the bathroom and I'll be right back."

She came out of the bathroom a few minutes later, then Matt went in and got rid of the first beer, afterwards giving himself a quick scrub with a washcloth, a gentlemanly courtesy he was certain Michelle would appreciate. When he came out Michelle was in the living room undressing. He opened the door a crack and threw Trumpeldor out into the darkness. "You're too young to see this, horrible beast that you are. Don't you want to come into the bedroom?" he asked Michelle.

"No, it's better in here," she said. "It's more like I've come home and found somebody in the house, or been abducted by some ruthless gangster type. Can you get this?" Matt unhooked her bra and the white globes of her breasts tumbled out, jiggling pleasantly. She slid off her panties. Her body was perfectly formed, unshaven dark fur at her armpits and her loins. Matt stepped out of his jeans and his boxer shorts. "Leave the T-shirt on," she requested. She turned around and brought her wrists together behind her back.

"Are you sure that's what you want, Mickey?" asked Matt. "I don't want the slightest shadow of doubt here."

"Put them on, please," she requested quietly. Matt fished his handcuffs out of his jacket pocket and snapped them around Michelle's wrists, pinioning her arms behind her. She turned around and nodded to the pistol on the table. Matt drew the gun from its holster, a .357 Magnum Colt Python with a six-inch ribbed barrel and custom grip to fit Matt's somewhat small hand. He flipped open the cylinder open, dropping all six rounds into his palm. "No, leave them in!" she urged.

"Absolutely not!" said Matt. "I told you before, Mick, there are going to be no accidents."

"Just one? Kind of a Russian roulette?" she pleaded.

"No!" He turned to her. "Look, another thing. The talk is fine, I'll lay it on you if you want, but I'm not comfortable with slapping you or pulling your hair, that kind of thing. I like you, and I don't enjoy hurting you, even in play."

"Okay," she said, looking at the .357. "You know that's really what I want. The gun. In the hands of a man who has killed with it."

"Ready for lights, camera, action?" he asked.

"Hold on, let me get into it in my mind." Michelle closed her eyes for a minute, then nodded. He held the gun barrel to her cheek. She jumped slightly as it touched her, and began breathing deeply. He caressed her face with the barrel, gently sliding it between her teeth, and she tasted it with her tongue. He slid the muzzle down her chest and held it against her heart, then circled each breast with it. Her nipples were erect, hard and pointed. He brought it back to her head. "Open your eyes, bitch." She obeyed, her dark eyes smoky with arousal. "You're going down, baby. You're going down or you're going to die. Do it, you slut!" he ordered.

"No," she whispered. "No. Please, please don't make me do it! Please don't!"

"Do it or I'll shoot you," he said. He brought the gun down to her navel. "I'll shoot you in the belly and watch you scramble around and die, slowly, in agony." He brought the barrel to her loins. "I'll put a round right up your cunt, cunt." He caressed her body up and down with the gun barrel. She quivered, breathing quickly and raggedly. He moved behind her and lowered the barrel to her buttocks, sliding it between her cheeks. "I'll give you a hot lead enema, bitch." She moaned. He moved back around in front of her, cocked the pistol and put it to her head. She trembled with ecstasy. "You know what I want, woman. I'm tired of telling you. Get on your knees now, bitch. Do it or pay the price."

She nodded and slid down to her knees in front of him. "Keep the gun on my head," she whispered. "I want to feel it the whole time I'm doing you." She leaned forward and took his erection into her mouth. For long minutes there was silence as she performed slow, expert fellatio. Matt kept the pistol pressed lightly against her temple whole time, although as the level of purest pleasure rose he found it difficult to concentrate on keeping it in place. Finally his body shuddered as climax hit him like a blow. She drained every drop from him and leaned back. "You know what, bitch?" said Matt by rote. "I lied to you. I'm going to kill you anyway."

"No, no," moaned Michelle in a low voice, swaying. Matt eased the hammer forward, then stuck the pistol against her forehead and slowly cocked it again. He grasped her hair and held her head against the muzzle. "Open your eyes, bitch. I want you to see it coming."

Her breasts heaving, she opened her eyes and he immediately pulled the trigger, snapping the hammer again and again onto the empty chambers. *"Yes, yes!"* she gasped, and she shuddered from top to bottom for more than a minute as multiple orgasms racked her body. Rivulets of sweat ran down between her breasts. When it was over she leaned her head against his hip. "Thank you," she whispered. "Thank you, Matt. God, I love doing this!" He tossed the empty gun onto the chair and ran his fingers through her hair. She sighed and got up. He took the handcuff key and reached around to free her, but she said "No, leave them on. I like the feel of them. I'm going to have to go soon. You can take them off when I need to get dressed." He pulled on his underwear and jeans and sat down in the armchair, and took a long pull of his beer. Michelle knelt beside him, and he held the Diet Coke to her lips while she drank thirstily. "Matt, there's something I'd like to talk to you about."

"What's that?"

"You're a policeman. You know a lot about deviate sexual practices, violence, about men and women like me who are turned on by violence. I've read that there are ways of beating people, ways of beating women, that don't leave any visible marks. Things pimps do to their whores, things that hurt like hell but don't damage the goods, so to speak. Next time I come, when we can plan ahead and make sure we have some time, will you do some of those things to me? It's not hurting me, Matt. It's a way of making love, the way I've always wanted a man to make love to me."

"Do you have any idea how dangerous that can get, Mickey?" asked Matt quietly.

"That's why I want to do it with you, Matt. I can trust you not to get carried away. I would never, ever ask Sid to do any of this. He'd agree in a heartbeat, I'm sure, but one night he'd flip out and I'd be dead or maimed for life."

"That's where I draw the line, Mickey," he said, shaking his head. "Mick, you forget Sid and I have that same extra Y chromosome we both got from that bastard down in Charleston. There's no guarantee *I* might not get carried away. You told me once it took you a long time to accept that you are a masochist. I don't dare *ever* accept that genetically I'm predisposed to sadism and cruelty. I'll tell you right now that I love the hell out of doing what we just did, but if I ever start enjoying it too much or making it a substitute for real sex I'm quitting. Look, are you going to be able to keep this under control? Please don't go taking out ads in the kinky classifieds in the *Independent,* for God's sake. You engage in this kind of sex with people you don't know and you're asking for a disaster which can destroy you in fifty-eleven different ways even if you survive physically. I can't give you that, Mickey. I don't dare hurt anyone who doesn't deserve it. It could too easily become a habit with me, and of all the things in the world I'm scared of, ending up like Sid and Daddy is the worst. I've made it a lifelong rule, I only hurt bad people."

"You hurt Sid last night," said Michelle.
"Now what did I just say?" asked Matt.

       *   *   *

That night Matt lay in bed in the darkness, staring at the ceiling. The stacks of papers from the SBI file were still on the table in the living room. He considered getting up and going in and looking them over again, but there was no point. He had been reading them for three years now, every chance he got, sometimes on his lunch break, sometimes after work, sometimes taking them out on weekends. On the second day after he had joined the SBI and received his badge authorizing him to use the archives, he had descended down into the records vault and asked for this file for the first time. He knew every word, every line, every name, every fact.

He remembered the first time he had come upon the photo of Mary Jane's murdered body. It was a shock, but then what had he expected to find? The sight of Mary Jane dead had hit him like a blow to the face. In a hundred classrooms and hallways at Chapel Hill High School, in as many adolescent fantasies and dreams, young Matt Redmond had dreamed of seeing Mary Jane naked, imagining the time when she would consent to reveal to him all the wonderful mysteries of woman, when he could take her unclothed in his arms and speak to her without words. Now he had his long-delayed wish. The naked body of Mary Jane Mears lay in front of him for inspection. Taped into a chair. Stiff and cold, not warm and soft and perfumed as he remembered it from that last night. Her face was the worst of all. Head lolling, eyes open, tongue slightly protruding, dead and empty. Mary Jane was gone forever; this was her shell. The photos were in color, eight-by-ten glossies, and the red line of the cord showed on the white neck he had kissed barely an hour before this abomination had taken place.

The forensic pathologist gave time of death as 11 P.M. plus or minus thirty, thought Matt in the darkness. *It would be more plus, because she and Jeannie pulled out of the CHHS parking lot at about twenty past. Ten minutes for them to get home. Then half an hour of terror and anguish. That makes it eleven when she departed from the world. As she died, I was listening to my father roar about whatever fault he had found with me that night. What the hell was it? Oh yeah, he took it upon himself to go through my room that night while I was out and he found my U. S. Army recruiting literature. Steve never admitted it, but I always figured he dropped a hint to Daddy. He wanted me to stay at home; he always blamed me for leaving him there in that house alone when I went into the service. God, Daddy ranted and raved that night, but I didn't care. I was thinking of her, and he just rolled off my back. But I didn't know that I would never see her again.*

That thought had obsessed Matt Redmond ever since he had read the file and understood the meaning of the medical examiner's report. He knew the seed of obsession with her death had always been there, down through the years, and finally it had brought him to the SBI. But ever since he had read the file that now rested in stacks on his table, Matt Redmond had lived in a kind of bizarre time warp. In every waking moment, everything Matt said or did, eating or working or practicing on the range or testifying in complex court cases, his life in 1996 had come to exist in a sort of simultaneous continuum in his consciousness alongside a period of about nine hours, every moment engraved into his mind and played over and over again like a recurring videotape. In some indefinable part of Matt Redmond's soul, it was still the afternoon and the evening of October 23rd, 1970.

IV

There had been doubt right up to the last minute whether 17 year-old Matt was going to make it to the dance that night.

He had learned always to ask his infrequent dates to meet him wherever they were going, and to make sure they had transportation home in case his father decided at the last minute that Matt wasn't going anywhere that evening. Along with his status as a county-resident tuition student, the Chapel Hill High School equivalent of a peasant, this arbitrary uncertainty as to whether or not he could ever keep any appointment of any kind had proven a formidable obstacle against Matt engaging in any extracurricular activities or forming any kind of deep or lasting friendships with anyone at Chapel Hill High, male or female. The fact that the 1964 Corvair Monza belonged to Matt, a gift from his grandfather, was irrelevant. All the components of Randall Redmond's personal universe, both living and inanimate, existed and functioned only in accordance with his desires. This was a law of nature as immutable as the daily rising of the sun in the east. If Matt's father did not want him going somewhere then he did not go. No reason for refusal would be given and Matt had long ago learned not to ask for any. The result of asking would possibly be a physical blow but certainly a twenty minute tirade of abuse and insults which must be listened to with silent humility. The surest way to provoke an assault was to attempt to escape, evade, or cut short one of his father's innumerable lectures on the error of Matt's ways.

Randall Redmond was not merely a tyrant, he was the most dangerous and terrifying kind, an inconsistent tyrant. The dynamics of survival in the Redmond household changed from week to week; tactics and techniques which worked like a charm once or twice or twenty times might provoke a rage and a beating the twenty-first. In the year since he had obtained his driver's license, cautious experiment had given Matt a feel for the best ways to get off the Plantation at night or on a weekend. He had to mention the event at least a couple of days in advance; for something as major as a school dance a week in advance was a good idea. Then there had to be a second mention, any time from a day to a few hours beforehand, some kind of reference which made it clear that Matt intended to go and gave his father the opportunity to veto it if he was in the mood, but which stopped short of flat-out asking permission. Timing on the second mention was crucial; Matt had to catch his father sufficiently preoccupied with something to give a grunt or noncommittal comment that could reasonably interpreted as permission.

Interrupting Daddy watching television was definitely a bad move, especially when he was more than halfway through a six-pack of National Bo. The trick there was to catch him on the first or second beer, then hit him with mention number two during the commercials, about thirty seconds before the program came back on, so that his father's preliminary grunts and mutters would subside as the program caught his interest again. Matt had learned through hard experience when using this technique never to get up and leave the room right at that point, and always to sit through the program until the next commercial break to see if his father would make a formal pronouncement. If he did not, it was usually safe to take permission as granted. Usually. One of the few consistent rules of the house was that anything at all could blow up in one's face, at any time.

Matt was determined to go to the Harvest Ball dance on October 23rd. The week before he had finally done it. After preliminaries going back to the previous spring, he had asked shy and lovely Mary Jane Mears to go to the dance with him. She had smiled quietly and said, "What took you so long, Matt?" He had walked around school on a cloud the rest of the day, and when he got home that afternoon he had fled into the woods behind the house. At the back of the 90-acre spread was his own secret place, an outcropping of rock above a small but swiftly flowing stream, and he had stayed there day-dreaming for several hours, almost losing track of the time and only slipping in the back door as his father's Cadillac pulled up in front of the house. The first thing Daddy did when he stepped in the door was to conduct an informal roll call; Mama had best be getting supper ready and all three of his sons had best be present, accounted for, and making some pretense of being busy with schoolwork. Watching TV was acceptable as well for the boys, although when Daddy walked in, his first beer of the evening in his hand, the channel was immediately turned to the news.

· That night after supper Matt went to his room and carefully plotted out his strategy. The problem was that it was a dance, and his father would be aware of the likelihood that he was taking a girl or hoping to meet a girl there. This was a delicate area. Since he was about 14 his father had insisted on full debriefing as regards anything to do with his son's nascent teenaged sex life, most specifically the identity of any girl Matt manifested even a faint interest in. (Daddy generally received his briefings on Sid's adolescent sexual episodes in the form of registered letters from law firms or visits from the sheriff). Matt had learned to conceal any such information at all cost, after various attempts on Randall Redmond's part forcibly to drag each girl into his universe and pound her into whatever square hole he fancied. When shortly thereafter the girl invariably fled from Matt as from a thing accursed, she became the subject of forced conversations and interrogations for the next six months. No way in hell was his father going to find out about Mary Jane Mears. His delighted efforts to pull the daughter of two of UNC's most prominent tenured professors into his gravitational field promised weird and cataclysmic events.

Matt had to decide whether to try to finesse the dance, or to take one of his two high-risk options. The first of these was to walk right up and ask his father's permission to go. The result was completely unpredictable. It was possible he'd get a casual, "Sure, just be back before eleven," but the odds were against it. Because of the coed nature of the event the response would almost certainly be, "Are you taking a girl?" If he answered yes a full interrogation would follow. Revealing Mary Jane's identity was out of the question, so he would either have to make up a completely fictitious date or claim he was taking someone else at school, both possibilities strewn with pitfalls and the chance of being caught lying. Daddy had been known to call the parents of girls he believed his son was interested in, and by now wild horses couldn't drag a girl's name out of Matt. If the answer was no, he was going stag, the response would be, "Then why the hell do you want to go? Why don't you ever take girls anywhere? You're seventeen, for Pete's sake!" which line of discourse usually ended up in a high-decibel assertion that Matt was a homosexual and a sissy as well because he did not play contact sports and he had not ridden a bicycle without training wheels until he was nine.

At the conclusion of the standard faggot speech, as Matt had nicknamed it in his mind, Daddy might tell him he was staying home and not gallivanting around in a car at night getting up to God knows what. Or he might say, "Get your ass to the dance then and try and figure out what the female of the species is for!" It was a toss-up, and if Matt could have been sure of winning it he would have sat through the faggot speech unblinkingly. But this was Mary Jane Mears, waiting there for him, at long last, her and Jeannie Arnold who was staying with her while her folks were in Washington...hey, since her folks wouldn't be home, maybe....maybe? The idea vanished from his mind as quickly as it had entered. For him to arrive home later than eleven o'clock for any reason at all, including flat tires and car trouble, was science fiction fantasy, something on the order of time travel. Things like that simply didn't happen in real life. So there was his second high-risk option; ask his mother for permission to go.

His mother's position in the family was roughly equivalent to a constitutional monarch or a European parliamentary democracy's president: nominally a person of authority, but no real power. In theory, Matt's mother was entitled to give him permission to go to the Harvest dance, and would most likely do so. Her one form of rebellion against her husband was very occasional assistance to one of her boys, although most of her efforts along that line usually involved trying to protect Sid from the consequences of his uncontrollable behavior. In actual practice, she would almost certainly mention Matt's request to his father. Even if she did not, he would be forced to sneak out of the house and hope he could get the car started and be down the long driveway of the Plantation before Daddy came storming and raving out of the house wanting to know where the hell he thought he was going. He could make it to the dance that way, but Daddy was quite capable of following him to the school, sneaking into some vantage point in the gym, seeing who Matt was with and watching him for a while in order to get whatever voyeuristic charge he got out of spying on his son with a girl, then barging onto the dance floor and dragging him away, as had occurred once before. In any event there would be hell to pay, directed at him of course, not his mother.

It was a sticky problem, one where failure was not an option since Mary Jane Mears was involved. Matt decided not to be creative; there was too much at stake. Finesse had worked the past six times or so, so Matt crossed his fingers and hoped he wouldn't crap out on throw number seven. He held off first mention until October 20th, which was a bit risky, but he hadn't liked the omens in the days before that. Daddy had been more morose than usual and had beaten Sid severely for burning trash in the barrel out back without permission. This was understandable in view of his brother's frequent pyromania and the proximity of the mansion's propane gas tank, but it didn't bode well for permission for Matt to go to the dance. Yet Matt's finessing skill held, or maybe it was only his luck. First mention on October 20th had produced a grunt and the sour comment of "maybe you can find a girl friend there", and second mention on the night of the 22nd produced a few more grunts and the magic words, "Make sure you're back home by eleven."

Matt was over the moon. He saw Mary Jane several times in school on the Friday of the dance, a vision of flower child-like beauty floating by in the hall in black leotards and skirt, a green sweater and granny glasses. He finally caught up with her in fifth period study hall. The teacher in charge was talking with another

student up front and Mrs. Weddle didn't keep order too well anyway, so a few minutes of conversation was possible. "You still
good for tonight?" he had asked breathlessly, suddenly terrified
she had changed her mind.

"Mmmm hmmmm," she said, looking away with the demure
shy smile that made Matt want to get down on his knees, draw a
sword and swear eternal devotion to her like a medieval knight to
his lady. "No band, but they've got Freddy Deal to play records.
Jeannie's bringing some of hers and I'm bringing my Jethro Tull."

"You want me to pick you up at your house?" asked Matt, a
daring ploy. He knew Jeannie Arnold had her own car, a 1968
Plymouth Fury which she would have taken to bed with her like a
teddy bear had it been possible, and nothing was going to persuade Jeannie to ride in the back seat of a battered old white
Corvair while she had her wheels. By picking Mary Jane up and
driving her home he would have more time alone with her.

"Nah, Jeannie's bringing her car. My mom made me promise
that Jeannie and me would stick together when she and Dad are
out of town. What would you like me to wear tonight?" The
question surprised him and confirmed that he was definitely in
the running.

"I think you look great in that maxi dress, the one with the
flowers on it," he told her. "You look beautiful in anything,
though."

"Naah, I'm dowdy as an old shoe. Jeannie's the sexy one," said
Mary Jane.

"I didn't say you were sexy, I said you were beautiful," said
Matt, before he realized the slip and almost bit his tongue.

"So you think I'm not sexy?" she whispered teasingly.

"You are, but that's not why I like you. I like you because
you're you, and I'd rather you were beautiful than sexy anyway.

Anybody can be sexy. Not everybody is beautiful like you, and I don't just mean to look at."

"That's sweet, Matt," she said. "Thanks." The bell rang and they gathered their books and left the classroom.

In the hall outside Matt said, "You got English literature with Jones now, right? I got history with Wilkinson. I'll walk you down there."

"Okay," she agreed. As they walked down the hall together Matt's mind was racing. Did he dare? Did he? She seemed so friendly, she was acting as if she really liked him. He glanced over, and saw that she was carrying her books with both hands against her chest. But wait, she was shifting them to one hand, now carrying them against her left side, leaving her right hand free, the slight motion of her breasts beneath the sweater in her graceful walk causing Matt to flush.

She'll think I'm trying to look down her dress! he thought, turning his head away quickly. *No, that's stupid, you can't look down a sweater. Better not look at all.* His heart pounding in his chest, he decided that he would dare. He reached out his left hand and brushed Mary Jane's fingers almost by accident, nerving himself to try and take her hand without grabbing at it. To his astonishment she quietly took his hand and interlaced their fingers without any further subterfuge being necessary. They walked hand in hand the full length of one corridor and half the length of another until they reached her class, and by then Matt knew they had been seen by three or four of the cliqued-up, key girls and guys at CHHS. By late afternoon the word would be out on a dozen humming phone lines, and the dance tonight would confirm it. Matt was on the home stretch. There was still the dance itself to get through, but barring some unforeseen disaster, he'd made it. The peasant youth had won the hand of the princess, in every sense of the term. After two long years, Matt Redmond finally had CHHS status; through her parents, Mary Jane Mears was purest blue-blooded UNC. That was his first, unashamedly gloating and prideful thought. His second realization was deep and wonderful and profound. He knew that he really loved her.

When they got to her classroom, she dropped his hand easily and pulled something out of a book, a folded piece of notebook paper. "I wrote you a note in study hall," she said, her eyes averting in embarrassment. Matt took it from her. "See you tonight then. It starts at seven but we'll be there a little early. See if you can get there early too, OK?" She turned and went into the class just as the bell rang for sixth period.

It was 2:30 P.M., October 23rd, 1970. Ahead of Matt Redmond lay twenty-six years of wandering the earth amid gunfire and bloodshed and ugliness. Mary Jane Mears had slightly less than nine hours to live.

$$*\qquad\qquad*\qquad\qquad*$$

Matt got up from his bed, turned on the light, and fished around in his drawer until he came up with a folded paper, a photocopy. The original note was preserved in a clear plastic document envelope in his private safe deposit box in Raleigh. In the pool of light from his bedside lamp, Matt sat on the bed and read the note again for the four or five thousandth time. At the top of it, Mary Jane had drawn a round, furry kitten face.

Hey, stud, I mean it, what took you so long? I like the strong silent type, especially cute ones like you. You're a DOLL! Matt, there's kind of someone else in the picture, but it doesn't mean anything. If you like me and want to go with me I'll break this other off. I swear, it's not serious. I really like you. No promises, but I think I could maybe more than like you, and I hope that's what you want too, and you're not just fooling around with me and we can get to know one another a LOT better if you know what I mean but we'll see. I had a dream about you and no I will NOT tell you what about 'cause I bet you can guess ha ha. See you tonight!

                                                              —Mary Jane

There followed a drawing of a heart.

    *   *   *

That October Friday afternoon Matt barricaded himself in the upstairs bathroom about four thirty. He shaved, showered and scrubbed before supper, made it through the meal with only a little casual needling from his father, then got back into the bathroom and applied the aftershave and cologne he had not dared to wear at the table. He dressed in his sharpest sport shirt and windbreaker, then debated quickly: front door or back door? He already had permission to go and protocol did not require him to check out, so to speak, but sometimes breaking contact and making the actual escape could be tricky. In 1970 the Southern Colonial style home his father had built was not yet the sprawling mansion it would become later, after Daddy got hold of his father-in-law's money and went berserk building himself a palace, and there were only two doors. Going out the front door would mean he would pass the TV den, and if his father was watching television there might be an incident. On the other hand, the back door led through the big kitchen where the family ate together, the formal dining room being largely unused because few people cared to be dinner guests in Randall Redmond's home. If Daddy was still sitting there guzzling beer there might be remarks passed which could lead to problems. Matt had noticed the refrigerator stocked

with a full case of National Bo, which had sinister implications.
Daddy usually got by on two six-packs a night. Matt sighed and
assumed he would catch hell about something or other when he
came in at eleven, but that was okay. He would have almost four
hours with Mary Jane Mears. But how to break contact and get
away now? It was quarter past six.

Sid was in his room, the door open a crack, sitting on the floor
in front of a small record player listening to his favorite classical
piece, Stravinsky's 1911 *Petruschka*, rocking back and forth
rhythmically, his eyes blank, his mind wherever it went when he
listened to the classics. There was a reek from the piles of filthy,
feces-caked underwear thrown in the corner. Matt stuck his head
into ten year-old Steve's room. The boy was reading a Spiderman
comic. "Hey there, Cheetah, got a mission for you. Tarzan say go
find Gorilla Man."

Steve jumped up and started making chimpanzee noises, then
ooked and eeked his way downstairs. This was a trick they had
done before when Matt wanted to sneak out of the house. They
both understood how dangerous it was; the most violent incidents, tantamount to bona fide assault and battery, always
occurred whenever Randall Redmond divined rightly or wrongly
that his sons were in any way colluding against him to do something, conceal something, or evade one of his rulings. There were
more monkey noises and the irate rumbling of his father's voice
downstairs. Steve came running back upstairs in his stocking feet.
"He's watching TV," whispered the boy. "Already got three dead
Marines on the coffee table." For some reason their father, an ex-
Marine himself with a chest full of medals from the South Pacific,
always referred to empty beer cans as dead Marines.

"Thanks, Cheetah," said Matt gratefully.

"Hey, Tarzan, you still going in the army?" asked Steve. The
boy had walked in on Matt in his room several weeks before when

Matt had been reviewing a pile of surreptitiously acquired recruiting pamphlets and literature on his bed.

"I think so, but I told you to keep your lip zipped about that," said Matt, perturbed. "You know what would happen if he finds out, Stevie. It will be bad, worse than anything we've either of us ever seen."

"You're telling me! I just figured I'd let you know I heard him and Mama talking about your application to UNC. He's going to fill it out for you but you've got to sign it or something."

"Great," sighed Matt. "Well, I guess it's going to come sooner or later. I'll hold it off as long as I can. Don't get caught up in it, Cheetah."

"I don't want you to go away," said the boy suddenly, looking away. "I don't want you leaving me alone with him and Sid. I'm scared of them, and Sid always smells like shit. Why can't you just get a job or something and take me with you?"

"If I have to stay here four more years while I'm in college I'll kill him," said Matt quietly. "I'm sorry as hell, kid. I just can't take it any more. Don't worry, your turn will come. You'll be eighteen one day."

"Yeah, in eight years!" said Steve sullenly.

"I know it seems like forever to you now, but it will come," said Matt soothingly. "Look, I've got to go. Thanks again." Matt made it out the back door, into his car, and down the driveway without incident. Twenty minutes later he pulled into the parking lot at Chapel Hill High School, and he saw Jeannie's Plymouth already there. Mary Jane saw him as he entered the gym. She ran up to him, her flowered maxi-dress billowing, and kissed him on the cheek. The magic began.

Matt could never fully remember everything they talked about that night. He remembered the dancing, the echoing rock music in the gym, the crowd and the noise, but mostly he remembered the feel and touch of Mary Jane's body, the electric thrill of her hand in his, standing along the walls with his arm around her, pressing her perfumed softness against him during the slow dances. In one sense he thought it would never end, in another sense it went by like a flash. All of a sudden he glanced at his watch and it was nine twenty. The dance ended at ten. He gulped. "Hey, ah, Mary Jane, isn't it kind of, ah, hot in here to you? I mean maybe you'd like to..."

"Let's go," giggled Mary Jane. Young couples slipping out of the gym at these functions was something that wasn't supposed to happen, hence the presence of a dozen teachers and parents as chaperones. Needless to say, it was a highly developed art form among the kids. "Let's go to the bathroom," suggested Mary Jane. Matt knew that was the first step, easily accomplished. The boys and girls' restrooms were in the large vestibule. One went past the door chaperones separately, through different exits. "Then I'll meet you in the band room," she went on. "They always watch the locker rooms, but there's a fire exit in the bandroom they never remember."

"How do you know?" asked Matt suspiciously.

"Jeannie told me. She kind of figured we might want to be alone for a bit."

"Ask an expert," agreed Matt. Five minutes later they were outside together, by the tennis court and the auto shop. Several other young couples were outside as well, under the trees or pressed against the wall in the moonlight.

"Oh, I don't believe that's Melissa Hardy! Who's she with tonight?" whispered Mary Jane.

"Who is she *not* with?" chuckled Matt. "Hey, that's Bob Ackerman with his hand in her bra! She's as bad as Jeannie!"

"Noooooo, Jeannie at least has good taste!" insisted Mary Jane merrily.

"You call that grit Riggsbee good taste?" asked Matt skeptically.

"Jeannie says getting it on with grits can be fun. Speaking of which...?" she went on suggestively, taking his hand and leading him beneath a tree. The air was crisp and chill, yet not too cold, and an October harvest moon hung full in the clear sky above them. In the classroom windows they could see glowing jack-o'-lanterns lit by the decorations committee kids.

"I didn't bring you out here just for that," said Matt. His chest hurt. He was afraid his heart was going to stop. His hands trembled. "I wanted to talk to you, Mary Jane."

"What about?" she whispered.

"Just listen," he said desperately. "I want to say some things to you, and I may be making a fool out of myself, but I'm going to risk it anyway. Better I come off like a jerk than not let you know how I feel. Mary Jane, I love you. I've loved you for a long time, but until today I don't think it hit me just how much I love you and how much I want to be with you forever. You're wrong about one thing, you are sexy. You're so damned sexy you drive me crazy every time I see you and you better believe if you keep on going out with me I'm going to do everything I can to persuade you to make love with me. But that's not all I want from you, Mary Jane. I want you to marry me. I want you to be the mother of my children, as corny as that sounds. Don't get me wrong, I'm not asking you to do anything stupid. I know we're both too young. I know you've got UNC coming next year, and then vet school. Me, I don't think I'm going to go. My Dad doesn't know that yet, but I'm going to go into the army, after I graduate if he'll sign for me, if not I'll just put up with his bullshit until I'm eighteen and then I'll go in anyway. But there's all kinds of training you can get in the army, I'll be making money, and when I get out I can go to college on the GI Bill. We could get married in a few years, once we're sure that's what we want. We wouldn't have to wait until you graduated…" He ran down. He knew he'd made a fool of himself. She would laugh at him. She would tell all her friends and they would laugh at him. His face flushed in the darkness with humiliation. "I just wanted you to know how I feel about you," he mumbled lamely.

"I go to college first, you go in the army and save money. You help me through veterinary school, then when I'm a vet I'll help you go through college, along with your GI bill," she said practically. "That'll work. A lot of young married couples do it like that." Matt was stunned speechless. She laughed in the chill darkness. "That was a yes, Matt," she said softly. "Aren't you gonna kiss me?" He gathered her in his arms and found her lips, crushing her to him.

They were back in the gym by five to ten. "Jeannie hasn't let it all hang out yet tonight," said Matt to Mary Jane. "I was sure we'd get one of her famous solos."

"Some of the teachers gave her some crap about it last time, so she told me she was going to wait until the last minute tonight to bust loose. She's talking to Freddy now." Matt saw Jeannie in conference with the DJ. Tonight she was wearing a red and gold sheath-like dress with high slits in the thighs that looked like it had been painted onto her magnificent body, her long blond hair roiling loose down her shoulders to the small of her back. She slid back to her escort of the evening, CHHS All-Conference football star Mike Malinsky, and all of a sudden music cut loose from the stand-up speakers, perceptibly louder and with more bass than previously that evening. It was Grand Funk Railroad's *Take Me,* a choice Matt always found chillingly ironic when he thought back on that evening. Jeannie kicked off her shoes and leaped forward. The word was obviously out; the kids jostled back to clear a space on the floor and coincidentally hamper the progress of any teachers who might try to make it to the record player and stop the performance.

Performance it was. Jeannie Arnold was a ballet-trained dancer since the age of eight, and the dance she gave now was up to any standards that Broadway or the Bolshoi could have demanded. There was no hesitation, no wasted or directionless motion, nothing indecisive or half-hearted. Her body's movement to the thundering rock music was an explosion in place, contained in a few square feet of polished wooden floor. It was a raging flame transformed into the image of a Valkyrie. It was powerful, awe-inspiring, overwhelmingly erotic. The girls were applauding and cheering her on, too carried away by the fiery beauty and spirit of her dance to be jealous or feel other than admiration for her beauty and her talent. The guys roared their approval, shouted out in unfeigned, honest open lust. Matt could not but be affected himself, but he looked at Mary Jane beside him, her eyes shining in happiness for her friend and for herself. He leaned over speak into her ear above the noise. "She's beautiful and fantastic, Mary Jane. But you're the one I will always love and want. I want you to know that. You don't ever have to be afraid of competition from Jeannie."

Mary Jane laughed out loud. "Neither do you!" she said, giggling merrily as if at some hidden joke. The music came to an end and Jeannie slumped to the floor to the accompaniment of thunderous applause and cheers. The harried Dean of Students, Mr. Strickland, finally bulled his way to the front of the crowd. "All right, kids, time to go home!" Strickland shouted, eyeing Jeannie disapprovingly. She winked at him, which seemed to fluster him. *"One more! One more!"* came a chanting shout from the assembled teenagers. "Okay, one more, then we call it a night!" conceded Strickland.

Freddy Deal fiddled with his 45s, then put one on. *"Slipping away, sitting on a pillow, waiting for night to fall..."* It was Three Dog Night. The couples paired off and embraced. Mary Jane slid into Matt's arms and laid her head on his shoulder, light as a feather, seeming to melt into him. Slowly they moved together around the floor, lost in the music, lost in their own world. He stroked her long black hair, bunching it in his hands, kissing it, kissing her face and her neck. *"Dress up tonight...why be lonely? Just stay at home and you'll be alone so why be lonely?"* For the first time in his life, Matt felt like a man. He swore to himself that he would make her happy, never hurt her, never betray her. "I love you," he whispered to her. "Every night I'm going to tell you I love you. If you can't be with me, I'll tell it to the moon, or the sea, or the trees or just the sky, wherever I am." *"Celebrate, celebrate, dance to the music..."*

"I love you," she whispered back. "I'm going to do that, too, Matt. Wherever I am, if we're apart, I will think of this night and I will say it out loud, every night, always." *"Celebrate, celebrate, dance to the music..".*

They hung around in the parking lot afterwards, embracing and talking, while the other kids left, the lights in the gym were turned off, and the jack-o'-lanterns in the windows were blown out one by one by the teachers as they went around locking up. Finally Jeannie blew her horn impatiently. "Hey, you guys, it's cold out here!" she yelled from the car. "I mean, like, tomorrow's Saturday, for crying out loud!"

"I'll call you tomorrow morning," Matt promised.

"I'll be there," she said. They kissed one more time, long and lingeringly. Jeannie blew her horn again. Mary Jane got into the car and Matt got into his Corvair and followed them out of the parking lot. At the edge of the lot they parted. Jeannie had to turn right, then left immediately onto Seawell School road to get up to

Airport Road and then on into Chapel Hill. Matt had to turn left, then left again onto Homestead Road to head back to the Plantation, his father, and his father's case of National Bohemian. *I wonder if I could get away with sneaking myself one or two of those tonight?* he wondered with a chuckle. Mary Jane's arm came out of the passenger side of the Fury, and she waved good-night. He could see the gold bracelet on her wrist. Matt beeped his horn and then waved as well. Jeannie pulled out and turned right, then left again, and he watched the red taillights through the trees until they disappeared, carrying the girls away from him into the darkness.

*   *   *

He had tried in the intervening years to keep his promise to tell Mary Jane he loved her every night. He hadn't been completely successful. Sometimes he'd been too occupied. Sometimes, for weeks at a time, he had simply forgotten. During the years of his marriage to Evangelina he had stopped. Even though it was something he could have done without his wife's knowledge, it would nonetheless have been an act of disloyalty and disrespect. Matt wouldn't have felt right about it, and he believed that Mary Jane herself would have understood. In the past few years he had resumed the practice.

Sometimes he would whisper softly, "I love you, Mary Jane," before he went to sleep; sometimes he would perform some ritual act like reading her last note to him, or going through his high school annual. He had carefully cut out her picture from the annual and had an enlargement made, and sometimes he would put in on a table in the darkness and light a fragrant scented candle in front of it. Tonight he put away her note and turned out the light. He didn't get back into bed but went to the window of his apartment and looked up at the October moon, wreathed in clouds. He was possibly two miles away as the crow flew from the tree behind Chapel Hill High School where that same moon had shone down on him and Mary Jane, a few weeks short of twenty-six years before. Softly he hummed a song he had memorized long ago, by the Scottish poet laureate Robert Burns:

"As fair thou art, my bonnie lass,
Sae deep in love am I,
That I would love thee still, my dear,
Till all the seas gang dry.

"Till all the seas gang dry, my dear,
And the rocks melt wi' the sun,
And I would love thee still, my dear,
Till the sands o' time be run.

"Sae fare thee well, my bonnie lass,
Aye, fare thee well a while.
But I shall come again, my dear,
Though it were ten thousand mile."

V

The next morning Matt pulled his fedora down over his brow at his customary rakish angle, left the apartment and started his leg-work on the case. Matt had gotten into the habit of wearing head-gear in the military and had done so ever since, but the somewhat notorious fedora was a special affectation of his. In his early SBI days he noticed that along with his cigars it seemed to irritate the hell out of the bureau's commissar of political correctness, Assistant Director Betty Springer, so he had begun wearing it all the time.

Ms. Springer formally complained about the hat in a memoran-dum with copies to the director of the bureau, the North Carolina Attorney General, the Governor, the state and Federal Equal Opportunity Employment Commissions, several liberal members of the legislature, the Raleigh *News and Observer,* and all three major RTP network stations. She asserted that Redmond's hat

"...projected a tactless, anachronistic and racially insensitive stereotyped image of Southern White male aggressiveness on the part of state law enforcement". Matt maxed out his Visa card and with some effort located and bought two dozen fedoras, which he gave to every black and female SBI agent in the name of racial and gender equality. Ms. Springer had not been amused, and when Matt had publicly presented her hat she had resisted with very bad grace repeated requests to try it on from her fellow officers and a camera crew from the local Fox network affiliate who had mysteriously shown up. She backed off when even the media saw the joke and the publicity started going sour on her, since she was eyeing a race for Attorney General in the Democratic primary. But it was a near thing. More so than the cigars, the fedora was pushing the envelope, and a junior agent without Matt's 100% clearance rate and his past reputation wouldn't have gotten away with it. But the hat and the cigars were his trademark and he never left home without either.

Matt's first stop in a homicide investigation would normally be the forensic pathologists from Duke Hospital who had performed the autopsies on the two victims, but one of them had died four years previously and the other was retired somewhere in Florida; it would take time and expense to track him down, and Matt decided that the lab work and path reports in the file were good enough for the moment. There seemed to be little mystery as to how each girl had died; the who and the why were what he was after. Next he approached the initial crime scene reports, from the time the Mears' black cleaning woman Katherine Lee had found the bodies at approximately 8 A.M. on the morning of October 24th. Photostats of the initial reports of Chapel Hill police officers Will W. Williams and J. D. Ellis were in the SBI file, but Matt decided he would do what he now had the authority to do since the SBI had officially assigned him the case; he would look over the Chapel Hill police department's in-house documentation on the murders. He got in his Taurus and drove to the Department of Public Safety building on Airport Road.

Matt had debated with himself prior to starting out whether or not to involve the Chapel Hill PD directly in his investigation, and after some thought he decided against it unless there was some pressing reason to do so later on, i.e. he came up with a viable suspect or suspects. In the first place, like all police departments the Chapel Hill cops were busy with present-day crimes. In the second place, right now he wasn't overly popular with the local constabulary in view of the fact that he had involved one of their officers quite undeservedly in an excessive force lawsuit.

Finally, while wary of the dangers of paranoia, in reading the SBI file and in his own memory of the events of 1970, it seemed to Matt Redmond that the initial investigation had stalled very quickly, perhaps too quickly. As 1970 had eased into 1971 Matt remembered his angry impression that the double murder of the two girls was fading from public attention with indecent speed, considering the sensational and bloody nature of the crime. Frenzied gossip and speculation among the students at Chapel Hill High had never ceased, in fact had overriden every other social topic among the kids for months, but by spring there was complete official silence. No arrests, no new developments, no articles or media coverage, no more police interviewing anybody in town, zip. At commencement exercises in June the graduating Class of 1971 had stood for a whole minute of silence in memory of Jeannie Arnold and Mary Jane Mears. *Thirty whole seconds each,* Matt recalled himself thinking bitterly.

Chapel Hill was an insular community even today, and in 1970 it had been still smaller and more insular, a town where unspoken consensus was not only possible but real. Like the wind, this consensus was felt, but never seen, never traced to its point of origin.

Within a short time after the death of the two girls Matt and everyone else at CHHS had become aware, without exactly knowing how or why, of the ruling that unofficial consensus had handed down: the events of October on Boundary Street were tragic and terrible, but they were over. They were part of the town's past, and it was time to move on. Matt understood that even now, twenty-six years later, swimming against the current of that subtle yet pervasive consensus was not a smart thing to do. He fully intended to violate as necessary the unspoken commandment of all consensus: "Thou shalt not open cans of worms", but he decided he'd best not broadcast his intentions if he could help it. It was entirely possible that whatever Chapel Hill wanted covered up in 1970, Chapel Hill wanted covered up in 1996.

So after he slid down into the basement, showed his ID, chatted brightly with the young black woman in the Records Department, made his request, and received the file he had asked for, Matt Redmond was not totally surprised to be handed a thin, dusty legal-sized manila folder possibly an inch thick. The complete SBI dossier on this same case consisted of five bulging files of the same size which had taken Matt almost an entire afternoon just to organize on his work table. *A one-inch file on the double homicide of two pretty teenaged girls in the middle of Chapel Hill's downtown residential area is purest bullshit,* he thought. *Something is going on here.* He took the file to a small table by a high window, sat down and went through it. He found the pathology reports, complete. There were the familiar crime scene photos, Mary Jane's shameful nakedness and empty dead face, Jeannie's beauty broken and smashed and bloody, the house inside and out, Jeannie's beloved Plymouth Fury in the drive and its interior. There were the newspaper clippings, the young black officer Matt remembered was named Will Williams looking sick outside the door with the crime scene tape strung all around. There were internal Chapel Hill police documents, a miscellany of time sheets and memos and press releases. And that was all. Matt walked up to the woman at the counter and smiled at her. "Hey, uh, LaVonda, I'm afraid I've got a problem. This file isn't complete. Sure there isn't more back there somewhere?"

"I looked very carefully in the file box I found that one in, Agent Redmond," replied LaVonda. "That's all there was under that case number for October 1970 Serious Crimes."

"Well, as you can see, it's a bit thin," said Redmond with a friendly smile. He knew it would do no good to badger the clerk; this wasn't her fault and he needed her help. "What's missing is essentially the guts of the investigation, the police interview reports. Presumably the Chapel Hill cops did question people about a double murder, and yet I don't find one single witness statement or interview sheet. If nothing else, there should be a report of an interview with me myself at age seventeen, conducted on the afternoon of October 24th, by Detective Bill Bass and Officer Will Williams. I don't even see any log sheets showing how the investigating officers spent their time, where they went, or who they spoke to."

"Oh, yes, I see what you mean," said LaVonda. "Yes, they certainly should be there. Isn't that strange?"

"Probably misfiled in another box or something," he said easily. "I hate to bother you, but could you have another look? I really need the complete file."

"Certainly," said LaVonda, and she disappeared into the remote bowels of the archives in the rear. While she was gone Matt studied something else which had caught his eye. On the front of the file was stapled a large form with neat black columns to record the file's handling history. It had been opened on October 26th, 1970, the Monday after the killings, no doubt the morning's first task for whatever clerical worker was doing the paperwork back then. It had been stamped "File Status Classified Open—Dormant", in other words sent down here to be buried, on February 6th, 1971. *Three and a half months?* exclaimed Matt silently, cursing in wonder. *Three and a half months and they feathered a double rape-torture-homicide? What the fuck was going on here? My God, SBI at least kept it open and active until 1975!* He looked at the checkout record. The file had been checked out several times in 1971 and 1972 by people, presumably police officers, whose names were unfamiliar to him. It had been checked out by Officer Will W. Williams three times in 1971, three times in 1972, and from then on once a year, always in October, until 1983. Beginning in 1977 onward the file was signed out "Detective W. Williams"; in 1979 it was "Detective First Class" and the last signout in '83 was to Sergeant Williams.

LaVonda came back, flustered, and swore that there was nothing else on the case lurking in her stacks in the back that she could locate. Matt handed the file back, not forgetting to sign his own name and date it with a flourish. There was no point in copying anything contained in the looted file; he already had it all in his. The thought occurred to him that the documents in his possession might be in some danger. *Good thing the bureau microfilms everything over five years old,* he thought. He left the building quietly by the back way, hoping his visit had been unnoted by anyone in authority.

He cruised back into Carrboro, stopped at Pizza Hut and munched on an early luncheon buffet he barely tasted while he thought hard. His impressions back in '70 and '71 had been on target, he reflected, not without a bit of pride. He'd had good copper's instincts even back then. Something had been wrong. Someone had decided to feather the investigation. Someone had apparently been so worried that they had gone into the case file and gutted it of every document that might conceivably hold a clue. Someone in the police department, or someone who had enough pull with the police department to gain access to the file. Now, was this done just as a paranoid precaution? *The guilty flee where no man pursueth, said the immortal Bard,* Matt thought to himself. Or was there actually something there, something which might give the game away? If so, did he have a copy of it in his SBI file? What could it be? What could he have missed? Matt decided he'd ask someone who seemed to be the closest person after himself to an expert on the case. He found a phone booth and looked up Williams, Will W. Luck was with him; Williams lived in black Carrboro just around the corner from Matt's apartment in white/University Carrboro. Matt dialed the number and was answered by a low, mellifluous James Earl Jones kind of voice. "Sergeant Williams, Chapel Hill PD?" he asked.

"Lieutenant Williams, retired. Who's this?"

"Lieutenant, this is Agent Matt Redmond of the North Carolina State Bureau of Investigation. I'm…"

"Not Two Gun Matt of the DEA? The famous Sherlock Holmes of the South?" asked the voice politely.

"I'm with the SBI now, Lieutenant. I've reopened the Mears-Arnold murder case from 1970. You may remember you and Bill Bass interviewed me at the time."

"Of course. I remember now. You're *that* Matt Redmond! Damn! Never made the connection before. How you doing, son?"

"I'd like to talk to you about the case, Lieutenant." There was a long silence.

"What, exactly, would you like to know?" asked Williams carefully.

"The first thing I want to know is where the hell are all the interview reports and the activity logs, who gutted the Chapel Hill PD's file of everything that might be useful, when, and why?" said Redmond, making very sure it didn't sound like an accusation.

"The where and the who I can't tell you," answered Williams. "The when was in 1982 or 1983. I used to look over the case once a year, close as I could get to the anniversary of the killings. The why? Presumably someone got wind of my habit of dragging that file out once a year and got scared I'd find something. Do you find that interesting?"

"Very," agreed Matt.

"And what do you think it means, Mr. Holmes?"

"Elementary, my dear Watson. The killer or killers were still in town as of 1983. Ergo there never were any crazed hippie cultists, any transient housebreakers who just got carried away, nor is it likely the killer or killers were students."

"Hmm, not bad," remarked Williams pleasantly. "Definitely up to Sherlock standards. Come on by the house. I got to be at work at four but I'm already up. I'd like to talk to you."

A few minutes later. Matt was sitting in a neat living room and Williams, older and more heavy but still recognizable from his 1970 photo, was pouring him an instant coffee. "My wife's at work. She's a nurse at Memorial Hospital," he said. "I work security for IBM over in the Research Triangle. Retired two years ago. Why are you digging up this old case? Got any new leads?"

"I knew both the girls, remember?" Matt told him. "I'm doing this on my vacation. It's just something I've wanted to do for them for a long time. I don't want them forgotten."

"That's why I looked at the file again every year for thirteen years," said Williams, stirring his coffee. "You've seen the crime scene pics?"

"Oh, yeah. Ugly, man."

"I saw it for real," said Williams, scowling at the memory. "I am ashamed to say that my first thought was, 'Oh, God, please don't let the men who did this be black.' Not just because of the usual racial reasons, but because I didn't want to carry the shame of belonging to the same race as someone who would do such a thing. I still feel that way a little, but whoever they are I still want to see them caught, real bad. That case is never going to be over for me until I know their names, at least. Look, ask me whatever you want. But could I ask you a favor in return? If you need anybody to do any extra legwork, give me a shout, will you? And if you find out anything, let me know. Nobody should have to die like that. God, it was a foul thing." He set his coffee cup down, trembling.

"First off, any idea who ripped off the file?" asked Redmond. "Who knew you checked it out regularly?"

"Anybody who took an interest in the department could have found out," replied Williams. "I raised holy hell when I went down there in '83 and found everything gone. All I got was blank looks, sorry Charlie, and soft shoe. I gave up when it became obvious that no one had any intention of finding out. Archives aren't all that secure. It was most likely somebody who worked in Public Safety, but it could have been a skillful outside job. I mean, who expects somebody to break into a police station?"

"What do you remember about the bulk material before it disappeared?" asked Matt. "I have a copy of the full SBI file, so I imagine I've probably seen most of what was there. It's the fact that it's missing at all that I find significant."

Williams started talking. Summed up in a nutshell, the interviews conducted by SBI and presumably by the Chapel Hill PD as well had been extremely frustrating and barren of anything remotely resembling a clue, and that was excluding even the bogus MacDonald diversion. State and local officers had conducted over a hundred interviews with friends, neighbors, students and teachers at Chapel Hill High, family doctors, co-workers and business associates of both girls' parents, Mary Jane's swimming coach, Jeannie Arnold's dancing and drama classmates, and every identifiable person who had been living, visiting, or passing through an eight square block radius around the murder house that night. "Zip," said Williams. "Zilch. Nada. Goose egg. Fuck all. Not a *damned* thing. Nobody saw nothing. Nobody heard nothing, not even Jeannie Arnold screaming in agony as she was whipped and burned and mangled. Scotty must have beamed the killers up to the Enterprise, for all the traces of their presence they left. No fingerprints. No fiber evidence, although that was pretty crude in them days. Not one object in that house which was identifiably theirs except for the common electrician's tape that bound Mary Jane Mears into the chair she died in. They may even have found that on the scene."

"I notice you keep saying they," asked Matt keenly. "You don't think it was just one guy?"

"Well...maybe. It could have been, sure," said Williams, shaking his head dubiously. "But I've always pictured two of them. I dunno why. You know how you can kind of *feel* a crime scene sometimes?"

"I know," said Matt with a nod.

"It just *felt* like a two man job. I'll bet you a year of breakfasts that when you find these guys there will be two of 'em."

"Thanks for not saying if I find them, Lieutenant."

"Call me Will. Hell, you the South's Sherlock Holmes," laughed Williams.

"I'm going to shoot that tabloid TV bitch on *Inside Affair* next time I see her," growled Matt. "Go on, please."

The police had learned that Jeannie Arnold slept around, which any kid at Chapel Hill High could have told them, and they had gotten some names of guys. Some of these confessed when the heat came down that they had been wishfully thinking and locker-room boasting, but some weren't and they admitted they'd actually gotten Jeannie into the back seat of her Plymouth or onto a sofa somewhere. Every one of these boys referred to Jeannie as "awesome" and every one of them had an unbreakable alibi. Besides, as Matt confirmed, everybody liked Jeannie, the ones who had tumbled her lovely passionate flesh more than most. From the SBI file Matt remembered one comment made by CHHS senior class jock Mike Malinsky: *"Look, officer, I swear none of us guys would have hurt Jeannie! We wanted to come back for more!"*

"That has the ring of truth to it," he told Williams. "Nobody who knew her ever thought it was any guy at CHHS who did her in. Jeannie wasn't the school tramp or a slut, at least we didn't think of her like that. She was an honest-to-God free spirit, and those who were honored with her favors considered it a privilege as well as a pleasure, if you'll pardon the pompous turn of speech."

"Were you so honored?" asked Williams, cocking an eye at him.

"Hell, no, I was a tuition grit from out in the county, no connection to the university at all. I supported the war, didn't use drugs, didn't burn the flag and I was generally politically incorrect. That term didn't exist back then, but the social chasm was there. Didn't matter how rich my father was, I was clean out of Jeannie Arnold's league," laughed Matt. "I was into Mary Jane, though, as you'll recall. She's my real reason for doing this. I've never forgotten her. Please, go on. What was the full scoop on the Riggsbee thing?"

The law had picked up and harassed Ronnie Riggsbee, Jeannie's bit of rough trade from the wrong side of the tracks, but it had been more *pro forma* than anything else. Jeannie went out with Riggsbee whenever she got tired of jocks and preppie UNC types and she wanted it a bit red around the neck. He was a 20-year-old dropout with tattoos who worked in a gas station, and who had a few juvy priors for joyriding and B & E. The year before he'd cut another man in a bar fight, but successfully pleaded self defense. This minor record of violence made Ronnie Riggsbee the only individual anywhere on the horizon who remotely resembled a suspect. Accordingly the SBI, the Chapel Hill PD, and the Durham County sheriff had grilled him up and down, but his alibi held. That October night he and another nubile 17-year-old, Miss Darlene Collins of Creedmoor, were cruising in his pickup truck and knocking back Miller High Life talls until about one o'clock, when they parked behind a Piggly Wiggly on the outskirts of Durham with the radio playing loudly. After ten minutes they were told to move on by a security guard on his rounds, who made a note of the license number of the truck and a description of the couple in his report, adding the comment, "on approaching vehicle observed female occupant nude to the waist and perform-ing oral sexual act on male occupant." The cops had attempted to construct a Charlie Starkweather-Caril Ann Fugate scenario that involved both Riggsbee and Ms. Collins in the murders, but there were too many people who had seen the truck rolling around and the time frame wouldn't work. The medical examiners were adamant that Jeannie Arnold had died at one A.M. plus-minus thirty minutes.

"They tried to diddle with the plus-minus thirty, but it just was-n't gonna fly," recalled Williams. "No way around it. The second victim was still alive or just being killed at the same time Ronnie Riggsbee was seen getting his knob job behind the Durham Piggly Wiggly." Beyond that every other attempt to create a scenario was nothing more than guesswork and desperate fantasy. The closest thing anyone had been able to come up with was some kind of right-wing death squad's revenge for Dr. Margaret Mears' strident anti-war activism and involvement with left-wing causes, but even in a town as liberal as Chapel Hill and as paranoid about anything or anyone to the right of Hubert Humphrey, the idea was simply too wild. "We were left with the obvious," concluded Williams. "A random burglary which turned into a violent sex crime because two good-looking girls came home at the wrong time and surprised the perps in the house."

"But that's absurd! No forced entry, nothing was stolen!" protested Matt. "How could the primary go for that?"

"A foolish consistency is the hobgoblin of little minds," admonished Williams..

"Ralph Waldo Emerson. I have that done up all artsy-craftsy on a computer and hanging over my desk at work," said Matt. "That's one item of info missing from the SBI file as well as yours, by the way. Just who the hell *was* the Chapel Hill PD's primary on this damned case?"

"A then Detective Sergeant Chuck Bennett," said Williams. "Did quite well for himself. Left the Chapel Hill department very soon after and went to work for...."

"The FBI," finished Matt, stunned. "Now Assistant Director Charles R. Bennett. Probably next in line for Director of the Federal Bureau. My next question was going to be what fucking imbecile feathered the case after three and a half months, but you just answered my question and explained a lot, a hell of a lot, about why this investigation stalled and died. Thanks, Will."

"You know him?"

"Oh, yeah. When I was in DEA we crossed swords, twice. Once he tried to get one of my guys framed for a murder committed by an FBI agent, a snitch of theirs they wanted to get rid of. Another time he wanted me to perjure myself on the witness stand to include a Cuban businessman in a case who so far as I know was legit, make him into a major drug player. They'd tried to get him to snitch on some anti-Castro exiles and he wouldn't play ball with them. I wouldn't either, and I threw Bennett through the window of a seafood place in Fort Lauderdale when he threatened me. I left DEA after that and went over to Justice Special Investigations until Waco happened, then I quit. Interestingly enough, our Chuckie was the SAIC on the ground at Waco, the man who got the word from Janet Reno on the closed-circuit phone and ordered the attack. He's the only man who can actually testify as to what the specific instructions were regarding the final assault. Three months later he's promoted to Assistant Director, and since then two Congressional committees, half a dozen tabloid TV programs and a dozen hotshot investigative reporters haven't been able to shake him, or even make him break a sweat."

Williams whistled. "Whew! Would you say that dude knows where some of Billyboy's bodies are buried?"

"Possibly in the very literal sense, yes. Looks like he's an old pro at that kind of thing. Damn, I never knew he was from Chapel Hill!"

"You think he might have something to do with the missing documents from the file?" asked Williams. "He left the Hill in 1971 and so far as I know he never showed his face back here. The reports didn't go missing until '83."

"I'll say this," said Matt somberly. "It already looks like this thing may be deeper than I thought. Will, what August body in the Southern Part of Heaven has the moral and political clout to hamstring a double murder investigation? The Mafia? The CIA? The Callé cartel? Multi-national banks? Saddam Hussein? The Catholic Church?"

"You talking the University, man," said Williams. "Hey, I'd rather mess with any of them cats you named than cross UNC inside the Chapel Hill city limits. But why would the university cover up a real piece of shit work like what happened in that house? I mean, you being a white man and all you might not like their politics, and me I don't like their money and their attitude, especially after having spent almost thirty years cleaning up their messes. But come on, they're not inhuman monsters! Every human being in this state with any shred of decency wants the men who did this caught and punished, even twenty-six years later!"

"Then where did the interview reports from the file go, Will?" asked Matt softly. "Who took them? What was in them? What could be so important as to justify the kind of influence that must have been used to put this case to bed after three and a half months of getting nowhere?"

"Guilt," said Williams immediately.

"No, no, no," said Matt. "Morality aside, a man like Chuck Bennett has everything to gain by cracking a spectacular case like this and arresting the guilty parties. Quite a feather in his cap. Someone persuaded him to forego that feather. Someone changed the equation, made it eminently worth his while to deep-six this case. Chuck Bennett to my knowledge is neither a lawyer nor a CPA, and you'll recall that in 1971 J. Edgar Hoover himself was still alive and those were still the basic requirements to join the FBI. Yet Bennett flushes this case and you tell me a few months later he's accepted for Quantico? Bullshit. Somebody leaned hard and heavy all across the board. Why? *Why, dammit?* What is so important about the apparently random sex murder of two high school girls?"

"Depends on who did it," observed Williams.

"Indeed. You have to get to work, Will. Thanks for the coffee." Matt rose and headed for the door.

"Hey, Two Gun," called Williams. "You know, I think maybe you better watch your ass on this one. If what you suspect is true it might not be too safe poking a stick at this even after twenty-six years."

"You still want me to call you if I need help?" asked Matt with a grin.

"*Hell,* yes!" answered Williams, shaking with a deep rumbling African laugh.

*   *   *

Matt's next stop was the University of North Carolina business office on West Franklin Street. There he spoke with a middle-aged woman administrator in personnel and flashed his badge. "I need any current addresses you may have on some people who are former employees of the university," he said. "Specifically Dr. Andrew Mears, who was a professor of anthropology here but who left in 1971, and a man named Leonard Arnold who was director of plant and facilities until probably the mid-1980s or so."

"Oh, yes, I remember Len Arnold," said the woman. "He retired in 1989. Let's see," she said, clicking away on her keyboard. A screen came up. "Sure, here it is. He lives out on Heritage Drive."

"Yes, I know it. You know, it never occurred to me they hadn't moved," said Matt. "I should have looked in the phone directory before bothering you."

"Not at all. Len hasn't done anything illegal has he?" she asked curiously.

"No, no, this has to do with an old case I'm working on," said Matt.

"Oh, yes. I see," she said gravely. "That was a terrible thing. I hope you can resolve it. I was very young, a sophomore here at UNC, in fact, but I remember it. That explains why you're looking for Dr. Mears as well. You know that Mrs. Mears..."

"Is now Congresswoman Mears. Yes, ma'am, I know where to contact her."

"I heard her speak last year at Duke on the administration's programs for the elderly," said the administrator. "She's quite a passionate advocate."

"She always was," said Matt. "Dr. Andrew Mears? Last I heard he was teaching at N.C. State in Raleigh, but that was many years ago and he might be anywhere now."

"Hmm...he's not drawing a pension or any benefits. But I'll bet he still gets the alumni magazine." She punched in a few more codes and another screen came up. "Ah! Here he is. Dr. Mears is still in Raleigh. Let me write out the address for you. Actually, I think I remember hearing that he was in poor health."

"Ma'am, I appreciate your time," said Matt, getting up. On his way out of the building he almost bumped into a tall, slender and graceful woman with long ash-blonde hair who was coming in. "Excuse me, ma'am," he said, touching his fedora as he left.

"Here's those forms you wanted, Ms. Thomasetti," said Heather, handing them to her. *Now who the hell was that?* she wondered. *Indiana Jones? Wonder if he works around here? With that hat he might be an archaeologist. Nah, probably some Sixties retread English prof. Don't know, though, he didn't look that old. Somehow not the professorial type, either. Veeeeery interesting. Definitely a possible. Should I ask? Better not. Don't want to get a reputation as Diana the Huntress, at least not quite yet. If he's UNC I'll see him around.*

                    *   *   *

The leaves were starting to turn along St. Mary's Street in Raleigh, but the air was still pleasantly warm, no fall crispness as yet. Matt found a place to park and walked up a stone-flagged walkway to the ivy-covered, two story brick home. He rang the bell and a middle-aged black woman in a nurse's uniform answered. "Ms. Rendell? I'm Matt Redmond, North Carolina State Bureau of Investigation." He showed his shield. "We spoke on the phone."

"Dr. Mears is in the study. I'll tell him you're here."

"Before you do, may I ask after his exact medical condition? Not just business, you understand. He and I have met before, long ago, and I always liked him."

"He's recovering from his second stroke quite nicely, but it's the cancer that's going to do him in," the nurse said frankly. "He moves very slowly but he's quite lucid. The cancer is extremely advanced and he could leave us at any time now, but he keeps to the bare minimum medication he can tolerate. The pain must be excruciating, but he says he prefers to have his mind clear so he can wind things up. He's a very brave and admirable man."

"I'm glad he's being taken care of," said Matt. "Insurance?"

"He believes so, but it ran out some time ago. His former wife, Congresswoman Mears, has quietly taken over paying for my services and the other two shift nurses as well. Please don't mention that. I think he may know, but..."

"It's not germane to my inquiry. I won't say anything to him," Matt assured her.

"This way. He's very eager to see you." Dr. Andrew Mears was sitting in a wheel chair in front of the open French windows of a large study or library, a room that looked precisely as an anthropologist's study should look. African masks and spears hung on the wall, and glass display cases held statuettes, bone fragments, pottery shards, and unidentifiable bits and pieces of stone and clay. The walls were lined with shelved books, and a large desk cluttered with books and papers and manuscripts filled the center of the room. The old man in the chair waved his hand cheerily at

Matt. "Good afternoon, Doctor Mears," said Matt, looking around him. "How many of these artifacts carry native curses?"

"Every damned one of 'em," said the old man in a chuckle that turned into a wheeze. Matt glanced over at the mantelpiece and rocked back as if slapped, a sudden tearing agony of pain and loss stabbing him to the heart. Mary Jane was there. The room was a shrine to her memory. Enlarged photos, small photos, everywhere. Mary Jane as a baby. Mary Jane as a three year-old child with her face smeared with birthday cake. Mary Jane as a six year-old in a church pinafore smiling like a little black-haired angel. Mary Jane with a hula hoop. Mary Jane aged eight holding an Easter basket full of baby chicks. Mary Jane, twelve years old standing by her bicycle. Mary Jane aged thirteen or so at a party. Mary Jane holding the puppy named Grouch in her arms. Mary Jane, growing tall and lissome and lovely. Mary Jane in a two-piece swimsuit at the beach, showing the long lithe body and high breasts to which even now his own body responded with long-forgotten desire, longing to fold her in his arms and lay her down on a soft bed and make love to her. Mary Jane's high school graduation picture, taken three days before she died, printed along with Jeannie's in the 1971 annual bordered in black. "God, she was beautiful!" Matt choked out. "I'm sorry, sir, that's not the way I intended to begin."

"Son, any man who comes into my home and says that is welcome here, always," said Mears. "Pardon me for not getting up. You sit down. And by the way, you're grown up now. You don't have to call me sir anymore. Andy will do fine." Matt pulled up a chair. "Before you begin, Matt, I have to ask you. It'll be twenty-six years this month. Do you think you can catch the bastards who took my child from me?"

"I don't know," replied Matt truthfully. "I can only promise you that I'm here in North Carolina to stay now, and I'll spend the rest of my life trying. I may not able to catch them and punish them, but I hope someday I can bring you some answers."

"You won't be bringing them to me, Matt. You're damned lucky you stopped by when you did. I'm all packed up, everything in my life been cleared out or put into storage, so to speak, the taxi's waiting outside, and I'm just about ready to head on down the road. A few more weeks might have been too late. You came to ask questions, son. Ask them."

"Actually I have almost no specific questions, Andy," said Matt. "If you'll pardon my bluntness, the fact is that you and your wife's alibis checked out. I'm here mostly just to let you know that Mary Jane's not forgotten and someone's taking an interest, but I also want you to just talk to me in general about the whole thing. Twenty-six years is a long time to really think, go over everything in your head."

"Over, and over, and over," said Mears tiredly. "Every day. It's always there in your mind, no matter what you may be doing. It's always there beating on your brain and screaming in the background. You just don't know, Matt."

"After all this time, sir...sorry, Andy...after all this time, I want you to tell me honestly, openly, frankly, what you think happened to your daughter and Jeannie Arnold. *Any* ideas, any suspicions you might have had, no matter how far-fetched, *anything* you remember about that time, no matter how trivial or irrelevant it may seem."

Andrew Mears sighed, then glanced over at Matt's shirt pocket. "Not trying to evade the question, Matt, but is that a Dominican cigar I see?"

"Yes, sir. Uh, are you allowed...?"

"Oh, God, I would die happy if I could go sucking on the burning butt end of one of those!" groaned Mears. "But if you were to give me one Marvella would kill me before I got in the first puff and then she'd kill you, and two guns or not, she'd pulverize you! But wait." He wheeled the chair over to the desk over to the intercom on his phone and buzzed it. "Marvella! My guest is about to light up what appears to be a very fine Dominican cigar, at my request. I am not going to smoke it, I just want to smell it. The windows are open and I will turn on the fan. You come in here and raise hell about it and he'll arrest you and I'll cut you out of my will!"

"You a crazy old motherfucker!" snarled the nurse on the intercom.

"Madam, you have two college degrees. Stop talking like Aunt Jemima. It's very patronizing and irritating."

"You still a ole fool," said Marvella's voice. He switched off the intercom.

"People are funny," said Mears. "Marvella genuinely likes me and she is having difficulty coming to terms with my impending death, so she recently started talking like a geechee. It's her way of putting distance between herself and the ole massa in de big house. She think's I'm joking about mentioning her in my will, but she's got a surprise coming. Now for mercy's sake, light up that stogie!" Amused, Matt did so while Mears turned on the desk fan. "Right," he said, inhaling the fragrance. "Now, let me answer you as best I can. To begin with, I believe that there was probably more than one murderer. That's just a feeling, and I have no evidence to back it up."

"That's my feeling as well," put in Matt, puffing on the cigar. "I base it on a slight difference in the MOs."

"Excellent," complimented Mears. "Secondly, it was not a burglary. Nothing was stolen."

"You are absolutely sure of that, Andy?" asked Matt keenly. "I've read the SBI file, of course, but this is the first time I've ever been able to question any of the principals. You didn't have any secret stashes of jewelry or cash or anything?"

"No, there was nothing like that and as nearly as Meg and I could determine they didn't take anything at all from the house. That indicates to me that they came into our home specifically to rape and kill, for which may God send their souls into everlasting hellfire. I could understand it, if not forgive it, if some thugs had been robbing the place, and all of a sudden were confronted with the opportunity to ravage two pretty girls. But this was deliberately done."

"Again, I agree," said Matt. "Go on."

"This leaves us with two alternatives," continued Dr. Mears in a professorial tone. "The first is that this man or men were sexual predators who selected Mary Jane and Jeannie as targets, were well enough informed to know they would be alone in the house, came in and killed them." Matt decided not to mention his theory that the rapes had been performed with blunt instruments as a red herring. "The second possibility is that they were killed by someone they knew. Someone they trusted enough to let into the house. Hence no sign of forced entry."

"I agree again," said Matt. "Sir, sorry Andy, do you have any idea who such a person might have been? Jeannie Arnold was promiscuous and she had a number of lovers at CHHS, including one teacher, as well as one older guy, Ronnie Riggsbee. All of their alibis checked. So far as I remember from that period in my life, Mary Jane went with Craig Roberts for a few months in the spring of 1970 but broke up with him early that summer, and she had no boyfriend at the time she died."

"Yes, she did," said Mears calmly.

"Who?" asked Matt in surprise, leaning forward.

"You," replied Mears. Matt leaned back. "Teenaged girls usually talk about their crushes with their mothers, but in the political climate of the times, for Mary Jane it was about like being the daughter of Joan of Arc. Meg was completely wrapped up in the Movement and very short on time for anything or anyone else. Mary Jane talked to me about you, the afternoon of October 22nd when we left for Washington, the last time I saw her alive. She wasn't gushing or silly, she was very calm and serious. She said she sensed something about you, and she thought she might be falling into genuine, adult love with you. That's the way she put it."

"We—-we talked about that at the dance," said Matt, his voice low. "I told her that I loved her. I asked her if she'd marry me one day. She said yes."

"Praise God!" cried the old man leaning back in his chair. "Thanks be to God that she was able to hear those words spoken to her by a young man before her life was cut off! Matt, thank you for coming and telling me this. You have made my own end so much easier to bear." He dabbed at his wet eyes. "I'm sorry, you're a police officer now with a job to do. In answer to your obvious next question, no, I have never been able to call to mind a single incident or hint that Mary Jane had any other boyfriends at all. I asked that afternoon point blank, but gently, whether or not she was still a virgin, and she got rather cagey about it. Her exact reply was, 'Well, yes and no'. She declined to discuss it any further and I didn't push it. That was one of the ground rules of our talks on intimate subjects. I always figured that she had gotten into what we used to call heavy petting with Craig or else with you."

"Not with me, no," said Matt. "The Harvest Ball dance that night was our first actual date. I don't know if you were told at the time, but the autopsy indicated that Mary Jane was *virgo intacta* before she was raped that night."

"Hmm. I wonder what she could have meant, then? We'll never know now, I suppose. Beyond that, Matt, I could not begin to give you the name of any suspect. I will say that I do not believe my daughter was the primary target of whoever came into our home that time. I was never given the full details of what was done to Jeannie Arnold, but I understand it was horrific. Was it?"

"It was," confirmed Matt. "It was also very meticulous and time-consuming. The medical examiner reported that Mary Jane died around eleven, right after they got back from the dance. Jeannie died about two hours later. They kept her alive and they methodically tortured her in addition to the sexual assaults."

"That might be your line of inquiry," said Mears thoughtfully. "Jeannie Arnold was a very beautiful and sexual young woman. Look for a man who was attracted to her, probably an adult, someone she spurned, a man who decided that he was going to take by force what she would not give willingly, that he would punish her for her beauty and her sexuality and her refusal to give him what she gave others pretty freely."

"It's a tenable theory," admitted Matt. "I don't know, though, it just..."

"Doesn't feel right," concluded Mears. "Yes, I know. But it's the best I've ever been able to come up with."

"A few more questions, Andy," said Matt. "They may seem impertinent and irrelevant, but I have to have a complete picture. They may offend and they may cause you pain."

"No more pain than I have endured every day since I was called to the telephone in the Washington Sheraton to learn that my daughter was dead," said Mears bleakly. "Son, you ask me any damned thing. You probably won't get many more chances."

"Were *you* attracted to Jeannie Arnold?" asked Matt bluntly.

"Hell, yes," laughed Mears. "When she and Mary Jane had been swimming and were running around the house in bathing suits I generally had to find something to do in my workroom that involved closing the door. But did I have sex with her? No. It was never offered and I never attempted to work my way up to such a thing. Jeannie wouldn't have gone for it, I'm sure. Mary Jane was her best friend, she liked and respected Meg immensely, and I think that even at 17 with all the hormones flowing she would have considered something like that unethical and disrespectful."

"Why did you and your wife divorce soon after the killings?" asked Matt.

"Ah," said Mears, "That is a bit delicate, yes. The fact is that I found out my wife was having an affair. It seemed too much on top of the strain of Mary Jane's death, plus to be honest I never shared her passion for politics."

"Like being married to Joan of Arc was the term you used," Matt reminded him. "Who the affair was with?"

"Would you take my word that it was totally irrelevant to anything involving the murders?" asked Mears. "No, of course not, only you can decide that. It was with one of her anti-war Mobilization Committee co-workers." Mears was silent. "It was with another woman. I never knew who. Meg would never tell me."

"Ah," said Matt, the cigar burning slowly in his fingers. "That must have been a pretty heavy scene back in '70."

"Heavy scene? God, I haven't heard that term in years!" laughed Mears.

"I seem to be getting sucked into a time warp," said Matt. "I may end up going around wearing bell bottoms and tie-dyes. I saw a lava lamp I almost bought in the mall the other day."

"Yes, Matt, it was a heavy scene in 1970, and it would be a heavy scene today to find out your wife was cheating on you, with anybody," said Mears morosely

"I know," replied Matt quietly.

"You do? I'm damned sorry for you, then. The fact is, Matt, that besides Mary Jane we never had much in common. It was quite amicable, though, us being civilized liberals. We are still on quite friendly terms."

"No, you're not," replied Matt. "I don't know how bad it is, but it's bitter and nasty. You've been doing great up until this point, Andy. I'm sorry you had to start lying to me now." Mears stared at him. "There are over a dozen pictures of Mary Jane alone on that mantelpiece," said Matt, gesturing. "There are four with Mary Jane and you. There is not one photograph anywhere in this room of your former wife." He decided against mentioning Marvella Rendell's comment about Meg Mears paying his medical bills.

"God damn," said Andrew Mears, shaking his head in surprise. "You really are the Southern Sherlock Holmes!"

"Why did you and your wife divorce, Andy?" asked Matt. Mears looked out into the back garden. A cloud went over the sun and a small cool wind sprang up. For a brief moment it was autumn outside. He sighed.

"The affair I told you about was true. Meg had been obviously losing interest in me sexually for some time, and she chose the period after our daughter's death to tell me she'd discovered, or more likely just decided because it was starting to be trendy, that she was a lesbian. She offered to continue the marriage on what she called an open basis. She seemed to think I'd welcome the opportunity to start banging my students guilt-free. She tore me apart and didn't even know or care she'd done it. She's almost seventy now and I believe she still has a live-in female companion."

"That wasn't the only reason, was it?" asked Matt gently.

Andrew Mears looked at him. "Son, I am going to tell you something that I have never told to any living soul. Not the police, not even to Meg herself."

"Go on."

"It is my belief," he said slowly, "That my former wife, Margaret Mears, knows more than she ever revealed about who murdered our daughter and Jeannie Arnold. That feeling began the day we learned of her death in Washington. I've never been free of it since then."

"On what do you base that feeling, Dr. Mears?" asked Matt formally, hardly daring to breathe.

"On one thing only. My wife was speaking at the breakfast when I was called to the telephone. It was the Chapel Hill police. I let her finish her address on the evils of imperialism and the sins of Richard Nixon. There didn't seem to be any hurry about giving her this terrible thing that we were going to have to live with for the rest of our lives. I called her out and asked the manager if I could take her into his office. I told her. She broke down into hysterics and she screamed out something I will never forget." The old man looked Matt square in the face. "She screamed out in her agony and her grief, 'No, no, no! It can't be! *They promised!*' That was all. Just that once. '*They promised!*' Sometimes I have been unsure I heard those words. But I did."

"Did you ask her what she meant?" Matt pressed gently.

"She claimed she didn't know what she was saying, that she meant to say the girls had promised to lock all the doors and windows or something of the kind. She was lying to me. I was sure of it then and I'm sure of it now. It took a while, but I realized I couldn't stay with her. The lesbian thing was just an excuse. If that had been all, then I loved Meg enough to work something out and stay with her. I had an out, and I took it. I asked for the divorce, Matt. Not her."

"Jesus!" whispered Matt.

"My sentiments exactly."

"Is there anything else you want to tell me, sir?" asked Matt, lapsing back into formality.

"There may be, yes. I am going to put a great strain on your patience, Matt. I am going to ask that you leave now and wait until you hear from me. Leave me a telephone number where you can be reached. I may wish to contact you again, I may not. I am going to call my wife's scheduling secretary and ask that she either arrange a visit down here to me or that she arrange to call me when she has time and privacy to conduct a conversation of some length. I am going to speak to her for the first time in many years, and I am going to say some things I should have said many years ago. That I did not speak before is a cowardly and despicable injustice to my daughter and to her dear friend, whom I liked and admired and whom I have mourned almost as much as Mary Jane. There's a possibility I can right that wrong before I die. Thank you for coming, Matt. This has been an important day in my life."

Matt stood up and laid his card on the table. "Thank you, sir. It's been instructive."

"Matt!" spoke up the old man. "I want you to know something. We talked about you. Meg considered you to be an entirely unsuitable young man for my daughter. I did not share that opinion, then or now. Mary Jane always had good instincts about people. I am truly sorry you never became part of my family."

Matt made a show of peeking around the door looking for Marvella, then he stepped over and pulled his second cigar out of his pocket, sliding it under the old man's blanket. "I only have one lighter, so you're going to have to solve the problem of lighting it and smoking it yourself," he said.

"A problem which will give me hours of intellectual stimulation in overcoming," chuckled the old man. "You are an angel of mercy, son." He reached up and gripped Matt's arm like a steel vise, his face twisted with years of pain and hate. *"In God's name, find them and kill them if you can! I can't die until I know they are dead!"*

⋆   ⋆   ⋆

Can I find them? Matt wondered. He was coming back into Chapel Hill from Interstate 40 down Franklin Street. When he reached the corner of Boundary, where the old library had been in his high school days, on a sudden impulse he turned right and two minutes later parked the Taurus across the street from the house where Mary Jane Mears and Jeannie Arnold had died. It was a cool autumn evening now, daylight dying slowly and lingeringly amid leaves turning gold. He stood on the sidewalk looking up at the room where the girl he loved had died. *How did that James Taylor song go?* he thought, as the pain and inconsolable loss washed over him for the ten thousandth time. Matt started to hum quietly, mouthing the words under his breath, singing to Mary Jane. *"...I've seen fire and I've seen rain. I've seen sunny days that I thought would never end. I've seen lonely times when I could not find a friend...But I always thought that I'd see you again..."*

"Mom, there's a guy in a cowboy hat standing on the sidewalk acting weird!" called out Tori inside the house. Heather was unpacking groceries.

"What do you mean weird?" she asked, putting cans in the cupboard.

"He's sort of rocking back and forth looking up at the sky talking to himself," said Tori.

"Probably one of the psychiatric out-patients from South Wing," said Heather. "Gail says they have a tendency to wander around when they overdo their medication. He's not actually standing on our lawn, is he?"

"No, just the sidewalk."

Matt stared up at the window. *"But I always thought that I'd see you again..."* he repeated to himself, the words echoing over and over in his mind. Then he did. Clearly, unmistakably, the face of Mary Jane Mears looked down at him through the window. She recognized him and smiled with infinite sadness.

"Now he's staggering around waving his arms like he's drunk," said Tori, looking out the living room window with interest. "He's putting his hand inside—-*Mom! He's got a gun!*"

"Oh, Lord!" cried Heather in alarm.

"He's coming toward the house!" hissed Tori. "Shit! He saw me! He's coming toward the window!" Tori bolted into the kitchen. Heather ran upstairs and jerked open the drawer of her nightstand frantically, fumbled around in the papers and Kleenex and pens and junk, and pulled out the snub-nosed Smith and Wesson .38 she'd bought when Bill had violated the court order, come to her home in Seattle and beaten her bloody. She ran back downstairs. "Call 911 and get the police here!" she ordered Tori. *"Now!"* Heather knew full well that going out to confront an armed intruder when all she had to do was sit tight and wait for the law was an incredibly stupid thing to do, but after she was last beaten by her former husband she'd resolved that she would never show fear of any man ever again, and to her own inner amazement she was evidently serious about it, scared to death but resolute. Even as she threw open the door she thought, *Dear God, what if he kills me? What will become of Tori?* Then she saw the man peering through the living room window. *Damn! It's the Indiana Jones character! The son of a bitch is stalking me!*

Matt thought he was losing his mind. He'd gone for his gun before he got a grip, but he'd put it back in the holster. Obviously he was having some kind of a breakdown, or mental surge of power of suggestion. Then he'd seen another teenaged girl looking out of the lower window and moved in to take a look, but she was gone when he got there. *Holy shit,* he wondered desperately, *Is losing her all those years ago getting to me that badly? Am I losing touch with reality?*

"Get your hands up, asshole!" rapped a harsh female voice. Matt turned and found a tall, slender blond woman covering him with a .38 snub. He'd seen her somewhere before. The personnel office earlier today, that was it. "My daughter's called the cops and you're staying here and waiting for them. She also tells me you've got a gun. You're going to get rid of it, by the numbers, doing just what I tell you to do and no more. Now get your hands in the air!"

"There's a law in Chapel Hill against private ownership of handguns," he remarked. "Seldom enforced, true, but it's still on the books."

"Shut up or I'll shoot!" she ordered fiercely. "I'm a woman, I'm a single mother, and I'm an abused spouse. In Chapel Hill that gives me triple victim status, buster. You're white, male, and Southern. I could shoot you down like a dog and the jury will throw flowers under my feet as I walk out of court!"

"Not if you shoot an SBI agent, ma'am," Matt contradicted her gently. "I think they'd dispense with the flowers, anyway."

"Bullshit!" said Heather, hesitating.

"I'm Agent Matthew Redmond. With you permission, I'd like to get my ID from my pocket," said Matt. She nodded. He slowly pulled out his shield and his ticket in their leather case. She studied it carefully, holding the gun on him, then lowered it. "I'd like to apologize, ma'am. I'm trespassing, but I'll be glad to tell you why. Can I offer you some advice first?"

"What?" asked Heather suspiciously.

"Next time you come charging out to confront an armed prowler, you might want to load your pistol first."

Heather looked down at her gun, fumbled with the release and dropped open the cylinder. It was empty. She turned scarlet with fury and shame. *If he laughs, he can go straight to hell. If he doesn't, I may just fuck him,* she thought, embarrassment mixing with relief. "May we step inside please?" came Matt's voice, soft and polite.

Gallows Pole

"...Your brother brought me silver,
And your sister warmed my soul,
But how I lied..." He pulled so hard
She's swinging on the gallows pole.

—Led Zeppelin*

---

*Copyright 1970 by Atlantic Records

VI

"I think perhaps first you should tell me what this is regarding, Mr. Redmond," said Heather in a cool tone.

"Certainly. I'm working on an investigation, an old unsolved case from many years ago. Without getting into the unpleasant details, this house was the scene of the crime."

"The murder of those two young girls!" said Heather, stunned. "You're investigating it now after all these years?"

"Ah, you know, then. That's good. I wasn't sure how you'd react to my walking up and telling you there was once a double homicide in your home," said Matt. "Yes, it was a long time ago, 1970 to be exact, but there's no statute of limitations on murder, ma'am, and I'm proud to say that the SBI never stops looking for those who kill in North Carolina. Not completely. Every now and then we pull out the old case files and take another look, go over the ground again, see if maybe we missed something. I dropped by to take a look at the place, see how it had changed in all those years, and I'm afraid I yielded to curiosity and stepped up to take a peek inside. I have no warrant and no real reason to come in, considering the time lapse involved, but I confess I hoped to cadge an invitation from whoever lived here now. I've never been inside the place."

"You sound like you were here when the killings happened," said Heather, interested.

"Yes, ma'am. I was 17 at the time, a senior in high school. I knew both victims."

"Well, I'm Heather Lindstrom," she said, sticking out her hand which Matt took firmly. "We'd better go inside. My daughter is probably waiting with bated breath to hear gunshots."

"Thank you, ma'am." She was about to ask him to call her Heather instead of ma'am, then decided she rather liked it.

"It's all right, Tori," she called as she entered the house. "This gentlemen is a state police officer." Tori peeped around the kitchen door dubiously.

"Funny uniform," she said, looking at Matt's fedora, windbreaker, plaid shirt and jeans. "You look like Indiana Jones."

"I'm with the North Carolina State Bureau of Investigation, miss," said Matt easily. "We don't wear uniforms. We mostly provide investigative and forensic backup for local police and sheriffs when they've got a serious crime to deal with. Closest I've come to the Temple of Doom was a crack house in Durham, but that was close enough, believe me. I could have used a bullwhip on that one right enough. I keep asking my boss for one, but he says the state's got no budget for it." Tori smiled and relaxed.

"You were acting weird outside," she said, still a bit skeptical. "I saw you had a gun and that's why Annie Oakley here came out there after you."

"I have a habit of talking to myself when I'm concentrating on something. Sometimes people who don't know me find it unnerving," Matt told her, which was partly true. "It runs in the family. My brother does it too, trouble is he answers himself back. Sometimes he argues with himself. And loses the argument. He's crazy as a loon, but don't worry, I'm merely eccentric." This time Tori giggled outright.

"This simpering gamine is my daughter, Victoria," said Heather. "We used to call her Vicky but apparently Tori is more fashionable nowadays."

"Hi, Tori. I'm Matt Redmond. I was telling your mother that..." Tori's eyes widened and she clapped her hands together.

"Oh, totally *cool!* You're Two Gun Matt! All *right!*"

"Oh, Lord!" groaned Matt, putting his hand to his forehead.

"Two Gun Matt?" inquired Heather archly.

"You know, Mom, you've seen him on TV on *America's Supercops* and there were those big articles about him in Time and People Magazine. You know, about all his gunfights with Dynamite Slim and Little Willie and Don Ramon."

"I used to be an agent for the Drug Enforcement Administration," explained Matt. "This was back in the days when Miami Vice was going strong. The damned tabloid TV programs decided the whole drug scene was hot stuff, and they descended on the agency like blowflies to chronicle our Don Johnson lifestyles and careers, which they didn't find much in the way of, so they made it up as they went along. I was involved in a couple of high-profile cases in this country and in Latin America, and I ended up getting my fifteen minutes of worldwide fame, as Andy Warhol put it. It was not an edifying experience, and it didn't do my relations with my fellow officers much good. Real cops hate prima donnas and publicity hounds. Two Gun Matt was the contribution of a lady anchorperson on *Inside Affair.* There's another one floating around as well."

"You're the Southern Fried Sherlock Holmes, too," volunteered Tori.

"That's just Southern Sherlock Holmes, and I'm nothing of the kind, miss," said Matt, slightly exasperated.

"Yes you are," replied Tori confidently. "You're here to find out who killed Jeannie and Mary Jane, aren't you?"

"Yes, ma'am, I am," replied Matt, surprised. "How did you know?"

"I told Tori all about the history of the house," interjected Heather. "She can put two and two together. Young lady, make yourself useful. Go make coffee. Would you like some, Mr. Redmond? I've got Diet Coke and orange juice as well."

"I'm the world's worst coffee hound, ma'am. I'd love some. And it's Matt."

"Well, then, I'm Heather." She eased him into the living room as Tori went into the kitchen. "Ah, could I ask you something? How did you know the gun wasn't loaded?"

Matt drew his .357 Magnum from his shoulder rig; Heather flinched and drew back a little. He smiled. "It's OK, ma'am. You're not Little Willie and believe me, my reputation is very exaggerated in any case. Now here, you see?" He held the weapon at an angle and pointed to the front of the cylinder. "You can actually see the bullets in a loaded revolver." He reversed the weapon, "You can see the cartridge rims from the rear as well. You were very brave to face down an armed man with an unloaded gun in trying to protect your daughter, ma'am, Heather I mean, but it was actually a very dangerous thing to do. If I had been a real criminal I might not have appreciated such maternal heroics. Nobody likes having even an empty gun pointed at them. In the future I think you should keep it loaded."

"That's very suave and chivalrous of you to spare my feelings, Matt," laughed Heather, "But I think you can guess that I was just so damned scared and flustered I forgot to check the damned thing. I usually do keep it loaded. I don't know why it wasn't loaded tonight."

There was a ring at the front doorbell, and a voice called out, "Hello in the house! Police officer!"

Tori came in from the kitchen. "Coffee's brewing. Oh, I, ah, kind of called the cops while Mom was outside. She told me to."

Heather opened the door. A lean, muscular white police sergeant stood outside. "We had a report of a strange man with a gun at this address. I see the report was correct. Howdy, Matt."

"Hey, Charlie."

"You gone from whupping up on your relatives to peeping in womens' windows? That's low, Matt, real low."

"Didn't you hear? I'm on vacation. Rest and relaxation."

"I think you should let me run him in, lady," said the sergeant gravely. "We know this man. He's a notorious pervert."

"Ignore him. He's on a sugar high and doesn't know what he's saying," said Matt. "Chapel Hill cops are the worst donut whores in the state. A box of Krispy Creme and they're anybody's. Can't you see the pink glaze on his shirt? The man's a user."

"I've just learned from my daughter that this gentleman is apparently some kind of gunslinger, but if the state of North Carolina trusts him I suppose I'll give him the benefit of the doubt," said Heather. "Sorry about the false alarm, sergeant."

"Bull," said Matt politely. "You did exactly what you were supposed to do. You had no idea on earth who I was. No apology necessary, believe me. I'm lucky you didn't shoot first and ask questions later."

"With an unloaded gun?" asked Heather. "Speaking of which, Tori, do you happen to know how my pistol got unloaded?"

"I'm always scared you'll hurt yourself or shoot me when I'm going to the bathroom at night," said Tori defensively. "You're a good mom and all, but I'm not sure you're responsible enough to own a gun."

"Tori!" Heather groaned, mortified. The sergeant laughed as he left; Matt, she noticed gratefully, again did not.

They sat down at the kitchen table and Matt accepted a large cup of espresso. "Cream but no sugar," he said. "Thanks, Heather. I saw you this morning down at the University personnel office, didn't I?"

"Yes, I was coming in as you were going out," she replied. "I had to drop off some personnel forms. What were you doing there?"

"Trying to locate current addresses on the parents of Jeannie Arnold and Mary Jane Mears," said Matt. "I saw Mary Jane's father in Raleigh this afternoon, and I'll see the Arnolds tomorrow morning. How long have you lived here, may I ask?"

"Actually, we just moved in over Labor Day. We came here from Seattle in June when I took a job as head accountant for the university. My oldest son is already here in North Carolina, down at Fort Bragg. He'll be getting out of the army in March and getting married. His wife-to-be is from here and Greg already has a job offer in the Research Triangle Park. I got downsized at Microsoft in Seattle last February, but I walked away with a pretty good settlement, enough to move across country on, and I just decided a change of scene would be a good idea for Tori and me both." *I figured maybe in North Carolina I wouldn't be 42 years old, single, working poor, and within two years of having my kids grown and being alone,* she thought bitterly. "We rented a cramped little apartment while we house-hunted, and this house was very reasonable indeed. It was only after the agency had us hooked that they told us why." Matt noted the absence of any mention of a husband, the absence of a ring on Heather's finger, and said nothing.

"Chapel Hill has very definite folkways," agreed Matt. "This house has been part of them for a while."

"Why is the SBI reopening the case after twenty-six years?" asked Heather.

"That's my doing," explained Matt. "I mean, it's true what I said about the bureau never closing an unsolved murder case, but I asked to be given this one. I had some vacation time coming and I'm using it to go back into these homicides. I may not be able to catch the killers after all this time, but I at least hope to satisfy my own mind as to what happened. That's mainly what's important to me."

"You say you knew the girls?" asked Heather.

"Yes, I did," said Matt. "They were classmates of mine at Chapel Hill High School."

"I think that is so *way* cool!" pronounced Tori, fascinated.

"Tori started at CHHS this year, in the eleventh grade," said Heather. "You say this is the first time you have ever been in here?"

"Yes, ma'am. I knew Mary Jane Mears fairly well, but I was never actually granted entrée into these sanctified walls. I was a grit, you see. An Orange County kid whose father paid tuition to send me to Chapel Hill High instead of Orange High in Hillsborough. Do they still call the country kids grits out there, Tori?"

"No, they're called peckerwoods, but I know who you mean," said Tori. "Shop kids, yokels. Their clothes are crap, they talk like Gomer Pyle, and the girls are all sluts."

"One can tell you're not from here," chided Matt gently. "Your mother is UNC now and obviously you've gotten mobbed up with the university kids at Chapel Hill High. I presume peckerwood a term you picked up from the blacks, but it's not a good idea to call white Southerners that to their face, at least not outside Chapel Hill. It can have unfortunate results."

"She won't," said Heather. "She will not be using *any* racial or ethnic slurs of any kind, about anybody. Do you understand that, Tori?"

"Oh, mom, it's OK to do it to white guys," protested Tori. "They can't do anything."

"I know, dear, but that is precisely why you mustn't use that word," said Heather severely. "It's like saying the N word to a black person would have been fifty years ago, abusing and insulting people with no power who can't fight back. It's crude and boorish."

"Tori, I don't guess you've been out in the county or around the state much," said Matt carefully, "But sometimes even in Chapel Hill you'll see a car or a pickup truck with a license plate or a bumper sticker that's got a flag on it, a red flag with a blue X and stars in it. Do you know what that means?"

"I've seen those around," agreed Tori. "What are they?"

"Oh, *Tori,* don't be stupid!" snapped Heather. "You've had American history in school!"

"What?" asked Tori, genuinely surprised.

"Growing up in Seattle she probably has never seen a Confederate flag unless she watches old movies," put in Matt. "They still teach the Civil War in the public schools, or at least a PC version thereof, but they usually remove all the illustrations of the flag or anyone like Robert E. Lee. Confederate images are considered racially insensitive and hurtful to minority students. I think that's pretty much standard everywhere nowadays. Anyway, Tori, just don't call anybody down here you don't know a peckerwood, or trailer trash, or grit, or anything like that, OK? I have accepted the world the way it is, but some haven't, and there's a message in those rebel flags you'd better learn to read. Otherwise you might cause yourself a lot of trouble, and you could get hurt. I know it's hard to believe, but there are still a few white men out in these woods who aren't ready to roll over and play dead yet. Understand?"

"Okay, Matt," she said with a nod.

"Anyway, getting back to what I was saying before that politically incorrect digression, no, Heather, I was never invited into this house. My father was pretty rich even then, but Chapel Hill's class structure isn't financial, it's intellectual. Mary Jane was UNC. Daddy was a homebuilding contractor, before he got really filthy rich by inheritance. UNC people asked Randall Redmond to build houses for them, but neither he nor his sons were ever invited into those houses when they were completed, which I think is about 50% of his problem. For some reason Daddy's life-long ambition was to be accepted by this town."

"What's the other 50%?" asked Tori, glued to Matt's conversation.

"The fact that he's a congenital asshole, but that's another story."

"Will you tell me about the gunfight with Don Ramon?" asked Tori eagerly. "And Little Willie? And Dynamite Slim? People Magazine said you were the greatest American gunfighter since Wild Bill Hickock and Wyatt Earp," she said.

"People Magazine is full of sheep dip!" replied Matt.

"She knows everything about Michael Jackson, Heidi Fleiss, O. J. Simpson, and every sleazy scandal since she was old enough to turn on a television, but she doesn't recognize a Confederate flag when she sees one!" exclaimed Heather in exasperation. "Okay, I'll bite, who are all these people?"

"Drug dealers," said Matt. "White trash, black trash, and brown trash respectively who were killed resisting arrest on serious felony charges, and no, you bloodthirsty little hellion, I will not tell you all about it! Violence isn't funny or aesthetic or stimulating." *Michelle would disagree,* thought Matt, *but hopefully this girl won't turn out like Michelle.* Suddenly Tori looked at a door across the kitchen, a door Matt remembered from the house plan in the SBI file led down to the basement laundry room where Jeannie Arnold died. The smile vanished from her face.

"You're right," she said, quietly and gravely. "It isn't funny or nice at all. Mom's right, I watch too much TV and I forget what's real sometimes. Thank you for reminding me."

"Ah...and you personally killed all these colorfully named individuals in the line of duty?" asked Heather, fascinated in spite of herself.

"I had no choice in the matter, ma'am," said Matt. "They were trying to kill me. I could really kick the butts of the damned media people who decided to make tabloid stories out of those incidents, and others. They were horrible experiences and I deeply wish they had never happened."

"I believe you said you wanted to take a tour of the house?" asked Heather.

"Just a quick walk-through," he said. "I've studied a floor plan in the SBI case file, and obviously there's not going to be anything left for me to find after all this time. It's purely so I can say I've been on the scene. This door goes down to the basement, I believe?"

"Yes, feel free," said Heather. "Go on down and take a look. I want to get the rest of my groceries put away and I'll join you. I won't be a minute." She opened the door and turned on the light, and Matt stepped slowly down the stairs. Heather turned to her daughter and whispered, "What is the *matter* with you, young lady? You are acting like a first-class geek! Talking about peckerwoods in front of a man like that, asking him about killing people! You're making a fool of yourself!"

"Yeah, I guess I kind of am," admitted Tori sadly. "I'm sorry, mom, but I just think he's *brutally* cool! He was in love with Mary Jane and now he wants to find her killer."

"How do you know he was...I mean...?" Heather stumbled. Since their first evening here, Tori and she had not spoken of the psychic presences Tori felt in the house or the weeping sound which Heather had heard on two further occasions since then. The topic frankly unnerved her. "Did...did someone tell you?"

"I don't have conversations with spooks in my room, mom," laughed Tori good-naturedly. "It's not like that at all. Can't you tell? Woman's intuition. Where's yours? Isn't it just so way totally *romantic,* the way he's coming back to find his teen angel's killer after all these years?"

"Well, I need to go down and show him around," said Heather. "Are you coming?"

"Ah, no, mom, it's pretty intense down there for me."

"Then you can finish putting the groceries away and wash those coffee cups," Heather said triumphantly. "By hand. Don't you dare start the dishwasher for just two cups and saucers!"

"That's sneaky!" protested Tori.

"You should have used your woman's intuition."

Matt was standing under the bulb in the laundry room, examining the heavy water pipes. By stretching up and rubbing them he exposed a thin scoring in the black iron, barely visible beneath the accumulated years of dust and lint and grease. "Find something?" asked Heather.

"Ma'am, how much do you know about the details of what happened down here in the early morning hours of October 24th, 1970?" asked Matt.

"I know one of the girls died down here, very violently," replied Heather cautiously. "Why do you ask?"

"Do you really want to know?"

"Ahhh, yes. I'm not sure I should say that, and I may regret it, but yes. What have you found?" Matt pointed up.

"Feel this scar or cut, right by the T-junction in the water pipe?" he asked. "Feel that rough edge, like someone cut into it with a hacksaw?"

"Yes," said Heather, reaching up, her blood chilled by having an actual physical contact with something from that terrible night. "I can feel it. What is it?"

"Unless I'm mistaken, that's where Jeannie Arnold was hand-cuffed and suspended by her wrists in the nude for two hours while she was systematically tortured in a number of gruesome and hideous ways. At some point in the process she was raped and finally she was ice-picked to death through her eye."

"Dear God, I had no idea it was like that!" whispered Heather. "Oh, poor wretched child! Tori told me she still suffers in this place. Now I know why."

"I beg you pardon?" asked Matt.

"What's your take on the paranormal?" asked Heather directly.

"Generally speaking, I think something's out there," replied Redmond deliberately. "I've had a few experiences which are hard to reconcile with the settled order of nature, as Conan Doyle put it. I do reserve the right to absolute open-minded skepticism about individual cases."

"Fair enough. My daughter has always been what might be termed psychic or sensitive. There are a number of incidents from her childhood that I'll tell you about if you ever have the time or the inclination to hear them. She knew about the two murders in this house before I told her, that the victims were two girls her age, that one died down here in great pain and suffering, and that another one died upstairs in what is now her room, a girl whose spirit she believes is still present. Totally freaked yet?"

Matt sighed. "Go you one better. I wasn't being totally truthful about my behavior on your sidewalk earlier tonight. I was indeed acting exceedingly weird in Tori's eyes. I thought I saw Mary Jane looking down at me from the window of the room she died in. I thought I was losing my mind, letting my obsession with this case work me up into seeing ghosts."

"I'll top that, if I can, a test of Tori's talents," said Heather quietly. "She says you were in love with Mary Jane Mears and you've come back to avenge your teen angel. Is that true?"

"Pretty much," admitted Matt. "Could I see upstairs, please? Then I promise I'll get out of your hair. I know I'm holding up your dinner."

"Actually I was going to ask you to stay for a bite," said Heather. *Then send Tori to a movie so you could slip into something more comfortable, like me,* she added in her mind. *Ah no, let's slow it down here, Diana. Softlee softlee catchee monkey.* Aloud she said to him, "Come on up." Heather stood at the door for a bit as Matt entered Tori's room and then, moved by a sudden diffidence, she quietly turned and went back downstairs. Matt understood that Heather accepted this as a private moment, and he was intensely grateful to her.

Tori's teenage taste had furnished the room in a manner eerily similar to what was shown in the old crime scene photos: stuffed animals on the bed, a dresser and vanity table with a big mirror, a fluffy bedspread and folded quilt. Matt opened the closet. He recalled something from the 1970 photographs which even now filled him with almost as much horror as the deeds themselves. The flowered maxi-dress that Mary Jane had worn at his request that night to the dance had been on a hanger in the closet. The moccasins in which she had danced her last dance in his arms were on the closet floor, neatly lined up with her other shoes, and her panties and bra were in the laundry hamper beside the shoes. The bed was neatly made, undisturbed; her killer hadn't even used it while he raped her. The gold crucifix and chain she had worn around her neck, along with the golden bracelet he had last seen on her wrist as she waved him goodbye in the headlights of his Corvair, had been found on the vanity table. There had been no indication that the man who had killed Mary Jane Mears had forcibly stripped her naked. Instead, it looked as if he had ordered her to disrobe and courteously allowed her to hang up her clothing and stow away her shoes and underthings. Presumably she had been ordered to bend over, the act of violation had been performed quickly and with brutal efficiency, and then she had been seated in the death chair, strapped and taped in, and executed. The whole procedure probably took less than ten minutes and seemed almost clinical. The only blood in the room had been a few splatters on the floor which the pathologist believed had come from her brutally ruptured hymen.

What was it like for you, my dearest love? thought Matt despairingly. *Was your dearest friend already screaming in agony down in that pit, as you went through the procedure whereby some unspeakable monster had decided your life should end? I know it's self-centered and ghoulish, but did you think of me in those moments?* Unthinkingly, Matt began to speak aloud. "I couldn't be here with you that night, my darling," he whispered. "I couldn't show you how much I loved you by dying for you, but I would have, Mary Jane. Without a regret or a second thought. I was fifteen miles away listening to that accursed foul voice while you died. But I have never forgotten our last night together, beneath the tree in the moonlight back behind the bandroom. I'm here now, Mary Jane. Twenty-six years too late, but I'm here for you at last. I will do what I can to give you justice and rest, my dearest love. I swear it!"

He glanced over into the mirror. Slowly a patch of fog appeared on it, as if someone were breathing on it with warm living breath. As he watched, the patch grew bigger, five or six inches across. A mark appeared in the center of the condensation, deftly drawn by an unseen finger.

It was a heart.

Matt's eyes filled with tears. Slowly he walked over to the mirror, leaned over, and kissed the already fading symbol of love from beyond the grave. Then he spoke aloud once again, in an iron voice. "I swear it!" He turned and walked out the door, taking with him some of Tori's Kleenex. By the time he reached downstairs he was dry-eyed again.

*   *   *

Matt accepted the dinner invitation and they had a pleasant, meal of microwave Chinese and some really good home-baked bread, washed down with Diet Coke and more coffee. By unspoken consent they kept the conversation general and wide-ranging over every topic except the murders. Heather talked about the wild and tempestuous bacchanalia which had been the accounting department at Microsoft, making it clear that after ten years there she had been bored out of her mind and was actually almost grateful to be laid off. Matt and Tori compared notes on Chapel Hill High School and found out that they concurred in the opinion that while there were some high points, basically the institution sucked, big-time. Matt told them a few of his milder DEA war stories and delivered an anti-drug lecture which Tori found amusing and Heather found edifying and illuminating. "I know you wouldn't tell me if you were using, especially not with your mother present," concluded Matt. "But if you are for Christ's sake, stop. It's idiotic. I've known that ever since my third or fourth day at CHHS when I wandered out back to the smoking area and found a girl I'd met my first day having a bad acid trip."

"I know exactly where you're talking about, except now you get jammed up worse if you're caught with a cigarette than if you get caught with dope," said Tori. "The loadies still hang out back there, all right."

"If she's using dope I'll give her this, she's slick. I haven't seen any sign at all of it," said Heather.

"May I be excused?" asked Tori. "I need to run upstairs and shoot up."

"Look, I'll head on out now," said Matt, rising. "I've taken up enough of your time. Thank you very much for the meal and again I apologize for my clumsy and unorthodox way of introducing myself this afternoon."

Heather stepped out the door with him. Both of them were looking for some excuse for him to return to the house. "I'd like to ask you a favor," she said. "You say you're working this case on your own. If you need a hand with anything, I'd like to be involved. This does affect Tori and me, after all, if only peripherally. Will you keep me posted on what you find? Maybe you could drop by over on campus and we can do lunch? I generally go around twelve."

"Sounds good," said Matt. "How about tomorrow, in fact? I'm going to try to catch the Arnolds in the morning, then I need to see a man on campus. He's a pretty senior muckety-muck there now, but twenty-six years ago he was a teacher at CHHS who admitted having a sexual relationship with Jeannie Arnold, who was one of his drama students."

"Sounds like a real creep," commented Heather. "I'm obviously sensitive on the subject. What's his name? Maybe I know him."

"Paul Lieberman," Matt told her.

"You're kidding! Hell, he's worse than a creep," said Heather sourly. "He's my boss."

VII

The next morning Matt sat in the tastefully furnished living room of Leonard and Susan Arnold. They were both waiting for him, an elderly retired couple living surrounded by the images of their children, including the one who was dead. Matt looked over and saw a color blowup of Jeannie in a spotlight on stage, wearing a long archaic dress and a kind of tartan plaid shoulder cloak with a big cairngorm brooch, holding two daggers in her hand and looking over her shoulder with a sinister scowl on her face. "That's from the UNC summer theatre project, 1970," said Len Arnold sadly, filling his pipe from a leather pouch. "Mostly it was college kids. They were ambitious enough to try Shakespeare, and Jeannie got the role of Lady Macbeth even though she was only just 17 and still in high school. I've often thought it ironic that the closest she came to fulfilling her dream before she was murdered was to play the most infamous murderess in all English literature. But she loved every minute of that last summer of 1970, and she was good, Matt. Broadway or Hollywood or London, wherever she wanted, she would have made it."

"I know," said Matt. "I saw her in a couple of things, and I believe there's still an early videotape of that production of *Macbeth* that's shown now and then on Channel 4 and a few other Public Broadcasting stations. She left behind a glimpse of what she might have been."

"I have a copy of that video," said Arnold. "Perhaps once every five or six years, the family gathers here on the anniversary of her death, and we watch it. Even though it's black and white, even though every word is agony, for a few minutes at a time throughout the play we can hear the sound of her voice here in this house once again. I've always wished that Shakespeare had given Lady Macbeth a bigger speaking role." He sat down. "You said you wanted to speak to us about the case. Have you talked with the Mearses yet?"

"I spoke with Dr. Mears yesterday afternoon over in Raleigh, in fact," said Matt. "Congresswoman Mears is in Washington and I'll have to speak to her by phone or fly up if I think it's important enough. He asked me to convey his regards to you both," which Mears hadn't, but Matt decided it would be a politic thing to say.

"How's Andy's health doing?" asked Arnold.

"Not good," admitted Matt. "To be honest, it doesn't look like he has much time left. I promised I'd at least try and bring him some answers. Same with you. I'm not promising any arrests or convictions, I can't promise you any kind of closure. That may be out of reach after all this time. I do give you my word that whatever I come up with, I'll share it with you."

"God bless you for doing even that much, Matt," said Sue Arnold with a sigh.

"You must also understand there's a flip side," said Matt. "I am going to have to ask you to discuss some things you may find upsetting and painful."

"We talked about that last night after you called," said Len Arnold. "We understand that goes with the territory. Please ask us whatever you feel you need to know." Matt decided to begin with something innocuous.

"Was it a fairly customary thing for Jeannie and Mary Jane to spend the night together without any parental supervision?" he asked. "How did that situation come about?"

"Well, Meg Mears was very anti-war, as you know, and she became very involved with the Movement. In those days it wasn't quite as acceptable for a wife to go around appearing on political platforms and leading demonstrations without her husband. Middle-class morality was in its last dying convulsions, but it was still alive. Now, I know that Meg did make a number of out of town trips on her own, if for no other reason than Andy had classes he had to teach, but for major things like that seminar they were going to she pretty much dragged him along."

"Why didn't she drag Mary Jane along?" asked Matt.

"Well, there you get into a kind of gray area of obscure half-gossip, mostly just what Jeannie mentioned in passing, but I gather Mary Jane simply wasn't that politically inclined. She was more interested in animals."

"She wanted to be a vet," put in Matt sadly

"Yes, I remember her saying so," put in Sue Arnold. "Meg Mears wasn't that attached to animals. I remember Mary Jane's little dog, Grouch, the one that was killed that night, was Meg's one concession along that line."

"Anyway, Jeannie was 17 and Mary Jane was 16, both of them old enough to take care of themselves. Chapel Hill was a virtually crime-free town in those days. We saw no harm in them staying together for a couple of nights. How could we know?" said Arnold with a deep sigh. "Christ in heaven, how could anyone have foreseen such a thing?"

"You trusted Jeannie?" asked Matt.

"In what way?" asked her father.

"I'm sure I will be telling you nothing you don't already know when I mention the fact that Jeannie was sexually active," said Matt, choosing his words carefully.

"She was promiscuous, Matt," said Sue. "We long ago accepted that. We even accepted it in the last months of her life, although it saddened us and worried us tremendously."

"The police found birth control pills in Jeannie's purse. Do you know where she got them?" asked Matt. "In 1970 it was illegal for any doctor to prescribe contraceptives for a minor without the parents' consent."

"We gave our consent, Matt," said Sue. "This was a couple of years before Roe versus Wade, you remember. We didn't want her getting pregnant and messing up her life and the bright future she had ahead of her. We knew she wasn't going to be good, so we made sure she was careful. I know that sounds flippant and derelict on our part, but you have to understand that Jeannie matured early and at 17 she was a young woman, in every sense of the word. It was hard for us to accept that, but eventually we did. Always hoping, of course, that she'd change."

"We first became aware of that aspect of her life when she was fifteen," said Len. "It doesn't matter how, it was long ago and it's water under the bridge. She was caught with the son of some friends of ours. I hit the roof, of course. I shouted and cursed at her, called her names, threatened to ground her until she was eighteen, threatened to lock her in her room at night, send her to a convent school, you name it."

"I seem to recall I put in my two cents' worth as well," Sue reminded him sadly.

"Yes, you did. Jeannie understood that we loved her deeply and we were acting like that because we were afraid for her. She let me blow myself out and then she told me simply, 'Daddy, if it makes you feel better I'll promise I won't do it any more, but I won't keep that promise. It's part of my life from now on. That's just the way things have turned out. What you and Mom need to decide is how much you want to know about it.' Very calm, very mature and thought-out, not sassy or defiant, just giving us the facts. I was always impressed as hell with that answer of hers. Well, Sue and I thought about it. I figured that we had a choice. It was two and a half more years until she was eighteen, and we could spend them trying to keep her under lock and key and making everybody miserable, or we could try to work out a *modus vivendi*. So we laid out a few rules, and so far as I know, with one notable exception she always stuck to them."

"And those rules were?" asked Matt, intrigued. He couldn't help wondering, *Damn, if I'd known what the rules were maybe I could have gotten some!* and was immediately ashamed of his reaction. *But lord, she was fine!* he couldn't help adding.

"First off, no catting around. She wasn't to cut class and she wasn't to let her grades be affected because of this kind of activity. Her first and only senior class report card was all A's and a B-plus. The second rule was never here in the house," said Arnold, lighting his pipe. "We didn't want her bringing boys here where her brother and her sister could see them, and we didn't fancy coming home and finding her in bed with somebody. By the way, Matt, if I recall that long article about you in *People* I believe you're a cigar smoker. Feel free." Matt gratefully pulled one out and lit it while Arnold continued. "Third rule, no married men, no home-wrecking. If some guy going through his mid-life crisis was going make a fool of himself over a well-stacked teeny-bopper it wasn't going to be her. Fourth rule, no grown men. I wasn't happy with that Riggsbee character; I thought she was toe-dancing along the line there and I told her so."

"Ah, sir, you are aware that there was a teacher...?" interposed Matt delicately.

"Paul Lieberman, yes, I know. The one exception I mentioned. Adult and married both. We didn't find out about that until after Jeannie died. About a month after that I went to his house. He opened the door, I punched him in the mouth and knocked him flat on his ass, and left. I waited here that evening for the police to show up, but they never did, and neither of us mentioned the incident ever again except once, a few years ago when he pushed a fairly hefty raise for me through the Board of Regents, a raise that really helped my pension when retirement came. I ran into him in the hall and told him quietly, civilly, that he didn't owe me anything. He replied, 'I owe you for not bringing a gun to my house that night. I had it coming.' Which is pretty much the way I feel about it."

"After she died, the police and the SBI interviewed a number of Jeannie's lovers," said Matt, deciding to use that term rather than the more stark designation sexual partners. "All of them had alibis that checked out, including Paul Lieberman. Basically, Mr. Arnold, Mrs. Arnold, there have always been two theories about your daughter's death and the death of Mary Jane Mears. The first theory is that she and Mary Jane walked in on a burglary in progress, and they were raped and murdered by common criminals."

"I never bought that," said Arnold, puffing meditatively on his pipe. "Nothing was stolen. No forced entry. It just didn't make sense. Also, although you're the law enforcement pro and I'm not, it's my understanding that ordinary thieves or hoodlums who do things like that seldom do so completely undetected. Eventually they're arrested for another crime and they brag about it to some jailhouse snitch, or one of their own underworld cronies turns them in to get leniency for whatever they've done. Isn't that true?"

"It doesn't always happen like that, but often enough so it's a noticeable lack in this case, yes," replied Matt. "I agree that if the killings had been committed by ordinary criminals there is a good chance that something would have broken before this. They are notoriously unable to keep their mouths shut. This brings us to the second standard theory, that the girls were killed by someone they knew, someone they admitted into the house voluntarily. I have been assured by Dr. Mears that Mary Jane had no known boyfriend, other than a tentative relationship just beginning with myself, and my own memory of that time confirms that. If this known-killer theory is correct, then it was most likely a friend of Jeannie's."

"One of Jeannie's lovers, as you so chivalrously put it, Matt?" asked Sue Arnold.

"Or someone who wanted to become one of Jeannie's lovers," said Matt. "If you will excuse my blunt terminology, folks, your daughter may have been highly sexed but she was not a slut. She was selective. The investigation in 1970 indicated that she said no at least as often she said yes. She might have said no that night and the man lost his self-control. Do you have *any* suspicions at all of *anyone* who might fit this profile? If you do, please, don't hold back."

"I just can't see any of the boys at Chapel Hill High behaving in that manner," said Arnold slowly. "You were there. You knew most of the boys involved with Jeannie. Can you?"

"No, sir. I am convinced that no student at Chapel Hill High was involved," said Matt firmly.

"There was Riggsbee, but I understand he was definitely cleared," went on Arnold.

"Correct," confirmed Matt. "His movements that night were traceable and there simply isn't any way a workable time frame could be constructed, plus he had another girl with him as an alibi witness. Riggsbee is the closest thing to a suspect they came up with throughout the whole case, because he had a record, but he just plain couldn't have done it."

"The only other possible would be Paul Lieberman," said Arnold, "But as much contempt as I hold the man in, I have never once suspected him of being the killer. I understand his alibi holds up as well?"

"He said he was at home in bed with his wife," said Matt. "June Lieberman confirmed it. She died six years ago in an automobile accident, and I can't ask her myself, but I'm sure she was telling the truth. I kicked Lieberman around in my mind for a while because of the affair with Jeannie and also because the Liebermans were the official faculty radicals at the high school, super anti-war and very tight with Meg Mears, working on the same committees and going to the same demonstrations. But I don't think a wife would lie to protect a husband who committed a double rape-murder of two young girls, one of them the daughter of a close friend and the other one of his own underage students he was banging on the side." *Oh, shit, what the hell made me say that?* Matt cursed to himself. "I'm sorry. That was a cruel and stupid thing for me to say. I completely forgot where I was. Please forgive me, both of you."

Arnold laughed, "Matt, in our private conversation down the years Sue and I have often referred to Paul Lieberman and the other young men who were *banging* our daughter. She wasn't a blushing maiden or a fallen flower, and even when we were most upset and afraid for her future we never considered her that. My wife is quite right. She was a young woman who was stubborn, willful, exasperating, infuriating, impetuous, unpredictable, and entirely too ready to go down on her back. But we loved her and we will always be thankful for the wonderful, magical years we had with her." For the first time his eyes began to water. "We should have had more years with her, Matt. She should be here now. We should be turning on the TV and catching her latest special or her latest movie at the theater. Someone took that from us, and from her. I'm sorry, I'm getting maudlin." His wife quietly wept, and he held her hand. "No, Matt, I can't give you any names. If ever we had harbored even the remotest suspicion against anyone, we would have been shouting that suspicion from the rooftops until something was done."

"I don't think that was the situation, anyway," said Matt. Arnold looked up sharply.

"What do you mean?" he inquired keenly.

"What do you know about exactly what was done to Jeannie?" asked Matt carefully.

"We know that she was fiendishly tortured until she must have begged for death," said Sue quietly. "Len raised hell with the police and medical examiners until they told him. He asked me not to force him to tell me, and I have respected his wishes. I think it's best."

"I won't get into it either, ma'am, but it's always struck me that Mary Jane was killed several hours before Jeannie and, although I hesitate to use the word, fairly mercifully by comparison," said Matt. "I have to be very blunt here. The torture inflicted on your daughter was so utterly horrific that in my opinion it goes even beyond a sex crime."

"You mean...*punishment?*" asked Arnold, stunned. "Why? In the name of all that's holy, what could Jeannie have done that someone felt compelled to make her suffer like that? It doesn't make any sense at all!"

"No, although my idea is almost as nonsensical as that," admitted Matt. "Not punishment. Interrogation."

"I don't understand," said Sue.

"Again, please forgive me for being graphic, but the injuries inflicted on Jeannie were too methodical and show too much sign of premeditation. Sex criminals usually lose their self-restraint completely either just before or during the act of rape. They beat their victims with their fists, choke them with their bare hands, or use a simple easy-to-hand weapon like a knife or a blunt instrument. In Jeannie's case instruments for the infliction of pain and handcuffs to restrain her were brought to the scene and removed from the scene by the killers, and they were used only on her, not Mary Jane."

"Don't certain sex criminals do that?" asked Arnold. "Go out hunting, as it were?" Sue Arnold stood up.

"Len, I think I'd better give the rest of this conversation a miss. I know it's necessary but I'd rather not participate any more." She leaned over and kissed Matt on the cheek. "Matt, thank you from the bottom of my heart for what you are doing." She left the room and went upstairs.

"I'm sorry," said Matt contritely. "I'm really wrapped up in this and I keep forgetting what hell it must be for you to remember and talk about."

"No, she's right, it's necessary," said Arnold, shaking his head. "And I'm really excited that you are wrapped up in it to this degree, Matt. If there's any chance at all of bringing this man or men to justice, then we will willingly go through it all again. Do I understand that you believe my daughter was tortured to death for *information*? Jesus, Matt, what kind of information?"

"I haven't got a clue," said Matt, spreading his hands. "This whole theory of mine could be pure moonshine. It's based on intuition alone. One of the more unsavory aspects of my job over the past few years has been to acquire a certain familiarity with the dynamics and mechanics of torture. It's common practice in the narcotics underworld, to a degree never seen before or since in any other kind of organized crime. One thing that seems to generate this kind of barbaric treatment of human beings is the immense amount of money involved in the drug trade. I remember we had a pretty heavy drug scene at Chapel Hill High, but by today's standards it was all penny-ante, no weight at all. I doubt if any more than a dime bag or a dozen joints or half a dozen tabs of acid changed hands at once. The idea of Jeannie being involved in the kind of six or seven-figure dope deal that I've seen men and women tortured over is ridiculous on the face of it, but I'm convinced it would have to be something on that order to result in what was done to her in that basement. Any comment or ideas?"

"Jeannie didn't do drugs, I'm sure of it," Arnold asserted. "She didn't want it to affect her dancing and she was dead set on making it as an actress, which is damned hard work if you're serious. We even had a kind of joke about it. We told her we wished she'd practice the same kind of total abstinence with men she did with drugs, booze, and cigarettes."

"Well, the only other time I've seen anything as bad as what was done to Jeannie it was political, in Colombia," said Matt. "The Colombian police worked over some left-wing guerrilla types pretty bad. Admittedly this outfit had just planted a car bomb in Bogota that had killed twenty people, and earlier that month they fed a village mayor to an anaconda, which event they videotaped *pour encourager les autres* and distributed the video to the media. Several of the rebels were women, but I have to admit I couldn't work up much sympathy for Marxists of either sex who feed live people to monster snakes."

"Holy Christ!" muttered Arnold, shaken. "What happened?"

"The Colombians shot them all. But the political idea doesn't hold water, either. We were in the middle of a revolution in 1970, but not the South American kind. If somebody had broke in and killed Meg Mears, okay, maybe that would be the Klan or some kind of right-wing terrorism, but none of those anti-war leaders were ever even threatened seriously. You said Mary Jane wasn't political, and that tallies with my memory of that time, but didn't Jeannie go on a couple of peace vigils down at the Franklin Street post office? With Meg Mears, among others?"

"Oh, yes, but that was just the whole Sixties gig. In my day we went to sock hops and stuffed guys into phone booths. Jeannie's generation protested against the war. Flower power and all that sort of thing. She wasn't all that serious about it, she was serious about her acting and her dancing. I do know she admired Meg Mears very much indeed and sometimes she'd go over to the Mears house even when Mary Jane wasn't home, just to talk to Meg, help her around the house, help her with typing and stuffing envelopes, that kind of thing. But it was hardly storming the Winter Palace."

"Jeannie was never involved with SDS or the Weathermen or any fringe groups like that?" asked Matt.

"Oh, no, not at all," laughed Arnold. "You're way off base there, Matt."

"Yeah, I figured, but you see how I'm grasping at straws," admitted Matt. "What was done to her was so *disproportionate.*"

"If it wasn't a sex crime, how do you explain the rape of both girls, Matt?" asked Arnold.

"One last time I have to ask you to forgive my being very graphic and blunt," said Matt. "According to the autopsy reports no trace of male semen was found in either victim."

"I never knew that," said Arnold with a frown.

"I believe the sexual assaults were carried out with a foreign object in order to make the medical evidence point to rape and divert attention from the true motive for the torture of Jeannie and the murder of both girls to silence them."

"I will be good God damned if I don't think you just may be onto something," whispered Arnold, twisting his pipe in his hand, dumping ash all over the carpet without seeing it or caring. "But why? In the name of all sanity, in the name of...*why?*"

*   *   *

Matt looked up the number of the university accounting office and asked for Ms. Lindstrom's extension. He heard her voice. "This is Heather, may I help you?"

"Hey, this is that peckerwood detective who was out at your place last night. You still interested in keeping up with my progress, such as it is?"

"Yes, that's right."

"Can't talk? Someone's in earshot?" asked Matt. "They bitch about your taking personal calls at work?"

"Yes, that's right."

"Sorry, I won't call you there again. I have a suggestion. Look at the person in the office you most dislike. Are you looking at them?"

"Uh, yes, with reference to what?" asked Heather suspiciously.

"Now I want you to imagine that person buck naked, committing a deviate sexual act with a goat," he suggested. There were smothered, choking snorts from the other end of the phone.

"Stop that! You're worse than Tori!" said Heather, breaking into a semi-giggle.

"An old, smelly goat, with balls the size of grapefruit."

"Stop it!" she hissed. "What do you want?"

"Kidding aside, I'm going to be rattling Paul Lieberman's cage and opening a can of his worms that's been sitting around nice and hermetically sealed since 1970. If Lieberman is really your boss it might not be a good idea for you and I to be seen together anywhere around campus, so lunch is out. You been to the Rat yet?"

"No, I haven't," she said. "I know it's the official Chapel Hill signature restaurant. Is the food there any good?"

"It varies from year to year depending on the quality of the help they get," said Matt. "It can be anything from mediocre to really good pizza-wise, but the beer is cold and the sandwiches are usually edible. I'm seeing Lieberman at two. How about you meet me there tonight and I'll tell you how it went. Is he really a creep? Seriously, anything you know that might be relevant?"

"I'll tell you later. Nothing major, it's just that's the individual involved with the goat. About seven-ish OK?" she asked.

"Fine." Matt hung up. *Hmm,* he thought to himself. *Wonder if there's any possibility of my getting any of that? Must admit I always liked them long and tall and willowy.*

"Goat, Ms. Lindstrom?" asked Paul Lieberman. Heather jumped in her chair.

"Oh, hello, Dr. Lieberman. Ah, just my personal commentary on one of my daughter's friends from the high school."

"Call me Paul, please," said Lieberman, flashing a smile of perfectly capped teeth. "Dear me, you don't seem to like the kid. Daughter's boyfriend, you say?" He was tall and handball-court trim, handsome, coiffed hair with just enough gray at the temple to merit the label distinguished, thousand dollar suit. The next

Chancellor of the consolidated state university system, Heather had heard, assuming the politics of it worked out and the Democrats could hold onto the state legislature by the skin of their teeth a month from now.

"He thinks he's her boyfriend," said Heather, winging a story while desperately trying to avoid thinking of this mature, distinguished man in a state of deshabillé, sodomizing a goat. She was still too new to afford giggling fits.

"Well, if she's as attractive as her mother I can understand the young man's feelings," said Lieberman with an unctuous and brittle gallantry.

"I should have a preliminary trial balance for you by this afternoon, Dr. Lieberman, er, Paul," said Heather, ignoring the clumsy insinuation. Heather knew perfectly well that other than her hair she was in no way conventionally attractive and men who started out that way were guaranteed to get nowhere. She could never trust a liar. "Will you be free to go over it?"

"Later I should be," said Lieberman carelessly. "I have a personal appointment at two, but that shouldn't take long. An old alumnus I'm going to try and squeeze some money out of." *That's two lies,* Heather thought, *And one of them completely unnecessary. I didn't ask who his appointment was. Why should he offer the information gratuitously? Why does he want me to think Matt's someone else?*

"Come on by my office at about four," he said, leaning over her and resting his hand carelessly on her shoulder. "We can talk then." He walked away, letting his hand lightly caress Heather's neck as he left. She scowled after him.

"Gail, isn't unnecessary touching a sexual harassment violation?" she asked in disgust.

"Not for Paul Lieberman it isn't," said Gail, a desiccated and intensely militant vegetarian woman who sat at the next desk.

Heather had obliquely admitted to Gail once over lunch that she
had bisexual tendencies; from then on she was certifiably PC and
had official clearance to hear all the campus gossip, rumor, and
intrigue, of which there was a sufficient amount to confound and
overwhelm the Papal court of the Borgias.

"Well, if he does it too many more times with me he's going to
draw back a bloody stump," snapped Heather. "Good grief, that
kind of thing hasn't been acceptable in an office environment for
fifteen years! Hasn't anyone ever filed a complaint against him?"

"One woman did, yes," said Gail neutrally. "Your predecessor
in this job, in fact. That's why she's your predecessor."

"What? That's awful!" exclaimed Heather, shocked

Gail took off her glasses and leaned over. "Look, I don't know
what the political situation was at Microsoft, but here in North
Carolina it's a snake pit and no mistake. This whole university
system is a vitally important part of the progressive movement.
UNC especially has a proud liberal and progressive tradition
going all the way back to Dr. Frank Porter Graham, whose name
you may have heard mentioned around campus. There are a lot of
powerful white males in business suits, the Jesse Helms crowd,
real crypto-fascists who have been trying to destroy that tradition
for a couple of generations, who want to gut everything even
remotely liberal or progressive. Womens' studies, rape crisis cen-
ters, abortion rights, gay and lesbian services, reserved enroll-
ments for minorities and women and gays, minority hiring, you
name it. They don't want to give us a single dollar for anything
that's not the product of dead European white males. We can't let
that happen. There's always the chance we're going to lose the
White House in a month. That means another four years of fighting a rearguard action against everything that's white and male
and bigoted and mean-spirited and intolerant, and in North
Carolina that's a hell of a lot. Paul Lieberman has some incorrect

personal habits, I'll grant you, but we need him. He's got the credentials and the track record and he's paid his dues. He was marching against the war back in 1964 even before it was trendy, for Christ's sake, and he's been on the right side of every issue ever since. Heather, we *need* Paul Lieberman as the next Chancellor. This university controls millions of discretionary dollars, money we can use for make up for the lost Federal funding we used to have before these reactionary Republican motherfuckers got into power in Congress and started confusing and agitating all the goddamned resentful Joe Six Packs in the country against us with their lies and their hate propaganda. To borrow a phrase from the enemy, Paul Lieberman may be a son of a bitch, but he's *our* son of a bitch."

What's all this "we" stuff, you arrogant old bag? wondered Heather. *Jeez, not four months in the South and already I'm thinking PI thoughts which would never have occurred to me in Seattle. Must be something in the water.*

*   *   *

"If you'll pardon the terrible pun, Matt, I think I can say you're one of my few former students who's had a dramatic career since they left CHHS," said Paul Lieberman with a chuckle. "Please, have a seat. I wish I could tell you to light up one of your famous cigars, but I'm afraid the university is really tight-assed about the no-smoking policy."

"I'll try not to take up too much of your time, Dr. Lieberman," replied Matt.

"Now, didn't I tell all of you to call me Paul right from the first day in class back in '69?" chided Lieberman.

"I wasn't a law enforcement officer in 1969, sir," said Matt quietly, "Nor was I interviewing you in connection with a double homicide." He smiled. "Having thrown that chilling caveat into the conversation, I suppose in all fairness I should add that both years I had you for drama it was my favorite class, and the productions we did and the good times we had are some of the few decent memories I have of that place. Thanks."

"You want to thank me, find Jeannie's murderer," said Lieberman grimly. "I'm astounded that the SBI is reopening the case after all these years."

"Not so much reopening," said Matt. "Unsolved murder cases are never closed. Call this a periodic review."

"Well, whatever it is I'm glad it's you they've assigned. You knew her, Matt, you knew both of them, so you'll be motivated. Maybe that's what was lacking before, when they never arrested anybody." He settled back. "I know what you're going to ask me about. Me and Jeannie Arnold. Aren't you going to take notes or record this?"

"My memory's pretty good," said Matt. "I just want to confirm what I've already got in the file and maybe pick up on anything else you may have to add. You'd be surprised how all of a sudden some little thing can just pop up in a conversation and assume significance after a long time has gone by. When you were interviewed by Detective Bass of the Chapel Hill PD and SBI Agent McCracken on Monday, October 26th, 1970 you admitted that you had been having an affair with Jeannie Arnold. Is that correct?"

"Yes," said Lieberman. "She'd been my student for two years, as were you yourself. The physical relationship, which I think is actually a more descriptive term than affair, was of much shorter duration, beginning in July of 1970 and consisting only of a few, ah, encounters. Jeannie and I had already decided that there would be no more of them."

"Did she break it off or did you?" asked Matt.

"You could say it was pretty much a mutual agreement kind of thing," said Paul. "We both realized that it was an inappropriate relationship. She was very mature for her age, not a starry-eyed adolescent with a crush at all. For another thing there was a logistics problem, in that once school opened in September we didn't have as many opportunities for, ah, dalliance."

"With June being a teacher at the same high school, I could see how you wouldn't," agreed Matt. "Would have been kind of hard to work up a passion when your wife might walk into your office or a dressing room and catch Jeannie sitting on your knee, or on your face."

"Crudely but descriptively put," agreed Paul with a small wry smile.

"May I ask how exactly the, er, physical side of your relationship with Jeannie developed?" inquired Matt. "And how you handled the logistics, as I believe you called it?"

"I was working with the UNC summer theater group, stage managing and assisting Ben Harrelson in directing *Macbeth* and a series of one-acts the students performed," said Lieberman. "June's summer job was a bit more prosaic; she was selling textbooks to school boards around the state, which entailed a lot of travel. Seldom overnight, but enough so she often wouldn't get back until nine or ten P.M. if she was driving home from Wilmington or Charlotte or Asheville or someplace. I had the house to myself a lot. One day I invited some of the students over for an informal cookout, and Jeannie stayed behind to help me clean up. I honestly can't recall who started it, but we ended up having sex on the sofa. Several times, in fact. For a while I was hooked on her magnificent body like a drug, and we found other opportunities, but by September I'd cooled down enough to remember that I was playing with dynamite that could cost me my job and my marriage."

"Not to mention your life if Len Arnold had been the gun-toting type," commented Matt.

"Yes, indeed," said Lieberman with a nod. "I see you've already talked to Len."

"That being the case, why did you immediately 'fess up to the affair on Monday afternoon, the 26th?" asked Matt. "I recall from reading McCracken's report that their interview with you was just *pro forma*. They were talking to everybody who knew the girls, including me. Then out of the blue you admitted you'd been committing statutory rape, since North Carolina's 16-year age of consent only applies to sexual partners 18 or under. If the man is over 18, she damned well better be 18. Why did you volunteer the information?"

"Surely you can guess that?" replied Lieberman. "Because I was scared shitless of being accused of her murder, that's why! I know that sounds calloused, and I'd hate for you to think I was thinking only of myself." Lieberman leaned forward across his desk, and his voice began to shake a little. "Matt, I want you to understand something. When I heard that Jeannie Arnold and Mary Jane Mears were dead, when I heard the monstrous way in which they died, that was the most terrible moment in my life, ever. The thought of those two beautiful young lives being cut off like that, the thought of them suffering what I was told they suffered, fills me to this day with a horror I cannot describe to you. I am not exaggerating when I tell you that I quite literally have nightmares about what happened in that house, even now, a quarter of a century later. But at the same time, Matt, I admit I was terrified for myself. I was a teacher screwing a student, worse yet a Jewish teacher screwing a beautiful blond WASP student in the South, and in 1970 there were people still living who remembered the Leo Frank case in Georgia. I had the weekend to think it over, and I knew that my one hope was to tell the truth, the whole truth, and nothing but the truth right from the start, nothing held back. I knew the police were going to pursue a case this serious with their full forces, and the one thing which might literally kill me would be to be caught out lying about anything, no matter how trivial. Once the police caught me lying they'd become convinced I did it, and you and I both know, Matt, that when the cops decide in their own minds that someone has done something they'll make the evidence fit. Ask O. J. Simpson. I was sweating, I can tell you."

"I can imagine," agreed Matt. "But you waited until Monday to come forward with your information. What did you do that weekend while the headlines were screaming and the town was swarming with police and investigators and media?"

"I put first things first, even ahead of saving my skin," sighed Lieberman. "I was married to a fine and noble woman whom I had carelessly and callously betrayed out of pure lust to have a wild beautiful young girl in my bed. The least I owed her was to tell her before I told anyone else what I had done and what was likely to come of it. My job was gone at the very least. I offered June the chance to clear out before the shit hit the fan, which she declined. She went in and taught her classes on Monday just like it was an ordinary school day. You have no idea on earth how much that took by way of sheer brass balls, Matt. June was one tough little cookie, and I always admired her for it."

"She forgave you?" asked Matt.

"I didn't say that," replied Lieberman grimly. "It was touch and go for a while. She told me that divorce was definitely on the menu but she wanted to take time to decide on something that serious and that as much of a rat as I had been, she declined to return the favor, and she wouldn't run out on me when I was in trouble. She said to wait and see how it played out and then when the dust settled we'd decide what to do about our future together."

"You were a very lucky man," replied Matt neutrally, thinking of Evangelina and an empty house in Fort Lauderdale he had come home to one day, without a single word of warning. Only the divorce papers so full of lies, lying on the kitchen counter. Not even a note.

"Well, it played out a lot better than I expected it to," said Lieberman. "June confirmed to the police that I'd been at home from about ten o'clock on that Friday night and they believed her. As I'm sure you recall, I left the school system. I handed in my resignation without being asked, which was the right thing to do. I broke the rules big time, Matt, and I behaved in just about the most unethical and unprofessional way possible for a teacher. I have never denied that, then or now. I was extremely fortunate to have a very good friend here at UNC, a professor we'd met as part of the anti-war protest movement. He got me into graduate school, lent me the tuition money, in fact, and hired me as his teaching assistant."

"And the name of this friend indeed to his friends in need?" asked Matt, fidgeting, longing for a cigar.

"Vladimir Nakritin, the exiled Russian writer, Pulitzer and Nobel Prizes for literature, at that time chairman of the Eastern European Studies department and co-chair of the Philosophy department. You remember, he spoke at the high school a few times during the annual Humanities Festival."

"Mmmm, yes, I remember. I heard him once. He bored the hell out of me. I had no idea on earth what he was saying," said Matt. "Sorry, Dr. Lieberman, I know he's recognized as one of the greats of twentieth-century Russian literature along with Pasternak and Solzhenitsyn. You say you met him in the anti-war movement? Odd thing for a Russian intellectual whom Stalin came with a dickey bird of shooting to be opposed to a war against Communism."

"Volodya opposed the Vietnam war for the same reason he opposed Stalin," said Lieberman. "At the time of his death in 1985 he was just as actively working against U.S. involvement in El Salvador and Nicaragua. I'd use the word saintly if I had to describe him. He was a deeply committed pacifist, a man truly and passionately dedicated to the proposition that all men should live together as brothers."

"I took great pleasure in kicking my brother's ass around the University Mall parking lot the other day and he is now threatening to shoot me next time he sees me," said Matt with a smile. "But I digress. If I recall correctly, Nakritin's most famous and critically acclaimed novel is about a teenaged sexpot who seduces and betrays one of her teachers, is it not?"

"Yes, *Louisa*. Why?"

"Was Professor Nakritin acquainted with Dr. Margaret Mears?" asked Matt.

"Yes, actually Volodya became pretty good friends with Meg and Andy both. He used to have dinner at their home quite often, and I believe both Mary Jane and Jeannie met him there. Hey, wait a minute, Matt, I see where you're going here, and frankly it's ludicrous!" Lieberman insisted. "It's also physically impossible! Vladimir Nakritin was born in the year 1898! That makes him seventy-two years old at the time of the murders, hardly capable of overpowering, raping and murdering two strong young girls, one of them a dancer and the other a competition swimmer, either of whom could have fought him off with one hand even if Volodya was a sex maniac, which he wasn't. He just wrote about it, OK?"

"Your loyalty to your friend and mentor is admirable, Doc," laughed Matt. "I wasn't making any accusations, just trying to put together an overview of the whole situation. So you ended up getting your Masters and your Ph.D. here and lived happily ever after. What was your doctoral thesis, may I ask?"

"Shakespeare as a literary agent of the ruling Elizabethan bourgeoisie," replied Lieberman. "By concentrating his characters and plots almost entirely within the upper classes of his day and portraying the nobility as being unhappy, tragic, and doomed figures, Shakespeare sought to gain them sympathy from the pits, as they were called, and to render the working and artisan classes content with their lot by showing them the doleful example and heavy burdens that the ruling elite supposedly incurred in life. Completely ignoring the oppressive economic and social reality, of course."

"But didn't you see that Fox television special the other night?" asked Matt in surprise. "They've now proven beyond doubt that Shakespeare's plays were really written by Christopher Marlowe. Was Marlowe an agent of the world bourgeoisie too? Shit, that tears me up. If you can't trust Kit Marlowe to be a true proletarian hero who can you trust?"

"What? What television special?" exclaimed Lieberman perturbed. "That's impossible! Marlowe died in 1593!"

"He escaped the tavern brawl," Matt told him. "The guy that Ingram Frizer knifed was really an actor from the Globe Theatre named Booth."

"Booth?"

"John Wilkes Booth."

Lieberman stared, then he chortled. "Really, Matt, forty-three years old and still playing the class clown?"

"I'll wrap this up, I know you're busy," said Matt. "I'll ask you the same general question I am asking everybody I can find who was alive and present anywhere around the case in 1970. What do you think happened on the night of October 23rd? Who do you think killed Mary Jane and Jeannie? Just pure gut check."

"Well, I have to confess I always felt the police made a mistake letting that white trash pump jockey off as cursorily as they did," said Lieberman. "I know Jeannie's sexual tastes were, ah, eclectic you might say, but I imagine she got tired of that grit pretty quickly and sought her own level of intellect and talent once again. I doubt he appreciated that, and the subculture of the Southern white male is the most violence-prone in the world. Someone from his background who found out that he was about to be dumped by a classy uptown girl like Jeannie might well have reacted very violently indeed."

"Dr. Lieberman, thank you for your time," said Matt, standing up and extending his hand.

"Not at all. I am only too glad to be of assistance. I hope you can come up with something new and catch the killer, even after all these years," said Lieberman sincerely.

"I'll do my damndest, Doc. And by the way, I should have mentioned this before, but please accept my very belated condolences on your wife's death. I never had her for any classes but I always liked her." This was untrue, since Matt had always considered June Lieberman to be an arrogant Yankee bitch and her New York accent had grated on his ears, but that was hardly the most politic way to conclude an interview with the man who would be Chancellor.

"Thank you, Matt, I appreciate that." Matt left, and Lieberman scowled after him. "Marlowe indeed! Doc indeed!" he muttered under his breath. *"Schlemiel!"*

"Asshole!" muttered Matt under his breath as he left the building. He looked into the outer office and saw Heather and several other women working away on computer terminals and calculators. He leaned his head in the door and bleated *"Baaaaaah!*

Baaaaaah!" They all jumped and Heather stared at him, her face turning red as she recognized Matt and almost doubled up with hysterical laughter. He turned and left the building.

"Who on earth was that?" asked Gail.

"Some alumnus Dr. Lieberman was trying to squeeze for a donation," replied Heather, desperately trying not to giggle. "Obviously from the School of Agriculture."

*   *   *

"You're going to get me fired!" said Heather in exasperation as she slid into the booth across from him at the Ramshead Rathskeller that night.

"Good, you're wasted as an accountant," said Matt cheerily. "The way you handle a gun you should be a policewoman. I asked around and I am assured that the Rat pizza is back in top-notch form this year. Care to split one?"

"If you will go over the whole 1970 murder case with me," said Heather. "I meant what I said last night, Matt. I want to be involved. Largely because there seems to be something left over, so to speak, in my house, but I'll admit my motives are also kind of Nancy Drew-ish, or maybe mid-life crisis related. I'm forty-two years old and I want some adventure in my life. You're an adventure. I mean, ah, you represent an adventure as far as looking into this." *Shut up while you're ahead, Heather, you're putting your foot in it!* she thought.

"I know what you mean," said Matt with a smile. "Hell, why not? Actually you can be useful if only as a second person to run all my theories and data by. The old saying that two heads are better than one is very true in police work. I've been obsessed with this case ever since it happened, and in the past three years since I joined the SBI I've come to live in it. I may well be so close I can't see the forest for the trees. OK, you may consider yourself appointed to the role of Watson to the Southern Sherlock Holmes. Tonight I want you to practice saying, 'Really, Holmes!' and "Good Lord, Holmes, what can it mean?' in a toffee-nosed British accent, and I'll start lugging my Meerschaum around instead of these cigars."

"Watson! I love it!" laughed Heather joyfully.

"Tell you what, I'll run this down for you while we wait for the Rat's good-this-year pizza via the Rat's consistently slow as molasses service, and when I'm through please give me your opinion. I promise I'll avoid any details which will spoil your appetite." For the next hour Matt talked, while they waited, then while they ate, and finally while they polished off a pitcher to wash down the indeed superb pizza. He told her the whole history of the case, including Dr. Mears' cryptic remarks about his wife's possible knowledge and his interview with Lieberman that afternoon. "He was slick, I'll give him that," said Matt. "Just the right combination of contrition and deceptive candor which wasn't really candid at all, if you know what I mean. Like he'd rehearsed his lines, which he probably had. Remember, he was an actor and a drama coach. But just because he gave me a canned presentation doesn't necessarily mean he's hiding something."

"You might add to your storehouse of information that Dr. Lieberman is a sexual harasser," said Heather. "I've learned that the woman who held the head accountant's job before me left because of some kind of incident with Lieberman."

"What kind of sexual harassment?" asked Matt keenly. "PC bullshit or something real, something serious?"

"*Any* unwanted sexual advance is harassment and any sexual harassment in the workplace is damned serious!" snapped Heather.

"No, no, I'm not trying to start an argument. I'm wearing my cop hat now, not my Buchanan for President hat. Liberal rhetoric aside, there is both a legal and a moral difference between a man patting some file clerk on the behind or telling a smutty joke and really forcing himself on her, tearing her clothes, holding her physically restrained while kissing her against her will, something that indicates actual violence. Is Lieberman just a boorish jerk, or is he capable of violence against women? Has he ever committed violence against a woman? I need to know if he has. Can you find out for me, without letting him know that you're checking up on him?"

"I'll try," agreed Heather. "Can't you find out if he has a criminal record?"

"I already ran him with the state and the NCIC this morning, before I went to see him," said Matt, munching on the last pizza crust. "He's clean. He's got some old political arrests in the Sixties and early Seventies, blocking the street and chaining himself to the White House fence during ant-war demonstrations, that kind of thing. Nothing from 1970 on except for some DUIs which he plea-bargained down to illegal turns and whatnot."

"I don't like drunk drivers any more than I like people who touch me without being asked," said Heather sourly.

"I agree on both counts, but it's really reaching to call him a suspect," said Matt. "His alibi is acceptable if unconfirmable, and quite logical. Most people *are* home in bed between the hours of eleven P.M. and three A.M. Also, there isn't any really convincing motive for him to murder the two girls. He had only a nodding acquaintance with Mary Jane from school and as the daughter of Meg Mears, no reason at all to kill her, and while his sexual relationship with Jeannie did pose a threat to his job and his marriage, the MO simply isn't right for that motive. If Jeannie alone had been found dead on the side of a road somewhere, this would be a much simpler crime. We'd be looking for a boyfriend, an ex-boyfriend, or a boyfriend wannabe. But that's not the crime we're dealing with. Any alternative suspects come to mind, Dr. Watson?"

"Hmm. There's the famous Russian literary exile. I find that Lieberman connection odd, anti-war compadres or not," said Heather. "Would they really have all that much in common, with Paul being a mere high school teacher?"

"What are you suggesting?" asked Matt.

"I don't know much about Nakritin personally, but I did read *Louisa* in college as part of a course on the contemporary novel," said Heather. "It's got some pretty raunchy sex scenes. Nakritin had a definite fixation on intellectual older men in bed with firm young flesh and bouncing boobies of generous proportion. He was a friend of the Mears family and Lieberman admits he met Jeannie Arnold in their home. Any lights flashing or bells ringing here?"

"He was 72 years old and probably physically incapable of the crimes, not to mention breaking a dog's neck with his bare hands," said Matt. "Close but no cigar. It could be he sympathized with Lieberman for the very reason that he was a man who had lived Nakritin's novel. Good reasoning, though. Keep 'em coming, my dear Watson."

"Are you absolutely sure Mary Jane couldn't have been the target, and Jeannie the one who got in the way?" asked Heather.

"Setting aside for the moment the excessive difference in the physical violence inflicted on Jeannie, what motive?" asked Matt. "I'm not being argumentative, Heather, I'm really asking. If you see something you think I'm missing, now or at any time, for Pete's sake tell me. There is a large sign around my cranium that reads Open For Suggestions."

"Revenge," said Heather. "The revenge of a cuckolded husband, who even as he dies tries to implicate the unfaithful wife who rejected him. The revenge of a frustrated lover, straight or gay, against a wife or a husband who would not leave their family and go with them. The revenge of a student one of the professors flunked. Have you checked into that angle?"

"No," admitted Matt. "It couldn't have been either Andrew or Meg Mears; they were both in Washington D.C. in clear view of hundreds of people and hotel staff during the whole 24-hour period, but you can always hire muscle. Kill their own daughter and her friend? I've seen worse things done, but why? I'll say this, if Andy Mears is the killer he's the best damned actor I've ever come across. The lover or student angle is more interesting. Is that what you think happened?"

"No, I'm just throwing out suggestions like you asked," said Heather. "I think the key is in Margaret Mears' words as the news of her daughter's death slammed into her mind, the first words she uttered. *'They promised!'* she said. Who are *they* and what did *they* promise? If I were you I'd go up to Washington and ask her point blank."

"I intend to do that, but Meg Mears is a bit out of my league unless I can get chapter and verse first," said Matt. "I don't mind pissing in the corridors of power. I've done it before. But before I go shouting the odds to the most politically powerful feminist liberal in the country after HRC herself, right in the middle of the most angry and violent presidential campaign in American history, I intend to have every i dotted and every t crossed. The waiter is giving us dirty looks; we'd better shift our asses. Welcome aboard, my dear Watson. I'll give you a ring tomorrow and see if I can't give you something to do."

"Look, why not come on back to my house?" asked Heather as they left the Rat. "We can kick all this around some more, and

Tori said she wanted you to help her with some kind of school project she's working on if I could inveigle you into coming over again. I walked here, but you've presumably got a car?"

"I'm parked in the deck out back. Let's go."

* * *

It was almost quarter past eight. Tori sat in her room at her school desk playing a video game on her computer, which she had finally gotten around to unpacking and setting up again that evening. She'd decided that the effort required a lengthy long distance call to a quondam boyfriend in Seattle who was also her former school's official computer nerd, a call which Tori knew would cause Heather to go through the roof when she got the phone bill. Tori sighed; it looked like some kind of part-time job after school or on weekends was definitely indicated, if only so she could call Seattle more than once every few months.

Cheryl Crow moaned on the CD player about the sun coming up on Santa Monica Boulevard while Tori, in the guise of a Warrior Princess dressed in a tasseled bikini, slashed and shot and blew up assorted space aliens, monsters, and villains on the terminal. *Wonder if Mom will be home from her date with Two Gun Matt soon?* she thought. *Wonder if they'll go back to his place? Hope so. Mom's been really stressed a lot lately. She needs to get laid.* Tori was convinced her mother should be rogered rigid on a regular basis, in the belief that this would result in a more laid-back atmosphere, beer-drinking and smoking privileges in the home, and an all around new and improved Mom. Besides, if Heather acquired a boyfriend or husband there was greater financial and domestic possibility that Tori would be allowed to return to Seattle and go to the University of Washington, a plan she was waiting for an opportunity to broach.

Her own anguished and desperate longing for a father in her life was a pain she had learned to suppress to nearly subliminal levels, something she instinctively knew was there but which she ruthlessly kept down because she knew she couldn't handle it if brought to the surface. All she remembered about her own father was shouting, her mother's screams and bloodied face, a disheveled figure shambling around the house smelling of liquor, and unending fear and anger and despair seeping into her mind despite every effort she had made to keep it out. Her mental defense system had created a kind of mnemonic v-chip that routinely pulled the plug on the memories of that time whenever they surfaced. Since his death Tori had often felt what she was sure was his presence, but the combination of pain and sadness and love which she sensed there was almost as upsetting to her as the bad times had been. Tori heard a car in the driveway, looked out the window, and saw Matt Redmond's Taurus. Matt and her mother were getting out of the car. "Cool!" she said. She stepped out into the hallway and heard a small scratching noise above her. She looked up.

A human hand was clinging to the ceiling. It was small, white, and slender, and appeared quite real. It crawled onto the attic trap door upside down, like a spider, and scratched the wood with the fingernail. Then it made a fist and swung down on the index finger. It was now pointing towards the door, suspended lightly in midair. The extended index finger began to tap on the door, striking and rebounding an angle like a bouncing ball attached to an invisible rubber band. The tapping grew more rapid, the hand now moving up and down like a demented woodpecker, taptaptaptaptap*taptaptaptaptaptap* on the attic door taptaptaptaptaptaptaptap faster and faster, now it sounded like a machine gun taptaptaptaptapTAPTAPTAPTAPTAPTAP faster,

faster, ever faster, the hand blurred now it was battering so rapidly at the trap door.

It was insane. It was hideous. Tori screamed in horror at the top of her lungs and fainted.

Matt and Heather were just coming through the front door downstairs. "I'll put some coffee on," she said as she fitted her key in the lock. They stepped into the front hall just in time to hear a wild scream of terror and a thud from upstairs. *"Tori!"* cried Heather in alarm.

"Let me go first!" commanded Matt, whipping out his .357 Magnum and taking the stairs two at a time. Tori, dressed in a sweatshirt and cutoff short jeans, was just staggering up off the floor in the hall beneath the trap door leading into the attic, white and shivering and tearful. "What happened?" asked Matt.

"I think Mary Jane wants us to look in the attic for something," said Tori miserably. Both adults noticed a puddle on the floor. Tori saw it too. "She *scared* me, dammit!" wept Tori, hiding her face in her hands, scarlet with shame. "I peed in my pants!" The girl fled into her bedroom and slammed the door, sobbing in utter humiliation.

VIII

After a while Heather knocked on the door. "You okay, honey?" she called.

"I'm going to take a shower and change my clothes," said Tori's voice, muffled through the door. The sound of the shower in her bathroom came on.

Heather turned back into the hall."Would you mind stepping downstairs, Matt?" she asked. "I'll be down in a bit." Matt nodded and went down.

Heather stood in the hallway, looking around, slowly growing angrier and angrier, debating whether to make herself look foolish, and then deciding she didn't care. "Mary Jane!" she snapped. "If you can hear me, I am really pissed off at you! I don't know what you did to Tori, but it was cruel and mean and stupid! You scared her and humiliated her in front of her mother and Mr. Redmond! I know you don't want to be here. Well, I'm not too happy about you being here either! But it's our house now, dammit all, and you don't belong here anymore! You should go on to wherever it is we go when we leave our bodies for good! I've heard you crying in the night, I know you're unhappy, and you've got reason to be, but why do we have to be frightened and miserable too? I can't make you behave, and you're actually lucky I can't get at you or I'd probably give you a good slap right now, sixteen or not! If you're going to hang around here, then show some consideration for others!" There was silence except for the hiss of the shower in Tori's bathroom. "Please!" she concluded.

There was a clatter from Heather's bedroom as something hit the floor, making her jump. For a moment Heather was frightened herself, thinking there was an intruder, and she stood irresolutely, but then the pure frustration and irritation of the situation overcame her again. "Oh, what are you doing NOW?" she cried. She walked into her bedroom and snapped on the light. The big ceramic urn of expensive talcum powder Tori had given her last Christmas, which had been sitting firmly on her dressing table, now lay on the floor, the top off. The white powder lay in a broad swath across the parquet floor. "Oh, no! " Heather screeched. "Is it going to be vandalism now? Are we going to play poltergeist? *Jesus!*" She stepped forward and suddenly stopped. Something had been clumsily written in the powder.

"IM SORRY MOM" it said.

Heather sat down on the bed, her eyes filling with tears, overwhelmed with terrible grief. She understood that there was a child in unimaginable pain, so close, yet so far beyond her help. "Oh, God," she whispered. "Am I your mother now? Have I been adopted? I don't know if I can handle that, Mary Jane. It...it seems like only yesterday I was sixteen myself. All the years in between seem like a blur and now I'm forty-two. That's absurd. How can I possibly be forty-two years old? There must be some mistake. I was supposed to have this wonderful life coming when I was sixteen. How did I miss it?" There was only silence. She watched the powder on the floor to see if any more writing would appear, but nothing happened. "I can't possibly conceive of where you are now, or how part of you continues to exist in this place," she said after a while. "I would give anything to help you stop hurting. If my being here helps you, if Tori's being here helps you, makes it hurt a bit less, makes you a little less lonely, then I'm glad. I'm sorry I yelled at you, honey. Just try to be a little more careful in the future, OK? You have to understand that this is kind of a freaky situation for us." There was no answer, and after a while she went downstairs for a broom and a dustpan.

Some time later, Matt knocked softly on Tori's door. "Are you decent?" he called out. "Can I come in?"

"Sure," said Tori dully. He opened the door. She was sitting on her bed wearing jeans and a blouse, her feet bare. She had one of her stuffed animals on her lap, a kangaroo. She threw it over onto her pillow, embarrassed. Matt pretended not to notice. "Your mother says you didn't eat any dinner so she's fixing you a sandwich," he said. "She also says tomorrow after she gets home you and she will go up and thoroughly clean out and organize the attic."

"Will you be here?" asked Tori.

"If I'm invited," replied Matt.

"Do you believe me, about Mary Jane?" asked Tori.

"Yes," said Matt. "Last night I had a pretty weird experience up here myself. Two weird experiences, actually. Out there on your sidewalk I thought I saw Mary Jane looking down at me from that window there. That's why I was acting like a loon when you looked out the living room window and saw me. It was a shock, I can tell you."

"Did you pee in your pants?" asked Tori bitterly.

"No," admitted Matt. He pulled up a chair and sat down. "Tori, your mother has mentioned you're a bit on the psychic side, but you're not comfortable talking about it to her. I'm a police officer conducting an investigation, and I regard you as a witness who can give me potentially very valuable information. I can't promise you how I'll evaluate that information, but I can promise you that you will be listened to carefully and you'll have my full attention. It's your duty as a citizen to tell me anything you know or think you may know about the serious crimes which took place here in this house. I need your help, Tori."

"Okay," she said, smiling slightly. "If I do my civic duty will you help me with a Twentieth Century Culture class report? We had a choice of topics today, and I picked drugs because I figured I could get some expert help from you."

"Sure," laughed Matt.

"Okay," said Tori, relaxing.

"The first question I want to ask is the obvious one. Do you know who killed Mary Jane Mears and Jeannie Arnold?"

"No," said Tori. "I wish I did."

"Is there any way you can find out for me from the psychic remnants of the victims which remain here? Ghosts or whatever they are?" asked Matt urgently. "Maybe with a seance or a Ouija board or something like that? It would never be admissible in court, of course, but if I could just get a name to go on I'd be halfway there."

"Ah, I don't think it would do any good. Jeannie down in the laundry room is incapable of telling anybody anything. It's really horrible for her. She doesn't know she's dead. She was in such pain, so distracted and incoherent, so crazy with terror that she just plain didn't notice when they finally killed her. She thinks she's still being tortured."

"Sweet Jesus!" groaned Matt. "God, no! What about Mary Jane? Tori, can she tell you or communicate to you who killed her?"

"No," said Tori. "Uh, Matt, I can't tell you how I know this, it's just an impression and maybe I haven't got it right, but I don't think she can do that." Tori paused. "I don't think she's *allowed* to. It's, ah, against the rules over on her side of the fence, if you get what I'm trying to say. Living people have to solve their own problems. The most she seems able to do is speak in riddles, really obscure hints, and not much of that."

"Like the oracle at Delphi, eh?" chuckled Matt. "No cosmic handouts, no divine welfare state, the human condition is strictly *laissez faire*? God is a reactionary? How politically incorrect. One last question, Tori, and then you need to get on down to your dinner," said Matt. "Can you feel any bad presences or psychic remnants of the killers in this house? Anyone or anything besides the two murdered girls?"

"No, just them," said Tori.

"Good," said Matt with a sigh. "That means they're probably still alive, and if they're alive I can still get them. Hey, you remember asking me about some of those flamboyant shoot-outs I was in? Still full of morbid curiosity?"

"Yeah," said Tori, smiling.

"Well, if you read that bullshit in People and Time you recall the business with Little Willie in that dive in East St. Louis? Biggest, blackest dope-dealing motherfucker you ever saw. Head shaved like Mr. Clean, and he wore one of those Lion of Judah type goatee beards. 1979, and he was still wearing a Superfly outfit."

"What's that?" asked Tori.

"Back in the Seventies it was the ultimate in threads among ethically challenged African-Americans," replied Matt. "Anyway,

Willie had an understandable habit of wearing a bullet-proof vest under his silk shirts, and my first shot just staggered him. A .357 slug right in the chest, for Christ's sake, and he just grunted and raised that sawed-off 12-gauge pump shotgun he carried in a sling rig under his jacket, chunked in a round and opened up. The whole thing was split-second; I realized he was wearing a vest and my next shot had to hit him in the head or I was a dead man, but he was so fast he fired before I did. Fortunately, Willie had a habit of alternating his ammo, double-ought-buck with every other round a slug. The shell he fired at me was a slug; I felt the wind of it going by my ear. If it'd been buckshot my head would have been blown off. I fired again just as he pumped another round into the chamber, I hit him right between the eyes, and knocked him flying, and the buckshot blew a hole into the barroom wall."

"Wow, just like a movie!" said Tori, eyes glistening.

"Yeah, well, if they ever make a movie out of that episode I bet there's one thing they don't include," said Matt with a wry smile. "That 12-gauge slug zipping past my ear must have done it. After Willie was down and it was all over, I noticed something. I'd peed in my pants."

Tori laughed out loud. "Thanks, Matt," she said shyly.

"Make you a deal," he said, "I won't tell on you if you don't tell on me. Come on down."

When Tori came downstairs she brought her tape recorder with her. "That's a good one," said Matt approvingly. "Same kind I've got with the long-play microcassettes. I used it to tape interview, make case notes, so forth and so on."

"Mom gave me this one for Christmas," said Tori. "I'll eat my sandwich and potato chips and you talk about drugs for my report while I eat." She turned the recorder on. Heather handed him a cup of coffee. "First, tell me about the gunfight in Mexico with Don Ramon."

"That has only peripherally to do with drugs and much more to do with satisfying your lust for sensation," said Matt, shaking his finger at her. "Little Willie was enough. You like shoot-em-ups, rent a Sam Peckinpah video."

"I confess I'd like to hear about some of this famous swash-buckling too," said Heather, sitting down at the table with her coffee cup.

"I was with the DEA for almost fifteen years, and most of it consisted of long hours of boring surveillance, writing endless reports, dealing with every level of bureaucracy, dragging through long court proceedings, busting low-level mules and addicts whose brains were so fried on heroin or crack or PCP that they were barely functioning human beings. Latin America was more of the same but complicated by the fact that I could seldom trust the local cops I was working with and never knew when one of them in the pay of the Medellìn or Callé crowds might put a bullet in my back, which did wonders for my paranoia factor. I seldom swashed my buckle. The most interesting work I did was with the Justice Department Special Investigations division. When I left I was becoming Federal law enforcement's official Russian Mafia guru. I learned some Russian, which may be useful if we find a clue in Vladimir Nakritin's handwriting."

"We have Russian gangsters now?" asked Heather.

"Absolutely. They're giving the Sicilians, the Colombians, and the blacks a run for their money, especially in New York, Los Angeles, and Seattle. Mostly it's penny-ante stuff like they did back home, hijacking, fencing, black-market consumer goods they smuggle back to Russia, currency speculation, some gambling and loansharking in Russian or Jewish immigrant communities. But they're enterprising bastards. They were the first to get into theft of computer chips in a big way, memory SIMMS and so forth. Aside from diamonds no commodity is smaller, easier to transport, or brings more profit than black-market computer chips. They're also suspected of dealing in nuclear weapons technology and plutonium stolen from the old Soviet missile silos and military bases."

"Oh, great!" moaned Heather.

"Why did you leave the Justice Department?" asked Tori.

"I resigned after Waco," Matt said. "I told Ms. Reno I wouldn't work for a government that used tanks and flamethrowers against its own people for the crime of practicing their own religion, however admittedly bizarre that religion was. In America you're supposed to have a right to be different. Oh, it wasn't just that. I'd had pretty serious doubts for a long time, like when DEA was warned off the Mena Airport situation in Arkansas, and the time we got a briefing on the Federal Emergency Management Agency's Civil Disorder Response Plan, which involves rounding up thousands of Americans and interning them without trial in camps on military bases. In theory as far downscale as people whose only crime was writing a letter to the editor criticizing the government."

"Right wing paranoia," scoffed Heather.

"Only for those on the A-list," replied Matt quietly. "They're the ones who get rounded up if a liberal president gives the order. If a conservative president gives the order we round up the B-list, progressives and feminists and gay activists and academic Marxists, which would probably include virtually every professor over there on campus. That's what's scary, Heather. Not the ideological orientation of the people who are making these preparations and drawing up these lists, but the fact that they *have* none. Federal power today is completely mercenary. It will serve whoever is signing the checks. I didn't feel like being a mercenary any longer. This is America. There aren't supposed to be any lists. Anyway, my attitude has been duly been noted. In the three years

I've been back down here the IRS has audited me twice, they've tried to screw me out of my severance package and my benefits, a BATF snitch tried to persuade me to buy illegal automatic weapons from him, and somebody regularly taps my telephone, which I cleanse with my bugsmasher and various other little tricks."

"Don Ramon!" said Tori insistently.

"Why, for heaven's sake?" demanded Matt.

"That's where you got your name Two Gun Matt," said Tori.

"I thought you only carried one gun," said Heather teasingly. He shook his head.

"All right," he sighed. "Here's your bedtime story, little girls. This happened in 1983. I was doing an intelligence-gathering run down in Ciudad Juarez, Mexico, right across the border from El Paso. The subject of the investigation was a man named Tommy Sandoval, a greasy Tex-Mex punk from Amarillo who called himself Don Ramon. It was pretty bogus. In the first place, he wasn't the real Don Ramon. There was another much more famous Don Ramon during the 1970s, a man named Carrasco, a really heavy dude who was killed in a prison break in 1976. I often wonder what he would have thought of Tommy using his handle. Secondly, he was so Americanized he had to re-learn Spanish when he started hanging out south of the border. Got the picture? Okay. We learned Ramon was running some serious weight across the river, so I was told to ease on my body on down Mexico way and take a quiet look around. No warrant, we're not looking to bust him yet, just take a peek at his operation, get a feel for his habits and his MO, so forth and so on. I was told to liase with a *Federale* named Jésus Molina, a detective sergeant in the Mexican national CID. Molina had a rep as being totally straight, incorruptible, very rare for a Mexican cop."

I first saw Evangelina's picture on his desk, Matt thought. *Her and Pilar and Diego. "Muy bella doña y pocitos", I told him. She reminded me of Mary Jane, a bit.* "We heard Ramon was in town and we started asking around," Matt went on, both women listening raptly. "We got a call from a regular snitch of Molina's who said he could get on the inside with Ramon, wanted to meet us in this sleazy bar down on the bad side of town, or since this was Mexico I should say the worse side of town. Molina didn't suspect anything. He'd met this guy before in the same place, it was one of his usual hangouts. Well, like most good players, Ramon had somebody in the police station on his pad, who told him a DEA *Norteamericano* was hunting him. We were set up. Molina drives me down there, we park, Molina has me slip ten dollars American to this young kid he knows to make sure the car is still there when we get back, and we head for the cantina. We're about fifty feet from the door when it opens and out steps Ramon himself, an AK-47 in one hand and a bottle of tequila in the other, with four of his crew behind him. Kind of an evil Freddie Prinze, he looked like."

"Who?" asked Tori, puzzled.

"Way before your time, dear," said Heather. "Go on, Matt."

"They'd been waiting for us. Ramon decided he wanted to play hombre, show his machismo. Molina pulled his gun and stepped in front of me. Ramon damned near cut him in half with a long burst from the Kalashnikov. Molina was a big man in every sense of the word, and his body shielded me from the first bullets."

"*...Set ye Uriah in the forefront of the hottest battle, and retire ye from him, that he may be smitten and die.*" The Biblical curse Evie had thrown at him the last time he had ever spoken to her, the filthy lie Matt's father had convinced her of, via Jack Conley. *Did she really believe it?* thought Matt in despair. *Could she really believe that of me? Why, Evie, why? Whatever did I do or say to give you cause to think me so evil?* "Right at the moment Sergeant

Molina fell the AK jammed," Matt continued, remembering the
heat, the dust, the smell of the beer from the bar, the popping of
the bullets on the crumbling asphalt street. "Ramon threw down
his tequila bottle to fiddle with the bolt and try to clear the
weapon. The others were waving their guns in the air, firing them
all around me not really aiming, yelling *andelez!* and *arriba*! like a
bunch of hoot-owl drunk Speedy Gonzalezes. Fortunately for me,
they'd spent their time waiting in the cantina chugging tequila and
snorting coke up their noses, and so they weren't very together
about it all. So I had a second or two to get my own gun out, the
same .357 I carry now.

"One of the gang was a woman named Sarah Baldonado.
Twenty years old, been a hooker since she was twelve, tough as
nails and probably less drunk than the rest. She had a 9-millimeter
pistol. She was the only one who actually hit me during the whole
exchange, which I suppose ought to be considered some kind of
feather in the cap of world feminism. Her first shot hit my left
foot; I still have a bad arch down there despite reconstructive sur-
gery and although I can walk and even run now, it often hurts like
hell. I dropped to the ground and grabbed Molina's automatic in
my left hand and brought it up. Fortunately he carried a round up
the spout so all I had to do was cock and fire. I opened up just as
Ramon got his jam cleared. We everybody emptied our weapons,
Sarah got me one more time, shattered my left collarbone, and
when the shooting stopped all five of them were down. The whole
incident from start to finish lasted maybe fifteen seconds. I have
no idea how I hit them all. I suspect they were so drunk a couple
of them shot themselves or their compadres. Sarah lived long
enough to look up and tell me in Spanish that my mother sucked
off syphilitic horses, then she died. And there you have the saga of
how Two Gun Matt got his moniker. Let me know what grade
you get on that report."

"Woooow!" said Tori, impressed.

"Did the Mexican officer die?" asked Heather.

"Yes. He saved my life. I tried to repay him by providing for his family. I ended up marrying his widow."

"*Way* neat! You really go out for romantic gestures," said Tori, impressed.

"Evidently," agreed Matt with a chuckle. "It lasted about four years. We divorced and she's back in Mexico now."

"Any kids?" asked Heather.

"Two of Molina's, whom I legally adopted, and two of our own," replied Matt

"Ever see them?"

"No," said Matt. "My father pays Evie five hundred dollars a month to make herself scarce. I don't even know where they are in Mexico. And don't get me into the subject of my father or I'll be here all night."

"I'm not exactly sure what all this has to do with your school work, young lady," said Heather. "Speaking of which, tomorrow is a school day. You need to get upstairs, brush your teeth and hit the sack."

"Matt hasn't told us about Dynamite Slim yet," said Tori.

"He was a redneck fool who liked to rob banks and sell drugs and throw lit sticks of dynamite at people, and that's all you need to know about him," said Matt.

"Upstairs!" commanded Heather.

"And what are you two going to be doing downstairs?" asked Tori sweetly.

"Don't be a smart aleck!" said Heather, pointing to the stair-case. "Move!"

Matt finished a final cup of coffee and got up. "Tomorrow's a work day for you too, my dear Watson, and I've kept you up," he said. "Tell you what, I'll drop by tomorrow night with the SBI case file and you can look that over, how's that?"

"Good," said Heather.

"One thing," he said seriously, "You're a grown woman and I'm not implying any weakness on your part, but I suggest in the strongest possible terms that you do not look at the actual crime scene photos of the victims or the medical reports detailing Jeannie Arnold's injuries. You have to live here in this house, and seeing such things in color in recognizable surroundings would be very disturbing for you. You might not be able to stay here. Heather, I won't withhold the pictures, it will be your call, but please, trust me on this one."

"All right," she said steadily. "Matt, there is something I would like to talk to you about, but I'm not sure how to approach it. Are you involved with someone now?"

"No," he said, shaking his head. Michelle didn't count. "I couldn't ask anybody to share my life, Heather. For one thing, it would mean involvement with my psychotic family. I tried it once and my father eventually succeeded in destroying my marriage and costing me my children. That won't happen again."

"*Why,* for heaven's sake?" asked Heather, stunned. "Why does he hate you so much?"

"That is a question which requires an answer so long and complex it would take me all night, and I'm not totally sure I'd get it right in any case," said Matt with a sigh. "In twenty-five words or less, I committed two crimes. I publicly embarrassed my father by choosing to live my life in a manner which does not revolve around wealth and the accumulation of wealth, and which involves my associating with people whom my father considers to be socially beneath our family. He was born poor Southern white trash and when he climbed and clawed his way out of the tobacco patch he became the world's worst snob. The precise nature of my job is immaterial, what matters is that it is not the career he chose for me. My second unforgivable act is that on several occasions down the years, I have *proven Randall Redmond wrong.* Since Randall Redmond is a godlike being, infallible and omniscient, this has upset the natural order of the universe. The earth has halted in its orbit, the stars have paused in the firmament above, the entire cosmos awaits with bated breath the correction of this unthinkable state of affairs. Randall Redmond must be proven right, and nothing else matters."

"That's a lot more than twenty-five words," said Heather. "He must be proven right in what way?"

"Right about me. First off, I am insane. Raving mad, psycho, nuts, prime cackle box material. I am a violent psychopath with a badge and a gun and a license to kill. I spend my days plotting to cause Randall Redmond, my sainted sire, all kinds of further embarrassment by getting my name in the papers and forcing him to acknowledge that I exist. I lie, cheat, steal, embezzle, seduce, plot to overthrow the government, trample defenseless women and children beneath my coal-black steed's iron-shod hooves and square dance in roundhouses. I am a murderer, of course. Every one of the felons I have apprehended is lily-pure innocent, framed, and more than one has walked out of prison due to expensive legal counsel provided by my father. One of them was part of a gang in Duplin County who subsequently killed a woman and her baby."

"Why in God's name would your father do something like that?" demanded Heather in amazement.

"To make me lose my job by ensuring that any court case I'm involved in gets tangled up like a Chinese fire drill. Eventually he hopes SBI will get the message. Fortunately, the bureau's director is a friend and admirer of my dashing derring-do, and he told

Daddy to go fuck himself. Oh, damn, Heather, I don't feel like getting into this! It makes me physically sick!"

"Matt, I haven't told you the much less exciting story of my
own life yet, but you need to know this much," she said quietly. "I
admit to having the hots for you, as Tori would say, but I cannot
and will not ever become involved with any man who hurts me or
hurts my daughter. I'm going to ask you flat out: is there anything
to your father's assessment? I know most police officers go for
years without ever even having to draw their guns. You seem to
have done an awful lot of killing, legal though it may have been. I
need to know why."

"First off, although I've occasionally had to manhandle women
who resisted arrest in order to subdue them, Sarah Baldonado is
the only woman I have ever really hurt," Matt replied. "I killed
her, but she was trying to kill me and she actually shot me twice. It
was her call, Heather. The same for all of them. Nobody forced
those five people to be in the place they were, doing what they
were doing, interfering with the lives of others, engaging in
morally reprehensible and illegal activities. This idea that all
human life is of equal value is hogwash. Of course some human
lives are of more value than others, and some are less, and sometimes other human beings have to make that judgment and act on
it. Through a combination of circumstance and being damned
good at what I do, I have been in that position more often than
most, and I don't believe I've ever called it wrong. As for my character and my philosophy about violence, well, did you ever see my
favorite John Wayne movie, *The Shootist?*"

"I never took philosophy in college, no," said Heather.

Matt grinned. "Anyway, there's a scene in there where the kid,
played by Ron Howard, asks the old gunfighter John Bernard
Books how he managed to come out on top in all those shootouts.
I'll try to repeat the Duke's little speech as best I can, because it

pretty much tells you about me. It's not so much being fast with a gun, or even accurate that counts. It's being *willing.* I learned long ago that most men, regardless of cause or need, aren't willing. They don't really have the instinct to kill; it's been bred out of them by so-called modern civilization. They'll blink an eye or draw a breath, hesitate just that fraction of a second before they pull the trigger. I won't. It may be genetic; apparently most men in our family are carriers of that extra Y chromosome you may have heard about. That may well make me some kind of mental case, but that characteristic in me is why I'm alive and Ramon and Slim and Little Willie are dead. All I can add is that I recognize the moral and ethical difference between necessary violence to defend what little remains of the shredded social fabric today, and criminal violence. The fact that I recognize that distinction is the reason I no longer work for the United States government, which no longer does. I hope you can handle my past, my present, and my future. Because I've got a fairly tempestuous case of the hots for you, too." He smiled and got up. "I'll head on now. Think about it, and have a good night."

Heather walked him to the door. "Quite a silver tongue you've got, Holmes," she said with a smile. "I gather you must have been just as silver-tongued in Spanish."

"Yo soy un hombre sincero, de la tierra de las cartas verdes," sang Matt, to the tune of Guantanamera. "No, that's not fair. I shouldn't have said that. Evie always leveled with me, I'll give her that much. She was a widow with nothing but an irregular pension, an unlivable pittance from a bankrupt government that rates widows' pensions pretty much last on its list of bills to be paid. Unfortunately for her, the stories of her husband's honesty were true. Molina wasn't on the take and so they had no savings to speak of. She was desperate for a way out and I was ridden with guilt that I hadn't been able to save their husband and father."

"Like you are ridden with guilt about Mary Jane," commented Heather quietly.

"Jesus, does it show that much?" asked Matt sheepishly.

"It's there, yes. You do realize that there was not a damned thing you could have done to foresee what happened or prevent it, don't you?"

"I know, I know," sighed Matt. "My mind has been telling me that for years. My heart just won't buy it. I've always wondered maybe if she hadn't been riding with Jeannie, if I'd brought her home that night..."

"If you'd brought her home that night they would have killed you too!" said Heather.

"Yes. I know very well that my guilt is unreasonable. It just won't go away, and I'm sure it got mixed in with what happened to Molina as well. But until the very last it wasn't a bad marriage. The hell of it was that we really were pretty compatible. I gave her a house in Fort Lauderdale and she kept it for me, gave me children and nurtured them, put up with my insane work schedule. She had already been widowed once by the dopers, yet she knew fighting them was something I had to do, and she never once asked me to quit or gave me any cause for worry. I've always respected her for that. Fact is, I got a hell of a bargain there. I've always been pretty grim company since Mary Jane died, and Evie was very dignified and serious in a Spanish kind of way, almost Victorian formal. We were suited to one another."

"Even in the bedroom?" asked Heather, then practically smacked herself in the head. *Christ, you're as bad as Tori!* she hissed silently to herself. "Matt, I'm sorry, that was a childish and stupid thing for me to say, completely out of line. Please forgive me. God, you must think I have a mind like a sewer!"

Matt shrugged. "Oddly enough, it was when we got sufficiently used to one another to unwind a bit in the bedroom that we first discovered we really liked one another, we started really talking, and all of a sudden it wasn't just a marriage of convenience."

"What went wrong?" asked Heather.

"A man named Jack Conley," replied Matt. "Florida beach bum type, claimed to be a free-lance photographer. I won't get into details as to how he wormed his way into my life and my home and my wife's bed, except that for about a year I honestly thought he was my best friend. Later I found out he was a private detective my father had carefully selected, hired, and briefed to seduce my wife and break up my marriage."

"What? Matt are you sure about that?" asked Heather, shocked. "I mean, isn't that a little, ah, how can I put it....?"

"Paranoid?" Matt filled in bitterly. "I did some checking afterwards, Heather, after Evie left me and Conley dumped her and disappeared. I used my Federal police powers and came damned near getting fired over it, but I found out what I wanted to know. I found his Florida bank account and I got photostats of checks, big checks, drawn on an offshore account by a shady lawyer in Burlington who's done all Daddy's really dirty shitwork for him down through the years. Set him back over two hundred grand to take my wife and children from me, but I have no doubt at all he considers every penny well spent. Can we change the subject?"

"I'm sorry, I'm pushing this too fast," said Heather calmly, looking him in the eye. "But I want you to know I'm interested." Matt grinned and decided she was kissable, and he had his arms around her waist when a voice came from the top of the stairs.

"Matt?" called Tori hesitantly. "Matt, is that you? Are you still there?"

"The very one," he called out.

"I think you'd better come up here," Tori said, coming down the stairs. "You have a message. From Mary Jane."

In Tori's room Matt and Heather stared at the screen on Tori's computer terminal. Across the blue screen, in large black letters and heavy, almost unreadable Gothic type were the words: MATT THEY KNOW ABOUT YOU BEWARE BEWARE DANGER DEATH.

Heather looked at her daughter. "Tori?"

"Mom, I swear to you both, I did not type in those words!" said Tori emphatically. "I couldn't have. The lettering in my screen is either red or white. Black isn't in the word processing or graphics software, and neither is that weird fancy type face."

"I believe her," said Matt, fascinated. "Mary Jane? Mary Jane, is that you?"

Words appeared on the screen. IPHEGENIA.

"Huh?" asked Tori, puzzled. "What's Iphegenia?"

"It's a rather uncommon woman's name," said Heather.

"Maybe it's the name of a female spirit!" suggested Tori excitedly.

"It's also an opera, *Iphegenia in Aulis*, based on Greek myth, by, ah, Verdi? Puccini? Italian, I think, but what the hell is the significance here?" wondered Matt out loud. "Ah, well, Iphegenia, can you give us a hand here?"

SEEK AND YE SHALL FIND came the Gothic letters.

"Who killed the girls who were murdered in this house?"

WHEN YOU KNOW WHY YOU WILL KNOW WHO. GOODBYE.

"Wait!" said Matt urgently. "Will you speak to us again?"

WHEN YOU HAVE READ IT. GOODBYE.

No amount of entreaty could induce any further reaction from the computer. When Matt asked Tori to run him a hard copy of the screen, the paper came out of the printer blank.

IX

Matt spent the next day in Raleigh testifying at the Ming Ho murder trial. Two suspected Triad gangsters, Lo Wang Pak and Chin Feng Ho, were accused of murdering a Chinese-American woman scientist who had worked in the Research Triangle Park because she had refused to pay a $120,000 drug and gambling debt incurred by her brother in New York. She had come to America when she was four years old and had forgotten the old ways of family honor and obligation. The two hoodlums and their gang boss had not, and so Ming Ho died the Death of a Thousand Cuts.

The apprehension of the suspects had been due to an alert New York state police sergeant who had seen the suspects profiled on *America's Most Wanted*. Matt was called by the prosecution as an expert witness on the Triads due to his DEA experience. The defense spent most of the afternoon in *pro forma* attempts to portray Matt as a redneck who was racially prejudiced against the defendants, especially after they learned he was a Vietnam veteran. They asked him if he had ever said the word "gook" and so on, but they were just going through the motions. The mens' attorneys knew who they were dealing with as well as Matt did, more so in view of their princely fees which were being paid in cashiers' checks drawn on a bank in Macao. Matt noticed with amusement that even though it was warm in court the defendants kept their jackets on and kept their hands below the table so the jury could not see any of the colorful and highly detailed tattoos of dragons, skulls, and Chinese characters which decorated their hands, arms, and shoulders. He took no offense at the lawyers' hectoring. They were just doing what they were being paid to do and probably intended to vote Republican in the coming election.

Matt gave a few sound bites to the news crews after court recessed and then met the director of the SBI for dinner, ironically at a Chinese restaurant in North Raleigh, to bring him up to date on the Ming Ho case. "About what I expected," grunted the director. "This ain't Los Angeles. Not yet, anyway. The jury will convict. Any progress on your personal project, the Mears-Arnold murders?"

"Not what you'd call progress, no, but I'm coming across some funny stuff which bears looking into. You weren't with the bureau then, were you?"

"Nope, I was still in the Marines in '70."

"Anybody from the FBI ever inquire about this case, Phil?" asked Matt carefully.

"As in whom?" asked Hightower, curious.

"As in a Special Agent Charles R. Bennett? Now Assistant Director Charles R. Bennett?" Matt replied.

"No, not that I recall," said the director. "I met Bennett once or twice. He's that Feebie you tossed through a window in Florida, right? He was down here working on some Federal stuff a few years ago. Didn't leave a very good impression. Damned near ended up getting himself shot by a security guard in the old building on Jones Street, I remember that. The fool was still in the building at ten o'clock at night, guess he wanted to impress us by working late or something. Bennett went through the wrong door and tripped an alarm, and Oscar Massengill, remember that old retired Raleigh cop we used to have on night shift? No, before your time, of course. Damn, I'm getting senile! Anyway Oscar thought somebody'd broke in, drew his weapon and give him until three to come out with his hands up, the whole drill. A damned FBI agent! You'd think he would have known better than to go wandering into a restricted area at ten o'clock at night."

"What restricted area?" asked Matt keenly.

"Archives, I think it was," said the director.

"Where the SBI case file on the murder was kept," pointed out Matt. "Would this have been in late 1982, early 1983?"

"About Christmas of '82, yeah," said Hightower. "Damn if you ain't right. Why? What's going on? You found something, Matt?"

"The Chapel Hill police department file was gutted of all pertinent documents, every last damned interview report, anything that could be of help, during that time frame," Matt told him. "You know who was the Chapel Hill PD primary on the murders? A certain Detective Sergeant Charles R. Bennett. You know what he did, Phil? He feathered the case in February of '71 after all of fourteen weeks. Then he quit the Chapel Hill force and bee-bopped on over to the FBI and fame and fortune."

The director leaned forward, his eyes blazing in anger, his jaw switching. "Fourteen weeks?" he demanded. "Two young girls I saw in those photographs butchered like animals, worse than animals, and you're telling me that son of a bitch gave up after *fourteen weeks?*"

"Got it in one," said Matt.

"And you think he tampered with the Chapel Hill file and tried to tamper with ours?" asked Hightower, ruminating.

"Most likely. Looks like we're lucky our security guard was awake and watching his board instead of napping."

"Bennett's connected up there in D.C. now," warned Phil. "Really connected. I know that much about him. He won't take kindly to being embarrassed. I know I don't have to tell you to be careful, Matt." He signaled the waiter for the check. "I'll get it, Matt. I think we can write this off as an official business conference."

The manager of the restaurant appeared at their table, a neatly dressed Chinese with thinning gray hair. "There will be no charge, genturmen," he told them. He pointed to Matt. "I see you on TV. You help put those two coolie dogs who kill that Chinese woman in prison. Buffet on house tonight."

Outside the restaurant, Matt got his car to head back to Chapel Hill. Before he did he called his answering machine on his cellular and checked for messages. There was a long, rambling threat from Sid, which he ignored, but there were two others. "Uh, Mr. Redmond, this is Marvella Rendell," came the voice of the black nurse. "I found your card in Dr. Mears' study, and I'm sure he would want me to call you. He's had another stroke. He had a long conversation with his former wife on the phone yesterday afternoon and it appears to have upset him so much it brought on another attack. He's in intensive care in Rex Hospital. I'll be visiting him there this evening and I wonder if you could meet me there? He left something for you."

The second message was: "Matt, this is Heather Lindstrom. Could you come by the house tonight? We've found something." There was silence. "Matt, we've found Mary Jane's diary." There was more silence. "There's some things in there that, well, I don't know how you're going to take them. Give me a call."

He dialed Heather's number first. "Hi, Watson. I'm in Raleigh. I had to be in court on another case today."

"I know," said Heather. "We saw you on the six o'clock news. Tori said you look gnarly, which is a compliment, I think. Did those men really kill her?"

"Yes. What's this about Mary Jane's diary? Are you sure?"

"Yes, Holmes, I'm sure. I've been reading it all evening. I know you'll want to read it too, but I need to point a few things out to you first."

"Only one question now, Watson," asked Matt. "Does Mary Jane give any indication who the killer might be?"

"Not that I can see, no, but since you remember the time and the place and the people maybe you can make more sense of it than I can. Are you coming?"

"I've got to make a stop here first. Dr. Andrew Mears had a stroke right after talking to his Congressional ex on the phone. The nurse says he left a message or something for me. I need to get that first; it might hold the answer."

"Okay. I'll wait up. No, Tori, Matt is going to read the diary first and then *maybe* I'll let you read it. I don't know about that, there are some things in here that might not be suitable for a girl your age."

"Mom, it was *written* by a girl my age!" came Tori's plaintive voice in the background.

"Can you hear that?" asked Heather, exasperated.

"Tell her a foolish consistency is the hobgoblin of little minds, Ralph Waldo Emerson," said Matt. "I've got to go to the hospital. I'll be by later on tonight."

He was unable to get in to see Andrew Mears at Rex, nor would it have done any good. Mears was comatose. Matt spoke with the floor nurse and got the name of Mears' hospital staff doctor. He located the doctor, on one of the wards, looking like he'd been awake for twenty-four hours, which he probably had. By flashing his badge and citing Mears as a possible witness in an investigation, Matt got the following prognosis: "Not good. He might, just might, survive this stroke, although the damage will be extensive. He won't survive the next." When Matt got back to the intensive care section, he found Marvella Rendell waiting for him. Courteously, Matt talked about Mears' medical condition first before bringing her gently to the phone call.

"About three o'clock yesterday she called," said the nurse sadly. "He took the call in his study. They talked for about thirty minutes. I could hear him yelling at her towards the end."

"Could you hear what he was saying?" asked Matt.

"Something about her not being a king," said Marvella.

"Huh?" said Matt, baffled. "You mean her not being a queen?"

"No, a king," she said. "He was shouting who the hell did she think she was, King Backgammon? and no she sure as hell was not King Backgammon. He yelled that several times. Eventually I heard him hang up. I knew he was upset, so I left him alone for a while. When I brought him in his supper he was slumped over his desk. I called 911 and then I was trying to give him first aid when I found this right under his hand." She pulled an envelope from her purse and handed it to him. Matt Redmond's name was written on the outside. He opened it up and found only two words written on a sheet of typing paper, sprawling, straggling, as if Mears had written them even as the stroke came on with a final effort of will before he lost control of his body.

Vladimir Nakritin.

                    *   *   *

Matt arrived at the Lindstrom house at about nine-thirty. "Tori's upstairs finishing her homework," said Heather. "I told her she couldn't come down until she did."

"Trade you, Watson," he said as he sat down and accepted Heather's proffered cup of Irish Cream coffee. "One Mary Jane Mears diary for one SBI file." He handed her the big sheaf of folders and documents, wrapped in heavy rubber bands. "Technically you're not supposed to see this, proprietary law enforcement information and all that, so don't go broadcasting the fact that I gave it to you, OK? I've removed everything regarding a completely useless subsidiary investigation the bureau made trying to find a link between this case and the Jeffrey McDonald murders in February, 1970. They didn't find any linkage and I am certain none exists. The crime scene photos and pathology reports are in a separate manila envelope, labeled. Again I urge you, don't open the envelope. No point in giving yourself nightmares."

Heather took the envelope with the photos and slid it up on top of a tallboy china cabinet in the corner. "If Tori finds these files she'll root through them no matter what I say, so I'll stash these up here," she said. "What about Doctor Mears?"

"Bad stroke and he may not make it, but at least we now have a named murder suspect." Briefly he recounted what Marvella told him and showed her the note with Nakritin's name.

"Who the hell is King Backgammon?" asked Tori curiously, coming into the kitchen at the end of Matt's report.

"That could be some kind of nickname for the individual who assisted Nakritin in committing the murders," said Matt. "I'm treating Nakritin as a suspect from now on because I can only view this as an accusation. I assume that after talking with his former wife, Dr. Mears now wishes to denounce Nakritin. Until he is able to speak again, this is all I've got to go on. It's highly unusual, but not beyond the bounds of possibility, that a reasonably fit man of 72 could have participated in a crime like this, but he would have had to have help from at least one younger and stronger man, help in subduing and restraining the girls and help with things like killing the dog. I hope to identify and arrest that accomplice. Unfortunately, Nakritin is dead now."

"Even more unfortunately, he couldn't have done it," sighed Heather. She looked at him sadly. "Sorry to dash your hopes, Holmes, but I'm afraid he's got an alibi."

"Eh?" asked Matt.

"Today I was thinking about things I could do to help, and I got so itchy to get stuck into all this I took the afternoon off. Told Gail I had a parent-teacher conference at the high school," Heather explained. She produced a big stack of microfilm prints. "I went to the public library and I photocopied every complete issue of what was then the Chapel Hill *Weekly* for the entire months of October and November, 1970, and after that every reference I could find to the murder case up until June of 1971." *I also asked for certain back issues of Time and People,* she reminded herself. "I spotted something. It was in the *Weekly* for Sunday, October 25th. Most of the issue was taken up with lurid accounts of the killings here in this house, but I caught a little item I knew you'd be interested in, so I marked it." She took out a page she had flagged with a yellow sticky note, and pointed to a small article from an inside page:

UNC NOBEL WINNER NOW PRIZE PANELIST (AP) Dr. Vladimir Nakritin, internationally acclaimed Russian novelist and winner of the 1954 Nobel and 1960 Pulitzer prizes for literature, arrived in Stockholm Friday in order to begin work with the 1971 nominating and selection committees for the prestigious Nobel awards....

"Nakritin was in Sweden, with crowds of reporters and witnesses all around him," said Heather. "He couldn't have done it. Sorry, Holmes."

"Damn!" muttered Matt. *"Damn!"* He sipped his coffee and scowled, then relaxed and smiled at her. "Good work, Watson. Thanks. That's saved me a hell of a long time chasing a dead end. Now this diary you found?"

Heather got up and took down a small cardboard carton. "I wish I could tell you that a ghostly hand pointed this out to us as we searched the attic," she said. "It would have been so much more dramatic."

"I've had enough of that kind of drama," said Tori darkly.

"I know, so maybe it's a good thing we just simply found this box," said Heather. "It was tucked back in a crawl space between some floor joists and so covered with dust I had to take it out back, clean it with a whisk broom and then a washcloth before I even attempted to open it." She did so now, and Matt looked in. "Just papers, as you can see. Old phone bills, old pay stubs, some junk mail, nothing special at all. It's all addressed to either Dr. Margaret Mears or Dr. Andrew Mears at this address. The dates run from late 1969 until February of 1971, which is when they moved out of the house."

"How do you know that?" asked Matt.

"There's a final disconnect phone bill and one from Duke Power as well with cut-off on February 10th," she said.

"Very good. I tell you, you're wasted in accountancy," laughed Matt. "After this you and me need to quit our jobs and form our own private detective agency."

"Like Cybill Shepherd and Bruce Willis in Moonlighting!" said Tori excitedly. "I can be your secretary!"

Heather drew the diary out from between the papers, bound in blue leather and locked with a small padlock. The leather strap had been cut. "I read most of it, but I put it back in the papers where I found it so you could see two things. This was found in papers dated after Mary Jane's death, and someone, not me, who didn't have the key has cut their way in so they could read it. You can see by the discoloration that the cut is old."

"You're saying that one or both of Mary Jane's parents has read the diary," said Matt. "I agree with your conclusion."

"If I can conjecture a bit further, I would speculate that only one parent, Dr. Margaret Mears, read the diary. She then concealed it in a place where her husband would probably not look, in the middle of a stack of innocuous junk mail and routine bills, like Edgar Allan Poe's purloined letter. Why she left it here I don't know. She might have simply forgotten it."

"Why not Andrew Mears?" asked Matt.

"First off, there are things in here he didn't tell you. Either he's lying or he didn't know them. You tell me you think he can be believed. But mostly I base my case against Meg Mears on the fact that the bulk of the utility bills and important mail is addressed to Dr. Margaret Mears. She must have handled all the household finances and had charge of all this stuff."

"You really are good, you know," said Matt quietly. "You can get night courses for a two-year degree in Criminal Justice at several local technical colleges. It's something you might want to consider if you're really bored with number crunching."

"Thanks," she said. "Tori, go upstairs for a bit, please."

"Mom! Just what is it in there you think is going to corrupt my mind or whatever?" demanded Tori in frustration.

"Please do as I say, Victoria, and don't try to sneak down and listen."

"I'm not a little kid anymore, dammit!" cried Tori angrily. Matt raised his hand in a gentle gesture, simultaneously conveying to Tori that he wanted her to obey her mother and implicitly promising that he would tell her at least part of whatever the secret was later. She cast a furious look at her mother and stomped upstairs.

"Thanks," said Heather. "That might have gone on all night. Matt, mostly I wanted her elsewhere because reading this is going to be a private and very emotional experience for you. I know it was for me. She was a sweet girl, Matt, and she would have grown into a lovely wonderful young woman. For her to die the way she did now pains me more than ever."

"I appreciate your consideration," said Matt sincerely.

"You are going to find out something about Mary Jane which may shock you, but I want to say before I show it to you that she loved you, Matt. She told her diary so."

"She told me so herself, the night she died," said Matt. "But yes, it will be wonderful for me to see it in writing."

"I want to show you two passages, one after the other. I've marked them with yellow post-it notes," said Heather. "This is the first one, from July of 1970. Read it, and then the last entry. She wrote it after she came home from school on October 23rd, 1970, the day she died." Matt took up the book and reverently opened the pages.

July 8th—Well, we finally did it! After months of just fooling around Jeannie and I went all the way, or as close to all the way as two girls can go. We were swimming and came back in the afternoon, Mom and Dad both were in class. We listened to records, and then Jeannie asked if I wanted to mess around and I said yes, so we took off our bathing suit tops and kissed for a while, then Jeannie said "Look, this is stupid, we've got all after-noon and a perfectly good bed upstairs, let's do this right for once," so we did. We went upstairs and took off our bottoms as well and got into bed and made love. Jeannie went down on me and it was FANTASTIC so I went down on her and she said it was good too, although I'm nowhere near as experienced as she is. She says she's sucked guys off before and I believe her. I guess I'm a dyke now. I still like Matt Redmond, though.

"Before you go on, I need to know what your reaction is," said Heather quietly. Matt understood there was a deeper reason for the question. *So she's done some carpet-munching herself in her time, eh?* he thought.

"Just as if I'd found out Mary Jane was having sex with a boy at the school," he told her. "Oh, hey, I'm damned surprised and make no mistake, surprised at Jeannie too. But do I love Mary Jane any the less and do I now consider the girls to be depraved perverts who should have been burned at the stake? No. Why? Did you think I would react that way?"

"I...kind of wondered," admitted Heather. "You seemed a little bit too fond of that Confederate flag the other night."

"I am," said Matt. "My ancestors killed American men, shed their own life's blood, starved and froze and died of disease and went charging into the very mouths of the Union artillery for that flag and for what they viewed as their sovereign Southern nation. You need to know that about me, Heather. Do I hate gays? No. Do I hate gays who molest children and who commit terrible sex crimes on occasion? Yes. Do I hate evil? Yes. What I see here isn't evil," he said, gesturing at the diary. "I think she described it correctly as fooling around. If Mary Jane had lived and this had gone on, would I have been angry and jealous? Probably, because I wanted her for myself and I couldn't have shared her sexually with anyone, man or woman. That's about all I can tell you. I hope it's good enough."

"More than good enough," said Heather with a smile. "Look, I'm sorry if I seem to be, oh, testing you..."

"I understand perfectly. You want to know if you can trust me to throw you down on the bed and fuck your eyeballs out without beating the crap out of you afterwards or going after Tori. Yes, you can, but by all means, take your time looking the vehicle over before taking it for a test drive."

"My, my, aren't we sure of ourselves?" laughed Heather.

"Yes, ma'am. Quite sure." He turned back to the diary, to the last page, his hands trembling slightly as he saw the date. She had written this a couple of hours after she had given him the note she'd written in study hall. There was a brown stain on the edge of the paper. *Surely not blood?* he wondered, but then he realized it was probably Coke or some kind of food she had been snacking on while she wrote, possibly lying on her bed on the quilt, and in a way the thought was even more depressing and painful.

October 23rd—I'm sure of it now. I'm sure Matt loves me, and I know I LOVE MATT YES YES YES! (There followed a drawing of a heart.) *I told Jeannie today after school that we couldn't be lesbians any more because I love Matt and it would be like me cheating on him just as much as if it was with a guy. I know Jeannie is my true friend because she says she is real happy for me and she hopes it works out, and I believe her. She gave me a kiss and a hug, not a dyke kiss any more but a friend kiss. I asked her if she had any more girls she was sleeping with and she really laughed her head off and she said not girls, no, so I guess she's back to guys and I was just a fling kind of, which doesn't bother me because I have to say I really liked it but I know it will be much better and true lovemaking with Matt. In study hall he asked me to wear my flowered maxi tonight. I gave him a note. Hope he tore it up. It was kind of silly. Mrs. Mary Jane Redmond. Dr. M.J. Redmond, Veterinary Practice. Does Matt like cats, I wonder?*

The diary ended. ·

"I'm very much a cat person, yes," he replied, answering her question after a quarter of a century. He put the book down. "Heather, thank you for finding this. It will have to be returned either to Dr. Mears or Meg Mears, but reading these words is enough. Is there anything you saw that might lead us to Mary Jane and Jeannie's killers?"

"No, but do you see where this sex thing is leading us?" asked Heather pointedly. "Did you catch the significance of Jeannie Arnold's flippant reply, when Mary Jane asked her if she had any other lesbian lovers?"

"And she answered no *girls*, and to quote Mary Jane, then she laughed her head off," said Matt. "Yes, I catch the drift. We know from Andrew Mears, whom I believe to be telling the truth, that Margaret Mears either discovered or altered her sexual orientation from heterosexual to lesbian sometime in 1970. I won't get into which since the question of whether lesbians are born or made, and in fact this whole lesbian angle with reference to a powerful woman like Margaret Mears has present-day political implications which I desperately want to avoid fouling up this inquiry, if I can help it. Dr. Mears mentioned in passing that Jeannie would sometimes come over here just to visit with Meg Mears when Andy and Mary Jane were out, ostensibly to help her with her anti-war paperwork. I think we need to add Margaret Mears to the long list of people who were having sex with Jeannie, at least hypothetically, and if that ain't a can of worms I don't know what is."

"There's also Meg Mears' lesbian lover from the anti-war movement, ostensibly the cause of her divorce," said Heather. "That can't have been Jeannie. You say Mears described this woman as a co-worker."

"I'm sure if Andy Mears had known about Jeannie and Meg, if there ever *was* a Jeannie and Meg, which let us not forget we still don't know for certain, then he would have told us," said Matt. "I can see why it didn't come up in the original investigation. Lesbianism was still considered a perversion in those days, at least in North Carolina. If Meg was getting it on with Jeannie then she was committing not only statutory rape but crime against nature, both serious criminal offenses back then. If she'd been found out it would have ruined her career. Dammit, if it was just Jeannie I could see Meg being the killer, but her own daughter as well? That doesn't make sense, and in any case Meg couldn't have done it. Her alibi is just as nailed down solid as Nakritin's. She was in Washington surrounded by people! Damn, this case is going to drive me nuts!"

"Matt," said Heather quietly. "She did it."

"Eh?" asked Matt. "How do you figure?"

"She did it, " sighed Heather, her eyes moisting. "Damn it, she did it, or at least she knows who did it and protected them! The evil *bitch!* Women all over the country have looked up to her for years! *I* looked up to her!"

"Tell me," said Matt gently.

"King Backgammon. It just hit me. I know what Dr. Mears was shouting at his wife." Heather sniffled and blew her nose with a napkin. "Nurse Rendell didn't hear it right. She probably doesn't have much in the way of a classical education, so she didn't understand. In the library today I also looked up Iphegenia, trying to figure out that weirdness on the computer last night. All of a sudden it makes horrible sense. Mears wasn't saying backgammon, he was telling his wife she was not King *Agamemnon.*"

"Oh, my God!" whispered Matt, stunned and horrified. "Of course! I remember now. The Trojan War! Agamemnon, King of Mycenae, who led the Greek armies against Troy! The original story is in the *Iliad,* if I remember right, but some years ago I read a great two-volume historical novel by George Shipway, a fictional biography of Agamemnon. It's all there!"

"Do you remember the story of Iphegenia? Actually, now I think of it I once heard a feminist lecturer ranting and raving about it in college as an example of how you horrible white males have been persecuting women since time immemorial."

"The Greek invading fleet were becalmed in harbor, waiting for weeks for a wind to send them on their way to attack Troy," recalled Matt. "They made sacrifice to all the gods, but to no avail. Finally King Agamemnon consulted an oracle, who told him that the Greeks were being kept in the harbor by Ouranos, the dark god of the Underworld, who could only be appeased by the most special and magically significant of sacrifices. A virgin maiden. Agamemnon's ambition, his hatred of the Trojans, and his longing for personal glory was so great that he determined to make the ultimate gesture."

"He sacrificed Iphegenia. His own daughter," concluded Heather sadly. "That's it, Matt. It has to be. It was the spirit of Mary Jane Mears in the computer last night, telling us that her mother was involved in her death."

"Tori told me she thinks the dead can only speak in obscure riddles, ironically like the ancient Greek oracles," said Matt, shivering uneasily. "I made an offhand comment to that effect when I spoke with her last night. I wonder if that's where Mary Jane or...or someone or something listening to us got the Iphegenia idea."

"That has to be what Dr. Mears was talking about, the way a scholarly man would accuse a woman who had sacrificed her own daughter for her ambition and so she could destroy her enemies. But *why,* Matt? What terrible god were those two poor girls sacrificed to, and what kind of mother could do such a thing?"

Matt took her hand and kissed it gently. "Such a mother as you would never be in a million years. I don't meet many good people in my line of work, Heather. You seem to be one of the exceptions. Thank you for feeling some part of my own pain and that of my beloved dead. I'd like to take this home now and read it from beginning to end. I'll return it, and you have my word I won't copy anything unless I believe it contains evidence of a crime. Then I think Tori deserves to read it, but not unless you say so."

Heather sighed. "I guess you're right. I remember how outraged I was when my own mother wouldn't let me go see some dirty movie or other and how it pissed me off when she told me some day I'd have children of my own I'd be frantic to protect against all the bad in the world."

"Is this bad?" asked Matt. "Is there anything in here she hasn't been taught in sex education class? You didn't object to her being taught about lesbianism in school, did you?"

"No, but that's school. The diary is..." Heather wound down.

"Real? In other words what's all right as a public policy for other people's children is not all right when one's own kids are concerned?"

"I know it sounds hypocritical," admitted Heather. "Hell, it *is* hypocritical." She was silent for a bit. "In more ways than one," she finally added, not looking at him.

"So I gathered." She glanced up at him sharply. "I'm a detective, remember?"

"Well?" she asked with a sigh.

"None of my business who you slept with before you met me. Do you want Tori to read the diary or not?"

"Do you think Mary Jane would have minded?" asked Heather.

"I think she and Tori would have gotten along great." He stood up. "Sleep on it and I'll ask you tomorrow." He leaned over and kissed her on the cheek. "Good night, Watson. Thanks."

   *   *   *

Matt spent the whole night reading the diary, finally laying it aside around dawn when he eased his physically and emotionally exhausted body into bed. He had to will himself to sleep, rather than wallow in his agony of loss. *She might have been my wife,* was the one thought that kept hammering into his brain. *Who took this beautiful person from my life? Why is she not here in this bed with me? Why will I never see her children and mine, never come home and hear how her day went and tell her of mine, never go shopping with her at K-Mart, never give her gifts under the Christmas tree? Who took her away from me? Why?* In his hand he had held the story of the last two years of Mary Jane Mears' life, schoolwork and swimming and animals and holidays, passing references to old Chapel Hill High School events and gossip that Matt had not thought of in years, all mixed in with the story of the growing polarization over Vietnam, her mother's gradual complete absorption in increasingly left-wing politics, and life at the center of the war resistance movement.

But Mary Jane's personality always came through. On November 15th, 1969, her parents had taken her with them to the Moratorium demonstration in Washington, the biggest anti-war gathering in the history of the movement and up until that time the largest political demonstration in the history of America. Mary Jane's diary devoted three pages to the event, wherein she revealed her disgust at being dragged out of bed at three A.M. to make the chartered bus, then the incongruous breakfast of chili dogs the travelling demonstrators had consumed at a rest stop on

I-95 outside Fredericksburg. There was a long conversation about nothing in particular she had with an elderly black man who was on her bus and who seemed to be along more or less for the ride, and finally an animated description of the horses ridden by mounted U. S. Park Police during the demonstration behind the White House on the Ellipse. This closed with *"slept on the bus from Richmond to Chapel Hill. The Student Union was open at two in the morning special for us when we got home, and we had cocoa and donuts."* Not a single political comment or opinion throughout the entire entry.

Then there were occasional poignant lines that almost broke his heart. His own first mention, first day of school, September 1968: *"There was this cute guy in homeroom this morning. Teresa says his name is Matt."* Matt tried to remember when he had first really noticed Mary Jane, and he was ashamed to find he couldn't recall. He tried to bring back a picture of his first tenth-grade homeroom in 1968 and simply couldn't. The memory was gone. Evidently he hadn't been all that irresistably cute to Mary Jane, either; there was nothing more about him until February of 1970 when she complained about Craig Roberts having "happy hands" in a movie and his clumsy attempts to make out. *"Matt Redmond in chemistry, now he's what I call kissable!"* came the comment out of the blue.

Oh, yes, Matt remembered chemistry class. So did she. One day soon after that entry Mary Jane had been careless while picking up a stock bottle of strong hydrochloric acid. She banged the bottle against a gas jet and broke it, splattering acid all over her cotton skirt and blouse and eating great holes in the garments. Fortunately she had been wearing plastic safety goggles which protected her eyes. The chemistry teacher immediately shoved Mary Jane into the emergency shower and washed her free of the acid, but she had emerged soaking wet and her skirt and blouse had large ragged holes burned in them, her bra and underwear showing through. The other kids had chortled and the guys had whistled and made suggestive comments; Matt had quietly taken the teacher's lab coat from a hook in the back of the room and wrapped it around her. He remembered her grateful look. *"Everybody was laughing at me, yelling at me to take it off, take it all off,"* she wrote. *"I felt like I really was naked in front of them all. I was a dumb klutz breaking the bottle, I wanted to die I was so ashamed. Matt didn't laugh; he covered me."*

From then on Matt read almost a daily log of his activities at Chapel Hill High, things he hadn't remembered in years. Classes and reports, sporting events and drama productions, Matt's brief term on the student council (a job nobody else in his homeroom wanted), student car washes to raise money for band uniforms, the local SDS hoodlums putting silver polish in the oil of his Corvair, catty jealousy when Matt was seen talking to Ellen Donnelly in the corridors, the famous incident where Matt and some of the other country boys pelted a Kent State protest demonstration on the high school campus with rocks and full half-pint cardboard cartons of milk. (Matt had to admit Daddy stood up for him on that one and prevented his expulsion. Randall Redmond's sons were *his* property, and nobody else messed with his property.)

One entry gave Matt a genuine laugh. *"Jeannie says she saw Matt out in the back quad smoking a cigar!"* wrote Mary Jane indignantly. *"Ick! Gross! He'd better never try kissing me with cigar on his breath!"* Matt remembered when he had first started indulging in his odoriferous vice, with Tiparillos. It was admittedly a ridiculous affectation for a 17 year-old and his father had pointed this out, loudly and often, but he'd kept it up precisely because it was a way of getting at Daddy. His grandfather smoked cigars. After that last line Mary Jane had written later, in red ink,

"Oh, who am I kidding? He's never going to try to kiss me at all, and if he ever did he could smoke a whole box of cigars before-hand and I'd still just melt in his arms! Oooh, the thought of it gets me wet! Good grief, what do I have to do to get this guy's attention? Hang out a sign saying 'Take me, I'm yours?' Dance on a table in the lunchroom with a rose in my teeth?"

God, Mary Jane, do you have any idea how scared I was to approach you? thought Matt. *I held you in awe. For months I hardly dared speak to you. It never occurred to me you might like me, too.*

The "fooling around" with Jeannie Arnold had begun in May of '70, kissing and caressing initiated by Jeannie. The two girls had been best friends since they were toddlers, and the idea that she and Jeannie could do anything wrong together was conspicuous by its absence throughout the entire episode. After the first full-fledged lesbian sex in July the girls had "gone all the way" again five more times between then and late October. It was purely recreational; neither was a true lesbian. Mary Jane mentioned that Jeannie had regaled her with graphic descriptions of sex she was having with Mike Malinsky and Ronnie Riggsbee, and Mary Jane herself continued to pepper her entries with salacious yearnings for Matt. Finally, on Friday, October 16th, *"ALL RIIIIIGHT! MATT ASKED ME TO THE HARVEST BALL! YAAAAAAY!"*

Matt looked hard for references to Vladimir Nakritin. Mary Jane didn't like the Russian writer, referring to him occasionally as "Dr. Nacreep-in" and "Creepy Cretin", but she recorded no reason for this animus. Nakritin's visits to the Mears home seemed to be mostly dinner invitations and entirely decorous. There was no suggestion in any of Mary Jane's passing references that Nakritin had made any sexual advances to her, or to Jeannie Arnold, or for that matter to her mother. The friendship seemed entirely political; Matt noted with amusement that on October 21st Mary Jane had written, *"Vladimoron Nacretinous came to dinner again tonight. I went to campus with Dad and helped him polish and label some Eskimo skulls and whalebone fishooks and other neat stuff, while Vladimucous stayed here with Mom talking all their Bolshevik bullshit."* Matt chuckled. He had no use for the politics of either Nakritin or Meg Mears, but a man who had spent two lengthy terms in the GULAG and who had been publicly denounced by Stalin as a traitor and and a capitalist lackey could hardly be called a Bolshevik.

Still, she definitely didn't like him, thought Matt as he fell asleep. *Why not, I wonder? Andy Mears said she was a good judge of character. I remember the guy was a boring old fart with an incomprehensible accent but that's all that struck me about him. Damn, I hope Andy Mears recovers enough to speak!*

Matt awoke about three o'clock in the afternoon, dragged himself out of bed, put coffee on, and climbed into the shower. He poured himself a full pint of thick black coffee with chicory into his favorite giant mug, then sat down to think. The fact was that he was running out of leads. The next obvious step was to contact Meg Mears and arrange an interview with her, which would involve flying up to Washington. But he was impressed with Heather's womanly intuition that Margaret Mears was involved, and the "King Backgammon" business had sent a chill through his blood. The parallel with the mythological story of Iphegenia was downright creepy. If it was true, then letting a woman with Meg Mears' current political power know he suspected her was an extremely imprudent course of action. She could well be alerted already; Matt had no way of knowing what Andrew Mears had told her about his investigation during the phone call which had evidently brought on his seizure, and Iphegenia had said "they" knew about him.

Matt could try to track down Ronnie Riggsbee, but it didn't seem that if even located, Riggsbee could contribute anything new. Hell, the guy was probably selling insurance now. That wasn't the direction that Andrew Mears had pointed him in; the name on the slip of paper had been that of Vladimir Nakritin, dead since 1985. Matt picked up the phone and called Will W. Williams. "Hey, Lieutenant, Matt Redmond here," he said when the retired detective answered. "Glad I caught you before you headed out the door for Big Blue. A quick question, if you don't mind."

"I always got time for this case, Two Gun. Shoot. Get it? Two Gun, shoot?"

"Uh, don't quit your day job, Lieutenant," said Matt. "The next Eddie Murphy you ain't. Look, during the Mears-Arnold investigation, did the name of Vladimir Nakritin pop up at all, anywhere, in any connection? You know, the Russian novelist, used to be a real big-knob faculty member over on campus?"

"Uh, no, not at all," said Williams. "He was a friend of the Mears family and he flew in from Europe to attend the girl's funeral, I remember that. Hell, Matt, he couldn't have done it. The guy was in his seventies at the time, for fuck's sake!"

"Yeah, I know, Will, but the thing is this." Matt sketched his conversation with Dr. Mears, the subsequent "King Backgammon" allegation, and finally Nakritin's name in the envelope. "I've also come up with Mary Jane's diary, and while there's no hint of the killer's identity in there she mentions Vladimir Nakritin with obvious dislike. Apparently he was a frequent visitor at the Mears home."

"Her diary?" asked Williams incredulously. "Shit, Sherlock, you already doing better twenty-six years on than any of us did at the time. What's your secret?"

"I have discovered a very capable Watson. Any thoughts on Nakritin?"

"Well, no. I remember the old guy. Real eccentric egghead type, he'd buy an ice cream cone and then get interested in something and put the cone in his pocket, stupid mess like that. He's been dead a good ten years now. Only time I ever remember him having any contact with the law was as a victim, sometime about '70 or '71. Some brothers from Durham mugged him on Franklin Street one night and snatched his briefcase. A patrolman gave chase and caught the one with the case, and man, that was one pissed-off nigger when they opened it up. That score would have been the high point in his larceny career. The old Russian dude was walking around with a hundred grand in cash! Said he was looking for a new house and he wanted to be able to go ahead and buy it when he found one he liked, like you or me would go shopping for a couple of shirts or a new golf club."

"Incredible," said Matt, shaking his head. "Uh, Will, a hundred grand—-I don't suppose it could have been a drug buy?"

"I very much doubt it, Matt," chuckled Williams. "An elderly European academic? Hardly fits the profile of a big player, and like I said, this was early 70s. Even today we don't do that much weight in Chapel Hill. It all comes over from Durham, but in small quantities directly to the users. So far as I know Chapel Hill PD never heard of any dope dealing on that level at all. UNC is a market, not a marketplace."

"Yeah, I suppose you're right," sighed Matt. "Old DEA man's instincts. Any time I come across a lot of green I smell drugs."

"Uh, Matt, I don't think Nakritin's your man. You know why not?" asked Williams.

"I figure you're going to tell me why not," said Matt.

"I quote from the annals of your illustrious English predecessor. It was the interesting matter of the dog in the night. You remember the quote?"

"Uh, yeah, from *Silver Blaze,* I think. The punchline is the dog didn't bark in the night, because he knew the criminal."

"Exactly. You say Nakritin was a familiar visitor to the house? *Then why did they kill the dog?* If it was somebody the dog knew there would have presumably been no problem, it could have been locked up. But the dog must have started barking or tried to bite one of the killers when they entered the house, necessitating that the animal be immediately silenced. So one of them grabs the snarling, snapping dog and breaks its neck with his bare hands. Kind of a difficult trick for a man in his seventies, I should think. We're talking a big, strong, mean motherfucker here. I can't think of anybody involved in the case who fits that description except Riggsbee, maybe, but he's clear. I sure can't see Paul Lieberman killing an animal with his hands. You dig what I'm saying?"

"Yeah, I'm afraid I do," sighed Matt. "Meaning that the killers were strangers in the house. Back to those old standard burglars again. Shit. Well, it's nice to know I've got a backup Watson when I need one." The black man chuckled on the phone.

"What's your next step?" Williams asked. "Better be careful about rattling Meg Mears' cage, man. She was on TV last night, out on the election stump with Hillary herself. Ain't nobody going to appreciate you digging up her old bones with Billyboy fourteen points ahead in the polls. They'll say you're in the pay of the Republicans."

"I know," said Matt morosely.

"So what you gonna do now?" asked Williams.

"Well, I may have located an eyewitness to the murders. I'm going to see if she'll talk to me tonight," said Matt.

"*What?*" roared Williams, stunned. "Man, what the fuck are you talking about? *Eyewitness?* Who? Who the hell..?"

"I'm going to hold a seance and see if I can get the killer's name from Mary Jane's ghost," said Matt calmly. There was a long silence.

"Hmm," said Williams. "Now, do I really want to know whether or not you're serious?"

"No," said Matt. "Look, I'm holding you up. You need to be off earning your crust, protecting the IBM yuppies from the forces of evil. Thanks a lot, Will."

"Wait." The black man was silent for a while. "You *are* serious, aren't you?"

"Yes."

More silence. "I want to be there," Williams said flatly.

"I thought you had to work tonight?"

"I'll call in sick," said Williams. "Look, man, you ain't jivin' me or anything, are you?"

"No. No jive. Look, Will, I have to tell you there are some pretty bizarre angles developing in all this. Are you sure you want to get involved?"

"I have been involved ever since I saw the murdered bodies of those two girls in that house one Saturday morning twenty-six years ago," said Williams, his voice trembling. "I got to know, man. I got to *know.* There's one thing in this world I'm afraid of, and that's the possibility that I will never, ever *know.*"

"You and me both," said Matt. "I'll call you back in a few minutes." He hung up and called Heather at work and briefly explained the situation. "Do you mind another guest at our private little mad hatter's tea party?" he asked.

"No, no, the more the merrier," said Heather. "Gail's in the can now so I can talk. I asked around as discreetly as I could about Paul Lieberman's sexual harassment practices. A lot of touching, some propositioning, and apparently it's understood that a female employee goes farther in this department the farther she's willing to go, so to speak. But to give him what little credit he's due, it's all very suave. No dirty talk, and nothing even remotely suggestive of violence. Sorry, Holmes, look like that one's a strikeout."

"It fits in with what I remember about him," said Matt. "He's a lecher and a seducer but not a rapist or a killer. See you tonight." He called Williams back. "Go ahead and call off, Will. I'll come around and fill you in. Be prepared to make like Alice and believe six impossible things before breakfast."

*   *   *

That night, having received a quiet wordless nod from Heather, Matt handed the diary to Tori. "Thank you," said Tori, looking at both of them.

"Tori, you haven't read the diary yet but I have," said Matt carefully. "Our, ah, source of the other night said that she would communicate with us again when I had read it. At least I assume the diary is what was meant. This is your call, Heather. It's your home, and I can well imagine what a completely freaky experience all this is for you. I'd like to see if I can get some more information upstairs from Tori's computer, but if you don't want to we don't do it."

"I've grown to have one strong feeling about all of this, Matt," said Heather. "It has to be resolved. I also admit I am now thoroughly hooked on the whole thing. Tori, I'm concerned about you. Is this going to frighten you, upset or damage you in any way?"

"No, I'm OK now, Mom," said Tori. "Mary Jane didn't mean to scare me the other day, she just hasn't been able to get through to anyone before and so she kind of overdoes things."

"I'm sure you think we're all quite mad, Mr. Williams?" asked Heather.

"I've long since come to the conclusion that the whole world is mad, Ms. Lindstrom," said Williams courteously. He was dressed in an impeccable business suit. "With individuals it's simply a matter of degree."

"What a cheerful philosophy!" said Heather.

"Uh, Matt, you remember what I told you about Mary Jane not being able to answer direct questions?" said Tori.

"I remember," said Matt. "Let's hope the metaphysics of the astral plane can have a harmonic convergence with earthly justice." They ascended the stairs and entered Tori's room. Tori took a deep breath and turned on her computer. She clicked the mouse a couple of time to set up the word processing program and get rid of the icons, and a blank blue screen appeared.

"Uh, I think we need to clear our minds here, and think about Mary Jane, invite her to speak to us," said Heather. "Just Mary Jane."

"Yeah," said Tori. "I don't think Jeannie can get out of the basement and she can't tell us anything anyway."

"Christ, that whole idea horrifies me!" muttered Matt. "Tori, you won't be offended if I say I hope unto God you're misinterpreting that situation?"

"I wish I was," said Tori sadly. They were quiet for a while. "Mary Jane," Tori whispered. "Hi. I'm here, my mom's here. Matt's here. Mr. Williams, one of the policemen who tried to help you once, he's here too. Matt wants you to answer some questions. Can you hear me? Do you understand? Are you here?"

The screen flickered strangely with barely perceptible colors. Letters appeared, not in Gothic this time but simple white block type. IM HERE. Williams gasped softly. He looked over at Matt.

"It's not us. I swear," said Matt. "Mary Jane," he continued softly, "I'm not sure how to go about this. You know I want to find the men who took your life, who took Jeannie's life and left you here. That's my first question. Was it two men?"

The computer screen replied YES AND NO.

"Shit!" muttered Matt. "Can you explain to me what you mean by that response?"

NO said the screen.

"Do you know the names of the men who killed you and Jeannie?" asked Matt

YES. Then came NO. "Shit again," said Matt again. "Mary Jane, can you give me straight answers? By that I mean are you allowed to do so by whatever forces now control your existence?"

SOMETIMES IF YOU ASK THE RIGHT QUESTIONS.

"Can you tell me what the right questions are?" asked Matt helplessly.

NO.

"Then how can I ever help you?" asked Matt in despair.

NOT FOR ME came the letters, appearing silently one after the other. FOR YOU AND MANY MANY OTHERS. TRUTH MUST BE TOLD. TRUTH. ONLY TRUTH. TOO MANY LIES TOO LONG. WRONG.

"Mary Jane, I want the truth to be known," said Matt. "So does Heather, so does Tori, so does Lieutenant Williams, so does your father. I'm not sure about your mother. Mary Jane, was your mother involved in your murder? Can you tell me that?"

YES. NO. "Great," muttered Matt. "Was Vladimir Nakritin involved in your murder?"

IN A MANNER OF SPEAKING.

"Thank you for clearing that up, Mary Jane," said Heather. "Sorry, honey, I didn't mean to be sarcastic."

"Matt, she *can't*," said Tori urgently. "I can't explain, but she can't tell you what you want to know, she can't just hand it to you on a platter. It's, oh, how can I put it, against the law where she is. If the dead interfere in human events it causes all kinds of problems!"

YES! said the computer.

"All right," said Matt. "Let's go at this another way. Mary Jane, I just want you to tell me, in whatever words you can, anything at all you can communicate to us regarding the men who killed you and Jeannie."

The screen responded in large letters, a good 60-point type, with the word KOMAP. "Huh? What the hell is a komap?" wondered Heather.

"I don't understand, Mary Jane," said Matt. "Again, please."

KOMAP.

"I have no idea what you mean," said Matt, in frustration. "Can you tell me anything else?"

CMEPT. "Oh, Matt, she's not making any sense at all!" said Tori. The screen started spewing letters, scrolling up page after page, endlessly. CMEPT. KOMAP. CMEPT. KOMAP. CMEPT. KOMAP.

"*Holy shit!*" breathed Matt, recognition suddenly dawning.

"What?" asked Heather.

"It's *Russian!*" exclaimed Matt. "The English equivalent of the Cyrillic alphabet! She's speaking Russian, of all the..."

The screen stopped scrolling. YAAAAAAY! appeared in large letters. Fireworks burst in the background. "My God, how does she do that?" whispered Will Williams in awe.

"What do the words mean?" demanded Heather.

"*Smiert* means death," said Matt grimly. "The C is pronounced S and the P is pronounced R. KOMAP would be *kamar*, and what the hell does that mean? Damn, it's been years since I had my Russian classes! I was getting reasonably good at it when I left Justice, got so I could pick up a lot of what was on wiretap and surveillance tapes, but I can't remember that word. *Kamar.* Seems to me it means bug or insect or something...mosquito! That's right! *Kamar* means mosquito!"

The screen exploded into YES YES YES YES! with more fireworks, pinwheels and starbursts and flowers flying about. Then came MATT THATS ALL I CAN GIVE YOU BE CAREFUL THEY KNOW ABOUT YOU GOODBYE I WILL LOVE YOU FOREVER. The screen went blank and the computer turned itself with a loud snap. No one had touched the power button. Matt closed his eyes, his heart breaking within him. "I'll love you forever too, Mary Jane," he whispered.

"The two girls were killed by a Russian mosquito," said Heather in stunned disbelief. "Now why didn't I think of that?"

"Maybe they were killed by Russian spies?" suggested Tori excitedly.

"That runs up against the same problem we've always had," said Matt. "What was the blasted, ever-lovin', carnsarned *motive?* Somehow I can't see the Kremlin dispatching a team of KGB assassins to America to kill two teenaged girls in a small Southern college town. Their mother was active in undermining the American war effort in Vietnam, hardly the type of activity Moscow would want to discourage, and so was Vladimir Nakritin, despite his former anti-Stalin activities."

"Matt, if it was Russians, could Vladimir Nakritin have been the real target?" asked Williams speculatively.

"You seem to be taking all this in stride, Will," commented Matt. "Can we assume from your remark you accept this phenomenon as genuine?"

"Until someone can show me a motive for you people making up a fraud so utterly bizarre, yes," replied Williams calmly. "Matt, I'm sure your various instructors in police science taught you the same thing mine did. The simplest explanation is usually the correct one. I cannot think of any rational explanation for what has

just occurred in this room other than to take it at face value. I
repeat, could not Nakritin have been the target and the girls killed
in some kind of inconceivable corollary bungle?"

"Nakritin was expelled from the Soviet Union in 1950 after
being sentenced to death for engaging in anti-Soviet propaganda
abroad, specifically smuggling an anti-Stalin tract to the West
which was subsequently published," said Heather. "Only direct
appeals to Stalin himself and threats of all kinds of boycotts and
sanctions saved Nakritin's life. Could the 1970 Soviet government
have decided he was a loose end that needed tying up?"

"I don't recall he actually did much anti-Soviet propagandizing
once he was out," replied Matt. "Mostly he wrote novels which
were half incomprehensible philosophical screeds and half pubes-
cent female flesh with bouncing young boobies, as you put it.
Hardly the kind of thing to bring down a death sentence twenty
years later from Brezhnev, who was a pretty mellow dude compared to Uncle Joe."

"Maybe Nakritin left some bad blood behind in Russia?" suggested Williams. "Something that took a while to catch up with
him? Or maybe he did something later on that we don't know
about but which pissed off the Russkies big-time?"

"That's entirely possible, Will. But if so, though, why come to
Chapel Hill to kill him, when they could have gotten him far more
easily in Stockholm or Paris? On the very day the girls were killed
here in America, Vladimir Nakritin was within half an hour's flying time of Soviet territory. And if the Russians wanted him dead
but got their wires crossed and came here instead of Stockholm,
why come to this house? Why would they expect to find Vladimir
Nakritin here at midnight? Why kill two young girls, torturing
one of them hideously, a girl who so far as we can tell had only the
most distant if any acquaintance with Nakritin?"

"I don't know," said Heather. "Put that way, it does sound pretty far-fetched and ridiculous. But why did Andrew Mears write Vladimir Nakritin's name in that note to you? Why the Russian words on the computer screen tonight?"

"Why indeed," ruminated Matt. "*Pachemyu ana gavarit pa-Russki? Kak raskaz zdyes?* What the hell is the story here?"

*   *   *

A heavy, gray-haired man in an olive-green uniform stood staring out over the broad cobbled square in the cold, crisp morning sunlight. Pigeons roosted on the statue of Feliks Dzerzhinsky, first founder of the Cheka, a mass murderer with ice in his veins whose very name was still so feared seventy years after his death that the pro-democracy mobs had not yet dared to touch his graven image. There was a knock on his door. "*Vkaditye!* Come!" he barked. A small, dapper man in a dark fur-lined overcoat and fur hat entered the room. He was an indeterminate fortyish and wore a neatly-trimmed black goatee beard speckled with gray.

"You sent for me, Citizen Colonel?" asked the little man. "Er, we are still Citizens now, aren't we? Or are we Comrades this week?"

"I think so," said the colonel, "Although we may be Comrades again soon. There's supposed to be a memo coming down, but it hasn't reached here yet. When you are through here go home, Citizen Major. Pack a bag. Be back here at noon and collect your diplomatic passport and airline tickets. You are going to America, to the province of North Carolina, which if I recall my geography correctly is in the South despite its name. I know there is also a South Carolina."

"Possibly that province is in the north?" suggested the little man.

"I've no idea. When you come back I want you to bring me as many razor blades as you can get into the country."

"Thank you, Citizen Colonel. I will be sure to do so. I assume I am not going to America solely for the purpose of procuring razor blades?"

"You are not," said the colonel. "One of our skeletons has come rattling out of the closet and threatens to cause a most embarrassing scene, dancing around the parlor in front of guests. A very old skeleton, from back in the days when you and I were Comrades rather than Citizens. You are to re-inter it, and make sure the earth over the grave is immaculately smoothed over."

"Does this skeleton have a name, Citizen Colonel?" asked the major politely.

"Vladimir Nakritin," said the colonel, pronouncing the famous writer's name as if it were an obscenity. He turned and went back to his desk. "Sit down, Rozanov. Late last night Moscow time, yesterday afternoon Washington time, our embassy there received a contact from a source we had long believed to be de-commissioned and extinct. The authentication codes used were so old the intelligence officer didn't recognize them and thought he was dealing with a crank, but one of the clerks there has made a hobby out of reading over old case files. He will probably defect and use the information he has gathered to write a best-selling book and make a million dollars, but that is neither here nor there. This scholarly underling happened to be passing by and recognized the identification codes from an operation that was closed down twenty-six years ago. The story that this suddenly reactivated contact has to tell is extremely disturbing. In 1970 a cock-up of monumental proportions occurred. It was sorted out, but now some provincial gendarme who appears to have an inordinate amount of time on his hands has decided to go digging up the cemetery. You will find the details in there," said the colonel, shoving a top secret file.

"Take that file into my conference room and read it. It will explain what happened in 1970. When you arrive in Washington you will be briefed on the current problem. You will have full discretion as to how to handle this problem, Rozanov. You are to approach this in what the Americans refer to as a proactive manner. Very proactive. It is imperative that this matter does not become public knowledge. You will understand the implications more fully when you have read the file."

"I will do so, Citizen Colonel," said Major Rozanov. "Before I do, may I call my wife? She will want to begin making up a shopping list, and she has promised several of our neighbors that when I go abroad next I will bring back various items for them."

"Certainly. Just don't forget my razor blades." In the distance, beyond the square, there came a low rattle of submachinegun fire and the crump of several explosions, tapering off into a few scattered shots. "Better take the Metro back to your flat rather than the streets," recommended the colonel. "Sounds like they're at it again."

X

For the next few days Matt spun his wheels in unproductive diversions. He haunted the university trying to learn everything he could about Vladimir Nakritin, speaking to faculty and former students who remembered the Russian and grilling them as much as he dared without revealing the true reason for his inquiries. He managed to locate the surviving pathologist who had worked on the case in his retirement retreat in Florida and spoke with him for almost an hour on the phone, but gained nothing in the way of fresh insight. He located Ronnie Riggsbee in Fayetteville, where he was now a newly-retired Army Master Sergeant starting in on his second career as a salesman for a huge, well-known GM car and truck dealer. Riggsbee made it clear to Matt on the phone that he wanted nothing whatsoever to do with any revival of the murder case, unless "you find the son of a bitch who killed Jeannie, in which case give me his address and I will personally track him down and tear him limb from limb," a sentiment Matt shared but which brought him no more forward. Matt decided not to bother driving down to interview Riggsbee personally; he recognized a dead end when he saw one.

With some effort Matt tracked down the few Chapel Hill High School alumni from the class of '71 he could find who had remained in town, which wasn't many. Chapel Hill prided itself on being cosmopolitan, but another word for that was rootless, and amazingly few of Matt's old classmates were still around. He batted the breeze with the few he could locate, hoping to mine any possible lodes of long-hidden knowledge, casual recollection or just plain rumor and gossip he might uncover, but there was nothing he hadn't heard before, other than a disturbing current of speculation which had run through Chapel Hill High that he himself had somehow been involved. "I know it was stupid," one now restaurant owner told him, "But you know, that old man of yours had a kind of weird reputation. Still does, and those of us with younger siblings were already hearing peculiar stories about your brother Sid setting fire to Guy Phillips Junior High, and that incident with the razor blade. You know the old saying about the fruit not falling far from the tree."

I don't recall anything like that directed at me, but I was hurting so bad I probably didn't notice, reflected Matt as he drove home after that visit. *If it's true I suppose it's for the best I didn't have any friends and didn't give a damn what they thought of me*

On a Saturday morning he called Heather and filled her in on such developments as there were. "This is what I was afraid of," he told her. "What we've been able to find is tantalizing, not to mention our cyberspectral evidence regarding the mosquito, whatever the hell that means, but the well has just about run dry. I don't know how to proceed any further other than go up to Washington and rattle Meg Mears' cage, and with her as busy as she is working for Billyboy's reelection I doubt she'd even see me. And what am I supposed to tell her? 'Hey, Meg, I was rapping with Mary Jane's ghost on a computer the other evening and she was laying this line on me in Russian about killer mosquitos. Care to shed some light on that?'"

"Suppose we kick it around over lunch?" suggested Heather.

"Suits me. What time do you want me to pick you up?"

"Oh, I'm at a loose end the whole day. Tori is on a school field trip to colonial Williamsburg. One big advantage of living on the east coast, I suppose. A lot more history around, and she evidently needs some remedial history if she doesn't even recognize a Confederate flag. Tell you what, why don't I come over to your place?"

"Fine, but make it about noon," said Matt. "I want to get the place cleaned up. I'm afraid I have tendencies towards bachelor slobbishness." He told her how to get to his apartment and hung up. *Right, do I try to put the move on her today?* he wondered. *No, better not. It's only been about a week. We've joked about it and all, but Christ, nowadays how can you tell what they really mean? I'm going to need her help and I don't want to mess things up.* But he changed the sheets on the bed and took a shower anyway.

The weather outside had turned Carolina Indian summer warm again, and Heather showed up wearing a low-cut sleeveless blouse, cutoff jeans, and sandals. "Come into my parlor, said the spider to the fly," Matt greeted her, carefully avoiding with his eyes the enticing white expanse above the top of her blouse. She stepped in and looked around.

"It's small," she said.

"The state of North Carolina isn't exactly extravagant when it comes to compensating us indefatigable public servants," said Matt. "Hence the understated decor."

"Do you always decorate your digs with dead cats?" asked Heather, pointing. Trumpeldor was lying on top of the television set on his back, his curled front paws and his hind legs vertically straight up in the air and his long furry tail hanging down the side. He was absolutely motionless, not even a whisker or tail twitching.

"That's Trumpeldor."

"*What?*" laughed Heather.

"Special Agent In Charge Irving Trumpeldor. We seized a drug boat in the Florida straits a few years ago, and the dopers had a pit bull, which I had to shoot. They amused themselves on the voyage by feeding a litter of kittens to the dog. Trump was the last survivor. I took him home for my kids, and I named him after my boss of the time. For some reason Irv always regarded me with suspicion afterwards. I don't *think* he's dead," said Matt. "Let's see." He walked over and scratched the soft furry chest and belly, and immediately a rusty purr emitted from the orange ball, like someone had fired up a chain saw outside.

"That is the loudest purr I've ever heard and the biggest cat I have ever seen," said Heather flatly. Matt stopped scratching and the purring stopped immediately. Heather reached out and scratched, and the purring began again, the cat remaining motionless with eyes closed.

"Want to see him move?" asked Matt. He went into the kitchen and softly opened the refrigerator. Trumpeldor rolled off the television with a fluid motion and hit the floor galloping. Heather followed him into the kitchen. Matt had a block of cheese out and Trumpeldor shrieked at the sight of it, attempting to leap up onto the counter. Matt blocked him with one knee while he cut a thick slice of cheese. "He's a living garbage disposal. He'll eat anything, even vegetables if you put some gravy or pan grease on it. That's why he's so overweight; not only do I feed him too much, he goes the rounds of the other apartments and begs all kinds of goodies from people. But the one thing he loves more than anything is cheese, good sharp cheddar." Trumpeldor was standing on his hind legs, getting ready for another leap, mrowing excitedly. "Watch this." Matt hefted the cheese slice and then threw it gently; Trumpeldor leaped into the air and caught it like a dog catching a Frisbee and ran off into the living room with the cheese in his mouth. Heather laughed. Matt put the cheese back in the fridge. "What did you have in mind for lunch?"

Heather put her purse on a chair, then slid into his arms, took his head in her hands and kissed him long and thoroughly. "That answer your question? Tori won't be home until late," she said. "I'll cook you supper, later."

He returned the kiss, lust welling in him. "You sure?" he asked. "I'd planned on a longer lead-in, the whole flowers, candy, and candlelight dinner scenario."

"Let's get a take on the sex angle first," she said. "If that doesn't work none of the rest of it will, and we'll have found out before we get in too deep." She pulled a pack of condoms from her purse and slapped it into his hand. "First hurdle. I'm not going to get any argument about your using these, am I?" Matt grinned and pulled his Red Cross blood donor card from his wallet.

"Sure, no problem, but just FYI note the date of my last donation," he said, reversing the card. "I was clean as of a month ago. Since I don't engage in the behaviors which transmit HIV you're medically safe. How about emotionally, Heather? Suppose it doesn't work out?"

"A few years ago I would have been a hell of a lot more cautious," she admitted. "But I'm forty-two, and I admit I'm getting scared. I don't want to be dependent on a man, but I don't want to be alone, either, and I'm finally admitting that to myself. This feminist mantra about how women don't need men in their lives is bullshit. Fortunately I'm skinny enough to where I don't have anything to start sagging, but I figure if I'm ever going to have a second go-round I'd better start taking some chances. How about you? Is this just going to be a roll in the hay or could it go somewhere? My offer's still good either way, but I'd like to know where I stand."

"I have no idea, Heather," Matt told her frankly. "After Evie I pretty much made up my mind it just wasn't going to happen for me, and considering who I am and what I do it may well be best for everybody concerned that it doesn't happen. I just can't say. But if I knew for certain it wasn't in the cards, I'd be honest enough to tell you, and I'd do it before we go to bed together."

"Fair enough," she said. She took him by the hand and led him into the bedroom, then turned to face him, unpinning her hair from the band that held it and letting it fall free. He reached behind her back and stroked it, slid it between his fingers.

"I have wanted to touch your hair ever since I first saw you," Matt told her. "It's beautiful." They kissed again. "Now, how does this go again?" he wondered with a sigh.

"Yeah, I know what you mean," said Heather with a giggle. "As best I can recall, we start by taking off our clothes."

Matt snapped his fingers. "Right! That's it! Hey, it's coming back to me now!" He unbuttoned her blouse, slid it off her shoulders, and tossed it aside, then unhooked her bra and did the same. He leaned her backward and teased her small hard breasts with his tongue until she moaned and panted.

"Ah, can we speed this up a bit?" she asked, gasping. Quickly they finished undressing and he laid her on the bed. She ripped open the condom box, tore open a packet, and slid the latex over him. He covered her, and she wrapped her long legs around his waist and guided him into her with her hand. Matt plunged downward again and again, hard and brutal, making her scream with rapture every time, three times, four times, a dozen times, until her body was racked with orgasm after orgasm while he still thrust into her. Finally his own time came and he groaned and collapsed onto her. They were both covered with sweat. She smothered his face with kisses. She finally said, "God, Matt, I suppose I come across as a real slut, but it's been so damned long. I didn't realize how much I missed how *good* it feels!"

"I know exactly where you're coming from, babe," said Matt. "No need to apologize."

"Oh, I see. One screw and I'm a babe now?" she laughed.

"Yep."

"I love it," she said, snuggling against him. She leaned over and took the condoms off the nightstand and tossed them in the trash. "Next time I want it for real. To my own amazement, I trust you. How long before you can reload, Two Gun?"

*   *   *

They coupled twice more that afternoon, the second time a long slow gentle lovemaking, the third time exchanging steamy oral sex as they showered together. About five o'clock Heather dressed herself in one of Matt's shirts and fiddled around in the kitchen with pots and pans looking for something to make supper with, until Matt came out, unbuttoned the shirt and dropped it to the floor, pinned her against the wall kissing her and caressing her for a while and then gently but firmly bent her over the kitchen table and took her from behind, long and slow and sensuously, keeping her aroused and moaning and begging for release for ages until he finally showed mercy and let her explode in another salvo of pleasure. Afterwards they lay in bed again, holding one another. "Now you'll have to shower again," he said, nuzzling her.

"Uh uh," she said sleepily. "I'm going home with your scent on me and your seed inside me. When I'm alone in my bed I want to know it's there." She looked at him. "Matt, I want more of this. It may never go beyond the bedroom with us, but I want as much as I can get."

"I want more too, Watson," he said. "You haven't told me about your ex yet. Feel like that part of the ritual yet?"

"Not much to tell," she said. "High school sweethearts, married early, kids and bills and obligations came along. Bill wasn't a bad guy, I think he was just genuinely unlucky. He could never settle down into eight to five routine, so he kept trying all kinds of commission sales jobs, get-rich-quick promotions, that kind of thing. He never hit his stride. All the investment of time and money and effort never seemed to pay off. I went back to school, got my masters, got my CPA, and I ended up making the money that paid the mortgage and the grocery bills. That humiliated him. He started drinking, he started imagining that I was cheating on him while he was gone, which I wasn't, and he started beating me. The rest is the usual downhill tale, separations, reconciliations, more beating, a couple of arrests, then court orders and injunctions, then finally divorce and a long process of trying to get him to pay his child support. One day he got stinking drunk in a cheap motel room in Orlando and killed himself. He left a note the cops in Florida sent me. He was so drunk when he did it he could hardly write. He apologized to me for being a failure. Not for hitting me, not for stiffing me out of money or making what should have been the best years of my life living hell, but for being a failure." Her eyes were wet and she turned away from him.

"Let it out, honey," he told her gently. "You can cry with me around. God knows, I understand." She turned back to him, put her head on his chest and wept for a while.

"Thank you," she whispered. "Matt, please don't hurt me. I couldn't take it if it happened again. It would kill me."

"No beating, no lying or abuse. You can take that to the bank. Beyond that you're going to have to take your chances." He was silent for a while, then spoke again. "You know, I understand that if Mary Jane Mears and I had gotten married, it might well have ended badly. We might not have gotten married at all, of course. Once we'd indulged in a few clandestine teenage sex encounters the fire might have died down. College for her and the army for me would have matured us and we might have decided to go our separate ways but stay friends. Or if we'd gotten married the marriage might not have survived my job or the general crap involved in life on the great American consumer plantation. I'm sure I could have forgone the beating part, but Mary Jane and I might be divorced by now too."

"Or you might have kept your love alive and still be just as caring and devoted to one another now as you were then," Heather reminded him. "It still does happen, you know. People do fall in love and marry and make homes and raise families and stay with one another until they die. God knows how, but it does still happen. Somewhere. Surely it must happen."

"It does," he laughed, kissing her. "The thing with Mary Jane is, I don't *know* how it would have turned out. I will spend my life wondering what would have happened between us. Some son of a bitch took it upon himself to intrude himself into our world, to take that decision out of our hands. People have no right to do that. Whoever did it has to be punished, if that's still possible. Not just for what he did to Mary Jane and Jeannie, not just for the dead. For me and Andy Mears and the Arnolds and Ron Riggsbee and everybody who survived and was hurt by it."

"The PC term is closure," said Heather.

"The real term is justice," said Matt. The telephone rang. "Let the machine get it," he said. "If it's anybody I want to talk to I'll call them back."

The taped greeting came to an end, and the answering machine hissed and squawked ghostly in the descending twilight of the living room. *"Look outside, motherfucker!"* came a wild male voice, half chortle, half sob. "Look out in the parking lot, murderer, liar, coward, pipsqueak! Don't mess with me, asshole! I'll kill you!" The caller hung up. Matt leaped up out of bed and began pulling on his clothes.

"Who the hell was that?" asked Heather in astonishment.

"Sid!" snapped Matt. "My fucking lunatic brother! Stay inside, Heather. He might be calling from a cellular. I don't know what he's done, but he might still be outside, and if he is there's going to be bad trouble!" Matt got his shoes on and drew his .357 Magnum from the holster, then flung open the door and peered cautiously outside. Heather, attired once again in Matt's shirt, appeared in the living room. "Get back in the bedroom!" commanded Matt sharply. "My father has already arranged for one sniper attack on me. The guy fired through that window there, you can see the bullet hole on the wall behind the chair. This may be an ambush of some kind, trying to lure me out. Get dressed. If you hear shots or any kind of commotion, call 911 and tell them an officer needs assistance at this address! Move!" Heather didn't argue but did as she was told. Matt was impressed.

He couldn't see anyone outside in the gathering darkness, so he slid out of his door and moved into the parking lot carefully, gun at the ready, to check his vehicle. There the reason for Sid's heckling call became apparent. The Taurus was slumped onto the asphalt with four slashed tires. Matt looked around but couldn't see Sid anywhere. "Damn!" muttered Matt, sticking the gun into his belt. *"Damnation!"* he cursed in frustration, and kicked at one of the slashed tires. A couple of college students who had been getting out of their car saw him and started edging away. "It's OK, I'm a cop," he called out to them. "A very pissed off cop. I left my shield inside, but I'm with the SBI. Look, did you guys see anybody out here just now, doing this to my car?"

"Uh, like, no, man," muttered the boy.

"Hey, they really trashed your ride, huh dude?" said the girl. "That sucks."

"It does indeed. When you two get inside, do me a favor, OK? Before you turn on Beavis and Butthead, call the Carrboro PD and ask them to send an officer out here, will you?"

"Uh, like, Beavis and Butthead isn't on until later, dude," said the girl, puzzled.

"Never mind, just call them for me, please?" Heather materialized at his side, fully dressed. "I thought I asked you to stay inside?" said Matt irritably. "Sorry, I'm a bit worked up. See what that shithead brother of mine did?"

"Oh, Matt!" said Heather, shocked.

"I've got the Carrboro PD on the way. They'll take a report but I doubt they'll be able to hang it on Sid."

"You've got his voice on the answering machine," pointed out Heather. "That's evidence."

"The voice of Randall Redmond's pride and joy," said Matt bitterly. "Anywhere in the state of North Carolina that's a certificate of immunity from the law. You think this kind of thing hasn't happened before, Heather? It happens at least once a year. Sometimes Sid hurts people, smaller weaker people, women, people who can't fight back. Never kills them, though. There's a good deal of method in brother Sid's madness. He knows exactly how far he can go. For example, you'll note he slashed my tires, a petty misdemeanor. If he had set fire to the car that would have been arson, a felony. Not so easy for Daddy to get him off on a felony, although it's been done."

"Matt, in God's name, what's it all about?" asked Heather, bewildered. "And how can your father wield that kind of influence? I mean, how rich can you get building houses?"

"Not just building houses," Matt told her. "I haven't told you about my mother, or more importantly my grandfather. The late Zebulon G. Bowman of Greenville, North Carolina."

"Who?" asked Heather, puzzled. "I never heard of him."

"You wouldn't have unless you were an expert on business and high finance in the American South from about 1940 onwards," said Matt, leaning on a car hood while they waited for the police. "Zeb Bowman, my mother's father, had the Midas touch to begin with and he chose an industry that rewards men with the Midas touch. Banking. He started a little savings and loan in Greenville, North Carolina around 1930, at a time when banks were closing their doors all over the country, and he succeeded. The man whupped the Great Depression's ass. He had one daughter who was heir to everything he owned. Gave her everything, Vassar, a debutante ball, you name it. Mama should have been married to a Senator or a captain of industry, but in 1949 she met a penniless, hard-drinking ex-Marine named Randall Redmond who had about fifty cents to his name, an extra Y chromosome in his genetic makeup and an eye to the main chance. Christ, I sound like a damned tabloid TV show. Sorry, I'll shut up."

"Tell me," said Heather. She gestured towards the car. "I need to understand this."

"Fair enough. My grandfather got Daddy's number real quick and did everything he could to try and stop the marriage. I heard one story about how Papa called Daddy into his study for a man-to-man talk and offered him a choice: a ten thousand dollar certified check to leave town or a bullet from a .44 revolver pointed at his head. Daddy tore up the check and then stuck his finger into the barrel of the pistol and told Papa 'If you pull the trigger the gun will explode and blow off both our hands.'"

"Who told you that story?" asked Heather, fascinated.

"Papa," said Matt with at thin smile. "He told me he'd always hated Daddy's guts, but after that day he never underestimated him again. Anyway, Daddy married Mama and spent the next thirty-five years trying to get hold of my grandfather's money. Papa tied it up in a million different ways, trusts and holding companies and corporate shells and you name it. In his will he established three trust funds, one for each of his grandsons. On his death the money, the corporate control and the power was to go in three equal parts to me and Steve and Sid. Daddy would never touch a dime. Papa told me so. But there was a flaw." Matt stopped.

"Please, tell me," said Heather softly.

"My mother was his sole executor," said Matt. "Papa died in 1983. His will had to be probated in 26 states. It took a long time. My mother died before the probate was completed and the trust funds established. Under the terms of *her* will, Daddy got it all." Matt sighed. "In some respects Papa Bowman was a Renaissance man, a buccaneer of business. But he wasn't Renaissance enough. The gun Papa pointed at Daddy that time was a bluff to see if he'd scare. Papa came from the old school where you might ruin your enemies financially, but you didn't destroy them, and neither his experience nor his expectations ever included murder. Papa was wrong. He did underestimate Daddy one last time, underestimated just how much Daddy hates to lose, especially lose a game he'd played for thirty-five years."

"Your father murdered your mother to get your grandfather's money?" whispered Heather in horror.

"Moral certainty is not legal proof, but every instinct in my body as a law officer and as a member of my mad, bad family tells me that is the case," said Matt. "The official story is that one morning in May of 1984 she had a heart attack. She was 56 years old, prime coronary age for a man but not for a woman. She fought a seventeen-year bout with breast cancer, including a mastectomy, and during all that time of close medical supervision and examination not one hint of heart trouble was ever detected by any of her doctors."

"Matt, medical science isn't perfect. That doesn't mean..."

"Her heart attack occurred at approximately eight in the morning," interrupted Matt. "At four o'clock that afternoon my father drove her to the emergency room in Burlington. That's about twenty-five miles as the crow flies from our house. The emergency room at Memorial Hospital in Chapel Hill is less than ten."

"But..." muttered Heather.

"My father and my brother Sid both admitted to being in the house that day. They say they never noticed her lying on the kitchen floor." Matt looked at Heather, his eyes black with despair. "The kitchen floor, Heather. You know what's in the kitchen? The refrigerator. That's where Daddy keeps his National Bohemian beer. What my father told the police was, in effect, that he went from eight o'clock in the morning until mid-afternoon without entering the kitchen and getting a National Bo. That's bullshit. It's not legal evidence, of course, and no one outside the family would ever comprehend the fact, but for Randall Redmond that's as good as a confession to murder. He must have stepped over her on his way to and from the fridge. He must have intimidated or bribed Sid, probably with music somehow. What brought on the heart attack in a woman with no previous coronary history? For a healthy person digitalis will do nicely. Of course, we'll never know now.

"You know how I was informed of my mother's death, Heather? By a registered letter from a lawyer. He made damned sure I never heard a word about it in time, so naturally my not turning up for the funeral is another in my long list of crimes against the family. I did some digging on my own, of course. The first thing I noticed was that there was no autopsy. I found out that the doctor who signed the death certificate shortly afterwards bought a $200,000 home for cash in the Bahamas, where he moved and set up practice, out of U. S. jurisdiction. Mama always wanted to be buried next to her parents in Greenville. She even said so in her will. Daddy ignored that and had her cremated the very next day after her death. Any possible evidence literally went up in smoke. The only possible witness is my brother Sid, whose handiwork we are even now admiring. Even if he were to talk, he has a psychiatric history going back to age ten and any good defense attorney would cut him up into hamburger on the witness stand."

"I don't know what to say," said Heather, stunned and wretched. "Family is the most important thing in all the world. I can't encompass in my mind what it would be like to live without it, let alone to live with this kind of poisonous situation. How can you exist with such horror?"

"Well, for one thing, Heather, it's always been like this," said Matt moodily, staring at the bright light of Venus in the deepening azure twilight. "You can't miss something you never had. My father was always the enemy, the adversary to be outwitted if possible and avoided whenever feasible. Frankly, in some respects my childhood was a very good prep school for my later vocation. My mother wasn't a bad sort, but she waved the white flag on Daddy and life in general long before I was born. What love she could muster she gave to Sid, the one who was obviously badly damaged and heading for serious trouble. It took me some years, but now I understand that's a natural reaction in a mother, to cherish the weakest and the sickest offspring the most, and I don't hold it against her. Nothing she really could have done about it all anyway. I don't know if Steve, that's my youngest brother, has successfully wrestled with that particular demon yet. In some ways he got the really shitty end of the stick; he had to stay in that house with Daddy and Sid on his own after I left and although he won't talk about it now I get the impression it was pretty hellish. Daddy took his anger and his hatred of me out on him. Steve turned out okay, though. He's a lawyer here in town, and so far as I know he either doesn't have that extra Y or he keeps it in an iron grip, much better than me or Sid have done. Never heard of him shooting anybody or setting any fires."

"You're supposed to be the best lawman in the country, if I can believe Time and People Magazine," said Heather with a wan laugh. "Can't you do something?"

"With no evidence at all, against the power of money which is this society's god?" replied Matt bitterly. "No. The only thing I could do that is in any way adequate to my father's crimes against us all would be to put a bullet through his brain. I admit I've considered that, but never seriously. I could give you some line about not sinking to his level or giving him the ultimate victory by destroying me even in death, blah blah blah, but that's not it. The simple fact is I don't think enough either of my mother or my wife and children to sacrifice my own life just to avenge them. That may be selfish and cowardly, I don't know."

"No, don't be ridiculous, it's just common sense!" protested Heather.

"Whatever. The fact is he's gotten away with it, and I've accepted that," Matt said. "This is one of those cases where simple vengeance could never be any substitute for real justice, and justice simply isn't going to happen. One of the hardest lessons in

life to learn, Heather, at least the hardest for me to learn, was
that good does *not* always triumph over evil. What happened to
Mary Jane and Jeannie showed me that, but for a long time I
never internalized it."

"Is that why you became a cop?" she asked. "Because you
wanted to do at least tip the scales on the right side?"

"Mmmm, you could say so, yes, although it was a bit more
complex than that. For one thing, I really do enjoy the work and I
have a talent for it. But I've become convinced down through the
years that there's kind of a pendulum swing of history between
good and evil, and that whether we like it or not, we are living in
one of those epochs which sees the near total triumph of evil, a
new Dark Age. The pendulum has really swung far over into the
bad zone this time, though, so far sometimes I wonder if it's stuck.
I hope things will be better for people someday, but it probably
won't be in our lifetimes."

"Whoo, what a cheerful philosophy!" said Heather.

"I consider it realistic," said Matt with a shrug. "My God,
Heather, look around you. You read newspapers, you watch television. Will Williams says he believes the world is simply
insane. I say it's evil. My father is living proof of that. He has
done utterly hideous things to me and to my children, beyond all
bounds of acceptable human behavior, and not only will not a
single goddamned thing ever be done about it, but his behavior
has been handsomely rewarded. He is going to end his life surrounded by every material comfort and luxury and bathed in the
fawning admiration of all around him. No doubt he enjoys great
sympathy as well among the family and his friends for his terrible tragedy in life, i.e. having me for a son. The official version
of all of these events I've described will be handed down into the
family folkways by those whom his wealth has blinded and
bought. I will be the villain of the piece and he the sainted patri-

arch upon whose bent and hoary gray head I heaped untold distress and embarrassment."

"Matt..." Heather didn't know what to say. It was dark outside now. She took his hand and kissed it, and held it against her cheek.

"The Carrboro cops should be here soon,"said Matt. "Once I get through filing the report, can I trouble you for a ride to an excellent Chinese place I know down on Franklin Street? I'll buy. That is if you still want to continue the relationship. Heather, I'm glad this happened. Now you know. Love me, love my dog. My dog is not housetrained, and it bites. Bites hard, sometimes. My father and my brother Sidney are vicious, dangerous psychopaths backed up by a fortune so vast I doubt anybody even knows how big it is."

"That little savings and loan in Greenville from 1930?" asked Heather, surprised.

"I saw some of your mail on the table back at your house. Who financed your mortgage, Heather?" he asked.

"DixieBank. Why?" she asked.

"You owe Daddy money," said Matt.

"What?" cried Heather. "But Matt, DixieBank is...it's..."

"The largest privately owned financial institution in the United States and the fifth largest in the world, exceeded only by three Swiss banks and one in the Cayman Islands. Not just banking but real estate, textiles, trucking, communications, agribusiness, computer software, you name it. One of the world's major conglomerates. Old Zeb built himself an empire and to be fair to him, Daddy has built it up even further. He may have gotten hold of my grandfather's money by murder, but he's never lost a dime of it. I've got to give him that."

"What about your other brother?" asked Heather. "What does he say about all this?"

"Steve and a variety of assorted in-laws are spineless hangers-on who feed off that fortune and who all cherish hopes of glomming onto the big bucks when my father dies. I suspect that in this they are mistaken, but in the meantime they form a solid protective wall around my brother Sid and my father, an ongoing conspiracy to cover up and deny their behavior, and to excuse and explain it away when it can't be denied. If you get involved with me there will continue to be incidents like this that may involve you and maybe Tori and Greg. Never underestimate the depth of my father's burning hatred for me and for anyone I care about. Are you sure you want to continue seeing me?"

"As long as I can keep on fucking you, your family can go fuck themselves," said Heather steadily.

"Succinctly put," laughed Matt. His eyes softened. "God, do you know how brave you are getting involved with me?"

"Make sure I don't regret it," she said.

"I'll prioritize that, ma'am. Thanks, Watson. Now I have a favor to ask you. Any chance you could take care of the Trumpeldor at your place for a while?"

"Eh?"

"My brother likes to do things to animals," said Matt. "Bad things. Trumpel's an idiot. He doesn't have sense enough to be afraid of people; he thinks everybody loves him and wants to feed him. Sid could catch him just by waving a hot dog in the air. As pathetic as this sounds, that grotesque cat is about all I have left from my old life, the home and the marriage my father destroyed. If Sid were to get hold of him...well, I don't know if I could control myself."

"And your father doesn't care if you kill or hurt his second son, just so that in doing so you are destroyed?" asked Heather softly, shaking her head in horror.

"You're catching on."

"Oh, Matt, the *pain!* Mary Jane, your wife and children, the way you father has made your life a living hell...how have you lived with it all these years?" she choked.

"I haven't had much choice in the matter," said Matt with a shrug. "It's like living with a missing arm or a leg, or a painful but never quite fatal disease. You learn to work around it. But I have to admit, I could use some help, Watson."

"You got it. Holmes," she whispered, leaning over and kissing him passionately. "Long as you want it. And Trumpeldor will be a welcome guest."

"Meow," said Matt.

*   *   *

In the darkness across the road, two men in well-tailored business suits sat in a long dark sedan under a pine tree in the parking lot of another student apartment complex. The man in the passenger's seat had watched with interest through a pair of binoculars minutes earlier, while Sid Redmond had slashed the tires on Matt's car, then jumped into his own luxury sedan and fled the scene. "This is sure a classy town," said the driver in admiration, unwrapping a pack of chewing gum. "Even vandals drive a Lexus. Who the hell was that bozo?"

"Either an irate dope kingpin with a remarkably petty sense of vengeance, or else one of Two Gun Matt's notoriously screwball relatives," said the man in the passenger seat. "From the file photos I'd say probably Dr. Sidney Redmond, the renowned Chapel Hill pianist and composer. We'll have to run the plates on the Lexus to make sure, but it opens some interesting possibilities."

"The one that's married to the good-looking S & M broad? So what's he doing slashing his brother's tires like some homeboy wannabe?" asked the driver, stuffing three sticks of Juicy Fruit into his mouth at once.

"He's crazy as hell. Kind of a clockwork orange type, heavy into Beethoven and ultra-violence. Likes to burn down houses just to watch the glow, then sit down for a hot session of trio sonatas." A few minutes later they saw Matt come charging into the parking lot with his pistol at the ready. "Make a note, subject is confirmed still to be armed with the Colt .357 Python we already have noted in the file." Heather came out of the apartment. "We'll need to get an ID on the woman."

"Skinny," said the driver. "You'd think a hotshot like this guy could scrape up a twitch with some tits on it." The men watched while Matt and Heather talked until the Carrboro police pulled up, Matt explained what had happened, and the officer scribbled in his note pad. When the police cruiser left they watch the pair get into Heather's green station wagon.

"North Carolina plate LCX-569," said the passenger with the binoculars.

"Want me to run it now?" asked the driver.

"No, don't use the radio. I don't want any of the local yokels picking up on the fact that we're in town. Wait until we get back to the Holiday Inn and then do it on-line from the laptop."

"Wanna follow 'em?" asked the driver

"No, let's go. We know where he lives. If he's banging the broad maybe that will give us our handle on him."

"Say, Bennett, we gonna whack this guy or what?" asked the driver, starting up the car.

"Jimmy, the Federal Bureau of Investigation does not 'whack' guys, whatever your own agency may do," explained Assistant Director Charles R. Bennett as they pulled out. "Our rules of engagement occasionally compel us, very much against our will, to use lethal force in order to enforce the laws of the United States against those who refuse to abide by those laws."

"Bullshit," said Jimmy. "You didn't answer my question."

"Special Agent Redmond's position as a state law enforcement officer makes this case a bit more complicated than it otherwise might be, but yes, I very much fear than a man of his violent reputation and known right-wing antipathy towards Federal law enforcement might create a situation where we have no alternative but to use deadly force to defend ourselves and the lives of innocent bystanders," said Bennett.

"Look, yes or no?" demanded the driver. "I don't mind, hell, I'd waste my own grandmother if the computer told me to, you know that. That's why they sent me. I'm just curious to know what the hell we're doing down here is all." He grinned. "And how big a favor you FBI schmucks are going to end up owing the Company."

Bennett sighed. "I haven't decided yet. A deadly incident involving a state investigator might be more trouble than we can handle and certainly more than we need in the middle of a presidential election. It depends on how close he gets. We're going to have to talk to him, try to warn him off and at the same time figure out how far he's gotten."

"I don't see what the fuss is about," said Jimmy as they rolled down Franklin Street through a massed UNC football home game crowd of cheering, yelling students. "Look, Nakritin's dead, you say the local end of it here is shut down and tied up tight and from what I see in the file I believe you. What the hell can the guy find after twenty-six years?"

"Redmond has a rep, and I'm not talking about that magazine horse hockey in the tabloids," said Bennett morosely. "The Southern Sherlock Holmes moniker isn't total hype. The bastard's good, I'll give him that. He finds one damned thread he can pull on, he'll unravel the whole ball of wax."

"Ball of yarn. Youse is mixing your metaphors," said Jimmy. He rolled down the window. "Hey!" he called. "Didja win? Didja beat Duke?"

"Twenty-one to seven!" called a group of joyous students of both sexes, already half drunk, rolling down the sidewalk.

"Awright!" bawled Jimmy. He rolled up the window. "I had fifty bucks on Carolina in our office pool at Langley, fourteen-point spread. OK, suppose we decide Deputy Dawg has found a thread he can unravel. What do we do?"

"Then we whack him," said Bennett grimly.

Neither noticed that they were being followed down Franklin Street by a nondescript compact rental car. Behind the wheel was a small man in a fur hat with a goatee beard, listening to a newly purchased Prokofiev CD while he dodged the revelling students and kept them in sight.

XI

Matt spent most of the next day arguing with his insurance adjustor on the phone, and then trying to find someone who would deliver four new steel-belted radials to his apartment on a Sunday, no easy proposition even through AAA. It was almost four in the afternoon when he pulled up in front of Heather's house, to deliver Trumpeldor and to take her and Tori out to dinner at a Greek restaurant in one the Chapel Hill's largest shopping malls. "I'll buy this time," Heather told him as he lugged in the cardboard box containing the cat. "Those tires are going to set you back a few bucks until your insurance comes through. Did the police talk to your brother about the vandalism?"

"Claims he was at home giving an impromptu recital for a few trendy friends," replied Matt tiredly. "Fund-raiser to save the whales or overthrow some South American government or something. Same old song, the verses change but the chorus remains the same. Daddy's money can buy as many witnesses as he needs, not to mention a few lawmen, I'm ashamed to say."

"Tori!" called Heather upstairs. "We are going to have a house guest for a while. Come down and meet him."

Tori came bouncing down the stairs shoeless in jeans and a pullover sweater. "Hi, Matt."

"Hi, Tori. How was Williamsburg?"

"Colonial. House guest? You and Mom going to shack up?"

"*Tori!*" snapped Heather, exasperated.

"Look, fine with me," giggled Tori. "You were right, Mary Jane's diary has corrupted me. I'm going to be a dyke when I grow up." Heather scowled at her. "Just kidding, Mom! I think she was cool, really," she said to Matt. "I wish I could have met her. What's this about a house guest?" Matt opened the cardboard box and looked in. Trumpeldor was curled up in an orange furball in the box, fast asleep and apparently content to remain there. Matt reached in and lugged him out, drooping in his hands like a wet dishrag, and plopped him onto the kitchen table. "*Cooooool!*" cried Tori.

"He's mine, but he'll be yours if you want," said Matt. "He's a shameless cheese slut. A few slices of cheddar or mozarella and he's anybody's. I've got his bowl, his litter box and a bag of litter and some cat food out in the car."

"What's his name?" asked Tori, stroking and meowing at the cat, who responded with one of his thunderous purrs.

"Trumpeldor," said Matt, following with the same explanation of the provenance of both animal and name he had given Heather. By then Tori had the cat on the floor on his back, spinning him around and squealing in delight while Trumpeldor purred and batted and chewed on Tori's hand. "You'll need to keep him in for a few days until he's used to this place as his new home, but once he learns he gets fed here you shouldn't have any problem," Matt told Heather.

It took half an hour to tear Tori away from the cat. They got to the mall where the restaurant was situated and decided they weren't really hungry yet, so the three of them ended up wandering around the Wal-Mart. Tori bought some diskettes and a computer video game, and Heather picked up a few household items. They were going through the checkout line when suddenly Tori giggled and pointed one lane over, whispering, "Look at that weirdo!" A small, dapper-looking man in his forties with a goatee, a dark coat, and an incongruous fur hat was at the next checkout counter. He had a shopping cart full of what appeared to be every razor blade he could find in the store, likewise every pack of size C and AA batteries, and two precariously perched cases of Charmin toilet paper. The clerk, a young black girl, seemed rather flustered by some request he had made. "Yes, I think we may have some more batteries and razor blades in the back, sir," she was telling him. "I'll have to ask one of the managers to check."

"I would be most edified," replied the little man in careful, almost unaccented English. "I have American dollars. I would like as many of all these merchandises as you can give me for five thousand dollars."

"You want five thousand dollars worth of razor blades, toilet paper, and batteries?" asked the girl, completely bemused.

"What can you do with razor blades and batteries that gives you diarrhea?" asked Tori with a giggle.

"I think I recognize the accent," said Matt with a wry smile. "Probably some visiting professor from the former Soviet Union, stocking up before he goes home. Scarcity is a way of life over there. I spent a week in St. Petersburg at an international conference on drug trafficking back in early '93. Got to see the Russian winter and Russian toilet paper. I think they make their own out of sawdust. You wouldn't laugh, Tori, if you'd ever had to use it, especially in an unheated communal bathroom in twenty below weather. And that was just our hotel! You guys hungry enough yet to dig into some moussaka?"

They had a leisurely and enjoyable meal. Matt guessed that one of the things Heather was watching for was how he interacted with Tori, and he had the uncomfortable feeling of undergoing something akin to his first drivers' license exam, all the more because he wasn't yet completely sure he wanted this particular license. He liked them both and had difficulty keeping his hands off Heather in the restaurant, but avoiding complications had become a habit with him. Simpatico in the sack did not necessarily translate into a lifetime contract; Matt knew it and he was sure Heather knew it, but he decided that the best and fairest thing he could do was simply to be himself and see how they meshed. It seemed to work. As they left the restaurant and paid the bill, Matt noticed the little foreign man sitting at a table all alone, reading a newspaper and sipping an espresso, an anisette bottle on the table beside the bone china cup. Something about him rang a bell in the back of Matt's mind. "So where is the case going now?" asked Heather as they stepped out the door into the crisp autumn evening. "About ready to make that trip to Washington to confront Margaret Mears?"

"With what?" asked Matt. "I have nothing to confront her with, although I'm hoping that our luck is about to change."

"Why? Have you got another lead?" asked Heather eagerly.

"I think so, yes. I'd like to ask both of you ladies to step back against the wall here. Our latest lead should be coming out of the door right about now," said Matt, gently easing them back and drawing his .357 from his shoulder rig.

"Huh?" exclaimed Tori, her eyes widening at the sight of the gun. "You gonna shoot somebody?"

"Matt...?" asked Heather, startled.

"Please, stay back, both of you," he commanded. "I don't think there's any danger in a public place like this, but this gentleman has a rather nasty reputation. I may be wrong about his identity, and I may end up making a fool out of myself, but even so I want you both out of the way." The door of the restaurant opened, the little foreign man stepped out, and Matt grabbed him around the throat and slapped the gun muzzle to his head. *"Dobriy vyechir, tovarich,"* said Matt. *"Kak dyela vyechirom?"*

"Karasho, kromye Amerikanski militsik s pooshka na moi ookha. Vi gavarit pa-Rooski?" asked the little man calmly, without surprise. *"Ya oodivilyon. Nikto razkazi etot o vam."*

"Da, ya gavaryu dastatachna Ruskamu yaziku, Kolya Nozh," Matt replied. *"Vi zavut Rozanov, GRU, prava?"*

"Da, no kak vi znait minya?" demanded Rozanov.

"Ya oozhnu vam ot Pitirboork, tri goda tomu nazat."

"Hello!" said Heather, waving her hand in the air. "Ah, guys, could Tori and I have some subtitles, please?"

"Pardon me, ladies," said the little man, quite unruffled. "You are quite right, courtesy dictates that we should speak English. Although I would be able to hear you far better, sir, without a pistol barrel in my ear. People will stare."

"This is North Carolina. We're used to it," said Matt. "Major Rozanov, if I remember correctly you don't habitually carry a gun, but I ask if you doing so now?"

"No," said Rozanov. "And if I was, I am in this country on a diplomatic passport."

"I'm not concerned about legal technicalities, I just want to make very sure you aren't entertaining any ideas about harming American citizens, present company especially. Now give me the blades, Major. Slowly, very slowly." Rozanov shrugged and flicked his wrist; a long thin metal dagger leaped into his hand.

"On the ground," commanded Matt. Rozanov dropped the knife. "Now the other one."

"I only need one, I assure you," said Rozanov huffily.

"Don't teach grandma how to steal sheep, Kolya," advised Matt. "I carry an extra pistol in my boot and I know damned well you carry another blade. Out with it, again I emphasize, very slowly." Rozanov sighed and opened his jacket, carefully sliding another slender stiletto-like weapon lengthwise out of a cunningly concealed sheath in his belt. "Step away," he commanded. Rozanov did so, Matt keeping him covered. The restaurant manager stuck his head out the door and stared, his dark Greek countenance turning white. "I'm an SBI agent," said Matt, fishing his ID out of his pocket and flashing it at the stupefied manager.

"Sir, I believe this man is an agent of a hostile international criminal organization of a greatly sinister nature, and he may intend to murder me," said Rozanov. "Would you be so kind as to contact the Russian embassy in Washington and inform them if I am killed or if I should disappear?"

"Cut the crap, Rozanov. If you disappear they can always follow the trail of Charmin and razor blades. Ignore him," Matt directed the restaurant manager. "I am investigating this man on suspicion of international toilet paper smuggling."

The manager muttered something in Greek and disappeared inside. "Tori, hand me those knives, please," requested Matt. Tori picked the weapons up and gave them to him. Matt hefted them. "These are beautifully balanced," he said in genuine admiration. "I'll have to try a few throws." He put his gun back in the holster and the knives in his pocket.

"May I ask again how you recognized me?" inquired Rozanov politely. "When were you in St. Petersburg?"

"1993, for the narcotics enforcement conference. I caught several of your training sessions on the Georgian and Afghan drug networks, Major. Very instructive." Matt told him. "We never met, but I noticed your habit of using anisette to try and repair that crankcase oil which passed for coffee, something I ended up doing myself as long as I was in Russia. I also got an earful of your exploits one evening in some hotel bar on Nevsky Prospekt from one of your drunken colleagues whose name escapes me. Actually we first noticed you earlier today in the Wal-Mart. We were one aisle over. I didn't recognize you right off, I figured you for some Russian academic type, but that didn't quite fit. Academics generally don't stock up on blue-collar stuff like ass-wipe and razor blades when they're over here, they go for CDs, liquor, computer supplies, that kind of thing. Then I remembered that some of the Russian cops I worked with at Justice a few years ago had the same toilet paper jones when they came to the States. I assume there's a shortage of razor blades and batteries as well in the CIS now?"

"Correct," admitted Rozanov

"But surely you can buy American toilet paper in Russia, now, can't you?" asked Tori in puzzlement. "I mean, what about glass-nose and all that?"

"I am afraid, miss, that we have progressed beyond glasnost to a state of primitive capitalism," explained Rozanov courteously. "The fact is I was purchasing some of those items as a bribe to my colonel for letting me come at all, and some for my friends and neighbors, but mostly to sell. My old Soviet salary is inadequate in today's Russian free market economy. It is an extremely annoying diversion when one is on assignment but..." He shrugged expressively.

"Actually, Tori, I imagine the Major could really clean up with those cases of Charmin, no pun intended." Matt told her. "It's a major smuggling item for the Russian Mafia in this country. I understand it's customary among Russian guys when asking some *devotchka* out on a date to show up at her doorstep not with flowers but with a couple of rolls of some nice soft Western brand. The way to a Russian girl's heart these days is through her ass, pardon the crudity."

"Ick, gross!" said Tori, making a face.

"Are you making this up?" asked Heather suspiciously.

"No, swear to God!" Matt said with a laugh. Rozanov looked discomfited.

"Are you going to introduce us?" asked Heather.

"Oh, sorry. This is Major Nikolai Yefremevitch Rozanov, of the GRU, which is Russian military intelligence. Aka Kolya Nozh, which loosely translated means Nick the Knife."

Rozanov bowed to both women. "How did you get that name?" asked Tori, fascinated.

"The same way I acquired Two Gun Matt," Redmond answered.

"So, you're a Russian?" asked Heather. "To quote the late, great Jerry Garcia, what a long strange trip this is becoming. We keep changing scripts. We started out with *Ghost Story* and now we've switched to *Gorky Park.*"

"You forgot *Last Tango In Paris,*" said Matt with a grin, and Heather blushed.

"Last Tango, eh?" said Rozanov smoothly. "I congratulate you, sir. It is a film of great virtuosity."

"Tango?" asked Tori, puzzled.

"Before your time, dear," said Heather. "So, you're a Russian with a dirty mind? Just who were you planning on sticking with those knives?"

"I most sinceriously hope, dear lady, that this problem may be resolved without any such unfortunate occurrence," said Rozanov. "Might you spare me a few moments, Mr. Redmond?"

"Why not come on over for a cup of coffee or something?" asked Heather. "It's getting chilly out here and no, Matt, I am not letting you sneak off with this guy somewhere without me! I want to know what's going on, too."

"I'm not sure it's a good idea inviting him into your home until we know the nature of his assignment here," said Matt.

"We've got Two-Gun Matt to protect us, and you have his knives," · said Heather practically. "My name is Heather Lindstrom, Mr. Rosenberg, and we live on Boundary Street. Do you have a car? Do you know Chapel Hill at all?"

"Rozanov," said the major. "I know the house, yes." Matt suddenly scowled and his hand began sliding towards the gun butt again. Rozanov caught the move. "No, it's not what you think. In 1970 I was an eighteen year-old conscript in the Soviet army shoveling yak turds in Chermolensk. I promise you I am not one of the men you are looking for, sir. I arrived here several days ago and I have been familiarizing myself with the locality. I confess I recognized you as well in the Wal-Mart, and I followed you into the restaurant in hopes that I could make contact with you later this evening, to see if we could come to an accommodation. I followed you about on Friday and actually came to your apartment yesterday afternoon for that purpose, but on both occasions I was rather put off by your escort."

"Escort?" demanded Matt.

"Yes. You are being intermittently followed by several men whom I believe to be American secret police of some kind, FBI or another agency. You didn't know?"

"I guess I'm not quite the Sherlock Holmes I'm supposed to be if I'm wandering around town trailing Feebies and Russian agents unawares, but it makes sense," said Matt grimly. "I know an Assistant Director of the FBI is involved in a cover-up at least, and since he was here at the time maybe in the murders themselves. Do you see them now?"

"No. They are probably watching your apartment or the possibly this good lady's house on Boundary Street."

"Just what we need in our lives," sighed Heather. "A little more paranoia."

"Do you think they made you?" asked Matt.

"Pardon?" asked Rozanov.

"Do you think these Federals identified you, are aware of your presence?"

"I don't think they noticed me, but someone in Washington may have learned I am in the country and so they may be looking for me."

"Do you have a rental car?" asked Matt. "I suppose if Heather doesn't mind you coming to the house, then you can follow us back."

"Actually, I would like to drop by my own hotel first," said Rozanov. "I must admit, I feel a bit foolish driving around with a car full of batteries and toilet paper."

"And pick up some more knives?" asked Matt.

"Am I going to need them?" asked Rozanov.

"Not unless you threaten me or these women, or break the laws of the United States around me," said Matt. "I'm not a Federal agent now, I'm a law enforcement officer. I don't have sanction to terminate any more. Do you?"

"Yes, but if you know anything about me you will know that I prefer not to do so without dire need," said Rozanov.

"How dire is the need?" asked Matt.

"Pretty bad," admitted Rozanov. "My government would very much appreciate it if you might be persuaded to pursue the solution to more modern mysteries. However, from what I have learned, I don't think that's the solution. Killing you or anyone else would simply draw attention to this matter of the kind we wish to avoid. Agent Redmond, I give you my word that I will not attempt to harm you or these ladies. In return, I would appreciate the return of my weapons. You I believe I can trust. The men who are following you I do not trust. My country gives men like that uniforms to wear, so everyone will know they are murderers and avoid them. Yours does not, but I know the type from long experience."

"And we hear this from a man called Nick the Knife who carries hardware to match?" inquired Heather archly.

"Some people call me Two Gun Matt, Heather, but that doesn't mean I go around shooting people or that I wouldn't do everything in my power to avoid it," replied Matt. He pulled out Rozanov's knives and tossed them to him; he caught them lightly and they seemed to disappear into thin air. "Okay, let's go to Heather's place and have a talk. I hope that drunken brother officer of yours in the hotel was right about you."

"*In vino veritas,*" said Rozanov.

*　　　　*　　　　*

When the returned to Boundary Street Matt kept an eagle eye out for any Federal surveillance but could see nothing in the dark streets. "That doesn't mean they're not around," he said. "They might have the house bugged."

"Oh, wonderful!" muttered Heather.

"I'll get a guy I know to sweep the place tomorrow," Matt promised. Rozanov showed up at the back door several minutes later. "I thought best to leave car some distance away." he told Matt. Heather had boiled water by then and handed Rozanov hot tea. "You Russians like it in a glass, with lemon, right?" she asked.

"Yes, thank you," he replied, sipping it gratefully. "Agent Redmond, I am in rather invidious position. You have correctly divined that my presence in this country concerns events that took place in this house twenty-six years ago, events which I again promise you I took no part in and which I find repellent and saddening. I have been informed by my superiors that you are investigating the murders of the two most unfortunate young women. May I ask why? Has someone directed you to do this?"

"No," replied Matt evenly. "I am on my holiday and doing it on my own time, although I have requested that the SBI director assign the case to me on an official basis, to give me authority, which he has done. I am from this town, I went to Chapel Hill High School, and I knew both the girls who died in this house that night. I wasn't fully aware of the fact when I was younger, but I became a police officer so I could avenge them someday. Someday is now. I have no intention of stopping until I find out who is responsible and bring them to justice."

"Ah, that is unfortunate," sighed Rozanov. "Your personal motivation, I mean. Not bribable at all, are you?"

"No," replied Matt with a thin smile.

"Not all Westerners are," agreed Rozanov. "My superiors often have difficulty understanding that fact."

"So how exactly did you get involved in this?" asked Heather, stirring a cup of coffee.

"My superiors discovered that Mr. Redmond's investigation has apparently led him to suspect none other than one of my country's greatest literary geniuses of this century, Vladimir Nakritin," replied Rozanov. "Nakritin is revered in Russia today, Madame Lindstrom, no matter how he might have been regarded by past Soviet authorities. We are deeply concerned that his good name might be slandered in public."

"Bullshit!" said Matt succinctly.

"Perhaps, but as you say in America, that is my story and I am sticking on it," replied Rozanov calmly. "My problem is, Mr. Redmond, that I am limited in what I can tell you. My activities here are covered by both old Soviet and present-day Russian laws regarding state secrets. If I were to discuss certain things with you, I would be in very serious trouble when I return home."

"How does the Russian word *kamar*, mosquito, enter into this?" asked Matt. Rozanov's eyes barely flickered, but Matt knew he'd scored a hit. A sudden inspiration hit him. "*Who* is the Mosquito, Rozanov? Or who was he? It's a code name for a person, isn't it? Was it Nakritin? Or was Mosquito the name of an operation you people carried out in this country? The name of the operation in which the girls were killed?"

"I don't suppose you'd care to tell me where you got that name?" asked Rozanov.

"No, I think I've given you enough information. Time you gave me something in return."

Rozanov sighed. "I can understand your desire for justice, sir. Again I say that I truly abhor what was done here on that night in 1970. I am not a monster. I have two daughters of my own, one at university and one aged fifteen." He looked at Matt. "Agent Redmond, would it be possible for you make yet another leap of faith, to accept from me my solemn word of honor that you will never, ever be able to apprehend the persons responsible for these crimes? I swear to you sir, that they are all beyond your reach. Or anyone's. And in return, to end your investigation? It's true, you know. You'll never catch them. You are dooming yourself to a lifetime of frustration and disappointment."

"You're trying to tell me the men who killed Mary Jane Mears and Jeannie Arnold are dead?" asked Matt.

"They're not dead," said Tori. "At least not all of them. I'd know if they were dead. It's not over. Mary Jane and Jeannie wouldn't...they'd know if it was over. It isn't."

Rozanov arched an eyebrow towards Tori in questioning. Matt ignored him. "I won't call you a liar, because I have no evidence that you are lying," said Matt. "But no, I can't just accept your word. I have to *know*, Rozanov. I can't live with anything less. Who did this? And above all, why? Men from your organization? *Why,* in God's name? We weren't at war with the U.S.S.R. in 1970. In the name of all sanity, what threat could two teenaged girls in Chapel Hill, North Carolina have posed to the Soviet Union? What threat can the truth coming out now pose to Russia?"

"It might possibly mean the destruction of my country," said Rozanov quietly.

"Huh?" asked Heather.

"This much I can tell you, since it is public knowledge," said Rozanov. "Right now Russia is absolutely dependent on aid from the West in general and America in particular. Expertise, investment, technical assistance, training and education in new technologies and skills, and most of all simple massive amounts of cash which keep us afloat economically. Life in Russia right now is little short of hellish, Madame. You find it amusing to see me, a Russian officer, standing in line in a departmental store to buy small inconsequential items that you take for granted. I do not find it amusing. It is pathetic and horrifying and deeply degrading to me. Nor will I attempt to describe to you the humiliation which every Russian feels now that we find ourselves dependent on our former enemies for survival. We envy America, but I will tell you that there is more hate for your country in Russia today than ever before, because of our humiliation and servile status, forced to come to you with our hats in our hands like beggars, to hand over to you the trees in our forests, the minerals in our earth, the fish in our seas, our national treasures of art and talent, anything America will accept so you will condescend to let us go without total collapse for another year on the national equivalent of a diet of black bread and sour goat's milk. Yet as bad as it all is, it would be cataclysmic if the American aid were cut off."

"And you're afraid that if the American public finds out that your government was somehow involved in these murders twenty-six years ago, they'd be so angry our government would cut off aid?" asked Heather. "Granted, it would be an ugly international scandal, but let's face it, the Soviets have had some dillies of international scandals in the past and they've survived, As embarrassing as it would be, I don't think a revelation of something that happened twenty-six years ago, even two horrific murders, would jeopardize world peace. Especially if you're telling the truth about the people responsible being dead."

"Unless the secret motive for their deaths was still valid today," said Matt thoughtfully. "Something so explosive it could have repercussions on a world-wide scale? It would almost have to be something Vietnam-related. What could possibly be left over from Vietnam that could still upset the whole apple cart?"

Rozanov got up a bit too hastily. "Sir, I am terribly sorry. I am unable to help you. I can only hope that..."

"Vietnam is it," said Matt flatly. "Vladimir Nakritin..."

"Nakritin was a scribbling fool who wrote silly dirty books," sneered Rozanov dismissively. "And a traitor to Bolshevism to boot. But the fact remains that the Russian government does not wish to see his reputation..."

"But was he?" ruminated Matt, leaning over to stare at Rozanov. "Was he indeed? Mary Jane remarked that only a few nights before she died Nakritin and her mother were here in this house talking their Bolshevik bullshit..."

Revelation struck him like a blow.

The pieces fell into place. Matt Redmond's face went white and slack. He couldn't breathe. He staggered back into his chair and collapsed, his head buried in his hands. "Matt?" cried Heather in alarm. "Are you sick? What's wrong?"

"*I know now!*" he whispered. He stared at Rozanov in horror. "You know too, don't you?" he demanded.

"Know what?" asked Heather urgently

"He knows why Mary Jane Mears and Jeannie Arnold died, and now I know as well!" said Matt Redmond, slowly rising to his feet again. "You're here to protect Vladimir Nakritin's reputation, all right. His reputation as an anti-Communist pacifist liberal. Because Vladimir Nakritin wasn't anti-Communist, or a pacifist, or a liberal, was he? He was a fucking Bolshevik and a Soviet spy, wasn't he? And I know what he was doing here, among other things. He was what we call in American law enforcement a bagman. He was delivering money, lots of it, on at least one occasion a hundred thousand dollars in cash to Meg Mears to finance the anti-Vietnam war movement in this country! I should have noticed it in Mary Jane's diary! Where is it, Heather?"

Heather stepped to the cabinet and took the diary from a drawer. Matt flipped through it. "November 1st, 1969. Vladimir Nakritin comes to the Mears home for dinner, ostensibly to discuss literature and pacifism over the fondue. November 5th, Meg Mears flies to Washington and then on to New York for a 24-hour visit. November 15th, 1969, biggest anti-war demonstration in history, buses and charter flights bringing in protestors from all over the country. Who paid for all those buses and planes? February 10th, 1970. Vladimir Nakritin for dinner. February 12th, Meg Mears flies out to Los Angeles, then San Francisco, then up to Seattle and she's back home within 36 hours. That's a lot of jet lag. For what purpose? What did she have to do in person that couldn't be handled by phone? May 5th, 1970, the day after Kent State, Volodya for dinner and Meg jets off to Washington, New York, Madison, Wisconsin, and Columbus, Ohio. Back in 36 hours again and that week this country is damned near on the brink of civil war! August 11th, Vladimucous again and Meg's off for Washington, New York, Boston, and Ann Arbor, Michigan, headquarters of the Weatherman faction of the SDS, if I recall correctly.

"Who paid for it all, Rozanov?" asked Matt rhetorically, closing the diary. "Who paid for the buses, the charter flights, the hotel accommodation, the meeting halls and banquet rooms, the office space, the supplies and equipment, the so-called underground newspapers with six-figure press runs but no paid advertising to speak of, the millions of leaflets, the pop-art posters of Che Guevara and Huey Newton, the postage and labor and material for mass mailings, the bail and the legal expenses and fines when thousands of people were arrested at a time? Who paid for people like Meg Mears to go flying all over the country speaking and doing media interview and agitating? I remember enough to tell you it damned sure wasn't Junior Hippy-Dippy and Little Miss Flower Child. Their allowance money went for dope and Jimi Hendrix albums and flower decals for the VW bug. You people paid for it all, didn't you, Rozanov? I recall some conservatives even asked that question at the time, but they were sneered at, belittled, shouted down in the media, abused and vilified as bigots and crypto-Nazis and every other goddamned way the liberal left demonizes those who oppose their agenda. How dare those rude men ask such hurtful questions of the Love and Flower Generation? But there really was Moscow gold, wasn't there, Rozanov?

"As for the brilliant novelist Vladimir Nakritin, his whole resumé was very carefully faked, dummied up for years by the Comintern to give him a credible rep among world liberalism of the day. Right? Our Volodya actually did his alleged stretches in GULAG at some remote but comfortable dacha down on the Black Sea or something of the sort, right? Stalin himself even got into the act. Nice touch, guys! I imagine it gave Iosif Vissarionovich a real chuckle. The death sentence was disinformation, black propaganda, so Nakritin would be turned loose into the West with all the right credentials to be welcomed with open arms, the nice progressive liberal intellectual with the perfect record to silence any paranoid right-wing suspicions, eh? Commie spies? Why, there's no such thing as Commie spies! Mythological creatures way out there with the tooth fairy and the boogeyman, products of horrible paranoid right-wing conspiracy theories! Alger Hiss and the sainted Rosenbergs were lily-pure innocent and anyone who voices the slightest skepticism or disagreement is a secret racist bigot with a shrine to Hitler in his garage. Have I got the *pravda, tovarich?*"

"You realize you're raving, don't you?" asked Rozanov anxiously. "Do you feel quite well?"

Matt looked at Heather. "Ah, you kind of are, a bit," she said sheepishly.

"Sorry," said Matt with a tired sigh, leaning against the wall. "I've had a bleeding wound in my heart for twenty-six years. I'm starting to understand why now and it's making me very angry." He looked up at Rozanov. "Somehow, Jeannie Arnold found out about Nakritin and what he and Meg Mears were doing. Meg possibly told Jeannie herself in the course of a lesbian sexual relationship. Mary Jane probably knew or guessed as well, given her reference to Nakritin's Bolshevik bullshit as she called it. Someone in the apparatus discovered that the girls knew. I can understand why a possible security breach in that operation would be viewed very seriously indeed by Moscow. In the climate of the times it could literally have dragged us all into World War Three. Meg

Mears thought the girls were safe because she extracted a promise from your people they would not be harmed, a promise that was betrayed. Dumb liberal bitch made the same mistake a lot of people in this century made. She trusted the Reds to keep their word. When they didn't, when they murdered the girls after hideously torturing Jeannie Arnold to learn who else she had told, Meg cried out 'They promised!' Who the hell did she think she'd been dealing with, Snow White and the Seven Dwarfs?"

"But she did nothing," said Heather in a desolate voice. "It makes sense. She shielded the people who butchered her child. The evil bitch! I hope she burns in hell!"

"She couldn't have turned them in without revealing that she herself was a traitor in the pay of a foreign power," said Matt practically. "Also, of course, there was the noble and sacred Cause itself. The war had to be stopped. They kept saying that over and over and over again until it became a kind of cult thing with them. Nothing else mattered in life beyond pulling every soldier out of southeast Asia helter-skelter regardless of the consequences, and publicly thwarting and humiliating Richard Nixon and Spiro Agnew. Stop the war, get Nixon, and the Age of Aquarius would descend upon the earth. All our problems would disappear in a puff of marijuana smoke. We would melt down all the guns, run naked through green flowery fields in a land of perpetual summer, copulating with anyone and anything, living in teepees and making candles, man. You remember, Heather?"

"I remember some," she admitted. "I never quite bought it all myself, but yes, I remember, and it was a nice dream for a while. I've still got my old Santana and Jethro Tull and Iron Butterfly albums up in the attic somewhere. I listen to them sometimes."

"So do I," admitted Tori.

"Well, they stopped the war and they got Nixon and Agnew both," sighed Matt. "Now Bill and Hillary are in the White

House, there's fifty-eight thousand names on a wall up there in D.C. of guys whose lives were pissed away for nothing, and I wasted almost fifteen years of my life in a hopeless effort to dam the tidal wave of drugs roaring through the floodgates they opened with their wondrous counterculture." He grinned at Rozanov. "Came back on you bastards too, didn't it? You've got crack in Kiev and meths in Moscow now, *prava?*"

"True," admitted Rozanov.

"I'm right, aren't I?" demanded Matt. "I'm right about the murders, aren't I?" Rozanov bit his lip.

"Surely you know I can say nothing about that."

"Who was the Mosquito?" asked Matt. "Was it Vladimir Nakritin? No, it couldn't have been. Of course! The Mosquito must still be alive, because someone had to contact your people in Moscow, probably through your Washington embassy, and warn them I was sniffing around, poking at sleeping dogs! That's why you were sent here! Is it a man named Paul Lieberman?"

"Who?" asked Rozanov. Matt couldn't tell if his puzzlement was genuine or affected.

"Is it a man named Charles Bennett, a police officer here in Chapel Hill?" pressed Matt. "Is it Margaret Mears herself? Someone else in the anti-war movement here? Who actually did the killings? I know Nakritin was in Stockholm and Margaret Mears was in Washington, and I know there were at least two killers here in Chapel Hill. Who were they, Nikolai Yefremevitch? If you were telling the truth and they're dead, what harm could it be for me to know? Was it Bennett? Lieberman? Hired assassins? Anti-war SDS types? KGB men from Moscow?" Rozanov spread his hands helplessly. Matt strode to the dining room, reached up on top of the tallboy and took down the manila folder there. He slid the crime scene photos out of the envelope and shoved them under Rozanov's nose and into his hands. Tori strained to see them; Heather gently pulled her back down into her seat.

"No, honey, please. I'm asking you not to look at those. I haven't seen them and you don't want to see them either. Please trust me on this, Tori." Heather begged her.

"You see what they did to Jeannie, Rozanov?" said Matt coldly. "She was seventeen, the most beautiful and alive person I've ever known. She wanted to be an actress or a dancer. You might have seen her movies in Moscow, Rozanov. She might have been the first American ballerina in the Bolshoi. She was good enough." Rozanov scowled at the photos. "She might have delighted the world, Nikolai Yefremevitch, but men from your country or else American traitors acting on orders from your country came into this house on the night of October 23rd, 1970 and turned her into a lump of hamburger. But this one's worse," he went on, pointing to Mary Jane's murdered body in the eight-by-ten glossy. "She was going to be my wife. That very night I had asked her to make her future with me, and she said yes. For a period of roughly twelve hours after that, I was happy, the first and only time in my life I have ever been completely happy. Then I learned that she had been taken from me forever. Now I know why. That's half of it. It's horrible and unfair and it makes me sick, but I can deal with it now. I have no choice. But I have to know who, Nikolai Yefremevitch, and if I can get at them at all I have to punish them. If you don't tell me who did this then you are just as much an accomplice of the guilty men as if you had been here that night."

Rozanov slowly put the photos back into the envelope, obviously shaken. "My friend, please, I beg of you to believe that I would tell you what you wish to know, as little comfort as it would be to you, if there was any way I could do so and still do my duty as a soldier and as a Russian. I would not see you destroy yourself in this terrible quest for what is forever beyond your grasp. But if I assist you, then I might be helping you destroy far much more. If what you have theorized is true, which I neither confirm nor deny, then even today the revelation of it could be catastrophic for my country and thence for the world. Another consideration: what do you think the revelation of such a thing, which I neither confirm nor deny, would be regarding the present presidential election in this country, with most specific regard to the re-election chances of the Clintons? Both of them being ultimate products of this same anti-war counterculture you speak of, which now American people would find out to have been financed by Moscow gold as you put it?"

"He's right, Matt," said Heather. "This whole thing is too big for us now." She looked at him. "Matt, I'm going to ask this for your sake, not anyone else's. Any way you can see your way to settling for what you know? You know the why and you know more or less who. After twenty-six years that's good enough, surely?"

Matt shook his head. "Sorry, Watson. I know you mean well, but what about Mary Jane? What about what Tori says is going on down in your cellar? What about Len and Susan Arnold, Andy Mears, Ronnie Riggsbee, Will Williams, Paul Lieberman if he's innocent? What about the law itself? Murder is a crime, Heather. My job is to investigate crime and apprehend criminals, all the way to the end. I can't stop half way."

Tori stood up. "Mr. Rozanov," she said quietly. "I think I may see a way out here. There's someone else who may be able to persuade you. Will you do something for me? I'd like to take you upstairs and leave you alone in my room. I ask that you stay there five minutes. Then come down. If you don't want to tell us what you know then, we'll have to accept that. But I think you might change your mind."

"I don't understand," said Rozanov, puzzled.

"It's the room where Mary Jane died," said Heather. "I think it's a good idea, Mr. Rozanov. How about you, Matt?"

"Rozanov, if you decide not to tell me what you know after spending those five minutes up there, then I'll let it go," said Matt. "I will keep on trying to solve the case, but without something specific to go on, I still have only a wild theory that can never be proven. I have one card left, which is to go up and confront Meg Mears in Washington. If she's enough of a hardened leftist bitch to sacrifice her daughter like Iphegenia, a simile which has been used in this case, then she's hard enough to brass it out, laugh in my face and have me thrown out of her office and probably charged with harassment. Beyond that, the trail has dried out. I'm due back at work after Thanksgiving and from that point on it's back to chasing murderous crack dealers, larcenous con men and chicken rustlers."

"Surely they don't send the Sherlock Holmes of the South after chicken thieves?" asked Rozanov politely.

"They do when someone pulls up a tractor-trailer and steals twenty thousand biddies in crates from a high-volume battery farm," said Matt. "Anyway, the fact is that without your help your country's secret is safe. If you should change your mind, I will give you my word that if there is any way I can camouflage or downplay the political aspect I will. All I want is for Mary Jane's killers to be brought to justice, at least such justice as is possible after a quarter of a century."

Baffled, Rozanov followed Tori upstairs. Tori came down a minute later. "I just left him up there. My computer is on, blank screen. He asked me what was supposed to happen. I said I had no idea, maybe nothing, but please think about how she died in that room and how she must have suffered, and whether he could maybe help her rest a bit easier if he told us what he knows."

"I'm impressed, honey," said Heather. "Sometimes it's hard for me to remember you're almost an adult now." She hugged her daughter warmly.

"Getting enough adventure yet, Watson?" asked Matt.

Heather shook her head in amazement. "You realize all this is absolutely ruining me for work?" she said with a laugh. "I don't know if I'm going to be able to go back to a career in accountancy after coming home to ghosts and Russian spies!"

"When were you guys doing the tango?" asked Tori curiously.

"Uh, you want to field that one, Matt?" asked Heather with a grin.

"Not right at the moment," said Matt. "Tori, just put it down to the obscure Russian sense of humor."

"Is the Russian sense of humor obscure?" asked Heather.

"I never noticed they have one. They tend to short and pithy sayings that express hideous concepts in a nutshell. Like Stalin's famous comment that one death is a tragedy but a million deaths is just a statistic. Heather, you once asked to what dark god of the Underworld Meg Mears sacrificed her Iphegenia? The dark god was a Georgian cobbler's son named Djugashvili, a man who became known to the world as Joseph Stalin. The girls were murdered to protect his legacy. They figure old Joe killed something on the order of forty million people in his lifetime and to that you can add Lenin's by no means inconsiderable body count, Mao's Cultural Revolution, Hungary, Czechoslovakia, Vietnam and the Khmer Rouge and a village mayor in Colombia who was fed to a snake. Stalin's statistics." Matt paused. "Mary Jane and Jeannie aren't going to be added onto that horrible twentieth-century statistic and forgotten. I intend to see to that. Isn't the Major's five minutes about up?"

"It's going on ten," said Tori.

Heather put the kettle on, but Rozanov did not descend the stairs until the water was boiling. He sat down at the table, his face expressionless but completely white. He accepted the glass of Russian tea with lemon that Heather silently handed him and gulped half of it down, scalding hot as it was. He set down the glass and looked at Matt. "Sergei Aleksandrovitch Greshkov. Zachar Vasilievitch Probdanichev," he said.

"I don't recognize the names," said Matt.

"Those are the men who came into this house on that night twenty-six years ago and murdered the two young women they found here," said Rozanov.

"Thank you, Nikolai Yefremevitch," said Matt with a long sigh. *Names at last,* he thought. *How strange it is to know at long last. Twenty-six years of wondering ended in a moment, with names that don't mean a damned thing to me.* "KGB?" he asked.

"GRU. Military intelligence. Flown in from Moscow. In and out in forty-eight hours."

"Where are they now?"

"Probdanichev died in 1980 in an airplane crash. I speak the truth, I promise you. He is dead. Serves the fool right for flying Aeroflot, which is the true Russian roulette. I came over here on KLM. Greshkov is a retired major general now. He is eighty years old and completely senile. He lives in a special government apartment in Moscow, cared for by a nurse. He has no family, and the nurse tends to leave him locked in the apartment while she goes out and stands in line for food and simple necessities, so he is often cold and dirty and ill-fed. I know this because before I came to America I went to see Greshkov on the chance that he could tell me something about the case. He is completely incoherent and is unaware of his surroundings. He did not understand who I was or what I wanted from him. He sang a childrens' song from the 1930s, praising Stalin and the First Five Year Plan. It was all he could remember, apparently. Any attempt to punish this man would be pointless, I assure you. He will not live much longer."

"The Mosquito?" asked Matt.

"I am sorry to disappoint you, Matthew Randallovitch, but the Mosquito is dead also, and that is the truth. A member of the Communist Party U.S.A. from New York who grew up in a Communist family, what was termed a Red diaper baby. A woman named Lieberman, June Lieberman. I was puzzled when you asked about a Paul Lieberman. Him I do not know."

"June Lieberman?" asked Matt, stunned. "Why...she was a teacher...she walked right into school and taught her classes that Monday as if nothing had happened...my God, the cold-hearted bitch! Look, what the hell was it all about? What happened?"

"I'm afraid it was even worse from your point of view than you so brilliantly theorized, my friend," said Rozanov grimly. "You are right. Vladimir Nakritin was a carefully cultivated agent of influence among the so-called progressive elements of the West, a deep-cover Comintern operative with a whole false identity. He was actually a lifelong Bolshevik, who under his real name fought in the 1917 October Revolution in Petrograd, including taking part in the attack on the Winter Palace."

"You don't get much more Bolshevik than that," agreed Matt. He remembered Len Arnold's unintentionally ironic comment that Jeannie's peripheral political activity hadn't amounted to storming the Winter Palace. In point of fact, her death had gone back to just that. "Go on."

"Nakritin was used both as a conduit for information and an instrument of manipulation for what Communists call useful idiots, liberals and so-called progressives who are so full of love for humanity in the abstract and hatred for the Right as individuals that they overlook our practice of violence against the former in order to support our violence against the latter." Rozanov told them.

"What did I tell you about their pithy little sayings?" said Matt to Heather.

"In 1970 he was more or less loaned to our comrades from Hanoi for the purpose of transmitting funds to the anti-war movement here in this country," continued Rozanov. "You see, it wasn't Moscow gold at all. It was Hanoi gold, taken in through assorted left-wing charities and foundations around the world, all devoted to wondrously humanitarian ideals, some of the smaller denominations taken from American prisoners of war or dead American soldiers. Some of the bank notes quite literally had American blood on them."

"Oh, my God," moaned Matt. "I can just see some proud blue-collar father in Oklahoma or worried mother in Harlem slipping a twenty dollar bill they'd worked overtime for into the envelope of their last letter to their son, and then that bill coming back here with the kid's blood on it to subsidize those scum marching in the streets screaming hatred against the president and everything in America."

"It's horrible!" whispered Heather.

"Who told Moscow that Jeannie Arnold was a security threat?" asked Matt.

"The Mosquito, the Lieberman woman. She claimed that our American contact, the Mears woman, had entered into a perverse sexual relationship with Miss Arnold and that the girl was blackmailing Mears for part of the money. Moscow sent the order to terminate Miss Arnold immediately, but Mosquito replied that no one here was capable of it and requested specialists. They sent Greshkov and Probdanichev. According to their report, when they arrived Mosquito told them that a girl friend of the target had been told for certain and that she may have revealed the secret to

others. She informed them that the two girls would be attending a
school function of some kind that night, but would be alone in
this house on their return. The termination scenario suggested by
Mosquito was a sexual assault of the kind so common in capitalist countries. Rape is a crime under the Soviet military code, so an
instrument was used to achieve that appearance, a hardened rubber truncheon, standard Soviet military police issue. Probdanichev
took the Mears girl friend upstairs and..." Rozanov hesitated,
glanced upstairs.

"We know what he did," replied Matt. "You saw the pictures."

"Yes, I saw. Again, I swear to you that I abhor and condemn
what happened here that night without reservation. It was all the
worse because it turned out to be unnecessary."

"*What?*" demanded Matt, incredulous.

"Things started to unravel during the interrogation of the
Arnold girl. Greshkov noticed that the girl seemed to know virtually nothing about Nakritin and in any case the questions she was
being asked had mostly to do with her apparently many and var-
ied sexual relationships..."

"Wait, wait, who was asking the questions?" Matt interrupted

"The Mosquito, of course."

"She was *here?*" whispered Matt, stunned. "June Lieberman
was here that night? Of course she was! That's how they got in.
The girls trusted a teacher from school and they opened the door
for her. June supervised the torture of Jeannie? And now she's
dead where I can't get her? I think God is playing some kind of
joke on me!"

"He is notorious for His rather strange sense of humor, *da,*"
agreed Rozanov. "Greshkov and Probdanichev learned to their
disquiet that the girl they had already killed was the daughter of
the primary American collaborator in the operation, which the
Mosquito had neglected to mention before. Then, as I said, they

noticed that the Mosquito seemed more concerned with the second prisoner's sexual activity with the Mosquito's husband and also with Margaret Mears. After a time it became obvious that the girl knew nothing and was not blackmailing Margaret Mears. The girl believed she was being punished by Mrs. Lieberman for her affair with the husband. Her recorded answers to the interrogatories consisted mostly of asking what had happened to Mary Jane, pleas for mercy for Mary Jane and herself, and promises not to have sex again with the husband. When at the end the Mosquito informed her, quite unnecessarily, that the Mears girl was already dead, Greshkov's report indicated that further interrogation became impossible."

"Oh, no!" sobbed Heather. "That poor child! She didn't even know why she was dying!"

"May God have mercy on her soul," muttered Matt numbly.

"By this time, Greshkov was convinced they'd been deceived by the Mosquito," Rozanov continued inexorably. "He called a halt. Notwithstanding the fruitless interrogation, he was under orders from his superiors to kill the girl, so he did so, and they left. There was a lengthy debriefing at the Lieberman home later on, and I gather from reading between the lines that Mrs. Lieberman was subjected to some of the same kind of intensive interrogation, if that assuages at all your thirst for vengeance, Agent Redmond. They learned that the whole botched mission was due to her almost insane sexual jealousy of the Arnold girl. It seems that Mrs. Lieberman was also having a lesbian sexual affair with Margaret Mears."

"The anti-war co-worker Andy Mears mentioned," put in Matt.

"Not only had the youthful and beautiful Miss Arnold poached both of the bisexual Mrs. Lieberman's partners male and female, but she rejected Mrs. Lieberman's own sexual advances towards

her with some flippant remark about screwing both husband and
wife being tacky, whatever that means."

"Yeah, it's tacky, all right," agreed Tori. "Gee, Matt, Chapel
Hill High sure has gotten dull since your day. I haven't run into a
single Communist, lesbian teacher or Russian spy yet."

"Wait until your senior year." advised Matt. "Go on please,
Major. What happened when Greshkov and Probdanichev found
out they'd been inveigled all the way from Moscow into a bisexual
lover's quadrangle?"

"To them the whole thing was just incomprehensible capitalist
degeneracy," remarked Rozanov. "These sex things weren't
allowed in Russia in those days. More wonderful thing we have to
thank your capitalist system for, my American friends: buggery,
hepatitis, and AIDS."

"I wondered what all the Charmin was for," put it Tori.

"*Tori!*" snapped her mother. "That is crude and homophobic!"

"You are a most ribald young lady," said Rozanov primly. "But
I digress. Main consideration now was to preserve the pipeline of
funds to the anti-war movement, intact and unknown to the
Americans. The two GRU operatives considered killing the
Mosquito but they had no authorization, and besides, her death
would link her to the other two in the mind of the American
police, so they told her she'd better sort things out and if the
Nakritin's cover was destroyed they would be back to deal with
her next time, which you can imagine she found a most unpleasant prospect, having witnessed what they inflicted on Miss
Arnold. Then they went home to Moscow. The Mosquito was
able to bribe a local sergeant of police to divert and eventually
suppress the investigation."

"I know, Charles Bennett," said Matt. "Now I understand why
all that time and legwork was wasted on the non-existent connection with the McDonald case. It was Bennett's red herring.

Curiosity question: do you know how Bennett managed to get into the FBI in 1971 without being a lawyer or a CPA?"

"At the Mosquito's request our people in Washington applied pressure on J. Edgar Hoover," said Rozanov. "Apparently our intelligence in this country had acquired proof of Hoover's involvement in some kind of corruption involving the theft of meat products."

"Huh?" said Matt.

"Meat products?" asked Heather, puzzled.

"I did not understand the reference in the file I read," admitted Rozanov. "Something about FBI Director Hoover and one of his top aides, a man named Clyde Tolson, concealing some sausage."

"Ah," said Matt with a nod. "Yes, that would do it." Tori doubled over in helpless giggling while Heather turned red and spluttered, then gave up and giggled as well. Rozanov stared at them, and then continued,

"This was actually something of silver lining to cloud, since this individual is now highly placed in FBI and has been of some assistance to us in the past. Nakritin's assignment was terminated and the funds cut off late in 1971 when it became obvious that we had succeeded and the Americans were going to pull out of Vietnam. Probdanichev is dead. Mosquito is dead. Greshkov is dead as well, he is only unaware of the fact. There is no one to arrest, my friend, no one to punish. God has punished them all for you."

"Paul Lieberman knows," said Matt. "It was the reverse of what we thought. He was providing the alibi for his wife, not vice versa. He told me she had real brass balls to go in and teach her classes that Monday like nothing had happened, like she hadn't just murdered two girls and been tortured herself by foreign agents that weekend. I have to agree with him. But he knew. Meg Mears knew, and she said nothing. That's accessory after the fact for both of them."

"You'll never prove it, Matt," said Heather dismally.

"I know," said Matt with a tired sigh, knowing it was true, knowing that other than knowledge he had gained nothing and the case was now effectively closed.

"What happened up in my room when you were up there?" asked Tori curiously.

"Ah, I would rather not speak of this, please," said Rozanov hesitantly. "I believe that in view of this experience I must re-examine certain aspects of my conceptions of life and death. I will simply say that I felt a great pain and fear in someone in that place, pain and fear because I was a Russian. I tried to convince her that not all Russians are like the men who came into this house that night and took her life. I don't know if she believes me. I hope you do."

"One final question, Nikolai Yefremevitch, and then I promise that I won't ask you to compromise yourself any more," said Matt. "If the Mosquito is dead, then who contacted your organization and informed you that I was reopening the investigation?"

Rozanov looked away. "You will not believe me," he said.

"Try me," urged Matt. "You'd be amazed at what I'm willing to believe about this case."

"I must first tell you, Matthew Randallovitch, that when I came here it was strongly hinted to me by my superiors that I should solve this problem by removing you," said Rozanov carefully. "You are fortunate that I am not like Greshkov or Probdanichev or certain others. I do not believe in killing without a very good reason, and I dislike walking into situations of this nature without knowing all the facts. I made it my business to ascertain all the facts before I left Washington for this town, and I remain most distrustful of one aspect of this business. Although the threat to my country's well being is genuine, I cannot escape the suspicion that like Greshkov and Probdanichev, I may have become involved in something I know nothing about." He was silent, embarrassed. Matt's blood froze as he suddenly comprehended.

"*Kolya, kak vi znait moi ochistva?*" he asked softly. Heather frowned and started to speak, but he raised his hand to cut her off. "*Ochin moi atyets kto izmenyat minya, da?*"

"*Da,*" said Rozanov, staring at the table. "*Ya nie panimayu etot. Ochin pakhosh Stalinschina.*"

"*Spasiba, Nikolai Yefremevitch,*" Matt stared at the floor, his face bleak, clenching and unclenching his fist, a red vision filling his eyes.

"Matt...?" said Heather hesitantly.

"I asked Major Rozanov how he knew my patronymic, my father's name. He knew it because my father, Randall Redmond, is the man who contacted the Russians and told them I was digging into their business," said Matt.

"What?" demanded Heather, stunned. "Matt, that...that can't be! Even if he's that bad a man, as you say he is, in the first place how on earth would he know what you were doing in your job, and in the second place how would he know that the Russians were involved in these murders at all?"

Rozanov shrugged. "These questions I cannot answer, Madame Lindstrom. All I know is that this man Redmond called our embassy about a week ago and asked to speak with the KGB resident, and he repeated the old authentication codes that were assigned to the Mosquito. By happenstance there was an individual in the office who recognized the authentication."

"But why would Meg Mears or Lieberman or this Bennett man use your father to do something like that?" wondered Heather. "And what did they tell him? 'Hey, go sick the Russians on your eldest son and they'll kill him for you?' They couldn't have done that without telling him the story of the murders!"

"They didn't get him to do it," whispered Matt. "He did it all on his own."

"I don't understand," said Heather.

"Nor I," said Rozanov. "Please elucidate."

"My father must have already known about the murders, who did them and why," said Matt, his voice shaking with anger. "He's probably known for years."

"But how did he find out you were investigating them again?" asked Heather.

"I had a visit from a member of the family a while back. I had the file out on my work table. This person must have conveyed the information to my father, for motives which will probably prove to be of a piece with everything that has gone before. You were close, Rozanov. This is indeed somewhat like the old days in your country when father betrayed son and vice versa. If my father and Joseph Stalin had ever met they would have hit it off like old fraternity buddies. Major, another question and this really is the last one. Those Feebies who are following me, would you happen to know where they are holed up?"

"Yes, I followed them to the Holiday Inn. I myself am in Hampton Inn, room 268. If you do not object, I think I will spend a few more days in your lovely little town. With its most fascinating shopping malls."

"How much toilet paper are you planning to ship back to Russia?" asked Heather curiously. "Surely they won't let you take all that back on the plane with you?"

"I have made the necessary arrangements with some people at our embassy in Washington for shipment," said Rozanov. "I brought with me dollars and Deutschmarks from a kind of syndicate put together by my co-workers and more from my neighbors in my block of flats when they learned I would be coming to America. I would like to obtain at least two thousand cases of lavatory rolls, but many other things as well. Perhaps the young lady here can recommend where is best place I can buy Levi's jeans?"

Before the Russian left he asked to borrow Tori's paperback copy of George Orwell's *1984*. "It is still banned in Russia," he explained with some embarrassment. "I never read it."

*   *   *

Later that night, after Tori was in bed, Matt asked Heather, "Can I make a long-distance call? I'll put it on my card. I'm going to put the call on the speaker phone. You have a right to know what you're dealing with if you get involved with me, Heather."

"I saw yesterday," said Heather.

"You saw the symptom. Now you will hear the disease." Matt dialed the number in Charleston, South Carolina. He had not spoken to his father for twenty-six years, ever since that sweltering day in August of 1971 when Daddy drove him to the bus depot in Chapel Hill with his cheap travel bag, his ticket to Raleigh and his enlistment papers in his pocket. After Matt had gotten out of the car Daddy leaned through the window and stuffed a $100 bill in his short pocket. "That is the last cent of mine you will ever see in your life," he'd snarled in a voice of lead. "You are not to call or write or in any way communicate with your mother or either of your brothers. Don't ever come back here. Not ever."

It was almost midnight, but his father was still up and answered the phone on the second ring. *Probably starting in on his second six-pack of National Bo,* thought Matt. "How long have you known?" demanded Matt flatly.

Randall Redmond was over seventy years of age, but his mind was still sharp and he knew his son's voice without asking, nor did he waste time pretending he didn't know what Matt was talking about. "Since a few weeks after it happened," he rumbled, his voice deadly with hate. "When I found out about you and that Mears girl I made it my business to find out."

"How'd you learn what the SBI and the police couldn't? I suppose you bribed Chuck Bennett, and when he made the June Lieberman connection he told you and you put it all together from there?" asked Matt, knowing the answer already.

Redmond chuckled. "You never did get it, did you, hotshot? Money can do anything. You just gotta know how to use it."

"And you do," said Matt.

"I do."

"You also know how to acquire it," said Matt.

"I do."

"Like leaving a woman who's just had a heart attack lying on the floor for eight hours, then taking her to a second-rate hospital in Burlington twenty-five miles away instead of a better-equipped ER only ten miles away in Chapel Hill?" demanded Matt. "I understand Sid played Rachmaninoff piano concertos while she lay there. What did you do, watch TV and drink beer?"

"You going anywhere with this or just running laps?" asked Redmond sullenly.

"I'm going to beat you on this one," said Matt calmly.

"Yeah? Pigs may fly, little boy. But I ain't holding my breath." Randall Redmond hung up the phone with a decisive click.

"Why?" breathed Heather, appalled. "Why? He must be crazy!"

"To hurt me," said Matt conversationally. "You see, he knew one day I'd come back here and look into this case. He knew I'd find out that he's known all these years, almost ever since it happened. While I've been wondering and agonizing and speculating and driving myself crazy trying to understand what happened, he's known all along. He was way ahead of me. It was just a matter of time before he let me know how far ahead of me he was. He's probably cackling into his beer with glee right now."

Heather walked over and knelt by his chair, taking his hand, kissing it. "Matt, I'm going to ask you something important. I'm terrified of what might happen now, what you might do if you go home to that empty little coffin of an apartment and you are alone. Please, stay here with me tonight."

Matt grinned on her. "Actually, I was planning on it."

Rocking

"...Hey, hey! You got me rockin' now!
Hey, hey! There ain't no stoppin' now!"

—Rolling Stones*

XII

It was raining outside when Heather and Matt woke up in one another's arms. A gray dawn was barely showing through the curtains of Heather's bedroom. Low thunder rumbled through the room in the dim light, growling in the distance. "Listen," whispered Heather.

"Summer tends to hang on for a while down here," said Matt. "Wish it was summer now. Nothing like lying in a cool dry bed with a good woman, listening to a full-blown rip-roaring Southern thunderstorm outside."

"Damn it!" she whispered. "I have to work. It *would* have to be Monday morning."

"Mondays mornings and Friday evenings are the same," said Matt. "They come and they go."

"I really shouldn't call in sick," said Heather. "I'm still pretty new on the job."

"Then don't," said Matt. "We've got time, Heather. Hell, I've got a lot of time now. My boss was afraid of this. I know what happened now, and there's nobody to arrest."

"I wonder if that will be enough for Mary Jane and Jeannie?" asked Heather. "For that matter, do you think Mary Jane minds us being together here, right under her nose so to speak?"

"She was always pretty practical about things," said Matt. "I think she understands that our lives here have to go on. At any rate, there were no apparitions or clanking chains and the bed didn't go levitating around the room last night, so I think we're okay."

"I didn't hear her crying last night," said Heather.

"I'm glad," said Matt. "I hope it's enough somehow. She has wept in this place for too long. What time is it?"

"Only six thirty," said Heather. She smiled up at him and slid her hand beneath the sheets, caressing him. "I feel like an early breakfast!" she whispered.

"Better keep it quiet or we'll wake Tori," chuckled Matt.

"We'll just have to make sure we keep our mouths full," giggled Heather wickedly.

Afterwards Matt got up and took a shower, toweling himself off vigorously. When he came back into the bedroom he slid back into bed. "Your turn," he said.

"Ten more minutes of cuddle," demanded Heather, snuggling up to him and laying her head on his shoulder. The ten minutes turned to twenty and they were both slightly dozing when the door opened and Tori walked in wearing her bathrobe.

"Mom, it's almost seven fifteen, you'd better...*ooops!*" She put her hand to her mouth. "Sorry! My mistake!" She fled down the hall and down the stairs, giggling wildly. Heather slapped her hand to her head and groaned, mortified.

"Oh, *shit!*" she moaned. "I forgot to lock the door!"

"Heather, Tori is sixteen, not six. A locked bedroom door and my car still parked in your driveway would have told her just as much as seeing us together did," laughed Matt. "Besides, I think she already picked up on Rozanov's tango remark. Be glad she didn't walk in half an hour ago and catch you on the downstroke."

"Oh, that would have been just great," said Heather, her face scarlet, laughing in helpless embarrassment. "I can imagine her telling all her new friends at school in the lunchroom, 'Guess what, guys? My mom gives head!'"

"Look, surely she doesn't have some idea that you're a totally sexless being who found her and her brother under a cabbage leaf?" asked Matt.

"No, but dammit, your kids aren't supposed to *see* you getting it on!" sighed Heather.

"Look, let me go down and talk to her first, OK?" suggested Matt. "You get showered and dressed for work, take your time, and when you come downstairs don't act like you got caught with your fingers in the cookie jar. Neither of us have anything to be ashamed about." Matt got dressed and went downstairs. Tori was chewing on a bowl of corn flakes and reading the comics section fro the morning's Raleigh *News and Observer.* NPR's Morning Edition was on the radio, with learned commentators explaining with chapter and verse why Republicans were all secret Satanists just waiting for a GOP victory to start shoving minorities and gays into ovens. Trumpeldor was crouched over his bowl noisily consuming a huge mess of assorted leftovers Tori had given him, topped off with a can of sardines. He ignored Matt. "Well, hello to you too, Trump, you slut," he said. "How quick they forget when they find another hand to feed them. I brought cat food for him," said Matt.

"Boy, *you* sure move fast!" giggled Tori. "It's not even a week since I told Mom I saw a weirdo outside."

"Cut the crap, Tori, and tell me what you think about your mom and me being together," demanded Matt. "Neither of us underestimate your power, young 'un. You can make things miserable for us if you want and you know damned well your mother will choose you over me if you make her choose. Is it going to be like that?"

"It would be with somebody I thought might hurt her," replied Tori seriously. "I don't think you will."

"Not deliberately, no," said Matt. "But in this day and age men and women do a hell of a lot of hurting one another that's completely unintentional. It just seems to happen. It's almost impossible in this year of our Lord 1996 for a man and a woman to have a normal, loving relationship. Everything from the brutal economic realities of the mandatory two-income family to tabloid TV is dead set against it. The world shouldn't be like this, Tori, but a couple of generations of people like Margaret Mears who were absolutely convinced they were doing good, have finally pushed Humpty Dumpty off the wall, and all the king's horses and all the king's men can't put Humpty back together again. The people who gave old Humpty the shove thought we'd have an omelette. Instead all we've got is a lot of rotten egg that stinks to high heaven."

Tori stared at him, fascinated. "I have no idea on earth what you're talking about, but it sounds really cool," she said. "I like listening to you."

Matt laughed. "It doesn't matter," he said. "Old people have a tendency to rant and rave and find fault. I have a suspicion as I get older I'm going to be worse than most. I'll probably end up by subscribing to Reader's Digest and writing letters to the editor, two infallible signs of senility. The third is working in your yard."

"You're not old," said Tori.

"Thanks, honey," said Matt. 'Look, I'll tell you what I told your mother. I can't guarantee nothing bad is going to happen or the relationship is going to go anywhere, especially given who I am and what I do. I haven't made Heather any promises."

"One thing," she said sternly. "You don't try hitting on me. You do and I'll kick you in the balls and then I'll tell Mom."

"I don't play the game like that, Tori," said Matt, shaking his head. "But curiosity question: does that happen often nowadays among your crowd?"

"Fairly often," admitted Tori. "What gets me is how many girls my age think it's cute or cool to steal their mother's boyfriend. I think it's bitchy and tacky, especially when they do it so they can sue the guy and get his money."

"Definitely ethically challenged young ladies," agreed Matt.

"I hope it does go somewhere with you and Heather," said Tori seriously. "I want to go back to Seattle to college at UW, but I'm worried about leaving Mom alone. Greg and Sheri will be here but let's face it, Heather is going to be like a third leg for them. They're going to want their own place. Just between you and me, I think Greg and Sheri would like to get out of coming up here and moving in here when he gets out of the army. They agreed to it to help out with my college, but still it's going to be a strain. Working CPA or not, Mom is going to think she's living with her children instead of them living with her, and that's going to make her feel unhappy and depressed and old. She's not old, any more than you. She's young enough to start over, if she can find a good guy. I've kind of hoped from the first afternoon you were here it might be you."

"That's a pretty tall order, Tori," Matt said, shaking his head doubtfully. "I come with a hell of a lot of baggage."

"Yeah, I know, dopers trying to kill you and a family of psychos," said Tori with a smile. "That's even better. You're not just a man, you're an adventure. I was kind of scared Heather might get hooked up with another accountant or something, out of desperation, or maybe even become a permanent dyke."

"Uh...," said Matt, not certain how to proceed.

"She thinks I don't know," whispered Tori conspiratorially. "She brought a couple of them home, pretending they were friends from work or whatever. Dykes think if they dress nice other women can't tell what they are, but every girl who ever had a gym teacher in junior high school can recognize the way they look at you. Like a guy, you know?"

"Let's keep it that way, OK?" asked Matt. "I don't think she's comfortable with the subject. If she ever wants you to know let her think it was her decision, all right?"

"Oh, don't get me wrong, they weren't bad guys." Tori hastened to assure him. "I'm not homofogey. I wouldn't be homofogey even if it was legal."

"Another curiosity question, Tori," said Matt carefully. "Do you understand that being homophobic, or holding any other kind of politically incorrect opinion, or criticizing the government, is not actually illegal? Have you studied the Constitution in school? Do you know what the First Amendment is?"

"Sure!" replied Tori nonchalantly. "The Constitution says black people are equal to white people and that's why we have to have civil rights and affirmative action and racist white people have to be put in jail."

"Noooo, not exactly," said Matt. "That's just the Thirteenth and Fourteenth Amendments, and that's not precisely what those amendments say, either."

"Oh, yeah, I know that!" said Tori, brightening. "'Four score and seven years ago, our fathers set forth...'"

"No, that's the Gettysburg address!" groaned Matt.

Tori hung her head. "You think I'm stupid," she said sullenly.

"No, no, honey, never!" Matt said urgently. "I think you're tragic. I think people over at that goddamned place on Homestead Road are teaching you politically motivated lies and they ought to be dragged out of those goddamned classrooms and and shot!"

"Hardly Constitutional tolerance of differing opinion!" said Tori, starting to giggle again.

"Hardly," said Matt, chuckling in spite of himself. "Maybe you know more than I give you credit for."

"I know it's going to come to that someday," said Tori seriously. "What you said. I hear all this hate in the election every day on the TV and the newspapers. Eventually they're going to settle it like they do in Yugoslavia and the Middle East, with guns and cannons and tanks and stuff. Probably by the time I'm you and Mom's age."

"Yes, I know," said Matt with a sigh. "And oh, God, it's such a tragedy. It didn't have to happen this way in this country!"

"Then why did it?" asked Tori. "You know a lot about this stuff, Matt. I want to know, too. If PI isn't against the law why do they punish you for it? Why do they kick kids out of school if they say nigger and put it on their record forever, so they can't ever get a decent job except flipping burgers or driving a truck or something?"

"The same reason two men from a foreign country came into this house and murdered Mary Jane and Jeannie," asked Matt. "Many years ago, Tori, before either you or I were born, some very smart and highly educated Americans, who weren't really half as smart or well informed as they thought they were, decided that an alien political and economic philosophy called Marxism was what America needed, and the very first Marxist principle they adopted was that the end justifies the means. Any means.

Tori, getting back to your alleged education, have you been taught anything in school about Joseph Stalin?"

"Ah, let's see," thought Tori aloud. "Ah, not much, I'm afraid. I know he was the leader of Russia before that guy with the birthmark, Gorbachev. That's about it, I'm afraid."

"A little bit before that, actually," explained Matt patiently. "Joseph Stalin died in 1953, the year I was born. Insofar as any one man has made the world of the twentieth century what has become, it is he."

"How come you know so much about him?" asked Tori.

"Stalin was without question the most completely evil man who ever lived on earth, and I have made a lifelong study of evil," said Matt. "I freely admit to a destructive and unhealthy fascination with evil in my nature. It started with the unsolved murder of Mary Jane Mears. I always understood that the power that took her from me was evil, and I have always wanted to know it, to understand it. I first really turned on to Iosif Vissarionovich when I got involved into this Russian thing at the Justice Department. Unfortunately, a couple of generations before mine were turned onto him and his evil as well. Margaret Mears, for one. People like Meg Mears who describe themselves as liberals and progressives know they have to make all the correct noises regarding mass murder. If you really push them they'll very grudgingly come up with a few remarks to the effect that okay, Stalin wasn't such a nice guy, he made mistakes but his heart was in the right place and after all he killed a lot of Germans, so that kind of excuses all the millions of other people he slaughtered. Stalin murdered about four times as many people as Adolf Hitler has even been accused of killing, and yet within a thirty-mile radius of where we sit I could find you a hundred respected men and women with academic degrees and professional qualifications out the wazoo who will bend over backwards to excuse and explain away everything he did."

"If he was so evil, why did Mary Jane's mother serve him?" asked Tori in fascination. "I've read her diary. She loved her mother and respected her, even if she wasn't really into all the political stuff. Is Mr. Rozanov evil? I kind of like him." Trumpeldor, his stomach weighted down to the ground and squishy with food, leaped up onto a chair and then onto the table, walked up and gently bit Tori's wrist in gratitude for his obscene feast.

"I'll tell you something, Tori," said Matt, "I've dealt with a lot of criminal scumbags in my day like Willie and Ramon and Slim and hundreds of others. They all had one redeeming feature and one only: they were thugs who were in it for the money, for themselves so they wouldn't have to work for a living, and they didn't make any pretense that they were selling drugs in order to save the world or bring in the Brave New World. I despise my father more than any human being on earth, but there is one thing I will always concede to him. He will lie without hesitation about anything else, but he has never pretended to serve any ideal or person other than himself. There's an almost Mephistophelean grandeur to him at times. It's like he's Lucifer on some onyx pedestal inscribed with the Miltonic motto *Non serviam*, 'I shall not serve!', meaning God. I'm losing you again, aren't I?"

"Yeah, but keep going," said Tori, her chin resting on her hand, the other scratching Trumpeldor's belly as he purred.

"The most terrible crimes in human history have always been committed by those who thought they were doing good," Matt went on. "Mary Jane Mears and Jeannie Arnold were murdered in this house by men who doubtless considered themselves soldiers of Stalin doing their duty to *naroda* and *rodina*, to the People and the Motherland. Margaret Mears and her kind believed without question that Richard M. Nixon was the source of everything that was wrong in the world, and that if the United States would just pull out of South Vietnam and hand it over to the Communists, everything that was wrong on earth would be made right. So they dragged out a war which might have been over and won by 1970 if they'd kept their damned traps shut and quit giving aid and comfort to the enemy. As a result all of Indochina was handed over to Stalin's Oriental franchises and untold millions of people died, not to mention about 58,000 Americans dead and God knows how many more wounded, in wheel chairs or psycho wards."

"I think it's Reader's Digest time for you," said Tori.

Matt laughed heartily. "Hey, look, if I'm going to be hanging around here banging your mom you better get used to my occasional soap box orations. I'll try to answer your question. From what I know about him, Rozanov isn't evil. He is a soldier who serves a régime that used to be evil and has now become senile and confused, rather like General Greshkov apparently has become. Is Margaret Mears evil? I don't know, because I don't know if it's possible to be truly evil without being aware of the fact. My father understands that he is evil, I'm sure. I think it's a fair bet Stalin did as well. I think true evil is a matter of conscious choice. That may even be the prime element in true human evil. Not what you do so much, or even why you do it, as whether or not you're aware of what you're doing."

"So if Margaret Mears still thinks she was doing good and that Mary Jane's death was just some kind of horrible accident, but in the long run necessary to this wonderful holy cause of ending the war in Vietnam, then she's innocent?" asked Tori in puzzlement.

"No, you're confusing evil, which is a metaphysical concept, with guilt, which is a legal one. She's guilty as hell and I still intend to lock her ass up if I can," said Matt.

"I hope you can," said Heather, coming into the kitchen wearing one of her fashionable business suits and carrying her briefcase. "I come down and find a grossly fat cat on the table *where he has no business to be, Tori,* and I find Two Gun Matt preaching strange metaphysics to my daughter who has a milk moustache and cornflakes on her lower lip. Definitely not the usual Monday morning routine."

"Well, I need to hit the road," said Matt, standing up. "Speaking of bad guys, I'm going to have a go at some today."

"Eh?" asked Heather.

"Major Rozanov tells me those Feebies are staying at the Holiday Inn. Five will get you ten one of them is Chuck Bennett. I am going to see if I can shake him loose of anything remotely resembling an admission he covered up a double murder, took bribes from Daddy, or is in the pay of the Russians himself."

"Is that wise?" asked Heather.

"No," admitted Matt. He looked at Tori. "Tori, can you tell us if Mary Jane and Jeannie are still here?"

"Uh huh," she nodded as she put Trumpeldor on the floor.

"Then it's not over for them," said Matt. He looked at Heather. "I'm damned if I know what I can do to bring closure here, but I've got to keep on hacking at it," he told her.

"I know," she said calmly.

"If any FBI men or other Federals come sniffing around, you are under no obligation to talk to them or give them the time of day unless they have either a search warrant or an arrest warrant," Matt told them. "Even if they have either of those things, don't speak to them except to ask for a lawyer. When the lawyer arrives, you still tell them *nothing at all.* People who go to prison on fabricated Federal charges get pulled under because they have this idea that it's all a horrible mistake, that all they have to do is explain it all and the Federals will release them. Uncle Sugar doesn't make mistakes. If your fate wasn't already decided they wouldn't have come to take you away. I know this because I used to be one of them, although I was never one of the politicals. The one chance you have to jump clear of the machine when it snags you and tries to suck you in is to have a sharp, sharp, very sharp lawyer who hates them enough not to take their money and is skilled enough to blow holes in their fabrication. Ask Randy Weaver. I don't think this business will get that far, because they'd draw attention to the very case they want covered up, but I could be wrong. If you run into these characters, tell them *nothing*, clam up, and holler for a lawyer. I recommend this guy." He scribbled out the name and phone number of a famous Duke law professor. "Ironically, he's probably as Red as Meg Mears, but he hates these people as much as I do and he lives for Federal judicial and police misconduct cases. If you have to call him, which I hope you won't, do not under any circumstances mention my name. He is not one of my gushing admirers. He thinks I framed Sacco and Vanzetti and started the Reichstag fire. Have you got all this?"

"Understood," said Heather, with a grim nod.

He leaned over and kissed her, not giving a damn that Tori was watching. "Have a nice day crunching numbers, Watson."

"Have a nice day getting involved in all kinds of hairy exciting adventures while I sit in front of a computer terminal ruining my eyes," said Heather with a sour smile.

"There are some kinds of adventure you don't want," said Matt.

After he left Tori got up. "I have to get dressed for school," she said. "I left you some corn flakes and there's some fruit in the fridge for breakfast." She put her hand on her mother's shoulder. "He's cool. I hope you can hang on to him."

"Thanks," said Heather with a smile. "I'm going to try."

Tori went upstairs, and without thinking Heather opened the refrigerator. There was a short padding rush behind her and then Trumpeldor almost knocked her over as he lunged into the fridge. The last Heather saw of him, he was gallumphing off into the living room with a piece of pumpkin pie in his mouth.

*   *   *

About nine thirty Matt pulled into the Holiday Inn, went to the desk and flashed his badge. He did not ask the young man behind the desk if there were any FBI agents staying there. Instead he gave a brief description from memory of Charles Bennett and ascertained that it fit a Mr. Baines, who was staying in 147. Mr. Baines had checked in with a Mr. Johnson, who was in 148. Matt thanked him and slipped quietly down the hall to 147. He heard voices within. He drew his .357 and knocked on the door. "Custodian, *señor,*" he called out. When the door handle turned Matt put his shoulder against the door and shoved his way in. Bennett's reflexes were fast, Matt had to admit; he didn't fall back but leaped back, his hand inside his coat jacket. A slim, hard-looking but nondescript thirtyish man was sitting at a table with a laptop computer in front of him. He was halfway to his feet and had a 9-millimeter automatic half drawn from his waistband before Matt's .357 got his attention. "You must be Johnson," said Matt. "Put it away. I came to talk."

"You always talk to people with that hogleg in your hand, hotshot?" said the man at the table, his voice quiet, unintimidated. *Definitely pro here,* thought Matt.

"That's to make sure you guys just talk as well," he said.

"It's OK, Jimmy," said Bennett, gesturing, taking his hand out of his jacket and straightening his tie. "We need to have a word with him anyway. You know these theatrics are bullshit, Matt.

Why didn't you just give me a call? We could have done lunch together at the Rat or something." Neither of them asked how Matt had found them. *Oh, yeah, pro,* he thought. *This does not look good.*

"After our last get-together in a restaurant I thought you'd be a little reluctant," laughed Matt, putting his .357 away.

"Look, I was a bit out of line and you were right to get pissed off," said Bennett, his voice conciliatory.

"I'd call trying to suborn perjury to swear an innocent man's life away out of line, yes," said Matt coolly. Bennett waved his hands dismissively.

"I think I just expressed myself badly that night," he said. "You have to admit you flew off the handle, but I understand why and I let it go long ago." *I threw you out a window and you've let it go, huh?* thought Matt. *This is bad, this is dangerous.* "Look, sit down, will you? It's a bit early but I've got a bottle of Black Jack, or we can call room service for some coffee and Danish. We've got some things to talk about."

"I want to know why you're following me," said Matt.

"You know why," said Bennett. "You're making waves and some people in D.C. don't want to get splashed. How far have you gotten on the Mears-Arnold case?"

"As far as Greshkov and Probdanichev," said Matt. *Tease them with tidbits, but don't tell them you know about Daddy and don't tell them about Rozanov,* he thought. *If they think you know everything maybe they'll talk about everything they know.*

"Who?" asked Bennett with a frown.

"The two Russian GRU men who murdered the Mary Jane and Jeannie," Matt replied.

"Damn! Didn't I tell you he was good?" said Bennett admiringly to Jimmy. "Hell, Matt, we didn't even know the guys' actual names. We just knew it was a couple of Russkie heavies."

"That still doesn't explain why you two are in town following me around, Bennett," said Matt. "Okay, so you feathered the case when you were a Chapel Hill police sergeant because June Lieberman and her Congressional buddy bribed you with a ticket to Quantico, without which you'd probably be a security guard at K-Mart today. I know that, but I can't prove it and even if I could your ass is covered up there in the District six ways to Sunday. You'd survive any wild accusations some redneck state dick might fling about. I know about Vladimir Nakritin, the Red money he was pumping into the anti-war movement through Meg Mears. I know how the two Russian goons were brought over here by June Lieberman on a false pretext because Jeannie was giving it to everybody but June and it blew a fuse in her mind. Treason, murder, espionage, corruption, perversion...that's one hell of a case you buried nice and neat down there in that basement over at Chapel Hill Public Safety, Sarge. Sure, I'd love to dig it all up again. Dig it up and shout it from the rooftops until they string you up by your balls from the Washington monument and I can watch you turn slowly in the wind. But everybody's dead or out of reach. Nakritin's dead, June Lieberman is dead, the Russians are dead if I can believe my source, and Meg Mears is so high up she's out of reach. I can't prove one damned bit of any of this. So why all the cloak-and-dagger?"

Bennett spread his hands expressively. "Politics, Matt. What else? It's an election year, or hadn't you noticed? A particularly passionate and uncertain election year. One of the major ideological icons of the party presently in power is the magic and wonderful anti-Vietnam war movement. Like, peace, man. Far out, man. Groovy. All that bullshit. Those long-haired dope-smoking freaks we had all the trouble with twenty-five years ago are now wearing thousand-dollar suits, carrying briefcases, and parceling out a lot of lovely tax dollars to needy civil servants like my humble self. A couple of them even made it all the way to 1600 Pennsylvania Avenue, and they brought a lot of their friends along with them. They've turned out to be political animals just like anybody else. They asked me for a favor."

"I take it you mean Meg Mears," said Matt.

"Sure, but she's not the only one by any means," Bennett told him. "A lot of people are concerned."

"Who? Hillary? Billyboy himself?" inquired Matt.

"You know me, Matt, the soul of discretion." He sat down on the bed. "Look, Matt, you have to realize that to the people who are signing my checks these days, what you're doing now is tantamount to blasphemy and desecration. It's like you're spitting on God, motherhood, and apple pie. To these people the anti-Vietnam war movement is their national epic, their golden age, it's almost a religious experience, like World War Two was with our parents. The last time they all fought the good fight and everybody was pure and uncorrupted, or so they like to think. The time of flower power and grazing in the grass, good acid and good vibes. Hendrix and Joplin and Woodstock. You're threatening to piss in the punch bowl, Matt. And it's not as if there's any practical purpose to what you're doing, is there? You yourself admit that all the perps are dead and there's nobody left to bust. Why do it, for Christ's sake? Why come along now, twenty-six years later, and resurrect something that's old, old news? My guess is the timing of this little crusade of yours isn't coincidental, am I right? We're going into the home stretch of a general election when the current administration needs every vote it can get, man or beast, alive or dead, in order to scrape back in. Somebody up in Washington put you up to this, Matt? Jesse Helms, maybe? The Republicans looking for an October surprise to embarrass the Clintons by claiming one of their oldest personal friends and political allies was taking Moscow gold back in her protest days?"

"Two dead girls butchered like hogs in your town never bothered you at all, did it?" asked Matt wonderingly. "Why not? Did you see their bodies at the scene, Bennett? At least you must have seen the photos?"

"I saw both," said Bennett. "Yeah, Matt, I grant you it was a hell of a mess and a rotten thing to do. Look, if it had been dopers or high school satanists or bikers or some niggers who came over from Durham to rip off, I'd have run them down and nailed them good. But once I understood what was at stake I didn't feel like being the guy who escalated that cluster-fuck in Vietnam into World War Three. Sure, I lost some sleep over it, but time has proven I made the right decision. We're all still here and not sitting in nuclear craters that glow in the dark."

"I'll concede that it would have changed history," said Matt levelly. "I don't think it would have quite come to a nuclear war if the truth had come out at the time, but it certainly would have been nasty as hell and it sure would have thrown a monkey wrench into the anti-war protest machine at a crucial juncture. The whole movement would have collapsed overnight, and not just through the loss of the Communist funds. Once the American people knew what they'd done, people like Meg Mears wouldn't have dared show their faces on the streets again. They would have been run out of town on a rail, everywhere in America."

"So you admit I'm right?" said Bennett soothingly.

"Hell, no, you're as guilty of treason as Margaret Mears!" snapped Matt. "If the anti-war movement had collapsed in 1970 and the President didn't have to worry about civil insurrection at home, he might have screwed his courage to the sticking point and we might have won the war. There would have been no mass murder in Indochina, no boat people, and millions of people from Cambodia to Nicaragua to Africa might still be alive because the Reds understood that we wouldn't stand for

Communist insurgency in the Third World. Countries like Angola and Peru might be functioning democracies now instead of basket-case dictatorships. Probably there would have been no Watergate because the Left would have been in full retreat, running for cover, and the media wouldn't have had the influence to bring down a President of the United States. No one would have taken them seriously after the way they'd sucked up to the protest crowd and then been made fools of. The counterculture would have become so discredited that the drug scene might have been containable, and God alone knows how many wasted lives and trillions of wasted dollars *that* would have saved us. The Democratic party wouldn't have been hijacked by all these goddamned weirdos and on the other end there would have been no need for the whole Reagan backlash. We might still have a real government instead of being headed down the road to civil war like some kind of high-tech ancient Rome. Nice play, Bennett! There's an outside chance you may have destroyed America in order to get your snout in the trough up at the Bureau!"

"Hey, you oughta run for office, hotshot," laughed Jimmy.

"One of your special boys from Waco, Bennett?" said Matt, gesturing in disgust.

"I'm not going to go over all that again!" growled Bennett.

"Judging from the way you gave that last Congressional committee the finger and got away with it, I'd say not," agreed Matt. "Look, I'm still not exactly sure why the hell you're down here?"

"We'd just like to determine if you can be made to see reason on this business," Bennett told him. "Everybody's dead except Meg Mears and like you said, she's untouchable and you can't prove anything anyway. But I have to give you an A plus on the detective, work, Matt. You're good. I mean that sincerely. Too damned good to be wasting your time down here in Dogpatch chasing moonshiners or whatever you do. Look, if it's curiosity that's motivating you, congratulations, you've found out what you want to know and you know there's nowhere to go from here. What say you come on back up to D.C., go Federal again where the real money and the real action is? Surely you miss being a player, being able to just hop on a jet and go anywhere in the world courtesy of Uncle Sam? I can get you back into Justice. Sure, you pissed Janet off with that insolent resignation letter of yours, but she's a practical woman and she always respected your abilities. We all did."

"How do you know Janet's still going to be there in a couple of months?" asked Matt with a slight curl of his lip.

"Well, now, that's what we're trying to ensure here, isn't it?" replied Bennett. "You help her keep her job and she gives you back yours. Can't get more logical than that. The Department still need a Russian czar, no pun intended. Or you can go back into DEA if you want. Hell, it'll take some doing, but I can even get you back your seniority and your accrued pension time. We can call this three years you've been down here detached duty or something of the kind."

"You're a real piece of work, Chuck," muttered Matt in disgust. "My God, what does it take to get through to you? I threw you out a damned window the last time you laid that crap on me, and you still don't understand that I'm not for sale?"

"Wise up, hotshot, or they'll be picking iron out of your liver," said Jimmy with a sneer.

Matt snapped his fingers. "Don't tell me, let me guess...yeah, I got it! Elisha Cook, Jr. in *The Maltese Falcon*! Jesus, where'd you get this asshole, Bennett? Central casting?"

"Look, let's see if we can't..." began Bennett placatingly.

"Fuck you, Chuckie," interrupted Matt rudely. "I'll cut to the chase. Get your butt back to Washington D.C. There is nothing going on down here that concerns you. Go back to kissing

Billyboy's ass or whatever you do to keep your job. Tell whichever of those Sixties retreads who sent you that I gotta, like, do my thing, man and I'm like, into this really far out justice trip for those two murdered chicks who never had a chance to grow up, man. And a word to the wise: my badge may not be as nice and shiny as yours but it's just as legal and it's good in all one hundred North Carolina counties. If you obstruct justice or tamper with evidence or try to bribe or intimidate any witnesses I will bust both of you and haul you to the Orange County jail in Hillsborough, where I will make sure the sheriff makes your stay very interesting. He's a fishing buddy of mine. I'm going to swear out a warrant on you anyway if I find any proof that you stole the Chapel Hill police file on the Mears-Arnold murder case, as unlikely as I admit that possibility to be. And if this idiot here decides he wants to go waltzing Matilda, then lay on, MacDuff, and damned be he who first cries hold, enough!"

"Who's MacDuff?" asked Jimmy, caught off guard.

"He's the guy who whacked Macbeth," said Bennett irritably.

"You mean that computer geek who was selling guidance systems to Libya?" asked Jimmy. "Nah, that was that Corsican guy who works out of Naples. I oughta know, cost us two hundred Gs."

"You borrowing your thugs from the CIA now?" asked Matt. "What's the matter, can't find anybody sleazy enough to do your dirty work for you in the Bureau? Never mind. Just both of you keep out of my way. Or nothing in your lives shall so become you as the leaving of it." Matt backed out the door swiftly and backed down the hall, .357 out, quite prepared to fire if either of them emerged from the door with a gun in his hand. He made it back to his car without incident. *Shit!* he moaned to himself. *CIA involvement within the United States means they're ready to kill to keep this a secret. The media keep screaming Billyboy and Hillary have got the election, but it must be a hell of a lot closer than anyone thinks. This might tip the balance.*

Back in the hotel room Jimmy was laughing. "Well, I must say you handled that very professionally, sir," he chortled. "A pleasure watching you work."

"I knew damned well he'd never back off, it was just something that had to be tried," snapped Bennett irritably.

"So we do the old extreme prejudice trick?"

"You think you can take him?" It was Bennett's turn to be sardonic.

"I assumed that was why I was here," said Jimmy.

"Look, Jim, no disrespect intended, I know you're very competent, but this is a delicate job and we are going to have to plan this carefully, make damned sure there are no slip-ups, and we're going to have to make sure it all looks righteous. He is after all a state cop. He will be missed. He can't just disappear, and when he goes west it's got to be absolutely clear that it's nothing at all to do with this investigation he's been working on. Something completely personal. I know a man who can help us arrange that and will jump at the chance to be of service to his country in this matter, but when it goes down I want some extra help. Call your boss. Use the scrambler. Tell him to send Tedtaotao down here."

"*Whooo hooo!*" cackled Jimmy with a laugh, throwing the morning newspaper up in the air. "Boy, you really want this hotshot done in style! Hey, this I gotta see! Teddy will eat that cracker alive and spit out the bones!" He frowned. "You really think he's that good?"

"Some years ago there was a Mexican pharmaceuticals entrepeneur who made the mistake of underestimating our Mr. Redmond," said Bennett. "He and four of his pistoleros are pushing up cactuses, as well as a number of other criminal gentry. I do not intend to join them. But there's more to this. I wonder where the hell he's getting all his information?" he went on musingly. "Jimmy, it was made clear to me before I left Washington that every leak in this damned thing has to be plugged. Mine isn't the only ass that's on the line. Redmond was right about one thing, we're shooting craps with history here. If the so-called progressive element get their tie-dyed butts kicked out next month they probably aren't going to make it back in. The present administration has been very generous with our budget and very understanding about the need for legislation giving the Bureau new expanded powers to deal with domestic terrorism from crazed right-wing fanatics who want to undermine our free institutions and our democratic form of government."

"Powers which you can then turn around and use on anybody you want," pointed out Jimmy. "Powers you can use like J. Edgar Hoover used them, to build nice little dossiers on the people who control your purse strings and who might interfere with you, crying about all that Bill of Rights crap. Powers you can use to make yourself the guy who really runs this country."

"Cynically put, but essentially correct. This is too important to leave any loose ends."

"So the skinny bimbo and the kid gotta go as well?" asked Jimmy.

"There's a retired Chapel Hill cop, a nigger named Williams who kept nosing around in the case for years after it should have been dead and buried," said Bennett. "I think we can take it to the bank Redmond's been talking to him too. We don't know what he might have told Williams. There's also our highly placed scholarly gentleman in the groves of academe, Dr. Paul Lieberman."

"He swore up and down he'd stonewalled Redmond," Jimmy reminded him.

"And we saw how well Redmond buys bullshit," said Bennett. "Do you think that stuffed-shirt asshole will stand up if it gets too hot?"

"That's a lot of dead bodies," said Jimmy shaking, his head. "Gonna attract attention in a town this size. Especially Lieberman. He's a big fish in this little pond."

"That's why it's got to be done right. There's a lot at stake," said Bennett grimly. "I think I see a way to kill two birds with one stone in Lieberman's case, though."

"Hey, I been thinking," said Jimmy. "You get to step into J. Edgar's high heels and be next Director of the Bureau if we pull this one off, Billyboy gets re-elected and all the Sixties crowd get to breathe a sigh of relief, but what do I get beyond the quiet satisfaction of serving my country?"

"What do you want?" asked Bennett with a tired smile, expecting a demand for money.

"That hat," said Jimmy promptly. "I want that Indiana Jones hat he always wears."

"Consider it yours," replied Bennett. "Just remember the old saying about selling the lion's skin while it's still on the lion, James."

"When Tedtaotao gets through with hotshot, that's hat's going to be the only thing left," answered Jimmy with a grin.

XIII

The next morning Matt drove out to a favorite spot of his by the shores of Jordan Lake, some twenty miles away, to do some serious thinking. The day was cool and the leaves were starting to turn color in earnest. On a Tuesday morning there were few fishermen or boaters on the lake, so he was able to sit down at a picnic table by himself and smoke a long, leisurely cigar, then walk along the red and gold lakeshore as he smoked another.

It was maddening, but Matt was forced to admit that for all practical purposes the case was at an end. In theory he could arrest three people as accessories to the murders: Bennett, Margaret Mears, and Paul Lieberman. In practice he couldn't even get a warrant issued for any of them, much less convict and send any of them to prison. He possessed not one jot of legal proof except the word of a ghost and a foreign agent. *This case has got to be numero uno on the weirdness scale for my whole career,*

Matt thought to himself with rueful amusement. He imagined himself testifying in court about the spectral messages from the murdered girl appearing on the computer screen and laughed out loud. He doubted he could even do it with a straight face, never mind what a jury would think. Rozanov was useless as a witness. He would never appear in court and his diplomatic immunity made it impossible to force him or even arrest him. Besides, Matt felt honor bound not to harass him. He understood that there was a tacit professional courtesy agreement between them. He liked the little Russian and wouldn't feel right bringing pointless heat down on him.

There remained the possibility of extra-legal steps to punish those who had covered up for the killers. Like every skilled and experienced law enforcement officer, Matt was adept at bending or breaking the rules where necessary in order to apprehend or thwart the plans of those who recognized no rules at all. It was simply a necessity of the job, and anyone who thought otherwise was a fool. Very often a lawman's career and reputation were built on the acute, fine-tuned sensitivity needed to recognize and understand just when, where, and how far he could go, and the delicate finesse to break the law in such a discreet yet effective manner that the criminal landed in jail and he didn't. Matt was good at it, and he prided himself that during his entire career he had never violated the rights of anyone who wasn't guilty as hell, or committed any Mark Fuhrmanesque screwups. Men like Bennett recognized no difference between drug kingpins and the children of Waco; to them a target was a target and one brought the target down for whoever was signing the checks. Matt had never been like that. He didn't give a tinker's damn about the rights of anyone concerned in Mary Jane's death, but there just wasn't any evidence for him to obtain, legally or otherwise.

There remained two possibilities, going to the media and fabrication. The media route was hampered by the same difficulty as legal prosecution: not one scrap of usable, hard evidence he could give to a reporter or a TV tabloid celebrity upon which even the most tenuous story could be built; in view of who was involved the idea was pointless. If nothing else, the legal department of any newspaper or television network would go into hysterics over any attempt to link the noble and beloved Congressperson for the Women of the World Meg Mears to the murder of her own daughter.

That left fabrication. Matt knew that the three were guilty, and if he could think of a way to manufacture evidence against them he would do it without hesitation. But he remembered something he had been taught in a certain officially non-existent Federal law enforcement course, covertly designated "Real World 101." The instructor who was no instructor was a retired U. S. Attorney and FBI agent who knew his stuff backwards and forwards and taught the short course which was no course for free.

"Total fabrication of a case from the ground up is the riskiest technique any Federal law enforcement officer can attempt," this man had told Matt's class which was no class. "Use it only as a last resort, when all else has failed and you are dealing with someone so dangerous that they must be taken off the streets at any cost. Bear in mind, boys and girls, that officially I am telling you none of this and this whole discussion is not taking place, but if it was taking place, I would advise you that total fabrication is like radioactive waste. No matter how deep you bury it, no matter how many years you think it's successfully buried, it can still spring a leak and start poisoning and contaminating everything. Fabrication can cost you your job, your retirement, your whole career in law enforcement, and if you really screw up it can even send you into those living hells where you have sent so many others. Fabrication is not just dynamite, it's nitroglycerin. Don't handle this particular nitro at all unless you absolutely must.

"There will be times when you receive pressure from above to fabricate cases against people the government of the day finds politically inconvenient. They may call it 'proactive enforcement' or 'creative investigation' or some such bullshit. What they mean is quit screwing around and frame this guy because somebody in a really expensive suit with an agenda wants him in jail. My advice is don't touch these cases with a ten foot pole. They are dangerous as hell. Political frames are the most volatile and unstable of all. They can explode in your face at any time and besides, destroying innocent people out of political motivations is a dirty thing to do. You'll find the dirt stays on your hands permanently. The most important thing of all I would tell you about fabrication is don't *ever* attempt it without fully informed consent from your immediate higher up. You're putting your boss's ass on the line as well as yours and he won't thank you for any surprises that come up in court. Don't put him or yourself in a position where he has to throw you to the wolves to save his own pension. The *only* time, in my view, that fabrication is justified is when you know damned well that people are going to die if someone isn't put away. That's if our ethical and conscientious Federal government ever framed people, which of course we all know they don't. If any of you ever repeat any of this to anyone outside this room, I will call you a liar to your face and file disciplinary charges."

I guess that's out, thought Matt morosely as he puffed away meditatively. A flight of Canada geese sailed majestically overhead on their way south, then eased down for a rest on the crystal clear water of the autumn lake. *Phil's given me a lot of rope in the past, but he's a straight arrow and he won't go for an out-and-out frame. So what's left? Just plain smoke 'em?* Matt understood himself well enough to know that when he began the investigation, some such idea had been in the back of his mind if he was able to prove to his own satisfaction but not the law's that he had found the guilty parties. He was forty-three years old. He was starting to get clear and unmistakable signs that his body was aging and slowing down. His dark brown hair was getting lighter and lighter and he had recently shaved a long-time moustache because the white hairs came to outnumber the brown and he wasn't quite ready to make the ultimate surrender of using dye. Two weeks ago the future had been an incomprehensible blackness, and the idea of gunning down the Assistant Director of the FBI, a world-renowned Congresswoman, and the next likely Chancellor of the University of North Carolina would have had a sardonic appeal to him as a suitable blaze of glory to go out in.

But now there was Heather. *I told her I wouldn't hurt her if I could help it,* he thought bitterly. *If I keep that promise I may have to break the one I made to Mary Jane and Jeannie and those they left behind. There's an interesting ethical question to kick around. Which count more, solemn duties to the living or the dead? Speaking of promises, I told Will Williams I'd let him know what I found out. Maybe he can think of something I can't.* He tossed his cigar butt into the lake, got in his car, and headed back to Carrboro, stopping for a lunch at a salad bar along the way. He pulled up to Williams' small white frame house about three o'clock. Will's car was still in the driveway. The neighborhood was quiet. Matt rang the bell and got no answer. After the third ring was met with silence an alarm bell went off in his head. He drew his .357 and gently tried the front door. It was unlocked. "Will?" he called out as he stepped inside into the front hall, apprehension growing. "Will, are you here? It's Matt Redmond." *Maybe he's in the shower or on can,* though Matt desperately.

He found Will W. Williams lying on the kitchen floor, dressed in his IBM security blazer, white shirt and slacks, but with no tie. On the kitchen table was an open microwave dinner, cooked but now cold, and a cup of coffee, also cold. Williams' eyes were open, staring vacantly at the ceiling. There was a small hole in his forehead, placed neatly between his eyes. A similar hole traced spidery tentacles in the pane of the window onto the back porch. "Damn, Will," sighed Matt softly, sick at heart. "Shit, I'm sorry. I never figured this." He looked at the bullet hole in the window. "Looks like .22, but a heavier slug than a long rifle," he said to himself. "Probably a silenced .22 Magnum, Ruger or Beretta. A CIA hit man's gun. I know who shot you, Will. I'll get him. You can bank on it." He looked down at the corpse and then around the room. "Will, I hope you're close enough to hear me. I'm sorry, I need to move fast and I don't have time to call the law and file a hundred reports and shit. I'm going to have to leave you here for your wife to find. I just hope to God none of your neighbors remember some white guy in a funny hat coming in here. I think maybe that's what these bastards are after, trying to pin it on me. I'll get them, Will. I promise." Matt carefully wiped his prints off every doorknob he had touched with a handker-chief, slipped out the side door and got in his car. The neighbor-hood remained quiet and looked empty, but Matt had to assume his white face had been noted. He drove a few blocks to his apartment, parking carefully and looking all around as he went inside. He dialed Heather's number at work.

"Accounting. This is Gail, may I help you?" said a voice.

"I need to speak with Heather Lindstrom, rather urgently," Matt told her.

"I'm sorry, Ms. Lindstrom will be out of the office until tomor-row," said Gail. "She had to go to her daughter's high school after lunch, some kind of accident. Is there something I can help you with, sir?"

"Is Dr. Paul Lieberman in, by any chance?" asked Matt.

"No, he never came back from lunch. Rather odd, he missed several appointments."

"I see, Thank you, ma'am." A quick call to Chapel Hill High School confirmed that there had been no accident. A young student office assistant told him that a man had called the office and left a message for Tori to come home immediately. "Did this man on the phone identify himself?" asked Matt keenly.

"He said he was an SBI agent named Redmond," the girl told him. Matt hung up. *Dear God, don't let them be dead too!* Matt prayed, his head in his hands, his body shaking. *If I have killed them, if they have died because of me then I will go mad, mad like my father and my brother, and my soul will become as damned as theirs.* He dialed Heather's cellular phone number. It rang and rang, on and on, with no answer. *They're dead,* thought Matt in purest agony of soul. *I will never see her again, never touch her beautiful hair, never hold her again. Tori will never play with Trumpeldor again. Like Mary Jane, she will wander in the twilight, forever sixteen. The phone is ringing in a hole scraped under the fallen leaves, out in the woods somewhere. I am listening to her phone ringing in her grave. I am going mad. I will go to Washington D.C and kill them all, Meg Mears and Bennett and Janet Reno and Billyboy and Hillary, as many of them as I can get before I die. They have filled my life and my country and the whole world with drugs and death and lies and filth. I will not live in the world they have created and I won't let them live on and enjoy it either.* The phone clicked. Heather's voice seemed far away. "Hello?" she said tightly.

"Are you and Tori all right?" demanded Matt.

"No."

"Is it Bennett?" he asked.

"That's right."

"Where are you?" he demanded urgently.

"You did a lot of talking yesterday morning, Matt," came Bennett's voice. "Now you're going to do some listening, after which you're going to do what you're told. First off, you seem to have forgotten that my nice shiny *Federal* badge is good in all fifty states, including your hundred pissant little North Carolina counties. Records in Washington will show that my colleagues and myself are down here investigating a major drug ring. We discovered a couple of keys of high grade coke in your lady friend's home, which we searched today under a quite legal Federal warrant. We also found another key or two in the kid's car. They can share a cell together in Alderson for a good many years if you want to go that route, *capiche?*"

"Yeah, I get it," said Matt tonelessly. *Bullshit. He's trying to buffalo me.*

"Tell you what, though, you bring us that damned SBI file you've been working off, just so we can make sure this particular sleeping dog is let lie, and we'll forget about the dope," Bennett continued suavely. *If they'd searched Heather's house they would have found the file there,* thought Matt. *The whole thing is bullshit. No planted dope, no Federal search warrant, not a damned thing on paper. They're planning to kill us all.*

"Okay. When and where?"

"The when is now," said Bennett.

"I'm going to have to drive to Raleigh and get the file," Matt told him. "I took it back a few days ago; they were getting antsy about my keeping it out so long. If I get going now I can just make it in time to check it out again before closing."

"Sounds like a stall to me," said Bennett warningly. "Not good, Matt. Not recommended at all. Don't think you're going to call somebody with some horse shit about how we've kidnapped your girl friend. This isn't kidnaping, Matt, it's perfectly lawful detention if we have to justify it. Read them their rights and everything. If we see any county mounties or other local yokel cops coming in they're going to try to get Jimmy's gun and we're going to have to shoot them, Matt. It will be legal six ways to Sunday and you know it."

"Just like Waco was legal?" asked Matt.

"You got it. Just like Waco. Don't fuck with me on this, Matt. It's hardball time now."

"I'm not fucking with you, dammit!" snapped Matt, allowing a bit of his genuine panic to creep into his voice. "I told you, I took the damned file back! I'll get it for you, but I've got to drive to Raleigh and I need to get going! Where do you want me to bring the file?"

"A place I believe you know," chuckled Bennett. "Out off Highway 54 West, just short of the Alamance County line. The address is Rt. #4, Box 45, Mile End Road. I believe you guys call it the Plantation? Very impressive home, by the way. Your father and your brother have excellent taste. Even Jimmy calls it a classy joint."

"I know the place," said Matt, his eyes beginning to burn, red rage filling his vision. *Daddy is in this, too. That's it. He's gone too far this time.* "I'll get the file. I'll call ahead to the archives to tell them I'm coming, and I'll bring it out to you, but it will take time. I should be there about seven o'clock. Now let me talk to Heather."

"Sure," said Bennett. "I'll hold the phone up to her ear, and I will hear you as well."

"Heather, have you or Tori been harmed?" asked Matt.

"Not yet," she replied, her voice calm. *She knows they're going to kill them,* Matt realized. "Our wrists and our ankles are handcuffed. We're seated in chairs and up until now we've both been gagged, but we haven't been physically harmed." *Bound and seated in a chair,* thought Matt. *Dear God, not again!*

"Heather, I've got to go, so I'll say this quickly," he told her. "One night twenty-six years ago, I wasn't there for Mary Jane when she needed me. As God is my witness, I will be there for you and Tori tonight. Stay strong." He hung up.

"You'd better hope he does the right thing," Bennett told her menacingly, the westward-slanting sun gleaming golden through the tall windows of Sidney Redmond's ornate music room where they were held captive. He picked up the gag to put it back in Heather's mouth.

"He will," she said quietly, before the gag slipped between her teeth and clamped her tongue down again. She looked over at Tori's terrified eyes, pleading to her mother for hope she tried to convey. *He's going to do the right thing, all right!* she thought fiercely. *I heard it in his voice. My magnificent lover is coming to kill you all! Death and destruction!*

Matt ran into the bedroom. The first thing he did was take off his shirt. From a closet he took a nylon acrylic Second Chance bulletproof vest which he carefully donned and strapped snug with velcro straps. Then he changed his shoes, putting on soft leather hiking boots. From his closet he took a leather hunting pouch with a strap on it, and a large canvas bag holding something long and heavy and metallic. He walked quickly to his car, and put these objects in the trunk, got in, and drove into Chapel Hill down Jones Ferry Road and onto Franklin Street through the maddening afternoon rush-hour traffic. It took him almost half an hour to reach the Hampton Inn on Legion Road near the 15-501 bypass. He parked and ran up to room 268.

Please let him still be there! Matt silently pleaded with God. *Please let him be sober! They're not bad guys, but they drink like maniacs. Please let him be sober!* He knocked on the door. Rozanov opened the door, wearing obviously new slacks and a polo shirt. The television was on behind him. Matt began speaking without preamble. "Those Federals you saw have got Heather and Tori Lindstrom. They're going to kill them. They have already killed one man here, a friend who helped me investigate the murders. They want to kill me as well, and they will try to kill you if you help me, all the more if they understand you know the secret. They want what your government wants, to keep what happened in that house twenty-six years ago buried forever. If you help me you will be risking punishment when you return home, and yet still I ask you to help. You say you are a decent man, that you are not like Greshkov and Probdanichev. Prove it. Prove it to me, to Heather and to Tori, to the spirit whose presence you felt in that room. Prove it to yourself."

Rozanov gestured back towards the rumbling television set. "And for this hazardous and dubious mission you expect me to miss Isle of Gilligan?" he asked politely.

*   *   *

Forty minutes later Matt drove the Taurus carefully down the bumpy, grass-grown firebreak road that ran behind his father's property. He reached a certain spot and then carefully turned the car around, pointing it back out the way he had come in, and turned off the engine. The two men got out of the car. Rozanov was wearing a light, supple black leather jacket, yet another new clothing purchase, and his soft Russian sable fur hat. Matt had on his windbreaker and his fedora. Around them the setting sun glowed golden in the crisp red and yellow autumn foliage around them, mixed with fragrant pines. A light wind rustled the leaves and brought a scent of wood smoke from somewhere. "This is a lovely land of yours, my friend," remarked Rozanov. "The drive out here alone is worth a certain degree of risk. What, precisely, do you wish me to do?"

"I'll tell you in a bit," said Matt. He opened the trunk, picked up the leather bag and slung the strap across his chest, tightening the buckle so the pouch rode high on his hip and didn't flap. He opened a box and took out a Llama 9-millimeter automatic. "This is actually my DEA government-issue sidearm, I just never used it. Always liked revolvers for some reason. You sure you don't want this?" he asked, offering it to Rozanov.

The Russian opened his jacket and revealed a leather case in his waistband like a tool belt, holding an array of six long, thin metal knives that looked like letter openers, in addition to the two Matt had taken off him the night they had met. "I am quite well equipped, thank you," he said.

"How come you don't carry a piece?" asked Matt curiously.

"The British historian Thomas Carlyle once wrote that gunpowder makes all men tall," explained Rozanov. "He was correct. Tall men make conspicuous targets. Guns tend to impart a feeling of power, and I decided early on that it is not good for a man of our vocation to feel powerful. He tends to rely on his power and not his mind, to shoot when he should be thinking. It is possible to die that way."

"I understand your point, but I don't know what you'll say about my Chicago typewriter," said Matt. He picked up the heavy canvas bag and pulled out the contents.

"Holy Peter, is that what I think it is?" asked Rozanov in amazement.

"It is indeed, *tovarich*," said Matt with a chuckle. "A blast from the past, quite literally. The gun that made the Twenties roar. A Thompson submachine gun, with two drum magazines, one hundred rounds of .45-caliber APC each." Matt cleared and checked the bolt on the Thompson, snapped one of the hundred-round drums into the feed well, chambered a round, checked the safety, then put the other heavy drum into the leather bag at his left side. "Ever since I had a run-in with a gent named Ramon down Mexico way, I've had this thing about finding myself out-gunned. I decided I need some reserve firepower handy. I have a Class Three permit for this, which costs me a bundle every year in Federal license fees and drives the BATF crazy knowing I have it, in view of some of the politically incorrect opinions I have expressed in the past."

"I thought you Americans didn't have to worry about political indiscretion?" queried Rozanov with a sardonic smile.

"We didn't, not until recently," sighed Matt sadly.

"It is a magnificent weapon!" complimented Rozanov in admiration. "One does not have to be a gun person to appreciate such terrible beauty. What else have you got in that bag?"

"A few odds and ends I may need. It's kind of a kit I made up in case I ever needed to get wild at heart and weird on top in a hurry. This situation qualifies. Ready? We'll go in a back way I know, through the woods, and I'll tell you what I want you to do while we move."

"Are you certain we should not wait until after dark?" asked Rozanov as they moved into the cool autumn forest, fallen pine needles cushioning their footfalls. "There is risk we will be seen approaching house."

"No, for two reasons," said Matt. "Both involving your end of this. I haven't been here in twenty-six years, at least not up to the Plantation itself, and I know the whole house is different now, about twice the size it was when I left. My father came into a lot of money when my mother died and he went on a building spree. But I do have intermittent contact with one member of the family, as I mentioned the other night, and she's told me some things. One is that there is a dog. A big dog, a rottweiler. He lives in a kennel behind and to the southeast of the house, and I'm hoping that's where we'll find him. There will be at least two strangers in there, and they'll be waiting for me to arrive, another stranger, so logically it would make sense for them to keep the dog locked up. But we need to know where he is; if he's loose I don't want a rott charging down on us in the dark. The dog has to be silenced quietly so he doesn't bark and give us away. That's where you come in. I don't have a silencer, they're completely illegal. I hope you're as good as people say with those blades of yours."

"I'm here alive," said Rozanov with a shrug. "Some are not."

"Watch the way we're going here. You're going to have to find your way back to the car on your own. That's the second reason we can't wait until dark. You might get lost." They came to a small, deep and swiftly-flowing creek by a rocky outcropping of boulders. "See that tree trunk? Use that to cross over the creek. I was out here about a year ago and I spent half a day tussling that log into place in case I ever had to get in and out of here quickly." Rozanov gave him an odd look.

"This is your father's house, you say?"

"My brother's now," said Matt, slinging the Thompson muzzle down over his shoulder while he climbed up the log, which lay across the creek at an incline. "My father lives in Charleston. Yeah, I know all this must seem pretty weird to you. I'll tell you all about it later, but this has been coming for quite some time. This little visit on my part is definitely past due. After you take out the dog, I want you to go back to the car. Here are the car keys, before I forget. Give me about five minutes from the time you get back to the vehicle, then drive back out the firebreak, turn right onto Mile End Road when you hit the pavement, then drive down about a third of a mile and turn into the second driveway on your right, the one with three mail boxes. That's the entrance to the

Plantation, although you won't be able to see the house from the road. Drive all the way down until you're almost to the house. You'll see a big wide lawn on your left, and to the right where the road jogs a bit you'll see a little stand of pine trees. I'll show you when we're out back. Don't drive right up to the house; we don't know what they've got waiting. Turn around facing back down the drive like I did and park the car under those pines, engine running, ready for Heather and Tori. Once I extract them they will be making a fast exit from the house. Be ready to pick them up on the fly, and then *get the hell out of here!* Don't worry about me. I grew up around here and I can find my way out through these woods in the dark. Have you got all that?"

"*Ya panimayu,*" said Rozanov with a nod.

"Right, you can just see the back of the house through the trees," Matt whispered, pointing. "From now on this is a covert entry. Keep down, keep quiet, and move carefully. We'll see if we can sneak up behind the dog kennel." A brief breeze rattled through the trees. Matt licked his thumb and held it up in the air. "Good, we're downwind. Have your weapon ready. Let's go." Rozanov slid one of the throwing knives from his belt and palmed it in his right hand; they crouched and moved cautiously from tree to tree. They reached the edge of the wide, downward sloping back lawn of the huge mansion; Matt was momentarily stunned by the profusion of new wings, extra rooms, prefab outbuildings, a house trailer near the kennel which Michelle had mentioned was servants' quarters, all kinds of additions to the sprawling home he didn't remember. The kennel was big, enclosed with heavy wire fencing strung on stout wooden posts a huge metal doghouse in the center. The rottweiler lay in front of the doghouse, head on his paws, surrounded by bones and toys and a huge food and water bowl. One of the men cracked a twig beneath his feet and the dog's head snapped up, alert. Instantly the animal was on his feet, head turning towards them, a low growl beginning in the throat, building up to a thunderous bark.

Rozanov wound up like a baseball pitcher and uncoiled like a steel spring, a single fluid motion, lightning fast. Matt didn't see or hear the knife fly. The rott dropped over like it had been poleaxed, quivered once and then lay still. Perhaps four inches of knife handle protruded from his throat. "God Almighty, I've never seen anything like that!" Matt whispered in awe. "That's fifty feet if it's an inch!"

"Pah, an easy throw," replied Rozanov carelessly.

"Do you want to see if you can get in there and get your knife back?" asked Matt.

"*Nichyevo*. Let them know afterwards that Kolya Nozh was here," said Rozanov with a wicked little chuckle.

"The man's got panache," replied Matt with a smile. "Okay, that's half your gig done. Can you find your way back to the...?" Suddenly the side door of the house opened. A man stepped out into the covered walkway leading between the house and the huge garage, lit a cigarette, and stood smoking it. He was tall, slim, well-built, with a handsome tanned face and curly blond hair. He wore a plaid shirt and tight jeans; what looked like a steel-plated .357 Magnum police special with a polished wooden grip rode in a holster on his belt. "Well, I'll be damned..." whispered Matt slowly, his heart surging in bitter hatred. "Hail, hail, the gang's all here!"

"You know him?" whispered Rozanov.

"Yeah. His name is Jack Conley. He works for my father. My guess is he's holding Daddy's watching brief for this evening's festivities. Long story. Can you find your way back to the car?"

"*Da.*"

"Give me some time, say five minutes once you get back, which will be ten or twelve minutes from now you should be pulling down that drive. See the pine tree stand I told you about? Pull in there and be ready to boogie. It will be almost dark by then. They'll hear you coming down the drive and that will get their attention. I'll have to be inside by then and ready to extract Heather and Tori. If my information is right, there should be several exits towards the front of the house. As soon as I can I'll send the women out to you. Go on back. Be careful, make sure Conley doesn't see you."

"*Zhilayu uzpyekaf, tovarich,*" said Rozanov. "Good luck." The little man slipped away from him, in complete silence.

I guess not all Russians are city boys, thought Matt. He was a bit leery of moving himself from behind his tree, loaded down as he was with vest, bag, ammo, and several heavy weapons. His leg started to cramp up, but Conley seemed in no hurry to go back in. He glanced over at the kennel and saw the dog lying there. "Lazy mutt!" he laughed, then sauntered into the garage. Matt moved swiftly and as quietly as he could to behind the huge propane tank supplying the house, then after ascertaining that there was no one looking from the darkened rear windows of the house he made a run for the corner of the building, which he made.

He was now on the north side of the long, rambling house of mixed siding and brick, the only side where there were no entrances, where the woods clustered closest. His first thought was to try and locate Heather and Tori. Matt opened his pouch and took out a long tubular object of black plastic, which he telescoped open. It was a periscope. The last rays of the sun setting in the west shone down on the house, providing him with ample light. He worked his way down the side of the house, the Thompson submachine gun slung over his shoulder, easing the tip of the periscope over the sill over every window, looking into each room. There was the small den with the second TV where Matt had so often retreated to avoid his father in the main living room.

There was the large, never used formal dining room. There was the luxurious downstairs bathroom where Matt had run and vomited his breakfast when he understood that Mary Jane Mears had been murdered. There was the former TV lounge that had once been his father's throne room where he had held court surrounded by his silent Praetorian guard of dead Marines. This room had been extended until it was a huge, ornately furnished salon, with three of the biggest sofas Matt had ever seen on a parquet floor. The old 20-inch Zenith color TV of 1970, although an aristocrat of its day, had been replaced by a mammoth home entertainment center with a big screen that almost covered one wall, fed from the satellite dish atop the garage. Every room thus far was empty of human life.

In Matt's day the TV lounge had opened onto the outside through the front door with a modest pillared portico, but tonight a whole new wing protruded which almost doubled the length of the Plantation. Michelle had described to him the massive music room Sid had added onto the house in the mid-1980s, through generous expenditure of his share of the liquid part of Mama's estate. It was an acoustically perfect, high-ceilinged wonder of architectural engineering, the size of a ballroom with floors polished to a gleam by a succession of Latin American groundskeepers of deficient documentation. It was often used to give private recitals and hold elegant soirées for Chapel Hill's liberal elite, in aid of every imaginable artistic and progressive cause. Daddy's move to Charleston with his second wife had allowed Michelle to blossom into a chic and fashionable hostess whose invitations were much sought after in the Triangle's academic and Democratic circles. Matt had never seen the inside of this stately pleasure dome by Kubla Sid decreed, and he curiously raised the periscope. He struck pay dirt.

The first thing he saw was the mighty grand piano at the far end of the room. The lights were on, and it gleamed darkly against the crystal chandeliers' glow. The room was largely empty except for a sofa near the French doors at the far end that opened onto a wide brick patio, and a row of stacked chairs along the near wall. The CIA man Jimmy Johnson was lounging on the piano bench, leaning on the closed keyboard. An Uzi submachine gun was slung carelessly from one shoulder. FBI Assistant Director Charles R. Bennett sat in an armchair, staring out the window at the drive, obviously waiting for a car to come down from the road to the house. An M-16 rifle leaned in a corner by his chair, and several extra magazines lay on the window sill. Matt slid the periscope down and eased on down to the next window. Through that he saw a long L-shaped wet bar running along the wall nearest to him. He stood up carefully to give the periscope more reach, and to his immense relief he spied Tori and Heather sitting in high-backed chairs, their hands pinned behind them, government-issue leather gags with red rubber balls as tongue depressors in their mouths. *Thank God!* he almost cried out in relief. *They're still alive!*

Then he caught sight of something else and almost dropped the instrument in amazement. Sitting bolt upright in a chair a little way from the women, completely motionless, was a gigantic brown-skinned man dressed in a square-cut, blue tailored suit and green tie that looked almost like they were cut out of cardboard. Even sitting down, he was the biggest man Matt had ever seen outside of a circus. His head was completely bald, and his fat cheeks and jowls bulged up out over his collar. His flat-faced expressionless features and thin, almost non-existent lips made him look like a frog. Half of his face was covered with strange whorls of blue tribal tattoos, and the hands the size of hams resting on his knees bore tattoos as well. Cradled in the apparition's

lap was a long, slender-barreled weapon with a fat drum magazine, a South African-made Stryker "Street-Sweeper" 12-gauge
shotgun, in the proper hands more lethal firepower than the Uzi
and M-16 combined. *Holy shit, that's at least four of them!*
thought Matt. *And what in the name of God is that? That's got to
be a Samoan!*

He glanced at his watch; minutes were ticking by, and he still
had to get into the house. He put the periscope back into his
pouch, unslung the Thompson, crouched down and headed back
down to the east end of the house; his best bet getting in would be
the door Conley had come out of, which led into what used to be
Daddy's workshop, or else through the kitchen door. He passed
the last window and stood up, about to peep around the building
to see if Conley was visible, when the man himself stepped around
the corner and suddenly felt the muzzle of Matt's machine gun
pressing his navel. "Whoa!" said Conley, sucking in his breath.
"Hey, that's some pretty heavy heat you're bringing to the table,
Matthew old buddy! We were hoping to work this out with a nice
quiet sitdown, a mutual exchange of favors."

"Shut up," grated Matt, stepping back. "Take your piece out of
the holster, forefinger and thumb only." Conley scowled but did
so, slowly. "Toss it," ordered Matt. He did so.

"Now what the hell are you going to do?" Conley asked. *Good
question, old buddy,* thought Matt, his face expressionless. *Just
gun you down? Alert everybody in the house and put myself
legally in the wrong forever by killing my wife's unarmed lover?
Why don't I just walk up to Bennett and say "Take me, I'm
yours"?* Aloud he said in a steady voice, "If I kill you now I'll
always wonder if it wasn't for the wrong reason. If I just kill you
because I want to, then someday Evie might point to your death as
proof that I am exactly the kind of man you told her I was. So I'll
make you a deal, Jack. You turn around. You walk into those

woods. You keep on walking, straight. Cross over the creek. About a mile on you'll come to a firebreak road. Turn left and about a mile on down there's a little convenient store where you can phone for a cab or hitch a ride. Don't ever come back here, Jack. If I see your face back here again tonight I'll kill you."

"Look, Matt, down in Florida, it wasn't anything personal with me," said Conley placatingly. "It was just business. No, no, hell, I can't lie to you, you're too smart for that," he suddenly laughed. "I have to admit, towards the end there was a good deal of pleasure in it too. You should have stayed home more. That was one hot tamale you had there, Matt, once I figured out which buttons to push. Or should I say lick?"

"You're trying to make me mad, aren't you, Jack?" said Matt with a lazy smile that made Conley blanch. "Good. That means you're planning on doing something stupid. I'm glad you're planning on doing something stupid, Jack." Matt heard the click of the switchblade and tried to parry, but the Thompson was too heavy and Conley lunged past his guard. The vest saved him; if Matt hadn't been wearing it the vicious thrust would have gutted him like a fish. Matt twisted and before Conley could recover gave him the butt of the Thompson full in the face. Conley went down with a thud. Matt was on top of him in a flash, Conley's head in his hands, twisting. There was a snap as Conley's neck broke; his dying body quivered and flopped. A smell of feces filled the air as his bowels emptied into his jeans.

Matt slid around the side of the house and went directly to the kitchen, or what used to be the kitchen; now there was an extra room protruding and a screen porch. Matt eased onto the porch and carefully looked inside. The extra room was kind of a breakfast nook, lower than the main kitchen he remembered. Michelle Redmond was sitting in the nook at a table, wearing jeans and a turtle-necked sweater, idly glancing through a magazine. Matt eased off the porch and went back to the connecting door between the garage and the house. The door Conley had come out of was locked; Matt opened his bag, slid out a small leather pouch, selected a lock-pick, and had the door open in ten seconds. He slid into the dimly lit room. In his youth this had been his father's workshop. Now it was a kind of study; the books on the shelves were mostly of the New Age, feminist, and psychobabble variety. The room was decorated with odd bits and pieces of Third World kitsch and garish paintings showing ungainly naked women with huge breasts and buttocks dancing about on tiptoe and playing catch with a globe of the world. A personal computer and printer sat on a polished desk in one corner.

This must be Michelle's little study or New Age sanctum whatever, he thought. He slid quietly down the hall and into the kitchen. Michelle was still sitting at the table, her back to him. She got up and went over to a coffee maker and poured herself another cup. He leaned the Thompson carefully against the wall and tiptoed down the three steps into the nook, quietly drawing his .357 Magnum from his shoulder holster. When she had set the cup down on the table he stepped out and grabbed her from behind, clapping his left hand over her mouth and pressing the gun muzzle against her head.

"You always wanted me to keep the bullets in, Michelle," he whispered, soft and deadly. "You've got your wish. All six of them are in the cylinder tonight, and this time it's for real. I'm going to take my hand off your mouth. If you scream or if you try to alert those men in there, I will kill you. I mean it, Mick. Unless you are so damned sick in the head that you really do get off on your own death, you'd better keep very quiet and answer all my questions with the truth. Do you understand that this isn't a game any more, that you really are going to die if you fuck with me?" Michelle nodded. He took his hand off her mouth and clamped it around her throat. The pistol barrel he pressed into her head just behind her right ear. "First question. I need to know whose side you're on. If you're on their side, tell me, and as long as you're honest with me about it I'll let you live. I'll choke you out, strangle you until you're unconscious so you won't interfere, but I won't choke until you're dead. You have my word. Now tell me."

"I'm on your side," she whispered.

"How many of them are there?" he asked.

"Four. Three Federal agents and a private security guy who works for your father."

"Yeah, Conley. I ran into him outside. He's not a problem any more." Michelle's breath hissed in and she shuddered.

"Did you...?" she whispered.

"Yes. I saw the three in the music room through the window, and the two women hostages. Are the women actually cuffed into the chairs or can they get up?" asked Matt, his voice so low as to be barely audible.

"Bennett let them go to the bathroom, with the door open and guarded. I think they can get up," answered Michelle softly.

"Why did you betray me to my father?" Michelle slumped in resignation.

"Randall knows about you and me. God knows how, maybe Conley followed me. I've been spying on you for Randall. He threatened to make Sid divorce me."

"Now that I see this place I can understand why you wouldn't want to lose it," sighed Matt. "Now that you've been lady of the manor and tasted the fruits of wicked capitalism it would be hard to start over again, go back to sharing an apartment with a couple of other arts groupies, taking night courses, any excuse to keep hanging around campus into your thirties and forties."

"You never met my last roommates or you'd understand how scary that prospect is," she whispered back. "It's not just the money, Matt. I know you won't believe me, but I really do love Sid. That's why I stayed here tonight. I was afraid to leave him alone with those men. God knows what they mean to do, especially that...that big one. Sid's up in his room listening to CDs, but I can tell he's afraid to come downstairs."

"Why is he here at all?" demanded Matt.

"He's supposed to be the one who kills you," said Michelle dismally. "The scenario is supposed to be that you and those women are some kind of psycho love triangle. You three allegedly break into the house, tie up Sid and me, do crazy sex things with me, Sid gets loose and gets a gun and kills all three of you."

"And you went along with this?" said Matt, even in a whisper his voice shaking with anger. She turned and faced him.

"I won't ask you to forgive me for the spying, Matt, but this thing tonight came out of the blue. If you will trust me to help you, I'll do what I can to get them out alive, even if it means I get hurt myself. Only please, please don't hurt Sid. He's not responsible. You know Randall has always been able to dominate him."

"I always figured you to give Daddy some competition there," said Matt.

"Maybe if this business tonight goes bad I'll have the wedge I need to pry him away from Randall," she whispered.

"As long as Daddy signs the checks you can forget that idea. Well, hopefully he'll have sense enough to stay upstairs and out of the way," said Matt. "Michelle, how strong is that wet bar in there? How well built?"

"Pure mahogany, not just paneling," she said with a touch of pride.

"All right, listen up. I saw four doors into the music room, right? One through what used to be my mother's sewing room beyond the kitchen here, one from main hall, one from the TV room or living room or whatever you call it now, and what looked like a little door just behind the bar. Where does that lead?"

"Large guest cloakroom and bathroom," she said.

"Can you get into there through the living room without being seen?"

"The salon, yes. There's a second door into the cloakroom at the far wall."

"Get in there and be ready to move fast, very fast," Matt ordered. "In a couple of minutes there's going to be a guy driving my car coming down the driveway. That will get their attention. Hopefully the three men will move a bit towards the windows and away from the women, wanting to get a look. When they do I'm coming in through the sewing room door. I'm coming in smoking, and I don't mean a cigar. I've got a little toy with me that should be able to take them all out, one two three. You've got to get Heather and Tori out of the line of fire. When the shooting starts, you run out, grab the women by their collars or whatever you can grab, get them on their feet and down behind that bar to give me a free field of fire. If they're tied to the chairs you'll have to drag them chairs and all. Then you need to get them loose from the handcuffs. Here's a cuff key," he said, reaching into his pocket and handing it to her.

"Thanks," she whispered. "I've got one of my own, but it's upstairs."

"Why am I not surprised at this? Anyway, get them out of their cuffs and at the first chance you see, get them out through the French doors in the front and over the drive to that little stand of pines. My car and a driver will be waiting. Can you do all this?"

"I can," she replied.

"Will you do it?" he asked.

"I will. Matt, one thing. I think they're all wearing bulletproof vests."

"So am I," whispered Matt. "God, this is going to be a bloody mess!"

"So is everything Randall gets involved in," replied Michelle drily. She moved up the stairs, then turned and whispered, "Heather's a lucky woman. I know Sid loves me in his own way, but he would never do anything like this for me. I envy her. Do you love her?"

"I think so," he replied in an undertone. "You really want to make up for the deception, the lying, Mick? Save them both for me." He put the .357 back into the shoulder holster, reached around the corner and and picked up the Thompson.

"Damn!" hissed Michelle in admiration. "That's a *big* one!"

"Curiosity question," said Matt. "Are you getting off on all this?"

Michelle rolled her eyes. "Am I *ever!*"

*   *   *

Matt slid through the kitchen door and into what used to be his mother's so-called sewing room, actually a general clutter room. Among other things Daddy had tried converting it into a home winery and a laundry room. Now it was the music library; the walls were lined with shelf after shelf of CDs, cassettes, old vinyl LP records, reel-to-reel tapes of Sid's concerts in cardboard boxes, carefully marked in black felt-tip pen. Inset into a shelf by the door was a large console CD player, the biggest Matt had ever seen. He crept up beneath it. He glanced at the controls and saw a toggle switch labeled "speakers" and taped labels for "music room only", "upstairs", "bedroom", "guest bathroom", and finally "whole house". *Damn, that's a hell of a system!* thought Matt enviously. *Wonder what it set Sid back?* The door into the music room was open just a crack. Outside the sun was almost down, and only the dimmest light illuminated the little room. He could hear voices from the music room.

"I don't like the delay," Jimmy was saying. "You shouldn't have let him stall like that. We don't need the damned state police file."

"How did Redmond find out about the Russian connection?" demanded Bennett.

"You said yourself, the guy's an expert on the Russian mob. So he probably just asked the birdskis," replied Jimmy.

"How did he know the right questions to ask?" replied Bennett. "He found something in that file, dammit! Something tipped him off! We have to know what it is, Jim. This whole episode has to be wrapped up tight as a drum and sunk where it will never come bubbling up to the surface again."

"This gig may not get us a damned thing," complained Jimmy. "The TV and the polls say Billyboy's got it all sewed up come November 5th. But what if they're wrong? Your bosses may not be your bosses any more in a few weeks, and we will have wasted all this goddamned effort."

"I've been thinking about that," replied Bennett with a chuckle. "I think we can salvage something here which would be of over-riding interest to an incoming Republican administration. That's another reason why we need that SBI file. Suppose we can figure out whatever the hell Redmond figured out, put the same pieces together he did, only put an FBI label on it? You remember, Jimmy, this whole Mears-Arnold murder case was mine originally, back in the days when I was a humble Chapel Hill cop. I was the primary. It was my greatest failure. I suddenly find that it has preyed on my mind for all these years, and I just can't rest until I get justice for those two poor dead girls. I'm sure any conservative administration that takes over in Washington would be very pleased if a dedicated civil servant inspired by a passionate love of truth and justice were suddenly to discover that the anti-Vietnam war movement of the Sixties was financed by the Communists, and that brutal Russian agents committed the terrible murder of two beautiful young American girls. Be a good excuse to cut the Russkies off at the knees, or more likely make 'em really pay through the nose for their foreign aid welfare check from Uncle Sam. A lot of business interests would be able to really put the screws on the bastards with a little moral leverage like that."

"Make you look pretty good," said Jimmy with a chuckle.

"It would make me look *damned* good, James. It would make me a lot of very highly placed friends in corporate boardrooms and among the geriatric Russophobic set alike. Of course, if the Democrats get back in, their gratitude for my suppression of that information will be boundless."

"Looks like you're going to be stepping into old J. Edgar's high heels no matter who wins the election," said the CIA man.

"You can take that to the bank, Jimmy," replied Bennett.

"I still want the hat, though," said Jimmy. "Hey, Tedtaotao, I got dibs on hotshot's Indiana Jones hat, but is there any particular souvenir you want?"

"I should rather like to acquire the gentleman's liver, if I might," came an astounding low, rumbling voice in a perfect Oxonian British accent. "Would that be agreeable to you, Assistant Director? The liver of a slain enemy has many interesting properties of a ritualistic and occult nature, and from what I know of Mr. Redmond, his liver will be a particularly valuable acquisition. Not quite the done thing in Western societies, I realize, but one's old habits die rather hard."

"Uh, certainly, Mr. Tedtaotao," said Bennett, surprised. "But I doubt that street-sweeper of yours is going to leave much liver in him."

"Not necessarily, sir. Correctly handled the shotgun is a far more precise weapon than is generally credited."

Great, thought Matt to himself. *The CIA asshole wants my hat, that Polynesian Frankenstein wants my liver, and Rozanov is late. I don't think he'd come this far and then run out on me. Doesn't strike me as the type. But he might have gotten lost, or gotten the car stuck. Okay, time to get this show on the road. Firefighting 101: when faced with one or more weapons always take out the shotgun first, it's the most dangerous, so the pineapple from the BBC goes down first. Lights, camera, action! Cue theme music from "The Shootist", final shoot-out in hotel bar. The character of Two Gun Matt will kindly refrain from crapping in his pants during the shooting, no pun intended. Hmm. Theme music. Those bastards will be able to hear every move I make on that hardwood floor in there or out in the hall if I have to shift position. At three to one I can use something to cover the sound.* Matt gently pulled down a small stack of CDs. *Dr. Sidney Redmond at the Albert Hall, London? Do I really want to kill people to the sound of Mozart? Naaah. Dr. Sidney Redmond at Julliard? Rachmaninoff is bit more murderous, but Rozanov might take it wrong. Oh, YES, yes indeed! The Rolling Stones, Voodoo Lounge CD! I know just the cut to get the joint really jumping!* Matt quietly opened the case, slid the CD into the machine, and flipped the toggle switch to "whole house", turning the volume up to maximum. Then he took out a cigar. *Why not?* he said to himself. *They'll smell it, but they're going to know I'm here in about ten seconds anyway. Odd to think this may be the last one of these I ever light up.* Matt silently unwrapped the cigar, bit off the end with his teeth and lit it with his Bic. The fragrant smoke curled into the air. He clicked the safety off on the Thompson.

"Somebody's coming!" came Bennett's voice, excited. Matt could hear the car rolling down the driveway and he saw the headlights reflecting in the window. He heard Jimmy get up. *Let*

Heather and Tori live, Matt prayed silently to whatever God existed. *My life is worthless. It has been since she died and I could not save her, since that day I was left with nothing but the memory of her last dance in my arms. These men are evil, the man who built this house is evil, and there is no way I would rather end my life than putting a stop to their wickedness. Let's do this right for once, okay? Let the innocent and the good live and the worthless and the evil perish. Let's see some of that justice raining down like water you talk about in the Bible.*

"What's he doin'?" asked Jimmy.

"He's parking away from the building," came Bennett's voice. "I don't imagine he trusts...wait a minute! That's not Redmond!"

Matt hit the button on the CD player, track number two from the Voodoo Lounge. "Gentlemen, do you smell a cigar?" asked the mellow British voice calmly. "An excellent aroma. Dominican, I should think."

All hell broke loose.

*   *   *

A clanging roar of electric guitars burst from the speakers, the music of the Stones shaking the house to the foundations. Matt kicked open the door, fedora at an angle, cigar jutting from his jaw, Thompson braced against his hip. *Damn, I wish I had a video of this!* raced the thought through his head. *I must look picturesque as hell!* Michelle hurtled through the bathroom door and grabbed Heather and Tori by their collars, one in each hand, dragging them backwards out of the chairs towards the bar. The Samoan was on his feet. He turned as fast as lightning toward Michelle, raising his shotgun. He would have blown her body in half, but then Matt cut loose with the Thompson.

The Thunder God descended to earth, and his song was heard among the Carolina pines. Mick Jagger howled along with him in a mad duet. *"I was a butcher, cutting up meat! My hands were bloody, I'm dying on my feet!"* The roaring .45 slugs ripped into the wall, plowed into the parquet floor, ricocheted into the ceiling, flinging wood and plaster into the air, blasting chunks of marble from the mantelpiece over the fireplace, shattering the glass in the French windows. The Samoan danced and capered and gyrated in the leaden hail like a demented marionette, his shotgun firing spasmodically in one fist, blowing huge holes in the wall and ceiling and shattering the mirror over the bar. He collapsed over his own chair. Matt whirled the machine gun muzzle to his left. Bennett dived behind the huge sofa and came up with the M-16, while Jimmy opened up with the Uzi from behind the piano. Matt leaped back just in time to avoid a spray of bullets that chipped away the doorframe and slapped into the walls around him. *Damn! They're faster than I thought, or else I'm slower!* cursed Matt silently.

He ran through the kitchen and across the hallway into the living room; as he leaped across the hall Jimmy appeared in the music room door and fired a burst of three or four rounds at him. In the living room Matt leveled the Thompson at the music room door. There was a brief motion in the doorway and Matt opened up, riding the bucking Thompson from the floor to the ceiling, physically slicing a huge chunk of the wall to the left of the door away. There was no sign of a hit. *"I was a surgeon, 'till I start to shake,"* bellowed Mick Jagger, the deep bass shaking the house along with the gunfire. Matt backed toward the hall door.

There was a motion behind him. Sid Redmond came trampling down the stairs and into the salon, his arms waving like a windmill, mouth gibbering. Matt gave him the butt of the Thompson in the mouth, splintering his teeth, then kicked him into the room.

"Get down and stay down!" he roared over the wild pounding Stones. *"Stay away from the doors! Take cover, go hide under something!"* Sid howled something unintelligible. Matt ran back to the door into the music room and eased his head forward to where he could see what was left of the mirror over the bar. Bennett was standing behind the sofa, a wild look in his eye, M-16 at the ready.

The Samoan was slowly rising to his feet. *JESUS!* cried Matt in his mind. *A full roll from a Thompson and that motherfucker is GETTING UP? That's impossible!*

"Tedtaotao! Get those bitches behind the bar!" yelled out Bennett. The Samoan hefted his shotgun and began lumbering towards the bar; none of the women were visible. Matt snapped around the shattered door frame and hit the giant again with the Thompson, knocking him down, rolling him like a barrel across the floor. Bennett almost cut his head off with a burst from the M-16; Matt jerked back. *Jimmy? Where the hell is Jimmy with the Uzi?* thought Matt.

"Hey, hey...you got me rockin' now!" chanted the Stones. *"Hey, hey...there ain't no stoppin' now!"* Matt whirled just as Jimmy came charging through the door from the hall, Uzi blazing. One bullet shot the cigar from Matt's lips, another went into the wall behind him and sprayed him with debris. Suddenly Jimmy tripped headlong over Sid, who was still crawling aimlessly around on the floor gabbling. He rolled and tried to come up firing, but Matt had the Thompson to his shoulder and blew the man to shreds, vest and all, firing long bursts into his flopping, rolling body as it skittered across the floor of the living room like a piece of paper blown down a windy street, until Matt ran out of ammunition and the bolt of the submachine gun locked back. The bloody mass of flesh came to rest against a wall, a red stain spreading across the floor. Sid shrieked mindlessly at the sight.

Ears ringing, choking on cordite fumes, Matt knocked the drum off the gun and pulled the second magazine from his pouch, slapping it into the feed well and chambering the first round. The barrel of the Thompson was searing hot to the touch. He debated whether he could get behind the bar before Bennett hit him with the M-16. The Stones went into a wild, orgiastic guitar break. Matt decided to try to reverse his route, go back in through the kitchen to the sewing room, and come out the door nearest Bennett with the Thompson blazing. Surely at least one of the heavy slugs would get him through the sofa he was sheltering behind. He ran for the hallway door, jumped over Sid. The stairs were on his right; he crouched and leaped for the kitchen doorway a few feet in front of him.

A shotgun blast exploding at close range blew away half the lower banister as Matt jumped into the kitchen. Incredulous, he slipped the periscope out of his pouch and telescoped it with one hand, then stuck it out into the hall. A second load of buckshot blew it out of his hand and splintered the door into Michelle's study room, but Matt had time to see the mighty bulk of Tedtaotao staggering down the hall towards him. *My God, this bastard makes Little Willie look like Tinkerbelle!* Suddenly furious at this enemy who would not die, Matt snapped around with his machine gun at the ready, determined to rip him apart, but Tedtaotao was moving too fast and was on top of him.

The Samoan's suit was in shreds and the Bakelite body armor he wore showed scored and dented beneath scorched cloth. One of his ears was shot away and he was bleeding from several leg wounds. Blood oozed from his mouth and his ears, indicating internal bleeding caused the by bruising battering blows of Matt's .45 bullets on the body armor. Tedtaotao grabbed the Thompson, the hot barrel sizzling the flesh of his hand, and wrestled Matt for the gun like a terrier shakes a rat. *"I was a hooker, losing her looks!*" screeched Mick Jagger. "*I was a writer, can't write another book!*" The Thompson fired wild, aimless spurts of bullets all through the kitchen. Tedtaotao ripped the submachine gun away from Matt, hurtling him against the pantry wall. As Matt stared incredulously the giant bent the Thompson in his hands, twisting the barrel like taffy. He threw it down and as Matt groped for his pistol he raised the shotgun, pointing it at Matt's head. His face had remained totally expressionless throughout the entire episode, nor had he uttered a sound. *Forgive me, Heather, my beloved,* Matt thought in utter despair, still clawing for his gun. *I have failed again. Tori, forgive me. You might have been the daughter I never had. I am so sorry.* The Samoan lifted the barrel of the shotgun gently and blew a hole in the pantry wall right by Matt's head, his body turning, slowly, turning until he fell over and crashed onto the floor like a felled oak tree in a forest, shaking the whole house beneath his hurtling bulk. A long, slender knife protruded from his right eye.

"*Hey, hey! You got me rocking now! Hey, hey! There ain't no stopping me!*" chanted Jagger. Rozanov stepped up from the breakfast nook. A sudden burst of M-16 fire from the music room door sprayed through the CD and tape library and pattered against the pantry walls; Rozanov hit the floor. Matt grabbed up the fallen Samoan's shotgun and fired back into the darkness, twice, before the weapon clicked on an empty chamber. One of his blasts hit the CD player and blew it to fragments. A sudden unearthly silence filled the house. "Good," panted Matt, his ears ringing like the bells of Notre Dame. "The next cut wasn't worth listening to."

"This is madness!" shouted Rozanov. He lowered his voice. "What by hell are you playing at? I pull up car in trees like you say, engine running, I am ready to bugger!"

"That's boogie," said Matt.

"Whatever hell! Suddenly I hear what sounds like Stalingrad on disco night! I investigate and I find you being bounced off walls by creature from deep lagoon dressed like Leonid Brezhnev! This is not hostage rescue mission, this is bad episode of Dr. Who! Where are women?"

"Sorry, Kolya, if I'd known it was going to be this dull I wouldn't have asked you to miss a Gilligan's Island rerun," said Matt, heaving himself to his feet, his body bruised and sore. "By the by, thanks for the assist. I've heard of the cavalry coming over the hill, but this time it was the Cossacks. The women are behind a bar in there. Thanks to your timely intervention we've only one opponent left, but he's entrenched behind cover, he's got an M-16 and now I no longer have the Thompson to dig him out with. Come on." They made it into the living room without incident. Sid was cowering in the corner, shaking and gibbering to himself. Matt picked up the late Jimmy's Uzi and fished around in the bloody shredded mess of Jimmy's coat pocket until he came up with an extra clip, which he wiped off on a priceless sofa brocade. "I know you don't like guns, but I need some covering fire. I have to get to the girls behind the bar and see if they're all right." They moved cautiously to the chewed-up door of the music room. There was a shred of mirror left hanging on the wall above the bar. "You see the sofa?" Matt whispered.

"*Da*," whispered Rozanov.

"He's behind there. I think. I'm going to sprint for the bar. Hose that area down, okay?"

Rozanov slid the bloodstained clip into the Uzi and chambered a round. "Go! *Bistra!*" he commanded. Matt charged into the music room. Bennett popped up behind the sofa and raised the M-16 but Rozanov snapped around the door and sprayed the corner with the Uzi. Bennett's burst went high and he dropped down out of sight. Matt lunged behind the bar, skidded and rolled into the three women huddled behind it. "Somebody call for a taxi?" he said cheerfully.

"Matt, cut the Wild West show and get Tori out of here!" urged Heather. They were free of their handcuffs. "Don't worry about me! Get Tori away from here!" He leaned over and kissed her lips firmly.

"We're all going out together, Watson. Now shut up and let me work." There was more rattling small arms fire as Rozanov and Bennett exchanged bursts, then silence.

"Matthew Randallovitch, *rhuzyo poostoy!*" called out Rozanov.

"*Panimayu!*" shouted Matt. "*Kolya, minya yest bomba! Birigees, vrzif! Ostarozhna!*"

"*Panimayu!*" yelled back Rozanov.

"You working with the Russkies now, Matt?" called out Bennett. "So that's where you got all the skinny on the case, eh? Who's your partner? Some KGB guy doing a little moonlighting? One of your Georgian Mafia types? Does he know how many American dollars he might take back to Moscow or Minsk or wherever the fuck he's from by working something out here? You *panimayu* all that, Comrade?" There was silence. "Jimmy? Conley? Tedtaotao?"

"Got 'em all, Bennett," called Matt. "You're next!"

"Look, Matt, now you're bluffing and I know it. Those guys were synthetics. They can disappear. An Assistant Director of the Bureau can't. Let's talk this out, Matt. You've made your point. Just what the hell is it you want?"

"Still don't get it do you, Bennett?" shouted back Matt. He fished around in his pouch and drew out a hand grenade.

"*Cool!*" squealed Tori. Michelle's eyes widened.

"Souvenir of beautiful Bogotà," Matt whispered. "I hope the damned thing still works. It's Vietnam surplus, appropriately enough." He crouched, drew his .357 from the holster and laid it on the floor beside him, then took the grenade in his right hand. "The detonators on these things have a five to seven second delay. Supposed to, anyway," he whispered. "I'm going to have to cut it real close, because I can't risk him throwing it back at us. Hold your ears." He popped the spoon and the detonator smoked. *One thousand, two thousand, three...*

"Jesus, Matt!" screamed Heather in terror, and Matt lost his nerve for the extra second. He leaped up and lobbed the grenade gently, sending it rolling across the floor under the piano. "That's for Mary Jane and Jeannie, you son of a...!" He dropped behind the bar as the room exploded in a white flash and wood from the shattered piano scored the walls like arrows. Ears ringing, Matt grabbed up the .357 and jumped over the bar. Bennett stumbled forward, wobbling, then fell to his knees. One shinbone stuck out of his pulverized trousers leg, blood pumping onto the floor. His face was sliced and dripping blood. The M-16 was still in his hands. He tried to level it and fired a convulsive burst into the wall. Matt calmly aimed and shot Bennett between the eyes. He fell dead to the floor. "It's over!" he called. "Kolya! That's the last of them! Heather, Tori, Michelle, you can come out." Calmly he drew another cigar from his pocket, bit off the end and lit it, filling the air with yet more smoke.

"Holy shit!" whispered Michelle, looking around her, stunned and awed.

"Are you all right?" asked Matt anxiously.

"We weren't physically harmed," said Heather, shaken, leaning against him, trembling.

"Praise be unto God!" whispered Matt.

"They grabbed me at the front door when I came home for lunch, then made me call Gail and tell her a story about an accident at Tori's school," she said, beginning to sob quietly with relief and pent-up terror. "Then Bennett called the school and left a message for Tori, he said he was you, and they got her when she came home. They handcuffed us and shoved us into the back of a van. I could tell they were going to murder us, Matt. I was so afraid they were taking us out in the woods to shoot us and bury us. They were going to murder you. But they were FBI agents," she went on in numbed shock. "FBI agents aren't supposed to kidnap and murder people!"

"Only one was an actual FBI agent," said Matt. "Remember what Bennett said about the other two being synthetics?"

"What's that?" asked Heather.

"They will be carrying legit Bureau credentials under false names, but they weren't really FBI agents. I know the white guy was borrowed from the CIA, God knows where the Polynesian came from. This was supposed to be a CDO."

"What?" asked Tori, wide-eyed and white-faced.

"A credibly deniable operation," Matt explained. "You're right. Who would believe that an Assistant Director of the Bureau would commit kidnaping and murder? No one. That's right-wing paranoia, baseless and irrational conspiracy theory, the kind the good Representative Schumer wants to make a crime carrying five years' imprisonment. We don't have to be afraid of our kind and benevolent Federal law enforcement agencies, who only want to protect us against evil extremist terrorism. Our government only exists for the sole purpose of making our lives better, kinder, and gentler. Haven't you been listening all these years?"

Rozanov laughed out loud. "Oh, come now, Matthew Randallovitch, I know Americans are politically naïve, but surely none of you ever seriously believed *that?*"

"I believed it, once," whispered Heather, clinging to Matt.

"The use of these two synthetics gives the whole thing credible deniablity," Matt went on. "As FBI agents those two officially don't exist. That's good for us, Heather, real good."

"What do you mean?" she asked.

"It means that if this was not an officially sanctioned operation, something Bennett was doing to keep his own as well as Meg Mears' butt covered, the government will shut up about it if we will. No questions, no arrests, no murder charges, no inconvenient courtroom proceedings, the less said about this evening's revels the better."

"And if it was sanctioned?" asked Heather fearfully.

"Then the next team they send down from Washington won't miss," Matt told her gently. He turned to Michelle. "Bet you came about twenty times," he chuckled.

"Twenty-one. You sure you and her wouldn't be interested in a threesome?" asked Michelle, inclining her head toward Heather.

"No. But thanks, Mickey. You did what I asked. They're alive with your help. Do you want to come back into town with us?"

"No. Somebody has to call your Dad and tell him you've littered his precious palace with dead bodies until the place looks like the last act of *Hamlet*." She smiled. "Matt, I wouldn't miss making that call for the world."

Sid staggered into the music room, staring, disheveled, bleeding from his face where Matt had slugged him. He looked over at the piano, shattered into matchwood by the Matt's hand grenade, and he staggered over to it, falling to his knees, ignoring the bleeding corpse of the dead FBI official on the floor. He began weep like a child, pawing at the keys. "My Steinway! Oh, God, Matt, you wrecked my Steinway! Why? What did I ever do to you?" he bawled. Heather shook her head in disgust and started to say something but Matt stopped her. He knelt down by his brother.

"Sid, I am truly sorry about the piano. If you keep on doing things like stealing and trashing my car, I'll arrest you and kick your ass, and if you had hurt either of these women I would have killed you. But the one thing I would never, ever do is deliberately harm your music in any way. It is the only connection you have left with the rest of humanity, Sid. I would never destroy it. Please believe me. Michelle, are you going to be all right here? What are you going to tell the Orange County sheriff?"

"It may not come to that," said Michelle. "You know better than anyone that Randall's connected. He may want to make a few calls before I report this."

"Hey, look, well connected or not, even Daddy can't finesse away a houseful of dead Federal agents including an Assistant Director of the FBI!" said Matt, shaking his head. "Plus one dead private dick out back."

"I can't say I'm sorry about Conley," said Michelle coolly.

"I would have thought he was just your lean and dangerous type," commented Matt, his voice low, looking at Sid, but his brother still wept obliviously over the destroyed piano.

"So did I, for a bit, but I should have listened to you, Matt. He liked the games a bit too much. I tried to call a halt and then I found out he wasn't above a bit of blackmail. Plus he told stories about your wife. Randall thought it was funny as hell. I didn't."

"He who laughs last laughs best," said Matt grimly. "Let's go home, guys."

Matt rolled the Taurus out the driveway, turned left onto Mile End Road and headed for Highway 54. "I won't apologize, Heather," he said. "I told you it might get rough. But I honest to God never figured on something like this."

"I walked into it with my eyes open," said Heather. "There's only one thing that concerns me now, and I need a straight answer." She turned to him and grasped his arm, her grip like iron, and she hissed at him, "*What the hell is the story on you and that brunette back there?*"

XIV

They pulled up in front of the house on Boundary Street and Matt cut the headlights. "Please come in and have a glass of tea, Mr. Rozanov," said Heather, then she started to giggle shakily. "God, it sounds like we've just come from a football game or a stuffy business dinner full of accountants and marketing gurus!"

"All of it starting to crash in on you?" asked Matt as they got out of the car, concerned.

"A little," she admitted. "My daughter and I were almost murdered today. It probably won't really hit me until about two o'clock this morning. I'll need my teddy bear. Don't even think of going back to your place tonight."

"I wasn't. How about you, Tori? How are you doing?"

"I was scared shitless," Tori admitted. "I was scared they would kill us before you got there, but once I knew you were in the house I wasn't afraid any more. I knew you'd get us out."

"Thanks for the vote of confidence, kid," he laughed softly, touseling her hair. "I wish I could tell you I wasn't scared myself or that I never had any doubts. We were lucky."

"I could do with a shower," Tori admitted. "Not because I...did what I did the other day, I just feel icky where that Oddjob character was handling me." Heather handed her the house keys.

"Go on in and get cleaned up, honey," she said. "I want to have a word with the guys." Tori went inside, and Heather turned to them. "Look, what happens now?"

"It's not like in a movie where the hero wipes out the bad guys and then rides off into the sunset with the leggy supermodel perched on the back of his Harley," sighed Matt. "There's more to it than what happened tonight, Heather. Will Williams is dead. They shot him at his home in Carrboro this afternoon."

"Oh, God!" moaned Heather, leaning against the car and burying her head in her hands.

"The Carrboro police will know about him by now, so there's already a homicide investigation underway involving the SBI. It means I've got to make an official report on what I know and don't ask me what I'm going to tell my boss. I haven't even thought about it yet."

"When did they kill him?" asked Heather.

"Well, Will was dressed for work and having his lunch in the kitchen. His body was still warm. Probably about two thirty. Hey...wait a minute! What time did you guys...?"

"I told you, they were waiting here for me when I got home at about ten past twelve...but if they killed Mr. Williams at two thirty...Matt, that's impossible! We were already out at your father's house by then!" Matt took her arms.

"Heather, are you *sure* that all three of those men were together at my father's house at two thirty? Most especially that CIA guy, Jimmy Johnson?"

"I'm not likely to forget someone who shoves me in and out of vans with a gun at my head, chains my daughter and me to a chair, and then tells me I wouldn't be a bad-looking broad if I had some tits on me!"

"Bennett and the Samoan as well?"

"I'm even less likely to forget them," she said. "Of all things, I was most afraid they would give Tori to that...but then who killed Lieutenant Williams?"

"When I called your office, Gail told me that Paul Lieberman hadn't come back from lunch, in fact had missed several appointments!" said Matt excitedly.

"He got a call about eleven," said Heather. "He was on the phone for a good thirty minutes, then he left in a hurry without even taking his overcoat."

"This Lieberman...the husband of June Lieberman?" asked Rozanov politely.

"I believe we mentioned him Sunday night," said Matt. "By the way, Nikolai Yefremevitch, a thought occurs to me. Why were you in your room and sober this afternoon? Why exactly is it that you have not returned to your embassy in Washington? I can understand your wanting to prolong a stay in the West and buy up every Wal-Mart in sight, but why in this small collegiate backwater instead of the fleshpots of the District? You can buy everything you want up there. Unless something is keeping you in Chapel Hill?"

"You are a perceptive man, Matthew Randallovitch," sighed Rozanov. "Your reputation does not belie you."

"Lieberman!" said Matt flatly. "You were waiting for an opportunity to kill Paul Lieberman, so I couldn't get at him and break his story."

"Let us say I was waiting for an opportunity to tie up a loose end you might unravel," said Rozanov. "I had not yet decided on how to approach the problem. I spent yesterday and this morning wandering around the university campus here with briefcase and books under my arm looking academic. It is amazing how much information one can pick up in that manner. Did you know I once spent three months wandering around the Pentagon every day with a false identification badge, wearing the uniform of a Bulgarian postman? Having coffee in canteens and lunchrooms, spending a lot of time in restrooms listening to snatches of overheard conversation, rummaging through every waste basket I could find?"

"Yes, I've heard the story," laughed Matt. "It's something of a legend. The first time you were deported, I believe. They didn't charge you because they were too embarrassed."

"The officers who saluted me every day were the most embarrassed. But you understand my meaning. I was able to determine that Dr. Lieberman has intense political ambitions to become the next Chancellor of the university system of this province. The exposure of his late wife's role as a Soviet agent and a double murderess would not enhance his chances. Under such circumstances he will do anything at all to prevent exposure. What you say of this policeman's death proves that. I have no need to kill Dr. Lieberman. His silence is assured."

"Bennett must have decided Lieberman was too prominent to rub out, but he wasn't really in deep enough for Bennett and the people who sent Bennett to be absolutely sure of him," mused Matt. "After all, it was twenty-six years ago. Five will get you ten it was Lieberman who snuck up onto Will's back porch and shot him through the window, with a gun provided by that CIA bastard! If I can find Lieberman and the gun together I've got him!" He looked at Rozanov. "I've got him, Kolya. Not you."

"As difficult as it may be for you to believe, I would have no objection to some modicum of justice for those two murdered girls coming out of this affair!" said Rozanov, exasperated. "But the public revelation of this business with Nakritin back in the Seventies might end up causing untold harm to my country!"

"Matt," whispered Heather, gripping his arm. "Look down there! Under the street light! I just noticed that dark Mercedes parked there. I think it's blue!"

"And?" asked Matt.

"Paul Lieberman drives a blue Mercedes!" cried Heather, turning towards the house. *"Tori!"*

"Let me go in first!" ordered Matt, drawing his .357. "You follow me. Rozanov, you go around the back. Is the back door locked, Heather?"

"I don't know," she said.

"I have credit card from embassy," said Rozanov. He disappeared into the darkness. Heather and Matt opened the front door and moved into the house. The light was on the sunken living room. Tori sat in a straight-backed chair at one end of the room, her hands folded tensely in her lap. Paul Lieberman stood behind her, tieless, his ordinarily elegantly coiffed hair disheveled. With his left hand he gripped her by the hair, and in his right he held a black Ruger .22 with a long silencer pointed at her head. Tori smiled weakly when she saw them. "Déja vu all over again," she said with a shaky giggle. "Didn't we do this scene once already tonight?"

"Where's Assistant Director Bennett?" demanded Lieberman in a shrill voice. "This silly child was trying to tell me some wild story about you coming through a door with a tommy gun blazing to the accompaniment of the Rolling Stones and killing them all in some fantasy shootout at the OK Corral. Don't try that bullshit with me. Where's Bennett?"

"What can I say? He got me rocking," said Matt, spreading his hands, hefting the .357. "Tori was telling you the truth,

Lieberman. Bennett and his crew are dead. You'll be dead in a few seconds, too, if you harm a hair on that girl's head. I'm afraid you've rather narrowed your options in life today, teach. The Chancellorship is definitely out now. You're looking at immediate death if you hurt her, or else spending the rest of your life in Central Prison with your pants down around your ankles. No Club Fed or work release for killing a cop, Paul, even a retired one. By the way, exactly why *did* you kill Will Williams, when Bennett brought enough muscle down here to do the job himself?"

"B-Bennett said if the Republicans get in on November 5th he'd need some conservative credentials," muttered Lieberman, the gun in his hand trembling. "He said he'd reopen the case, that he'd find a way to implicate June and then me...but if I helped him, if I became part of the solution, so to speak...."

"And you *believed* that nonsense?" asked Matt incredulously.

"Who was I going to turn to? The law? When the law in this godforsaken state is a crypto-fascist killer like you?" demanded Lieberman, a little hysterically.

"I see," said Matt gravely. "You didn't want to trust a crypto-fascist policeman, so you went out and murdered a black police-man. Oh, yes, I see it all, now. That makes a *hell* of a lot of sense! You were a loose end, you idiot, and Bennett tied you up into a nice, pretty bow! If he'd won out tonight he would have had you dancing on his string for the rest of your life!"

"I never thought I could kill a man," Lieberman babbled, his thoughts meandering. "I was amazed at how easy it was. I met Bennett in my car in the parking lot. He had this little guy with him who gave me this gun and the silencer. I drove around for a while, trying to work up the nerve, and then I went to the address in Carrboro they gave me, I stepped up onto the back porch of the house and I saw him sitting at his kitchen table eating lunch. His head wasn't five feet away from me. He turned and looked at me just as I pulled the trigger. I couldn't miss. I never understood how easily men die. Did you find it easy, your first time?" he asked Matt, in an odd detached voice, the apprentice to the expert.

"I know how easy I'm going to find it if you hurt Tori," said Matt. "Put the gun down, Lieberman. You've still got a lot of money and a lot of pull. Put the gun down and they might still be of help to you."

"You're going to kill me anyway," Lieberman gabbled. "I know you will. You're going to kill me for Mary Jane and Jeannie."

"I want justice for Mary Jane and Jeannie, yes," said Matt soothingly. "But that doesn't necessarily mean your death, Paul. After all, I need a confession from someone who was there. You can't confess if you're dead, can you? You see, if you put down that gun I have every reason to let you live."

"Bullshit," said Lieberman uncertainly. "I don't believe you killed Bennett. You just escaped from him. He'll be here any minute now."

"Paul, *please!*" begged Heather. "Bennett is dead! He's not coming! You'll never get away with this! There's no reason for you to hurt Tori, you can't gain anything out of it! That night in 1970 two girls Tori's age were murdered in this house, because of your wife and because of what another wicked woman was doing with your friend Nakritin. You told Matt you never forgot what happened here that night. Now we know why. Mary Jane and Jeannie never got to grow up. They were snatched from the lives of the people who loved them, leaving nothing but emptiness. Now they're only photographs on a wall or in some old album, sixteen forever, frozen in time, all their hopes and their dreams and their chances to be and to live and grow gone! Paul, I beg you, don't do it again! Don't do that to Tori! Don't do it to me! I couldn't bear it!" Tears were streaming down her face.

"I...I couldn't believe it when June told me what she'd done," whispered Paul Lieberman in horror, his eyes wide as he remembered. "She came home that night at one thirty in the morning. I was worried about her, but she had these two men with her. She just said casually, 'These are some comrades from the Soviet Union. We've had to liquidate two infiltrators'. I was totally freaked out, man, once I understood that they had killed Jeannie Arnold and Mary Jane Mears. We were Marxists, of course, all the best anti-war people were, even if we couldn't admit it for tactical reasons, but I never understood before how serious she was, how deep in she was, until I saw those men that night, those Russians...my God, those men! They looked like they were chiseled from square granite blocks, dressed in cardboard suits. One of them had stainless steel teeth. I'd never understood what it all meant until that night. Do you know they flogged her? June, I mean. Flogged her while I watched, told me not to interfere or they'd kill me, it was a Party disciplinary matter. She was quite calm about it. They strung her up to a door and and beat her bloody because she'd brought them over here on a wild goose chase. June didn't even scream, just bit into a piece of carpet and took it all without complaint, because she'd broken the rules and she knew it. She went into class Monday morning with her back swathed in bandages and didn't stumble or wince once. God, she was dedicated and tough!"

"And Meg Mears?" asked Matt softly. "How dedicated and tough was she when you murdered her daughter?"

"She came to our house that Sunday she got back, as soon as she could get away from the police and the reporters," Lieberman recalled. "She was hysterical, cursing us, calling us as bad as Nixon, as bad as American pilots dropping bombs on Vietnamese babies, crazy stuff like that. She threatened to expose us even if it meant she went to prison herself. June stopped her with a few sentences. 'Fine,' she said. 'You go to the police, we go to prison, the people of Vietnam keep on dying. You shut up and stay at your post, we can stop this goddamned bloody imperialist war. There are casualties in every war and now you've suffered one. How dare you place a higher value on the life of your daughter over the son or daughter of a Vietnamese peasant woman? What incredible white American chauvinism! Now you know how it feels you should fight all the harder to bring the war to an end!' Meg couldn't argue with June politically. She never could. So she kept on doing the cash runs for Nakritin, kept on fighting to end the war."

"Insane!" whispered Heather. "Evil and insane!"

"You have to understand the times," pleaded Paul. "Our generation had a historic mission! The war had to be stopped! Nixon had to be stopped! The politics of stopping the war was more important than any other consideration. We had no right to live for ourselves!"

Quietly, Nikolai Rozanov slid into the room through a side door, just behind Lieberman's range of vision. He twisted his wrist slightly, and Matt saw the knife slide down into his palm from the sheath in his sleeve. "Please don't," said Matt in a quiet, level voice. "He's admitted to a murder and he's holding a hostage at gunpoint. He's done for, he'll go to prison no matter what. You can't silence his story now."

"What are you gibbering about, you redneck *putz?*" snarled Lieberman, jabbing the gun into Tori's ear. She winced, trembling. "You think you're going to trick me? Bullshit! We're all staying here until Bennett and his men arrive!"

"Bennett is dead," said Rozanov in a cold voice. Lieberman whirled, surprised.

"Who the hell are you?" he demanded.

"If he doesn't confess in public the world will never know!" pleaded Matt.

"If the world comes to know then there will certainly be more suffering and possibly more death, my friend," said Rozanov, never taking his eye off Lieberman. "I felt her spirit in that room above us. She was gentle and loving. Would she want others to suffer in her name, even people from the land of the men who murdered her? Would she have hated Russia so much that she wished terrible vengeance on all of us? Do you?"

"You know it's not that!" cried Heather. "Mary Jane told us she wanted truth, not vengeance! She said it wasn't for her, it was for all of us still living! Please don't kill him!"

"Hello? I should like to point out that I'm the one with the gun to this little teeny-bopper's head," sneered Lieberman. "Don't you think it might be rather appropriate to include me in the conversation? Now you in the hat, who the hell are..wait a minute, that accent...you're a Russian, aren't you?" Lieberman seemed to sigh with relief. "Bennett must have sent you to help me! Welcome, *tovarich*, welcome! What's your name?"

"My name to you is Nemesis," said Rozanov, his face like iron and his voice like a leaden weight. "Don't call me comrade, *gryazhny zhid!* You wouldn't make a pimple on a Bolshevik's ass. Release that child at once, you coward!"

Paul Lieberman's mind snapped. He screamed like a woman and jerked the gun upwards, firing a wild shot at Matt. The silencer coughed and the bullet shattered a window. Rozanov's wrist flicked like a striking cobra. Lieberman's right arm jerked and pulled him off his feet, knocking him against the wall, the pistol flying out of his hand. He slumped limply onto the floor, right arm in the air, the knife pinning his wrist to the oaken paneling of the wall. Tori ran to her mother and embraced her. Lieberman saw his wrist transfixed by the blade, streaming blood down his arm, and began to scream again and again. Matt walked up and smashed him in the teeth with the barrel of his .357, stunning him into silence. "Paul Gordon Lieberman, I am placing you under arrest for the murder of Will W. Williams, kidnaping, unlawful restraint, assault and the taking of a hostage," he drew in his breath, "And I am also arresting you for the murder of Mary Jane Mears and Alison Jean Arnold on these premises on the night of October 23rd through 24th, 1970. You have the right to remain silent…" After the Miranda speech he turned to Rozanov. "Thank you, Kolya," he said.

"How do you know I just didn't miss?" asked the little Russian. "I do, sometimes, you know."

"Did you?" asked Matt. Rozanov shrugged and spread his hands in a gesture that could have meant anything.

"You still can't really prove he was involved in the killing of the girls," said Heather sadly. "And I'm not a lawyer, but isn't the proper charge against him for killing the girls accessory after the fact? And isn't there a statute of limitations on accessory?"

"Yes," sighed Matt. "That's why I arrested him for murder one. That and the fact that I have wanted to say those words ever since I pulled up outside this house that Saturday morning in 1970 and saw them taking Mary Jane and Jeannie away in body bags. It probably won't stick, but the charge will be filed and even if the D.A. or a judge throws it out, I'm getting this story on the public record. Andy Mears and the Arnolds and everybody in this state will know what he did. Kolya, your government has had lots of practice denying things. They'll just have to deny all this. He won't go unpunished. This is the gun that killed Will Williams and we have eyewitnesses to his restraining and threatening Tori. He's going down to a place where he can really get into an ethnically diverse gay lifestyle." Lieberman whimpered and began to sob incoherently. "That is, of course, unless you decide to cooperate, Paul," added Matt genially. "You confess and describe the whole Nakritin setup, and you tell us exactly what Margaret Mears was doing and how she covered up the murder of her own daughter and another innocent girl for her precious Vietnam protest movement and I'll see what I can arrange for you by way of a little better institution than Central, someplace where you won't be getting buttfucked in the shower by the homeboys every night. I can do that for you, Paul. How about it? You ready to roll on Meg Mears?"

"Fuck you," said Lieberman dully, staring at the floor. Softly he began to sing to himself. *"Look what's coming up the street! Got a revolution, got a revolution...we're Volunteers of America, Volunteers of America..."*

"He has decided to become a good Bolshevik," said Rozanov in sour disgust.

"We heard him confess!" protested Tori.

"A dope-dealing homeboy from the Durham projects with a court appointed lawyer would be crucified by that," explained Matt. "Within a matter of hours this fine flower from the groves of academe is going to be surrounded by the best lawyers money can buy, and with that kind of legal firepower in his corner what we heard him confess is hearsay," said Matt. "A guard in the Los Angeles jail overheard O. J. Simpson shouting out that he'd killed two people. O. J. had the Dream Team, so Ito ruled it hearsay. Inadmissible." There was a loud click from the bookshelf behind Lieberman. "What's that?"

"That's the sound my tape recorder makes clicking off when the tape runs out," said Tori, puzzled. "But..." Matt leaped to the shelf and located the recorder sitting there unobtrusively. He hit the rewind button, then the play button. Paul Lieberman's voice boomed out through the room, clear as a bell. *"She just said casually, 'These are two comrades from the Soviet Union. We've had to liquidate two infiltrators'"*. Matt leaped over and hugged the girl in excitement. "Tori, you *genius!*" he shouted joyfully. "How did you turn it on without him catching you?"

Tori's brow furrowed. "Ah, Matt, the last time I saw my recorder it was on my closet shelf," she said. "I didn't turn it on. I don't even know how it got down here!"

There was a surprised silence. Then upstairs, quite clearly, they heard the door to Tori's room softly pull closed.

*   *   *

"We need to call the law now, and things are going to get very hectic," said Matt quietly. "But before we get the ball rolling, there's one more thing I want to do. Nikolai Yefremevitch, will you do us the favor of keeping an eye on our suspect here while I make a call?" He went into the kitchen and put Heather's phone on the table, ran the tape back a couple of times and found the section he sought. "There is one more party to be heard from in this business," he said grimly.

"Margaret Mears," said Heather

"Yes. I was planning on flying up to Washington and confronting her personally, but now that's out. I'm going to have to stay here and help get this end sorted out with the Chapel Hill PD and the SBI. I took the precaution of providing myself with Margaret Mears' private unlisted number in case I needed it." He dialed the number and listened to the ring. A Hispanic-sounding woman answered the phone. "Probably a maid," he told them. "*Buenos noches, chica. Necesito hablar à Señora Mears, por favor,*" he said. "*Mi nombre es Matteo Redmond. Ella me conocera.*" There was a long pause. Matt put the call on the speaker phone, and they could hear voices and music and the clinking of glasses in the background. "She must be having a cocktail party. Probably a fund-raiser for Billyboy and Hillary."

"Hello?" came Margaret Mears firm contralto voice. "Is this Matt Redmond?"

"Hello, Congresswoman. We haven't spoken for a while."

"A long while, Matt. Let me close the door. I've got some people in and it's a bit noisy." The voices in the background faded. "I'm glad you called, Matt. I wanted to have a word with you. I understand that you came to see Andy a few days ago, and after you left he was very upset. You evidently told him some rather wild and in my view completely unnecessary..."

"Shut up and listen, bitch," interrupted Matt. He turned on the tape recorder. Paul Lieberman's voice again filled the room. *"She came to our house that Sunday...she threatened to expose us....Meg couldn't argue with June politically. She never could. So she kept on doing the cash runs for Nakritin..."*

Matt snapped off the recorder. "That's your old buddy Paul Lieberman, Meg. He's under arrest for murder. He killed a retired Chapel Hill police officer, a man you may remember, a black guy named Will Williams. He also kidnapped a young girl, and to top it all off I've also charged him with his participation in the murder of your daughter and Jeannie Arnold on 1970. He's headed for some really hard time and I think once he realizes what's waiting for him over there in Central Prison he'll be really happy to tell us all about what happened back then. However it plays out with Paul, it's over for you, Meg. I may not be able to get you arrested and charged and tried, what with statutes of limitations and all, but I'm going to do my best, and even if I can't everybody's going to know what you did. Enjoy whatever little soirée you're throwing up there tonight, Meg. It's your last." There was total silence for a long time. "Did you think you'd gotten away with it, that no one would ever know? Surely you knew that someday this call would come?" asked Matt quietly.

"If you know all this, why are you calling me at all?" she asked, her voice totally calm.

"Meg, there are two other people listening now, but they're not police officers, just people who are involved and who have a right to hear this. I give you my word that this call will not appear in any official report or document. Common decency and the fact that you are the mother of someone I loved long ago dictate that I at least let you know what's coming. For my own sake, I have to know why you did what you did, how you possibly could justify it in your own mind. Please, tell me."

There was another long silence. "The war had to end. Nixon had to go and he had to go in disgrace. The world had to change. Racism, sexism, imperialism, capitalism, homophobic bigotry against gays and lesbians, the destruction of the environment, patriarchy, child abuse in the so-called traditional nuclear family, all of these things must be destroyed. I have suffered every day of my life over what happened to Mary Jane and Jeannie, but I have also known every day that June Lieberman was right. That's why I couldn't argue with her politically, as Paul put it, because she was right. Mary Jane died so the world could become a better place, and everything I have done since then has been her monument, her legacy." Heather stepped forward, tears flowing, about to shout at her, but Matt grabbed her arm and shook his head sternly. "Does that tell you what you want to know, Matt?"

"In a way, yes, it does," he said. "I asked you why you acquiesced in your daughter's murder and shielded those who killed her, and you responded with a political diatribe. You, madam, are a Marxist. That explains everything."

"I see you understand more than I gave you credit for understanding," she said coolly.

"My God, you evil bitch, doesn't the death of your child mean anything to you at all?" cried out Heather, unable to restrain herself any longer.

"One of your concerned parties, Matt?" asked Meg. "Of course it does, Ms. whoever you are. Lenin defined death as the permanent cessation of political activity, nothing more and nothing less. Mary Jane's life was cut short before she could become politically active for progressive change and the betterment of the human condition, and that is a terrible tragedy which I have lived with all these years. Is there anything else? I should get back to my guests."

"Yes, there's something else, although you probably won't understand what I am about to say," said Matt carefully. "I don't want you entertaining any political notions about me. I am utterly opposed to everything you stand for. I was then, even before I understood why I was against it, and I am now. But I want you to understand that I haven't done any of this out of any kind of political grudge or desire to get you because of your ideology. I have done it because I loved your daughter more than life itself, because losing her at seventeen and having to live my life without her left an emptiness and a wound in my heart which will never heal, because finding and punishing her killers was all that remained in this world I could do for her. Now go back to your party. I will arrest you and put you in prison if I can, but I don't want to talk to you any more. You sicken me." He hung up the phone. Sobbing and shaking, Heather walked unsteadily over to the kitchen sink and vomited. "Thus spake King Agamemnon by the shores of Aulis," said Matt in a flat voice

"Damn!" moaned Heather as she dry-heaved. "I haven't anything to eat all day, nothing to bring up!" Matt walked over and enfolded her in his arms while she wept.

"Whatever happened to that King Backgammon guy in the myth?" asked Tori curiously, after her mother had calmed somewhat.

"He won his war against his enemies, after many years and a lot of slaughter," said Matt. "He used the Trojan Horse to deceive them to their destruction, as Meg Mears used the anti-war movement she helped finance with Communist funds. A Trojan princess named Cassandra tried to warn her people, but she was ignored. They brought the wooden horse within the walls, and Troy fell amid massacre and plunder. Agamemnon sailed back to Mycenae in triumph, bearing the captive Cassandra with him as his slave, but he didn't live to enjoy his victory for long. He and Cassandra were murdered in his bath by his wife Clytemnestra. She chopped him up with an axe to avenge her daughter Iphegenia, whom he had so cruelly sacrificed to the dark god of the Underworld. The gods granted Agamemnon the victory and the glory he craved because of his sin, but they would not let him off the hook, and in the end he had to pay the price. So will Meg Mears. I'll make the 911 call now. Then I want to call my boss in Raleigh. He'll want to be in on this personally."

$\star$ $\star$ $\star$

It was almost two o'clock that morning before Matt and Heather climbed wearily into bed with one another. There had been police and SBI agents in the house for hours, and it had taken all Matt's influence to prevent them from arresting Rozanov. He took a long hot shower, but he was still feeling battered and bruised from his fight with the Samoan assassin. "I'm going to be sore as hell tomorrow from all the exercise," he said with a wry chuckle. "Running through the woods lugging that Thompson and all that ammo."

"Matt, I....thank you doesn't come close to what I want to say to you," she whispered, taking his hand in both hers.

"Since I was the one who got you and Tori into that situation, the least I could do was get you out of it," he told her. "Like I said, we were lucky."

"What you said on the phone this afternoon, about not being there for Mary Jane, Matt...well, you were as good as your word. You were there for Tori and me tonight. Is it over now? Have you purged yourself of guilt for something that was never your fault? You married Evangelina because of that kind of guilt, because you couldn't save her husband's life. You've lived all your adult life weighed down by guilt because you're not some kind of Superman who comes flying down from the sky to save the day. Well, tonight you broke the hoodoo. Are you going to be able to let it all go now, Mary Jane and Evie? Can you start life over again, once we get all this cleaned up?"

"Well, there's still a lot of cleanup left to be done, and it could get very nasty," Matt warned her. "I understand what you're asking, though. Heather, I just don't know. I've lived with this monkey on my back for twenty-six years. I have no idea what life without it will be like, what kind of man I will be without it. I might not like the result. *You* might not like the result."

"I'll take that chance," she whispered. "Come here to live with me, Matt, here to this house. I don't want you to go back to that coffin in Carrboro again. You can bury your dead now. You don't need to live in a coffin because she lies in one. I want to be able to reach over and touch you, every night from now on. I want to smell those godawful cigars when I come in the door, and know that you are here. Whatever happens, I know one thing, and that is that from now on I have to have you in my life. I'm willing to pay whatever price tag comes with that."

XV

Matt and Heather slept like logs, too tired even to make love, and they didn't awaken until a little after eleven o'clock in the morning. Tori knocked on the door. "Hey, you guys, how about hitting the deck?" she called out.

"Why aren't you in school?" called out Heather sleepily.

"Same reason you're not at work," retorted Tori. "Getting kidnapped and almost murdered twice in one day gets me one comp day off school. It's in the CHHS handbook."

"Sorry, hon, that was a stupid question," said Heather.

"Besides, I don't think it's a very good idea to go outside now," added Tori. "We're kind of under siege."

"What?" asked Heather.

"Look out the window," said Tori. Matt pulled on his trousers and went to the window.

"The boys and girls of the Fourth Estate," he said, peeping out between the Venetian blinds. "Looks like camera crews from Fox and CNN and, ah, I think that's the local CBS affiliate. They're camped out on the front lawn."

"My God!" moaned Heather. "I suppose it's a good thing I didn't try to go into work. Not to mention that fact that I had my boss arrested," she added with a giggle. "I wonder if I'll have a job after today? I'm still in my probationary period, and Paul Lieberman was the one who had to do my six-month evaluation to get me vested. I wonder if he'll recommend me for permanent staff now?"

"The media's claiming you and Paul Lieberman were getting it on," said Tori.

"*What?*" cried Heather.

"They've been calling all morning," said Tori. "Some reporter from the Raleigh paper asked me that. I told her no, you were getting it on with Two Gun Matt."

"*Tori!*" shouted her mother in exasperation. "Don't talk to any of those people at all, not about anything!"

"You're catching on fast, Watson!" said Matt with an approving chuckle.

"Well, I haven't said much," said Tori. "Their questions are so stupid I've started letting Trumpeldor talk to them."

"I beg your pardon?" queried Heather.

"I put him on the table, cut him a slice of cheddar and tell him to sing, and when he starts meowing for it I hold the phone up to his mouth. NPR actually played it over the air. It was fun until I ran out of cheese just now."

"You fed that cat a whole 12-ounce block of cheese?" demanded Heather. "Tori, that's bad for him! He's too overweight as it is. Cats can have heart attacks too, you know."

"Well, I had to give it to him once I showed it to him and he sang for it, didn't I?" protested Tori. "Teasing him is mean."

"It's big news, Heather," said Matt. "Lieberman was looking good for next Chancellor of the consolidated university system. Tori, any public comment on the connection with Margaret Mears, and most especially any news on what happened out at Mile End Road yesterday?"

"Ah, yeah, that's what I came up here to tell you, Matt," said Tori. "You're not going to like it. There's not going to be any follow-up with Margaret Mears or with that Feebie creep Bennett. You'd better come down and hear for yourself."

When they arrived downstairs, Heather in her nightgown and robe, Tori had CNN on the television. An elegantly dressed woman telejournalist was standing in front of the Capitol in Washington with a microphone in her hand, a stricken look on her face, talking to someone named John in her studio. "Washington is reeling in shock this morning, John, from the news of not one but two sudden deaths by apparent suicide among top associates of the Clinton administration. Democratic Congresswoman Margaret Mears of New York was found dead early this morning in the basement of her Georgetown home by her long-time companion and domestic partner, Washington attorney Helen Lloyd. Congresswoman Mears apparently took her own life sometime in the early hours of this morning by hanging herself from a pipe."

"Like Jeannie was strung up to a pipe in the basement," growled Matt. "How appropriate. Poetic justice!"

The newswoman continued, "Also, this morning at approximately seven o'clock A.M. a jogger discovered the body of FBI Assistant Director Charles R. Bennett, lying alongside a trail in a national park in Northern Virginia. U.S. Park Police have issued a statement that Bennett apparently died of a self-inflicted gunshot wound to the head sometime last night…"

"They forgot to mention the self-inflicted hand grenade wounds," commented Tori sarcastically. Matt clicked the remote and the TV fell silent. "What stupid lying dorks!"

"Damn," Matt muttered. "Damn! *Damn!* DAMN!"

"Dear God!" whispered Heather in horror. "Matt, they killed her! A Congresswoman! Will they be coming after us next?"

"I don't know," said Matt. "Let me make a call."

"To whom?"

"I still have a few friends up there who might talk to me about this," said Matt. "There's one guy in particular who would be in a position to know." Matt dialed. He got a switchboard and asked for the man he wanted to talk to by name. Heather and Tori's jaws both dropped in stunned amazement when they heard the name. Matt held his finger to his lips and put the call on speaker phone. He was on hold for a long time. A man's voice finally answered the phone. "Thanks for taking my call, Al," he said. "I wasn't sure you would."

"Jesus fucking Christ on a raft, Matt!" yelled Al. "You bastard's ghost, where the hell do you get off wasting an Assistant Director of the FBI? Not to mention two of the Company's top choppers? We're all supposed to be on the same side, last I heard!"

"Bennett didn't see it that way," said Matt. "The man was committing kidnaping and conspiracy to murder. He also covered up two murders here on my patch twenty-six years ago. Come on, Al, everybody inside the Beltway knew damned well that Chuck Bennett was the dirtiest Fed there was, long before Waco. He was holding two women hostage and he and his crew were going to kill them and me."

"Holy shit! Why the hell didn't you call me, Matt? I owe you big time, I've never denied that. I would have sorted it out if you'd just given me time!"

"There wasn't any time, Al, and this wasn't something that could have been sorted out," said Matt. "Do you know what it was about? How'd you hear about it?"

"I just got back from the White House. Where the hell do you think I heard about it?" said the man on the phone. "Hillary is damned near hysterical. She wants your hide nailed to the barn door, Matt, and it was all Bill and me between us could do to keep her from calling up Janet and ordering you hit on the spot! Nobody's shedding any tears over Bennett, I gotta admit, but Meg Mears was a close friend of Hillary's from way back when they were both chewing on Richard Nixon's leg."

"That's what I'm calling about, Al. I need to know how bad this is going to get. Look, I know you may not feel you can tell me this, and if not I understand, but what about Meg Mears? Did she really kill herself or was she terminated?"

The man on the other end seemed to reflect. "Matt, I'll level with you. I just don't know. I don't think so. Sounds to me like she offed herself. You know that lawyer dyke she was shacking with found her hanging in the basement. She told the Georgetown cops that Meg was very upset because of a call she'd received from you last night. No mention of any unusual visitors wearing dark suits. Bill and Hillary believe she did herself in because you dug up all this old stuff about her daughter's murder. If it was a hit nobody's informed them of the fact. I know Janet would never order a termination within the United States on her own."

"Next question. Are they coming after me, and are they coming after Heather and Tori Lindstrom?" asked Matt.

"Honest to God, Matt, I just don't know," said Al. "You know I'm not exactly in the loop over there, even less so than normal for the guy in my slot."

"Al, I need to see them coming," pleaded Matt quietly. "I appreciate the fact that I'm asking you to put your ass on the line if you help me. I've never asked for any quid pro quo over that business in Panama. The way I see it I was just doing my duty. I can live with the sword of Damocles hanging over my head, I'm used to it, but these two women can't, and dammit, they shouldn't have to! They haven't done anything except stumble onto the counterculture's dirty little secret by accident."

There was silence for a bit. "Matt, that other business, with Vladimir Nakritin and Margaret Mears. I just heard about that this morning for the first time. You could have knocked me over with a feather. I have to ask you, is it true?"

"Yes," said Matt.

"The North Vietnamese financed most of the anti-war movement through the Soviet espionage network in this country?"

"Yes. I don't know how much money came in from Hanoi but it must have been well over a million dollars. That's 1970 dollars," Matt reminded him.

"Damn!" whispered Al. "I was a captain in 'Nam, you know."

"Yes, sir, I know."

"You were there too, weren't you?" asked Al.

"Yeah, I was an E-5, just caught the tag end of it in '72, didn't do a full tour. Spent most of my time in the NCO's mess in Bien Hoa drinking beer," said Matt.

"When Hillary laid that little bombshell on me this morning all of a sudden I remembered this black kid named Derrick," said Al, his voice quiet and far away. "I am ashamed to say I can't remember his last name. He saved my life, although not intentionally. One day in Quang Tri he stepped on a land mine about three seconds before I would have. His leg was blown off clean at the hip, no way anybody could have saved him. He died in my arms. Hillary was crying this morning, ranting and raving about how you had killed her friend. The 58,000 names on that wall a few miles from here didn't even enter her mind."

"They wouldn't," said Matt.

"Matt, I'll tell you this much. Right now we've all got a lot on our plate, as you know unless you've been living in a cave for the past twelve months. Hillary's calmed down and she's got sense enough to understand that now is not the time. She can't afford the slightest whiff of any more scandal and she knows it. That last grand jury came too close for comfort. If we get back in on the fifth, though, you watch out for Hillary. She wants you dead and I gather Janet wouldn't be too upset either if you had an accident. Something about an insubordinate letter of resignation you wrote."

"Just between you and me and the wiretaps, Al, how do you rate your chances next month?" asked Matt curiously.

"Well, we've got those two million brand new citizens we've had the INS and every other bureaucratic body we could scrape up processing like mad all summer," said Al. "We called it Citizenship USA."

"Yeah, I heard. The Republicans have been bitching about it."

"Fuck 'em if they can't take a joke. We've concentrated on five cities, New York, Miami, Chicago, L.A. and San Francisco. That's New York, Florida, Illinois, and California, almost enough electoral votes to win. Most of our new Americans are from Third World countries, of course, so they understand the *quid pro quo*. As a public service we've even got voting registrars on hand at these massive swearing-in ceremonies. We filled Candlestick Park the other day."

"Yeah, I saw it on the news," put in Matt.

"The mayors in Detroit, Atlanta, Los Angeles and St. Louis are pulling out all the stops for us, since Janet whispered the magic words 'Federal indictment' in their ears. A lot depends on whether or not Daley in Chicago can deliver the goods like his old man could and make damned sure we get those Illinois electoral votes like in '60 and '76," Al went on. "I know Bill's sure as hell no Jack Kennedy, but if Daley and some of the other city bosses can do the old Lazarus trick and raise the Democratic dead, with the blacks and the fems and what's left of the unions up north, and all that lovely disposable gay income keeping our war chest nice and topped up, we just might slip back in by a hair. Love that electoral college! Of course it doesn't help the GOP that their candidate is Mr. Baker the Undertaker. We were sweating bullets that Buchanan's peasant uprising might succeed and we'd be facing somebody with charisma and some actual principles, but the country club Republicans did him in for us quite neatly. They'd rather lose than allow the peasants into the country club."

"Somehow I don't think you're going to get much of the American Legion vote this year," commented Matt.

"Politically partisan rumor-mongering, Matt," warned Al. "Some university egghead went off the rails, killed a guy and held some teeny-bopper hostage, now he's trying to muddy the waters and save his ass. I don't know if Margaret Mears died by her own hand or not, Matt, but now she's dead she's officially a martyr for the Movement and of course she's also conveniently beyond questioning. That's what this morning's meeting was about, basically. Damage control. The spin doctors are already spinning, Matt, the media feeding frenzy is gearing up and you and your lady are both going to get stripped to the bone like you've been attacked by piranhas. You've got no proof, and by tonight Dan Rather will be telling the whole country there's no proof. NPR will be leading the chorus screaming bloody murder and by Sunday night Sixty

Minutes will have exposed the whole thing as a right-wing hoax that probably originated with Jesse Helms. It's rotten and it makes me sick, Matt, it's spitting on the grave of every man who died over there, but there it is."

"I know," replied Matt wearily. "Won't be the first time those guys have had their graves spit on by the Usual Suspects."

"Ain't that the truth? Even if we are tossed out on the fifth, you're still going to have a problem with the Company. They don't take kindly to country bumpkins in fedoras knocking off their guys. I will do this much for you: while I'm here I'll make it my business to keep my ears peeled and if I can possibly warn you of any impending problems I will. If I leave office I'll make sure somebody reliable takes over the listening post."

"Thanks, Al." said Matt. "I appreciate that."

"I owe you, buddy. I remember that every time I look at my wife. And Matt...?"

"Yes, Al?"

"Any chance of picking up your vote on November 5th?" Matt laughed out loud.

"No chance at all," he replied.

"Didn't think so. Take care, Matt," he said.

"You, too." He hung up. Heather stared, waving her hands inarticulately, questioning. "That was one that didn't make the papers or the tabloids," explained Matt. "National security, diplomatically sensitive and so forth. A few years ago his wife was on an official tour of Panama. Some muchachos from Medellín got the idea of snatching her and trying to exchange her for Pablo Escobar. I was able to dissuade them. I got that grenade I used yesterday off one of them. He didn't need it any more."

"Oh," said Heather weakly. "Matt, what will Margaret Mears' death do to the case itself? About the girls, I mean? All we have is Paul Lieberman ranting and raving on a tape recording while he's obviously emotionally distraught. Even I can guess that recording will be suppressed by the court. Apparently the story is out, like you wanted it to be, but there is still not one bit of hard proof."

"You can lead a horse to water, Heather, but you can't make him drink," sighed Matt. "We've done all we can. The horse is standing at the water's edge and it's there if he's ever thirsty. I just hope it will make the dead and the living both rest a bit easier."

"One is resting easier already," said Tori quietly. "I went down into the cellar this morning. Jeannie's gone."

"God be praised!" said Heather fervently, her head bowed.

"Amen!" seconded Matt. "Mary Jane?"

"She's still here. I'm not sure why. I get the impression she's waiting for someone," said Tori.

"Her father," said Matt. "He's probably not going to be with us too much longer."

"Say, does the Federal government really operate like a bunch of gangsters all the time?" asked Tori with interest.

"In a word, yes," said Matt.

"I have a civics paper I'm supposed to do," said Tori with a grin. "I wonder…"

"Put down whatever orthodoxy your teacher wants you to put down and get an A on it," advised Matt quietly but firmly. "If you want to fight it when you're an adult then more power to you, but for the next few years your mission in life is to cop a couple of pieces of paper off the system, girl, starting with your high school diploma and then a college degree. I never had the chance to go to college, but I've always regretted it. Don't rock the boat until you've got those pieces of paper in your grubby little paw."

"I agree," said Heather. The phone rang. Heather picked it up. "Hello?"

"Ah, is this Ms. Heather Lindstrom?" said a female voice. "Ms. Lindstrom, this is Lindley Beatty from the Los Angeles *Times,* and I'd like to ask you a few..."

"*Meow!*" said Heather, and hung up.

*   *   *

Matt stepped quietly into the hospital room. Len and Susan Arnold were there. He sat down beside them and Marvella Rendell and took the old man's hand. Dr. Mears turned sluggishly towards him. "Y..y..ou did....it," he gasped. "I....saw...TV..."

"Don't try to talk, Andy" said Matt. "Thanks for coming Len, Sue. I promised you all some answers. I know you're hearing all kinds of rumors on the news, but this is what I have learned. Mary Jane was murdered by a man named Zachar Vasilievitch Probdanichev. Jeannie was murdered by a man named Sergei Aleksandrovitch Greshkov. They were officers in Soviet military intelligence. They were brought to the house that night by June Lieberman. Probdanichev is dead and Greshkov is in terminally ill health in Moscow. Paul Lieberman is under arrest. He may not be convicted for his part in covering up the murder of your daughters, but he'll be going to prison for other crimes. The police officer in charge of the 1970 investigation, Chuck Bennett, deliberately covered up the crimes. He is dead as well." He turned to Marvella and silently mouth the words, "Does he know about Meg?" She nodded. "Andy, I don't need you to tell me that you didn't know what your wife was doing with Nakritin," Matt went on. "I know you wouldn't be a party to treason."

"S...s...suspected," gasped Mears. "S...s...said nothing. Loved...her. God forgive us...both." Tears rolled down his withered pale cheeks. "Matt...from bottom of my...soul...I...thank you...."

"We second that, Matt," said Len Arnold. Both he and his wife had tears in their eyes

"For what comfort it may bring you, because Jeannie died the way she did, the world will come to know the truth about one of the worst times in our country's history," he said gently. "Maybe not now, because it is still in the interest of people in power to cover it up, but someday the truth will come out. She didn't die for nothing."

"Knowing that is so wonderful!" sighed Sue.

"It's over now, darling," whispered Len, hugging her. "Matt, we owe you a debt which can never be repaid."

"There's something else I want to tell you, Andy," said Matt to Mears. "You're tired and you need to rest, so I won't go into a long story, but during the course of this investigation I found out something for sure, and that is we don't have to fear life's end. Mary Jane loves you, and she's waiting for you. You will be with her soon, my friend."

"Always...knew...that..." he whispered.

*   *   *

Several days later Matt and Heather and Tori stood in the departure lounge at Raleigh-Durham airport. "That is my flight being called now," said Rozanov, standing up, hefting a large plastic shopping bag in his hand. "Matthew Randallovitch, my thanks for making my stay in your lovely Southern land an interesting one."

"I'm glad you're not staying any longer as a guest of the state," said Matt ruefully.

"Not at all. This is my third *persona non grata*," said Rozanov proudly. "That, I believe, is now the record for my service. Of course, who knows? I may try for a fourth."

Heather stepped forward and kissed him on the cheek, and shyly Tori likewise followed suit. "I have you as well as Matt to thank for my life and the life of my child," she said. The second boarding call came. Matt gripped Rozanov's hand.

"*Spasiba balshaye*, Nikolai Yefremevitch," he said. "Many thanks. *Das vidanya*".

"*Das vidanya*," said Rozanov, gallantly kissing Heather's hand and picking up his shopping bag. A roll of toilet paper slipped out of the well-filled bag and rolled across the departure lounge floor. Tori giggled merrily. Matt looked down and then picked up a new leather briefcase.

"Kolya!" he called out. "You forgot your briefcase!"

Rozanov turned at the entrance to the boarding ramp. "That is not my briefcase!" he shouted, and waved again. "But perhaps the contents will prove of interest! Stay well!" He vanished into the aircraft's covered boarding ramp.

Matt and the women went to an airport coffee shop and sat down at the table. "What's he talking about?" demanded Tori. "That's his case. He brought it in with him!" Matt snapped the case open. The first thing he took out was Tori's paperback copy of George Orwell's *1984*. A piece of paper protruded from the book; Matt opened it and read it.

Matthew Randallovitch,

I almost neglected to return this excellent work to Mademoiselle Lindstrom, he read. *I am growing old and I am always forgetting things. I believe you will find something else here which I have forgotten.*

That night in Mademoiselle Lindstrom's bedchamber I was overwhelmed by the presence of one whom men of my country so terribly victimized, and I understood that what I was experiencing through her must be multiplied by countless tens of millions of

victims of the past eighty years when my nation and my people,
for reasons I have never fully been able to explain to myself, went
mad and tried to inflict their madness on all the world. Humbly
and in anguish, I asked of her what I might do, what I might give
her to make up in some tiny measure for what had been done to
her and so many others. Upon the screen of the computer
appeared one word:"Pravda". I do not believe she was referring
to the Russian newspaper of that name.

There have been enough lies in this most terrible of centuries,
Matthew Randallovitch. Let at least one of them be demolished
before the coming new millennium begins. I hope that thus she
may find rest.

—*N. Rozanov*

He handed the note to Heather. "Pravda means truth in
Russian," he explained. He lifted from the briefcase a heavy, dark
manila folder stamped and written in Cyrillic lettering. He opened
the yellowed pages and glanced through them.

"What's that?" asked Tori.

"It appears to be a GRU file from the embassy in Washington,"
said Matt calmly. "It details the whole operation involving
Vladimir Nakritin, Margaret Mears and June Lieberman. There
are lists here of amounts of money and delivery dates. Looks like
there was a lot more money involved than I thought, and I see that
Nakritin and Mears weren't the only conduit. I see some names I
recognize from today's elevated strata in the political and media
and academic worlds. And here on these pages is a detailed report
from Greshkov and Probdanichev on the events of October 23rd
and 24th, 1970. Can you say 'written confession'? Sure you can!"

"Can you say 'proof positive'?" whispered Heather joyfully.

"I can indeed." Matt stood up. "Where's a phone? There's a
reporter I know with the Washington *Times* I need to call."

On the way to the phones he looked out over the gangway and saw Rozanov's face in a window on the aircraft, just as it began to pull away and taxi onto the runway. Matt hefted the briefcase high in his hand, then he stood to attention and saluted, his fingers touching the brim of his fedora. Rozanov returned the salute, his face expressionless, and the plane moved away toward the tarmac and the sky that would bear him back to the vast and tragic motherland of Tolstoy, Tchaikovsky, and Stalin.

"Though It Were Ten Thousand Mile..."

XVI

It was a cold and clear late afternoon in early November. Matt finished loading the first boxes and bags into his car to be moved into the house on Boundary Street; within a few days more he would be completely out of his apartment. Hesitating at first, he decided to go ahead and do something he had been planning to do for a while. He dialed a number in South Carolina. His father answered the phone.

"I stopped by out at the old home place a couple of weeks ago," said Matt. "Pity you decided to absent yourself that evening. You missed the party. You might say we brought the house down. I saw something funny while I was out there. It was a flying pig."

"You are a murdering psychopath," said his father in a deadly voice, hardened with decades of hate. "You are a disease. You have to be eradicated."

"Save it, Daddy," said Matt. "It's been a long, long time since I gave a damn about anything you have to say. But I'm going to tell you something now. There will be no more Jack Conleys. Heather and Tori Lindstrom are off limits to you. You so much as lift one finger to harm them or involve them with your sick and twisted scene in any way, then I'm coming down there to Charleston and I'm bringing my Rolling Stones soundtrack, and you and me and Mick Jagger are going to go rocking. I don't expect you to answer. But you'd damned well better listen, and you'd damned well understand. I'm forty-three years old and it's time this bullshit ended. It ends now, tonight. Heed what I say, old man." Matt hung up.

At Heather's house they all three lugged Matt's boxes in and plunked them down in the room he had selected for his private den and study. On their lapels both adults wore little stickers saying "I Voted '96." "How was it at your polling station?" asked Matt.

"I thought I'd go in early, before they opened," she said. "I ended up having to park four blocks away and stand in line for over an hour."

"Mine was mobbed, too," he remarked. "I voted at noon and I was number one thousand and twelve. Heather," Matt continued gravely, "You know there's one unresolved problem between us. I've been afraid to broach it, because it's such a sensitive and divisive issue..."

"Why do I get the impression you're having a hard time keeping a straight face?" asked Heather. "Oh, all right! You can light up those damned things in this room *only*, and keep the windows open! I don't care if it's thirty degrees out...!"

"You're letting him *smoke?* In the *house?*" cackled Tori with glee. "You got it bad for this guy, Mom!"

"Well, it is kind of his trademark," said Heather defensively.

"Well, if Matt can have a smoking room then..."

"You're not old enough!" chorused both Heather and Matt in unison.

"Hey, no fair you two ganging up on me!" protested Tori.

"I owe you guys a dinner," said Matt. "What say we do a Chinese buffet and then come back and watch the elections on the tube? Speaking of which, how's your phone been running?"

"It's picked up during the last few days as we get nearer the election," said Heather. "TV tabloids and television news, mostly, but a couple of investigative reporter types as well. They're still trying to claim the Russian file is a hoax, a sinister plot by the Republicans to smear the Clintons and their progressive values."

"That's the Party line, yes, no pun intended," sad Matt.

"They keep asking about you, about your politics, wanting to know if you know Jesse Helms or if you've been having secret meetings with Pat Buchanan, that kind of thing," said Heather disgustedly. "They also claim Major Rozanov is secretly a supporter of Vladimir Zhirinovsky and we're all part of some international fascist conspiracy. Anything to distract people's attention from the contents of the file and that series of articles in the Washington *Times.*"

"Nobody is stupid enough to believe all that bullshit!" protested Tori.

"It's called shooting the messenger. They obviously feel the best defense is a good offense," said Matt. "They may be right. I guess we'll find out tonight whether or not they can pull it off. How's it been going at work?" asked Matt in concern.

"Gail doesn't speak to me any more, which is no loss. I'm a heroine to half the campus because I'm allegedly a strong woman who was victimized by a man with a gun known to be a sexual harasser, and to the other half I'm a sinister right-wing Mata Hari who carried out a *coup d'etat* against a beloved liberal administrator. Total polarization, complete partisanship. No middle ground, no attempt on anyone's part to ascertain the facts or deal with the real issues."

"America, 1996," agreed Matt. "Thought any more about that two-year criminal justice and police science course? If this all works out you and me may go moonlighting yet."

"It gets more tempting every day," admitted Heather. "Let me change clothes and I'll be right down. I just hope we don't run into any more damned media at the restaurant. Never thought I'd have to worry about paparazzi!"

Heather went upstairs to change and Matt availed himself of his newly acquired smoking privileges, lighting up a cigar and opening a window. "Tori, look, you're cool with me being here, aren't you?" he asked.

"Sure, but..." She paused.

"But what?"

"When are you and Mom going to get married?" she asked anxiously. Matt laughed.

"Boy, ain't that a switch from the days when I was your age?" he chuckled. "Tori, we need to see if it's going to work out. We need to see if we really have anything in common outside this case and outside physical attraction. Why? Don't tell me there's now a stigma attached to cohabiting parents among your generation? If so, I'm all for it!"

"It's not just that, it's...I want you to get married before I'm eighteen," said Tori, biting her lip and looking at the floor. "I want to call you Dad, but it's got to be true, all legal and every-thing. I want you to adopt me." She looked up, her eyes wet. "Will you adopt me, Matt?"

Matt exhaled slowly. "I haven't had very many good things happen to me in my life, Tori," he said after a while. "Your mother is one. You're another. Yes, honey, if that's what you want. As soon as your mom and I know we're going to make it, I'll make an honest woman out of her and I'll file a legal adoption request on you. How will your brother feel about that? How will he feel about me and your mom, for that matter?"

"Greg will be happy for both of us,"said Tori. "Besides, I've already told him if he gives you any problems I'll kick his ass." She hugged him and for her trouble got a hot cigar ash down the back of her blouse.

When Heather and Tori were ready to go out to dinner they went out to the car first. As he had taken to doing every time they left the house, Matt checked all the doors and windows to make sure they were locked, and made sure everything was off in the kitchen. As he stepped into the front hall he stopped in his tracks, stunned with amazement

Mary Jane Mears stood at the top of the stairs, dressed as he had last seen her on their final night together so long ago, her raven hair and flowered maxi-dress billowing in an unseen wind from some unconceivable place, golden bracelet on her wrist and crucifix around her neck. She smiled at him and waved gently. Matt stared, his jaw slack, gulping. Finally he spoke, softly and carefully, afraid she would vanish.

"Hi, Mary Jane. I did the best I could, for you and Jeannie. There's not much justice and there won't be much truth left when they get through with it, but it's all I can do. I hope it's enough. I...I guess this is that goodbye we never got to say back in '70, huh?"

She nodded to him tenderly.

"Thank you for coming. I'm grateful for the chance. Honey, maybe I'm wrong, but I think we'll meet again someday, in another place and time, in another life, different people but the same souls. When we do, I only hope I love you then as much as I have always loved you in this life." She drew her hands to her lips, kissed her fingers and extended them to him in farewell. He returned the gesture, slowly, his heart breaking. "Goodbye, my dearest love," he whispered. "Sorry we couldn't be together this time, but I'll catch you next time around. Rest in peace until then." For a final time she nodded, for a final time in his life he saw her smile and saw her lips silently form the words,

"I will love you forever!"

Then she was gone.

Matt spoke quietly into the silence.

> *"Sae fare the well, my bonnie lass,*
> *Aye, fare thee well a while.*
> *But I would come again, my dear,*
> *Though it were ten thousand mile."*

A little later Matt quietly stepped out the front door and locked it. He joined Heather and Tori in the car. "I think we'll hear a bit later on tonight that Andrew Mears died in the hospital earlier this evening," he said.

"Mary Jane?" asked Heather quietly.

"Yes. She's gone now." Heather took his hand. "I don't know about you guys, but I am definitely in the mood for some fried rice and Kung Pao chicken," he said, starting the car and backing out of the driveway. The red taillights of the Taurus disappeared down Boundary Street.

Upstairs in the silent house a dim light glowed in the window of Tori's room for the last time. Slowly it faded, until finally it was gone, leaving only the light of a full harvest moon in the quiet darkness, and the sound of fallen leaves rustling gently along the sidewalk.